MW00441789

NED MYERS;
OR,
A LIFE BEFORE THE MAST

CLASSICS OF NAVAL LITERATURE

JACK SWEETMAN, SERIES EDITOR

This series makes available new editions of classic works of naval history, biography, and fiction. Each volume is complete and unabridged and includes an authoritative introduction written specifically for Classics of Naval Literature. A list of titles published or currently in preparation appears at the end of this volume.

NED MYERS;
or,
A LIFE BEFORE THE MAST

Edited by
J. Fenimore Cooper

with an introduction and notes by
William S. Dudley

NAVAL INSTITUTE PRESS
Annapolis, Maryland

This book was originally published in 1843
by Lea and Blanchard, Philadelphia.

Library of Congress Cataloging-in-Publication Data

Myers, Ned, ca. 1793–1849.
Ned Myers : a life before the mast / edited by J. Fenimore Cooper : with an introduction and notes by William S. Dudley.
p. cm.— (Classics of naval literature)
Originally published: Philadelphia : Lea and Blanchard, 1843.
Includes index.
1. Seafaring life. 2. Meyers, Ned, ca. 1793–1849. I. Cooper, James Fenimore, 1789–1851. II. Title. III. Title: Life before the mast. IV. Series.
G540.M94 1989
910.4'5—dc19 89-30546
CIP

ISBN 0-87021-417-9

Printed in the United States of America

CONTENTS

Scourge (drawing by Ian Morgan, © *Hamilton-Scourge* Foundation)

INTRODUCTION

THIS IS THE TRUE STORY OF THE SAILOR NED MYERS, as told to James Fenimore Cooper, an old friend and former shipmate.[1] Some readers of this book may never have heard of *Ned Myers* nor have known that James Fenimore Cooper wrote anything other than romantic novels. Certainly, his literary reputation is based on the famous "Leatherstocking Tales," mostly set in New York state during the eighteenth and early nineteenth centuries. But Cooper wrote more authentically than most authors about the sea and seafaring men.[2] He knew them well; he had been one

1. The editor wishes to acknowledge his debt to Professor Robert Madison of the U.S. Naval Academy English Department, a Cooper scholar who has generously shared perceptive insights on Cooper, his composition of *Ned Myers,* and his authorship of *The History of the Navy of the United States*.

2. For a general introduction to Cooper and other writers of his period, see Emory Elliott, ed., *Columbia Literary History of the United States* (New York, 1987). In this volume, H. Daniel Peck's essay, "James Fenimore Cooper and the Writers of the Frontier," pp. 240–61, provides a balanced view of Cooper's craft.

of them, having served as a midshipman in the U.S. Navy during 1808–1810.[3]

To prepare himself for a naval career, Cooper spent a year as a common seaman before the mast, 1806–1807, in the merchant ship *Sterling* (or *Stirling*), under the command of Captain John Johnston of Wiscasset, Maine.[4] It was during this voyage from New York to England and the Mediterranean that Cooper became close friends with the subject of this book, a 13-year-old cabin boy named Ned Myers. Cooper's early nautical novels, sometimes called sea romances, *The Pilot* (1824), *Red Rover* (1827), *The Water Witch* (1830), and his later ones, *The Wing and Wing* (1842), *Two Admirals* (1842), and *Afloat and Ashore* (1844), demonstrate his mastery of the seafaring world and its strange, colloquial language. Cooper created and developed the American nautical novel. Thanks to his command of the language of the maritime world and his emotional link to American history, Cooper made an essential contribution to American maritime nationalism, reflecting the country's pride in the accomplishments of the small but very skilled navy of the War of 1812. He realized the power of the past and harnessed it to the conflict between man and nature inherent in the maritime environment.[5] His two-volume *History of the Navy of the United States* is itself a classic, the first complete account of the navy's operational history from its inception in 1775

3. James Franklin Beard, ed., *The Letters and Journals of James Fenimore Cooper,* 4 vols. (Cambridge, Mass.), vol. 1, 3–22.

4. Cooper was a bright, well-read, high-spirited boy who entered Yale University in 1803, at the early age of 14. He was soon in difficulties, being younger than most of his classmates but more advanced in his studies. He participated in pranks and fights that led to his expulsion in 1805. His father, Judge Cooper, decided a year or so at sea might provide his son with some self-discipline and also prepare him for a naval career and so made the necessary arrangements for his voyage in the *Sterling*. Beard, *Letters and Journals,* vol. 1, 4–5.

5. Thomas Philbrick, *James Fenimore Cooper and the Development of American Sea Fiction* (Cambridge, Mass., 1961).

through the end of the War of 1812.[6] In *Ned Myers,* a non-fiction work, Cooper provides the reader with the same realistic, unvarnished view of seafaring life that he had used as the basis of his early novels.

Cooper's time in the navy was short, but sufficient to acquaint him with its traditions and several of its rising officers.[7] He obtained a midshipman's warrant in 1808, at the age of 19. The Navy Department first assigned him to duty in the bomb ketch *Vesuvius* at New York City. From there, he was sent northward to assist Lieutenant Melancthon Woolsey, who was superintending the construction of the brig *Oneida* at Oswego, New York. This vessel was intended to enforce the embargo laws on Lake Ontario. (At the outbreak of the War of 1812, she was the navy's only vessel on the lake.) Cooper's last assignment was service on board the *Wasp,* commanded by Lieutenant James Lawrence, who sent him on recruiting duty at New York City. Despite the difference in their age and rank, Cooper and Lawrence became good friends, possibly because they shared a mutual birthplace, Burlington, New Jersey.

In May 1810, Cooper requested a year's furlough from the navy for personal reasons. His father, Judge William Cooper, had died, leaving an extensive landed estate in cen-

6. The first "history" of the naval aspects of the War of 1812 was that of Thomas Clark, whose *Naval History of the United States from the commencement of the Revolutionary War to the present time,* 2 vols., 2nd ed. (Philadelphia, 1814), does not include a complete account of the War of 1812. The second edition is merely a reworking of the first volume (edition), with a few documents added, bringing the war up to January 1814. Several documentary volumes appeared before Cooper's *History,* but his was the first based on primary sources, including eyewitness and participant testimony, that attempted a cohesive, interpretive account of American naval operations since 1775.

7. William Branford Shubrick, later rear admiral, and Cooper became lifelong friends as a result of Cooper's service in the *Wasp,* under Lieutenant James Lawrence. Beard, *Letters and Journals,* vol. 1, p. 69, note.

tral New York. As co-beneficiary with four brothers, Cooper inherited $50,000, 23 farms, and a one-fifth "residue" of the estate. At the same time, Cooper was courting Susan de Lancey, the daughter of a socially prominent but no longer wealthy New York family. He resigned his commission a year later, explaining his reasons as "private," by which he meant his increased financial responsibilities and probably the wishes of his new wife.[8] Though he left the navy, Cooper never lost his fondness for the service and his naval friends.

Ned Myers spans the better part of its subject's life, from his birth in Quebec about 1793 until the end of his seagoing days in the 1840s. This period encompassed some of the most difficult times in the life of the early American republic, its naval wars with France and the Barbary States, and finally the War of 1812, often called "The Second War for American Independence." Then came years of exuberant growth for commerce. The American shipping industry flourished during the years 1815–1860 as it never would again. The seamen's unbridled, nomadic instincts were channeled and used for profit. For them, the seagoing life presented a harsh world where nature and domineering masters controlled their destiny. Yet even the seamen benefited, for American shipowners paid higher wages than foreign companies to a labor market short of experienced hands.

Ned Myers's memoir offers an unparalleled view of life on the lower deck. By Cooper's tally, Ned had been a crew member of 72 different vessels, in some of which he made

8. Beard, *Letters and Journals,* vol. 1, pp. 15–23. On 1 January 1811, Cooper married Susan de Lancey (1792–1852), a member of one of the great New York colonial families that had lost its holdings during the American Revolution because of Tory sympathies. Her father, John Peter de Lancey (1753–1828), served as a major with the Pennsylvania Loyalists during the Revolution, and afterwards as a captain in the Royal Irish Regiment. He resigned and returned to America in 1790.

several voyages. When to that figure is added the number of ships in which Ned was embarked as a prisoner or passenger, the total may have been closer to 100. His life afloat amounted to 25 years out of sight of land. Ned, for reasons he will reveal, preferred to sail "before the mast" as a common seaman, despite years of experience which might have qualified him for command. He had his turns as first and second mate and showed his proficiency in numerous dangerous situations, saving his ship, cargo, and crew. He usually rejected offers of greater responsibility. His life held much inner conflict, and he expresses unrequited desires for greater companionship and closeness to family. It was characteristic of Ned, however, that when these opportunities occasionally arose, he turned away. He mentions only one relationship with a woman and apparently did not indulge in the promiscuity commonly associated with sailors. If he did, he does not disclose it, though Cooper may have exercised editorial discretion, omitting to mention adventures that might make readers blush.

Ned had many acquaintances but few close friends, perhaps because so many died relatively young from accidents, disease, and dissipation. He was good company and easily established rapport with strangers, even those one might expect to be antagonistic. Between voyages, he spent his hard-earned dollars freely on friends, meals, and liquor. He seemed to own nothing but his clothes and a few nautical instruments. Still, he knew how to lay away a little property and a few dollars, leaving them in safekeeping with a friendly landlord to be reclaimed on return from his voyages. He could read and knew enough mathematics to navigate. He does not say much about writing letters, but he became fond of the Bible, tracts, and other religious works as he grew older. He possessed an active though frequently dormant conscience, which came back to haunt him as he sensed how his opportunities had evaporated. His bondage to liquor became acute. Ned was fortunate that by the

1820s and 1830s, churchmen had founded organizations to minister to seamen.[9] Thanks to these influences and his own survival instincts, Ned became, by the end of his seafaring days, a reclaimed soul. It is very unlikely that this memoir would have been written had not Ned had a conscience and a strong will to set things right. Aged nearly fifty in 1843, he probably looked older than his years when Cooper took down his life's story.

Though Ned spent most of his career in the merchant marine, he also served in the navy. He enlisted in 1812 at New York and was assigned to the gunboat flotilla based at the New York Navy Yard in Brooklyn. When the yard commandant, Captain Isaac Chauncey, called for volunteers for service on Lake Ontario, Ned stepped forward. His love of the service and his patriotism ring clear, and there is never a harsh word for his treatment, though he does note that the navy did not pay as well as merchantmen. It is in part because of Ned's service as an able seaman assigned to the schooner *Scourge* on Lake Ontario during the War of 1812 that this reprint of Cooper's work has appeared. Ned virtually leapt from the pages of the *National Geographic* in 1983, when the Society published a remarkable article on the underwater discovery of the U.S. Navy schooners *Hamilton* and *Scourge.*[10] As a result of a search spear-headed by Daniel A. Nelson of St. Catharines, Ontario, these war vessels were located by sonar 280 feet below the surface of the lake in 1973. Two years later, a side-scan sonar search in the same area provided a more positive identification of the *Scourge* on the lake floor and then of the *Hamilton,* 1,500 feet away. In 1982, a team of archaeologists, underwater scientists, and

9. Roald Kverndal, *Seamen's Missions: Their Origin and Early Growth* (Pasadena, California, 1986).

10. Daniel A. Nelson, "Ghost Ships of the War of 1812," *National Geographic,* vol. 163, no. 3 (March 1983), pp. 289–313. See also Emily Cain, "Building *Lord Nelson* [*Scourge*]," *Inland Seas,* vol. 41, no. 2 (Summer, 1988) and Emily Cain, *Ghost Ships* (New York & Toronto, 1983).

National Geographic Society representatives photographed the schooners with a remotely piloted vehicle.

On the night of 8 August 1813, Commodore Chauncey's squadron was becalmed at the western end of the lake when a squall suddenly hit and capsized the *Scourge* and the nearby *Hamilton*. Ned Myers was one of the few sailors to survive the schooner's sinking. His narrative, which the *Geographic* excerpted in an illustrated five-page spread in the midst of Nelson's article on the discovery of the schooners, vividly describes his escape. Linking Ned's account with the archeological discovery was, for many maritime historians, as exciting as finding the schooners themselves, for it provides the only detailed explanation of what happened to the schooners lost 176 years ago. What a few Cooper enthusiasts and literary scholars knew all along, many others had to rediscover. Cooper's own *History of the Navy of the United States,* published in 1839, contains only a summary of the tragic sinking of the *Scourge.*[11] In addition, Ned gives us a unique account of the capture of the U.S. schooners *Julia* and *Growler* a few days later.

Ned's naval career, as distinguished from his many merchant voyages, is an important though interrupted theme and deserves summation. Ned was rescued by the U.S. armed schooner *Julia,* but, soon after, she was captured in company with the schooner *Growler.* Ned spent the next 19 months in prison ships and in a prison camp on Melville Island at Halifax, Nova Scotia. Freed in March 1815, he entered merchant sail and did not return to a naval vessel for 12 years. In 1827, he signed on the *Delaware,* 80 guns, under Commodore John Downes, for a three-year enlistment that took him to the Mediterranean and back in 1831. Next he joined the frigate *Brandywine* and patrolled the Gulf of Mexico. In 1832, he found himself in the Revenue Cutter Service, a seagoing branch of the Treasury Department, off

11. James Fenimore Cooper, *The History of the Navy of the United States,* 2 vols. (Paris, 1839; reprint, Upper Saddle River, N.J., 1970), vol. 2, p. 262.

Charleston, South Carolina, during the Nullification crisis, serving for most of the time in the cutter *Jackson*. The cutters, augmented by two navy vessels, the sloop-of-war *Natchez* and schooner *Experiment,* were assigned to prevent South Carolina vessels from leaving port without paying the fees established by the Tariff of 1832.[12] South Carolina's legislature had declared that it had the right not to comply with U.S. laws that usurped the authority granted the states. The federal government, under President Andrew Jackson, responded with force. The excitement ended with a compromise in March 1833, and the government discharged the extra hands it had hired for the cutters.

After a three-year stint in merchantmen, Ned returned to the navy and signed on the frigate *Constellation,* in which he saw duty in the Gulf of Mexico during the "Florida War" (Second Seminole War) in 1835–36, and later transferred to the sloop-of-war *St. Louis.* After a severe injury, he spent some time in the Pensacola Naval Hospital, and was finally invalided back to New York. He traveled to Washington, D.C., where he visited the navy yard and paid a call on Commodore Isaac Chauncey, then serving on the Board of Navy Commissioners. The old Lake Ontario commander was much interested in seeing Ned and questioned him at length about the sinking of the *Scourge.* Navy Department clerks set him to work on a pension application, but it was several years before Ned obtained anything more than a small sum in compensation for the injury that had put him in the Pensacola Naval Hospital.[13] In August 1840, Ned was sailing on his last merchant voyage, from Rotterdam to

12. This small force was put under the command of Commodore Jesse Duncan Elliott from November 1832 to March 1833.

13. According to documents in Ned's pension file, he had fallen and broken his clavicle (collarbone). This he duly reported to the Navy pension office and was awarded a monthly pension of $3.00, as of 16 October 1838. National Archives, Military Service Branch. See pension file of Edward Myers, Seaman.

Java on board the Dutch ship *Stadtdeel.* Under way, he fell while on deck and broke his hip. Though he was in great pain, the ship's captain and mate believed that he was malingering and refused to provide treatment. On arrival in Batavia (Djakarta), Ned finally gained admittance to a hospital but almost died before he was properly diagnosed. He regained his health except for a bad limp and returned to the United States in the merchantman *Plato.* He obtained admission to the Sailor's Snug Harbor, a well-endowed home for retired mariners on Staten Island near New York City.[14] The Navy Pension Office had by this time approved his application, and the money was waiting for him.

By the time Cooper met his former shipmate in 1843, he had firmly established his literary reputation, and had produced his nautical novels and *The History of the Navy of the United States.* Ned wrote Cooper a letter from the Sailor's Snug Harbor, asking if he were the man Ned had known as a boy on board the *Sterling.* To Cooper, Ned's arrival on the scene was a gift from the gods, and he quickly replied that this was so. They met briefly in New York City, and Cooper invited Myers to his home in Cooperstown on Lake Otsego, where the two spent five months closely reviewing Ned's seagoing career. Here the famous author could see himself through another's eyes and at the same time share his experiences.

At the time Cooper and Ned were collaborating, the American public's taste for seafaring literature was changing. The popularity of the "romance of the sea" was being replaced by harsher, more realistic portrayals of seamen who risked all manner of dangers and lived with minimum comfort, rudderless in the face of almost dictatorial authority, nature's whims, and ill-educated, occasionally degraded companions. Richard Henry Dana's *Two Years Before the Mast*

14. Kverndal, *Seamen's Missions,* pp. 518–19.

had appeared only three years before, and the navy's investigations of the infamous *Somers* mutiny and Captain Alexander Slidell MacKenzie's shipboard executions of the alleged conspirators were the cause of national debate. Progressives and churchmen were beginning to promote the cause of reform within the U.S. Navy and the merchant marine. Their chief goals were the elimination of corporal punishment and the consumption of alcohol on board ship.[15] With Ned Myers's story, Cooper had the materials to equal Dana's literary triumph and ride the crest of the new literary trend. For all of Cooper's efforts, though, *Ned Myers* was not as well received as *Two Years Before the Mast.*[16] Dana's memoir had set the standard, and the critics did not applaud Cooper's work, even though *Ned Myers* had wider scope, being an entire life "before the mast," global in its seafaring. With *Ned Myers,* Cooper responded to Dana's book, replicating its maritime realism and reinforcing the technical authenticity of his early sea novels. Despite the critics' ambivalence, Cooper's work had a certain popular success and went to many editions, including French and German by 1862.[17]

Literary scholars have raised questions as to how Cooper wrote *Ned Myers.* He does not explain whether he wrote it

15. Harold D. Langley, *Social Reform in the United States Navy, 1798–1862* (Urbana, Illinois, 1967).

16. Philbrick, *James Fenimore Cooper,* pp. 117–20; Hugh McKeever Egan, "Gentlemen-Sailors: The First-Person Sea Narratives of Dana, Cooper, and Melville" (unpublished doctoral dissertation, University of Iowa 1983), pp. 137–40, 177–78,

17. Although popular in its own day, *Ned Myers* is now one of Cooper's least known works. There were 13 different reprints and editions after it first appeared in 1843. Most were published before 1860. There was a French edition of 1844 and a German edition of 1862. Many "complete" editions of Cooper's works did not include *Ned Myers.* In recent years, literary scholars have been re-evaluating Cooper and writers of his generation. In the process, *Ned Myers* has become better known, to the benefit of maritime historians.

as Ned narrated or made notes and composed it later. The conversations with Myers at Cooperstown lasted several months, allowing much time for reviewing the facts and renewed questioning over forgotten or confused episodes. Ned himself could not have "written" it, even though the author uses the first person voice. Ned could read but could barely write. One of the documents in his pension file shows an "X" where he was to sign his name. His letters to Cooper in the late 1840s indicate he employed an amanuensis. The literary conventions preserved in the work are Cooper's, but the terseness of the passages, the harshness of the scenes, and the honesty of characterization are very authentic. It would have been very difficult for Cooper to have "invented" *Ned Myers*.[18] Cooper himself claims that he seldom "interposed his own greater knowledge of the world, between Ned's more limited experience and the narrative; but, this has been done cautiously, and in only a few cases in which there can be little doubt that the narrator has been deceived by appearances, misled by ignorance." As Hugh M. Egan states, by writing in the first person, Cooper's assumption of Ned Myers's identity "dictates its own willful pattern in the prose."[19]

If *Ned Myers* had a "happy ending," with Ned completing his searoving and swearing off liquor, the rest of his life did not. Cooper paid Ned an advance on his share of the royalties and helped him find a job at the Brooklyn Navy Yard. After Ned married a widow with children, Cooper took in one of the step-daughters as a domestic servant. Two years later, Ned relapsed into his old habits and died, probably of alcoholism, in 1849. Cooper had assisted in writing Ned's will and later helped his family with their bills.[20] After

18. Egan, "Gentlemen-Sailors," pp. 158 ff.
19. Ibid., p. 162.
20. Ibid., p. 155.

Ned's death, his widow applied for the arrears of a pension that Ned had requested, based on a War of 1812 injury. While Ned was struggling for his life during *Scourge*'s capsizing, the jib sheet struck a heavy blow on his left arm. A tumor developed on that spot and was surgically removed 30 years later.[21] The records indicate a pension was paid but not its amount.[22]

The importance of *Ned Myers* for modern readers is what we learn about the subject and his companions on the lower deck. The social history of seafaring is still in its infancy, in regard to both naval and merchant ships. We need to know why men went to sea, how they looked at their captains and mates, what they thought about their treatment, when and why they got sick, who took care of them when they did, and what happened to them in their old age. The dangers of seafaring in the age of sail may be familiar to some readers, but to others the fragility of that existence may not be apparent. The recent capsizing and sinking of the schooner *Pride of Baltimore,* designed along the authentic lines of a War of 1812 privateer, brought home to many observers that this event was quite common in the early nineteenth century. For men like Ned Myers, the possibilities of piracy, dismasting, shipwreck, impressment, punishment by flogging, alcoholism, insanity, unfaithful landlords, and penury ashore were altogether real.

The study of American maritime culture includes the mental life of the seaman, his worries, his concept of duty,

21. Cooper, *Ned Myers,* pp. 64, 213–14, and 237.

22. See letter from James Otterson, Jr., to J. L. Edwards, Commissioner of Pensions, dated 9 July 1850. Otterson, who was probably a lawyer acting on behalf of Myers's widow, argues that despite Myers's death, the money was owed during his life and ought to be paid to the widow. He adds, "This case is the more interesting from the fact that this man was the hero of the well-known work of J. Fennimore [sic] Cooper's entitled "Ned Myers: or A Life before the Mast." National Archives, Military Service Branch, Pension Files.

his reading habits, his concerns for his shipmates, his legal rights and responsibilities, and his thoughts on religion. All these can be gleaned from accounts like Ned Myers's. Beyond this, *Ned Myers* is a remarkable tale of adventure on the high seas. It has suspense, excitement, retribution, suffering, remorse, and moments of happiness. In this historian's view, *Ned Myers* is a work of both art and social comment, and its influence will last far longer than its author would have dreamed.

WILLIAM S. DUDLEY

NED MYERS;
OR,
A LIFE BEFORE THE MAST

PREFACE

IT IS AN OLD REMARK, that the life of any man, could the incidents be faithfully told, would possess interest and instruction for the general reader. The conviction of the perfect truth of this saying, has induced the writer to commit to paper, the vicissitudes, escapes, and opinions of one of his old shipmates, as a sure means of giving the public some just notions of the career of a common sailor. In connection with the amusement that many will find in following a foremast Jack in his perils and voyages, however, it is hoped that the experience and moral change of Myers may have a salutary influence on the minds of some of those whose fortunes have been, or are likely to be, cast in a mould similar to that of this old salt.

As the reader will feel a natural desire to understand how far the editor can vouch for the truth of that which he has here written, and to be informed on the subject of the circumstances that have brought him acquainted with the individual whose adventures form the subject of this little work, as much shall be told as may be necessary to a proper understanding of these two points.

First, then, as to the writer's own knowledge of the career of the subject of his present work. In the year 1806, the editor, then a lad, fresh from Yale, and destined for the navy, made his first voyage in a merchantman, with a view to get some practical knowledge of his profession. This was the fashion of the day, though its utility, on the whole, may very well be questioned. The voyage was a long one, including some six or eight passages, and extending to near the close of the year 1807. On board the ship was Myers, an apprentice to the captain. Ned, as Myers was uniformly called, was a lad, as well as the writer; and, as a matter of course, the intimacy of a ship existed between them. Ned, however, was the junior, and was not then compelled to face all the hardships and servitude that fell to the lot of the writer.

Once, only, after the crew was broken up, did the writer and Ned actually see each other, and that only for a short time. This was in 1809. In 1833, they were, for half an hour, on board the same ship, without knowing the fact at the time. A few months since, Ned, rightly imagining that the author of the *Pilot* must be his old shipmate, wrote the former a letter to ascertain the truth. The correspondence produced a meeting, and the meeting a visit from Ned to the editor. It was in consequence of the revelations made in this visit that the writer determined to produce the following work.

The writer has the utmost confidence in all the statements of Ned, so far as intention is concerned. Should he not be mistaken on some points, he is an exception to the great rule which governs the opinions and recollections of the rest of the human family. Still, nothing is related that the writer has any reasons for distrusting. In a few instances he has interposed his own greater knowledge of the world, between Ned's more limited experience and the narrative; but, this has been done cautiously, and only in cases in which there can be little doubt that the narrator has been deceived by appearances, or misled by ignorance. The reader, however, is not to infer that Ned has no greater information than usually falls to the share of a foremast hand. This is far from being the case. When first known to the writer, his knowledge was materially above that of the ordinary class of lads in his situation; giving ample proof that he had held intercourse with persons of a condition in life, if not positively of the rank of gentlemen, of one that was not much below it. In a word, his intelligence on general subjects was such as might justly render him the subject of remark on board a ship. Although much of his after-life was thrown away, portions of it passed in improvement; leaving Ned, at this moment, a man of quick apprehension, considerable knowledge, and of singularly shrewd comments. If to this be added the sound and accurate moral principles that now appear to govern both his acts and his opinions, we find a man every way entitled to speak for himself; the want of the habit of communicating his thoughts to the public, alone excepted.

In this book, the writer has endeavoured to adhere as closely to the very language of his subject, as circumstances will at all allow; and in many places he feels confident that no art of his own could, in any respect, improve it.

It is probable that a good deal of distrust will exist on the subject of the individual whom Ned supposes to have been one of his godfathers. On this head the writer can only say, that the account which Myers has given in this work, is substantially the same as that which he gave the editor nearly forty years ago, at an age and under circumstances that forbid the idea of any intentional deception. The account is confirmed by his sister, who is the oldest of the two children, and who retains a distinct recollection of the prince, as indeed does Ned himself. The writer supposes these deserted orphans to have been born out of wedlock—though he has no direct proof to this effect—and there is nothing singular in the circumstance of a man of the highest rank, that of a sovereign excepted, appearing at the font in behalf of the child of a dependent. A member of the royal family, indeed, might be expected to do this, to favour one widely separated from him by birth and station, sooner than to oblige a noble, who might possibly presume on the condescension.

It remains only to renew the declaration, that every part of this narrative is supposed to be true. The memory of Ned may occasionally fail him; and, as for his opinions, they doubtless are sometimes erroneous; but the writer has the fullest conviction that it is the intention of the Old Salt to relate nothing that he does not believe to have occurred, or to express an unjust sentiment. On the subject of his reformation, so far as "the tree is to be known by its fruits" it is entirely sincere; the language, deportment, habits, and consistency of this well-meaning tar, being those of a cheerful and confiding Christian, without the smallest disposition to cant or exaggeration. In this particular, he is a living proof of the efficacy of faith, and of the power of the Holy Spirit to enlighten the darkest understanding, and to quicken the most apathetic conscience.

CHAPTER I

IN CONSENTING TO LAY BEFORE THE WORLD the experience of a common seaman, and, I may add, of one who has been such a sinner as the calling is only too apt to produce, I trust that no feeling of vanity has had an undue influence. I love the seas; and it is a pleasure to me to converse about them, and of the scenes I have witnessed, and of the hardships I have undergone on their bosom, in various parts of the world. Meeting with an old shipmate who is disposed to put into proper form the facts which I can give him, and believing that my narrative may be useful to some of those who follow the same pursuit as that in which I have been so long engaged, I see no evil in the course I am now taking, while I humbly trust it may be the means of effecting some little good. God grant that the pictures I shall feel bound to draw of my own past degradation and failings, contrasted as they must be with my present contentment and hopes, may induce some one, at least, of my readers to abandon the excesses so common among seamen, and to turn their eyes in the direction of those great truths which are so powerful to reform, and so convincing when regarded with humility, and with a just understanding of our own weaknesses.

I know nothing of my family, except through my own youthful recollections, and the accounts I have received from my sister. My father I slightly remember; but of my mother I retain no distinct impressions. The latter must have died while I was very young. The former, I was in the habit of often seeing, until I reached my fifth or sixth year. He was a soldier, and belonged to the twenty-third regiment of foot, in the service of the King of Great Britain.[1] The fourth son of this monarch, Prince Edward as he was then called, or the Duke of Kent as he was afterwards styled, commanded the corps, and accompanied it to the British American colonies, where it was stationed for many years.

I was born in Quebec, between the years 1792 and 1794; probably in 1793. Of the rank of my father in the regiment, I am unable to speak, though I feel pretty confident he was a commissioned officer. He was much with the prince; and I remember that, on parade, where I have often seen him, he was in the habit of passing frequently from the prince to the ranks—a circumstance that induces my old shipmate to think he may have been the adjutant. My father, I have always understood, was a native of Hanover, and the son of a clergyman in that country. My mother, also, was said to be a German, though very little is now known of her by any of the family. She is described to me as living much alone, as being occupied in pursuits very different from those of my father, and as being greatly averse to the life of a soldier.

I was baptized in the Church of England, and, from earliest boyhood, have always been given to understand that

1. The writer left a blank for this regiment, and now inserts it from memory. It is probable he is wrong.

His Royal Highness, Prince Edward, the father of Queen Victoria, stood for me at the font; Major Walker, of the same regiment, being the other god-father, and Mrs. Walker, his wife, my god-mother. My real names are Edward Robert Meyers; those received in baptism having been given me by my two sponsors, after themselves. This christening, like my birth, occurred in Quebec. I have, however, called myself Edward, or Ned, Myers, ever since I took to the sea.

Before I was old enough to receive impressions to be retained, the regiment removed to Halifax. My father accompanied it; and, of course, his two children, my sister Harriet and myself, were taken to Nova Scotia. Of the period of my life that was passed in Halifax, I retain tolerably distinct recollections; more especially of the later years. The prince and my father both remained with the regiment for a considerable time; though all quitted Halifax several years before I left it myself. I remember Prince Edward perfectly well. He sometimes resided at a house called the Lodge, a little out of town; and I was often taken out to see him. He also had a residence in town. He took a good deal of notice of me; raising me in his arms, and kissing me. When he passed our house, I would run to him; and he would lead me through the streets himself. On more than one occasion, he led me off, and sent for the regimental tailor; directing suits of clothes to be made for me, after his own taste. He was a large man; of commanding presence, and frequently wore a star on the breast of his coat. He was not then called the Duke of Kent, but Prince Edward, or *The* Prince. A lady lived with him at the Lodge; but who she was, I do not know.

At this time, my mother must have been dead; for of *her* I retain no recollection whatever. I think, my father left Halifax some time before the prince. Major Walker, too, went to England; leaving Mrs. Walker in Nova Scotia, for some time. Whether my father went away with a part of the regiment to which he belonged, or not, I cannot say; but I well remember a conversation between the prince, the major and Mrs. Walker, in which they spoke of the loss of a transport, and of Meyers's saving several men. This must have been at the time when my father quitted Nova Scotia; to which province, I think, he never could have returned. Neither my sister, nor myself, ever saw him afterwards. We have understood that he was killed in battle; though when, or where, we do not know. My old shipmate, the editor, however, thinks it must have been in Canada; as letters were received from a friend in Quebec, after I had quitted Nova Scotia, inquiring after us children, and stating that the effects of my father were in that town, and ought to belong to us. This letter gave my sister the first account of his death; though it was not addressed to her, but to those in whose care she had been left. This property was never recovered; and my shipmate, who writes this account, thinks there may have been legal difficulties in the way.

Previously to quitting the province of Nova Scotia, my father placed Harriet and myself in the house of a Mr. Marchinton, to live. This gentleman was a clergyman, who had no regular parish, but who preached in a chapel of his own. He sent us both to school, and otherwise took charge of us. I am not aware of the precise time when the prince left Halifax, but it must have been when I was five or six years old—probably about the year 1798 or 1799.[2]

From that time I continued at Mr. Marchinton's, attend-

2. Edward, Duke of Kent, was born November 2, 1767, and made a peer April 23, 1799; when he was a little turned of one-and-thirty. It is probable that this creation took place on his return to England; after passing some six or eight years in America and the West Indies. He served in the West Indies with great personal distinction, during his stay in this hemisphere.—EDITOR.

ing school, and busied, as is usual with boys of that age, until the year 1805. I fear I was naturally disposed to idleness and self-indulgence, for I became restive and impatient under the restraints of the schoolmaster, and of the gentleman in whose family I had been left. I do not know that I had any just grounds of complaint against Mr. Marchinton; but his rigorous discipline disgusted me; principally, I am now inclined to believe, because it was not agreeable to me to be kept under any rigid moral restraint. I do not think I was very vicious; and, I know, I was far from being of a captious temperament; but I loved to be my own master; and I particularly disliked everything like religious government. Mr. Marchinton, moreover, kept me out of the streets; and it was my disposition to be an idler, and at play. It is possible he may have been a little too severe for one of my temperament; though, I fear, nature gave me a roving and changeful mind.

At that time the English cruisers sent in many American vessels as prizes. Our house was near the water; and I was greatly in the habit of strolling along the wharves, whenever an opportunity occurred; Mr. Marchinton owning a good deal of property in that part of the town. The *Cambrian* frigate had a midshipman, a little older than myself, who had been a schoolmate of mine. This lad, whose name was Bowen, was sent in as the nominal prize-master of a brig loaded with coffee; and I no sooner learned the fact, than I began to pay him visits. Young Bowen encouraged me greatly, in a wish that now arose within me, to become a sailor. I listened eagerly to the history of his adventures, and felt the usual boyish emulation. Mr. Marchinton seemed averse to my following the profession, and these visits became frequent and stealthy; my wishes, most probably, increasing, in proportion as they seemed difficult of accomplishment.

I soon began to climb the rigging of the brig, ascending

to the mast-heads. One day Mr. Marchinton saw me quite at the main-truck; and, calling me down, I got a severe flogging for my dexterity and enterprise. It sometimes happens that punishment produces a result exactly opposite to that which was intended; and so it turned out in the present instance. My desire to be a sailor increased in consequence of this very flogging; and I now began seriously to think of running away, in order to get to sea, as well as to escape a confinement on shore, that, to me, seemed unreasonable. Another prize, called the *Amsterdam Packet,* a Philadelphia ship, had been sent in by, I believe, the *Cleopatra,* Sir Robert Laurie. On board this ship were two American lads, apprentices. With these boys I soon formed an intimacy; and their stories of the sea, and their accounts of the States, coupled with the restraints I fancied I endured, gave rise to a strong desire to see their country, as well as to become a sailor. They had little to do, and enjoyed great liberty, going and coming much as they pleased. This idleness seemed, to me, to form the summit of human happiness. I did not often dare to play truant; and the school became odious to me. According to my recollections, this desire for a change must have existed near, or quite a twelvemonth; being constantly fed by the arrival and departure of vessels directly before my eyes, ere I set about the concocting of a serious plan to escape.

My project was put in execution in the summer of 1805, when I could not have been more than eleven years old, if, indeed, quite as old. I was in the market one day, and overheard some American seamen, who had been brought in, conversing of a schooner that was on the point of leaving Halifax, for New York. This vessel belonged to North Carolina, and had been captured by the *Driver,* some time before, but had been liberated by a decision of the Admiralty Court. The men I overheard talking about her, intended taking their passages back to their own country in the craft. This seemed to me a good opportunity to effect my purpose, and I went from the market, itself, down to the schooner. The mate was on board alone, and I took courage, and asked him if he did not want to ship a boy. My dress and appearance were both against me, as I had never done any work, and was in the ordinary attire of a better class lad on shore. The mate began to laugh at me, and to joke me on my desire to go to sea, questioning me about my knowledge. I was willing to do anything; but, perceiving that I made little impression, I resorted to bribery. Prince Edward had made me a present, before he left Halifax, of a beautiful little fowling-piece, which was in my own possession; and I mentioned to the mate that I was the owner of such an article, and would give it to him if he would consent to secrete me in the schooner, and carry me to New York. This bait took, and I was told to bring the fowling-piece on board, and let the mate see it. That night I carried the bribe, as agreed on, to this man, who was perfectly satisfied with its appearance, and we struck a bargain on the spot. I then returned to the house, and collected a few of my clothes. I knew that my sister, Harriet, was making some shirts for me, and I stole into her room, and brought away two of them, which were all I could find. My wardrobe was not large when I left the house, and I had taken the precaution of carrying the articles out one at a time, and of secreting them in an empty cask in the yard. When I thought I had got clothes enough, I made them into a bundle, and carried them down to the schooner. The mate then cleared out a locker in the cabin, in which there were some potatoes, and told me I must make up my mind to pass a few hours in that narrow berth. Too thoughtless to raise any objections, I cheerfully consented, and took my leave of him with the understanding that I was to be on board, again, early in the morning.

Before going to bed, I desired a black servant of Mr. Marchinton's to call me about day-break, as I desired to go out and pick berries. This was done, and I was up and dressed before any other member of the family was stirring. I lost no time, but quitted the house, and walked deliberately down to the schooner. No one was up on board of her, and I was obliged to give the mate a call, myself. This man now seemed disposed to draw back from his bargain, and I had to use a good deal of persuasion before I could prevail on him to be as good as his word. He did not like to part with the fowling-piece, but seemed to think it would be fairly purchased, could he persuade me to run away. At length he yielded, and I got into the locker, where I was covered with potatoes.

I was a good while in this uncomfortable situation, before there were any signs of the vessel's quitting the wharf. I began to grow heartily tired of the confinement, and the love of change revived within me in a new form. The potatoes were heavy for me to bear, and the confined air rendered my prison almost insupportable. I was on the point of coming out of prison, when the noise on deck gave me the comfortable assurance that the people had come on board, and that the schooner was about to sail. I could hear men conversing, and, after a period of time that seemed an age, I felt satisfied the schooner was fairly under way. I heard a hail from one of the forts as we passed down the harbour, and, not long after, the *Driver,* the very sloop of war that had sent the vessel in, met her, and quite naturally hailed her old prize, also. All this I heard in my prison, and it served to reconcile me to the confinement. As everything was right, the ship did not detain us, and we were permitted to proceed.

It was noon before I was released. Going on deck, I found that the schooner was at sea. Nothing of Halifax was visible but a tower or two, that were very familiar objects to me. I confess I now began to regret the step I had taken, and, could I have been landed, it is probable my roving disposition would have received a salutary check. It was too late, however, and I was compelled to continue in the thorny and difficult path on which I had so thoughtlessly entered. I often look back to this moment, and try to imagine what might have been my fortunes, had I never taken this unlucky step. What the prince might have done for me, it is impossible to say; though I think it probable that, after the death of my father, I should have been forgotten, as seems to have been the case with my sister, who gradually fell from being considered and treated as one of the family in which she lived, into a sort of upper servant.

I have learned, latterly, that Mr. Marchinton had a great search made for me. It was his impression I was drowned, and several places were dragged for my body. This opinion lasted until news of my being in New York reached the family.

My appearance on deck gave rise to a great many jokes between the captain of the schooner, and his mate. I was a good deal laughed at, but not badly treated, on the whole. My office was to be that of cook—by no means a very difficult task in that craft, the camboose consisting of two pots set in bricks, and the dishes being very simple. In the cabin, sassafras was used for tea, and boiled pork and beef composed the dinner. The first day, I was excused from entering on the duties of my office, on account of sea-sickness; but, the next morning, I set about the work in good earnest. We had a long passage, and my situation was not very pleasant. The schooner was wet, and the seas she shipped would put out my fire. There was a deck load of shingles, and I soon discovered that these made excellent kindling wood; but it was against the rules of the craft to burn cargo, and my friend the mate had bestowed a few kicks on me before I learned to make the distinction. In other respects, I did tolerably well; and, at the end of about ten days, we entered Sandy Hook.

Such was my first passage at sea, or, at least, the first I

can remember, though I understand we were taken from Quebec to Halifax by water. I was not cured of the wish to roam by this experiment, though, at that age, impressions are easily received, and as readily lost. Some idea may be formed of my recklessness, and ignorance of such matters, at this time, from the circumstance that I do not remember ever to have known the name of the vessel in which I left Nova Scotia. Change and adventure were my motives, and it never occurred to me to inquire into a fact that was so immaterial to one of my temperament. To this hour, I am ignorant on the subject.

The schooner came up, and hauled in abreast of Fly Market. She did not come close to the wharf, but made fast, temporarily, at its end, outside of two or three other vessels. This took place not long after breakfast. I set about the preparations for dinner, which was ready, as usual, at twelve o'clock. While the crew were eating this meal, I had nothing to do, and, seeing a number of boys on the wharf, I went ashore, landing for the first time in this, my adopted country. I was without hat, coat, or shoes; my feet having become sore from marching about among the shingles. The boys were licking molasses from some hogsheads, and I joined in the occupation with great industry. I might have been occupied in this manner, and in talking with the boys, an hour or more, when I bethought me of my duty on board. On looking for the schooner, she was gone! Her people, no doubt, thought I was below, and did not miss me, and she had been carried to some other berth; where, I did not know. I could not find her, nor did I ever see her again.

Such, then, was my entrance on a new scene. Had I known enough to follow the wharves, doubtless I should have found the vessel; but, after a short search, I returned to the boys and the molasses.

That I was concerned at finding myself in a strange place,

without a farthing in my pockets—without hat, shoes or coat, is certain—but it is wonderful how little apprehension I felt. I knew nothing, and feared nothing. While licking the molasses, I told the boys my situation; and I met with a great deal of sympathy among them. The word passed from one to the other, that a "poor English boy had lost his vessel, and did not know where to go to pass the night." One promised me a supper; and, as for lodgings, the general opinion seemed to be, that I might find a berth under one of the butchers' stalls, in the adjacent market. I had different projects for myself, however.

There was a family of the name of Clark, then residing in New York, that I had known in Halifax. I remembered to have heard my sister, Harriet, speaking of them, not long before I quitted home, and that she said they lived in, or near, Fly Market. I knew we were at Fly Market; and the name recalled these people. I inquired, accordingly, if any one knew such a family; but met with no success in discovering them. They were strangers; and no one knew them. It was now near sunset; and I determined to look for these people myself. On this errand, then, I set off; walking up the market until I reached Maiden Lane. While strolling along the street, I heard a female voice suddenly exclaim: "Lord! here is Edward Myers, without anything on him!" At the next instant, Susan Clark, one of the daughters, came running into the street; and presently I was in the house, surrounded by the whole family.

Of course, I was closely questioned; and I told the whole truth. The Clarks were extremely kind to me, offering me clothes, and desiring to keep me with them; but I did not like the family, owing to old quarrels with the boys, and a certain sternness in the father, who had made complaints of my stealing his fruit, while in Halifax. I was innocent; and the whole proceeding had made me regard Mr. Clark as a sort of enemy. My principal motive, in inquiring for the family, was to learn where a certain Dr. Heizer[3] lived. This gentleman was a German, who had formerly been in the army; and I knew he was then in New York. In him I had more confidence; and I determined to throw myself on his kindness.

After declining a great many offers, I got the address of Dr. Heizer, and proceeded in quest of his residence, just as I was. It was moonlight, and I went through the streets with boyish confidence. My route lay up Broadway, and my destination was one of its corners and Hester Street. In 1805, this was nearly out of town, being near Canal street. I had been told to look for a bridge, which then stood in Broadway, and which answered for a landmark, in my new navigation. The bridge I found easily; and, making inquiries at a house, I was told the family I sought lived next door.

The Heizers were greatly surprised at my appearance. I was questioned, of course; and told them the naked truth. I knew concealment would be useless; was naturally frank, notwithstanding what I had just done; and I began to feel the want of friends. I was fed; and that same evening, Dr. and Mrs. Heizer led me down Broadway, and equipped me in a neat suit of clothes. Within a week, I was sent regularly to school.

I never knew what Dr. Heizer did, in relation to my arrival. I cannot but think that he communicated the circumstances to Mr. Marchinton, who was well known to him; though, Harriet tells me, the first intelligence they got of me was of a much later date, and came from another source. Let this be as it might, I was kindly treated; living, in all respects, as if I were one of the family. There was no son; and they all seemed to consider me as one.

3. This is Ned's pronunciation; though it is probable the name is not spelt correctly. The names of Ned are taken a good deal at random; and, doubtless, are often misspelled.—EDITOR.

I remained in this family the autumn of 1805, and the winter and spring of 1806. I soon tired of school, and began to play truant; generally wandering along the wharves, gazing at the ships. Dr. Heizer soon learned this; and, watching me, discovered the propensity I still retained for the sea. He and Mrs. Heizer now took me aside, and endeavoured to persuade me to return to Halifax; but I had become more and more averse to taking this backward step. To own the truth, I had fearful misgivings on the subject of floggings; and I dreaded a long course of severity and discipline. It is certain, that, while rigid rules of conduct are very necessary to some dispositions, there are others with which they do not succeed. Mine was of the latter class; for, I think, I am more easily led, than driven. At all events, I had a horror of going back; and refused to listen to the proposal. After a good deal of conversation, and many efforts at persuasion, Dr. Heizer consented to let me go to sea, from New York; or affected to consent; I never knew which.

The *Leander,* Miranda's flag-ship, in his abortive attempt to create a revolution in Spanish-America, was then lying in the Hudson; and Dr. Heizer, who was acquainted with some one connected with her, placed me in this ship, with the understanding I was to go in her to Holland. I passed the day on board; going up to my new employer's house, for my meals, and to sleep. This course of life may have lasted a fortnight; when I became heartily tired of it. I found I had a mistress, now, as well as a master. The former set me to cleaning knives, boots, candlesticks, and other similar employments; converting me into a sort of scullion. My pride revolted at this. I have since thought it possible, all this was done to create disgust, and to induce me to return to Mr. Marchinton; but it had a very contrary effect.

My desire was to be a sailor. One Sunday I had been on board the ship, and, after assisting the mate to show the bunting fore and aft, I went back to the house. Here my mistress met me with a double allowance of knives to clean.

We had a quarrel on the subject; I protesting against all such work. But to clean the knives I was compelled. About half were thrown over the fence, into the adjoining yard; and, cleaning what remained, I took my hat, went to the doctor's, and saw no more of my mistress, or of the *Leander.*[4]

4. A private armed ship belonging to Francisco de Miranda (1754–1816), Venezuelan-born soldier and revolutionary who believed that the Spanish-American colonies were ready to revolt. Unsuccessful in obtaining significant assistance from the English, he purchased *Leander* at New York, armed and supplied it with American assistance, and sailed with 200 men and munitions of war in February 1806. Landing near Caracas, he proclaimed Colombia a republic but was betrayed and imprisoned. He died a prisoner of the Spanish at Cadiz. For a sketch of his life, see William Spence Robertson, *Rise of the Spanish American Republics as Told in the Lives of Their Liberators* (New York, 1946), pp. 41–81.

CHAPTER II

An explanation took place. Dr. and Mrs. Heizer remonstrated about my conduct, and endeavoured, once more, to persuade me to return to Mr. Marchinton's. A great deal was told me of the kind intentions of that gentleman, and concerning what I might expect from the protection and patronage of my god-father, the Duke of Kent. I cannot help thinking, now, that much of the favour which was extended towards me at that early period of life, was owing to the circumstance that the prince had consented to stand for me at my baptism. He was a great disciplinarian—so great, indeed, I remember to have heard, as to cause more than one mutiny—and my father being a German, and coming from a people that carried military subordination to extremes, it is highly probable I was indebted, for this compliment, to a similarity of tastes between the two. I cared little for all this, however, in 1805, and thought far less of being protected by a prince of the blood royal, than of going to sea, and especially of escaping from the moral discipline of Mr. Marchinton. Finding his arguments vain, Dr. Heizer sent me to school again, where I continued a few months longer.

All this time, my taste for ships rather increased than diminished. At every opportunity I was on the wharves, studying the different craft, and endeavouring to understand their rig. One day I saw a British ensign, and, while looking at it, with a feeling of strong disgust, I heard myself called by name. A glance told me that I was seen by a Halifax man, and I ran away, under the apprehension that he might, by some means, seize me and carry me back. My feelings on this head were all alive, and that very day one of the young ladies said, in a melancholy way, "*Edouard,*" "Halifax." These girls spoke scarcely any English, having been born in Martinique; and they talked much together in French, looking at me occasionally, as if I were the subject of their discourse. It is probable conscience was at the bottom of this conceit of mine; but the latter now became so strong, as to induce me to determine to look out for a vessel for myself, and be off again. With this view, I quitted a negro who had been sent with me to market, under the pretence of going to school, but went along the wharves until I found a ship that took my fancy. She was called the *Sterling,* and there was a singularly good-looking mate on her deck, of the name of Irish, who was a native of Nantucket. The ship was commanded by Capt. John Johnston, of Wiscasset, in Maine, and belonged to his father and himself.

I went on board the *Sterling,* and, after looking about for some time, I ventured to offer myself to Mr. Irish, as a boy who wished to ship. I was questioned, of course, but evaded any very close answers. After some conversation, Capt. Johnston came on board, and Mr. Irish told him what I wanted. My examination now became much closer, and I found myself driven to sheer fabrication in order to effect my purposes. During my intercourse with different seagoing lads of Halifax, I had learned the particulars of the capture of the *Cleopatra,* 32, by the French frigate *Ville de Milan,* 38, and her recapture by the *Leander,* 50, which ship captured the *Ville de Milan* at the same time. I said my father had been a serjeant of marines, and was killed in the action—that I had run away when the ships got in, and that I wished to be bound to some American ship-master, in order to become a regularly-trained seaman. This story so far imposed on Capt. Johnston as to induce him to listen to my proposals, and in part to accept them. We parted with an understanding that I was to get my clothes, and come on board the vessel.

It was twelve at noon when I got back to Dr. Heizer's. My first business was to get my clothes into the yard, a few at a time; after which I ate my dinner with the family. As soon as we rose from table, I stole away with my bundle, leaving these kind people to believe I had returned to school. I never saw one of them afterwards! On my return to New York, several years later, I learned they had all gone to Martinique to live. I should not have quitted this excellent family in so clandestine a manner, had I not been haunted with the notion that I was about to be sent back to Halifax, a place I now actually hated.

Capt. Johnston received me good-naturedly, and that night I slept and supped at the Old Coffee House, Old Slip—his own lodgings. He seemed pleased with me, and I was delighted with him. The next day he took me to a slop-shop, and I was rigged like a sailor, and was put in the cabin, where I was to begin my service in the regular way. A boy named Daniel McCoy was in the ship, and had been out to Russia in her, as cabin-boy, the last voyage. He was now to be sent into the forecastle, and was ordered to instruct me in my duty.

I was now comparatively happy, though anxious to be bound to Capt. Johnston, and still more so to be fairly at sea. The *Sterling* had a good, old-fashioned cabin, as cabins went in 1806; and I ran about her state-room, rummaged her lockers, and scampered up and down her companion-way, with as much satisfaction as if they had all belonged to a palace. Dan McCoy was every day on board, and we had the accommodations of the ship very much to ourselves. Two or three days later, Capt. Johnston took me to the proper place, and I was put under regular indentures, to serve until I was twenty-one. I now felt more confidence in my situation, knowing that Dr. Heizer had no legal authority over me. The work I did, in no manner offended my dignity, for it was on ship-board, and belonged properly to my duty as a cabin-boy.

The *Sterling* soon began to take in her cargo. She was to receive a freight of flour, for Cowes and a market. Not only was the hold filled, but the state-room and cabin, leaving barely room to climb over the barrels to reach the berths. A place was left, just inside of the cabin door, for the table. Passengers were not common in that day, while commerce was pushed to the utmost. Our sails were bending when the consignee, followed by another merchant, came down to the ship, accompanied by a youth, who, it was understood, wished also to be received in the vessel. This youth was named Cooper, and was never called by any other appellation in the ship. He was accepted by Capt. Johnston, signed the articles, and the next day he joined us, in sailor's rig. He never came to the cabin, but was immediately employed forward, in such service as he was able to perform. It was afterwards understood that he was destined for the navy.

The very day that Cooper joined us, was one of deep disgrace to me. The small stores came on board for the cabin, and Dan McCoy persuaded me to try the flavour of a bottle of cherry-bounce. I did not drink much, but the little I swallowed made me completely drunk. This was the first time I ever was in that miserable and disgraceful plight; would to God I could also say it was the last! The last it was, however, for several years; that is some comfort. I thank my Divine Master that I have lived to see the hour when intoxicating liquors have ceased to have any command over me, and when, indeed, they never pass my lips. Capt.

Johnston did not flog me for this act of folly, merely pulling my ears a little, and sharply reprimanding me; both he and Mr. Irish seeming to understand that my condition had proceeded from the weakness of my head. Dan was the principal sufferer, as, to say the truth, he ought to have been. He was rope's-ended for his pains.

Next day the stevedores took the ship into the stream, and the crew came on board. The assembling of the crew of a merchantman, in that day, was a melancholy sight. The men came off, bearing about them the signs of the excesses of which they had been guilty while on shore; some listless and stupid, others still labouring under the effects of liquor, and some in that fearful condition which seamen themselves term having the "horrors." Our crew was neither better nor worse than that of other ships. It was also a sample of the mixed character of the crews of American vessels during the height of her neutral trade. The captain, chief-mate, cook, and four of those forward, were American born; while the second-mate was a Portuguese. The boys were, one Scotch, and one a Canadian; and there were a Spaniard, a Prussian, a Dane, and an Englishman, in the forecastle. There was also an Englishman who worked his passage, having been the cooper of a whaler that was wrecked. As Dan McCoy was sent forward, too, this put ten in the forecastle, besides the cook, and left five aft, including the master of another wrecked English vessel, whom we took out as a passenger.

That afternoon we lifted our anchor, and dropped down abreast of Governor's Island, where we brought up. Next day all hands were called to get under way, and, as soon as the anchor was short, the mate told Cooper and myself to go up and loose the foretopsail. I went on one yard-arm, and Cooper went on the other. In a few minutes the second mate came up, hallooing to us to "avast," and laughing. Cooper was hard at work at the "robins," and would soon have had his half of the sail down in the top, had he been let alone; while I was taking the gaskets from the yard, with the intention of bringing them carefully down on deck, where it struck me they would be quite safe. Luckily for us, the men were too busy heaving, and too stupid, to be very critical, and we escaped much ridicule. In a week we both knew better.

The ship only got to the quarantine ground that day, but in the morning we went to sea. Our passage was long and stormy. The ship was on a bow-line most of the time, and we were something like forty days from land to land. Nothing extraordinary occurred, however, and we finally made the Bill of Portland. The weather came on thick, but we found a pilot, and ran into St. Helen's Roads and anchored. The captain got into his boat, and taking four men pulled ashore, to look for his orders at Cowes.

That afternoon it cleared off, and we found a pilot lying a little outside of us. About sunset a man-of-war's cutter came alongside, and Mr. Irish was ordered to muster the crew. The English lieutenant, who was tolerably bowsed up, took his seat behind the cabin table, while the men came down, and stood in the companion-way passage, to be overhauled. Most of the foreigners had gone in the boat, but two of the Americans that remained were uncommonly fine-looking men, and were both prime seamen. One, whose name was Thomas Cook, was a six-footer, and had the air of a thorough sea-dog. He filled the lieutenant's eye mightily, and Cook was very coolly told to gather his dunnage, as he was wanted. Cook pointed to his protection, but the lieutenant answered—"Oh! these things are nothing—anybody can have one for two dollars, in New York.[1] You are an Englishman, and the King has need of your services." Cook

1. A document attesting to the American citizenship of the bearer, usually including a physical description of the individual and signed by a notary. The possession of a "protection" was almost the only way a seaman could claim exemption from service in the British navy on the basis of being an American citizen. If a seaman's protection was lost, stolen, or confiscated, he was legally powerless to prevent impressment.

now took out of his pocket a certificate, that was signed by Sir John Beresford, stating that Thomas Cook had been discharged from His Maj. Ship *Cambrian,* after a pretty long service in her, because he had satisfactorily proved that he was a native-born American. The lieutenant could not very well dishonour this document, and he reluctantly let Cook go, keeping his protection, however. He next selected Isaac Gaines, a native New Yorker, a man whose father and friends were known to the captain. But Gaines had no discharge like that of Cook's, and the poor fellow was obliged to rowse up his chest and get into the cutter. This he did with tears in his eyes, and to the regret of all on board, he being one of the best men in the ship. We asked the boat's crew to what vessel they belonged, and they gave us the name of a sixty-four in the offing, but we observed, as they pulled away from us, that they took the direction of another ship. This was the last I ever saw, or heard, of Isaac Gaines. Cook went on with us, and one day, while in London, he went with Cooper to Somerset House to get an order for some prize-money, to which he was entitled for his service in the *Cambrian,* as was shown by his discharge.[2] The clerk asked him to leave the certificate, and call a day or two later, when he would have searched out the amount. This was done, and Cook, being now without certificate or protec-

2. Prize money was awarded to captors of enemy vessels, if the capture were legally made. The captured ship or "prize" would be sent in to a port that had an admiralty court. The local marshal would take possession and schedule a libel hearing. Captors would provide the court with captured documents and give testimony as to the facts in the case. If prisoners were available, some of them might also be examined. The judge, finding the capture legal, would condemn the vessel and have it sold at auction. The proceeds, less court fees, would be awarded to the capturing ship's officers and crew. If the captor were a naval officer, the commodore of the squadron would be entitled to a healthy share, even though not actually present at the capture. If the capturing ship were a privateer, the proceeds would be divided fifty-fifty between shipowners and ship's company.

tion, was pressed on his way back to the ship.[3] We never heard of him, either. Such was often the fate of sailors, in that day, who were with you one day, and lost for ever the next.

Captain Johnston did not get back to the ship for four-and-twenty hours. He brought orders for us to go up to London; and, the wind being fair, and almost a gale, we got under way, and were off as soon as possible. The next morning we were in the straits of Dover; the wind light, but fair. This was at a moment when all England was in arms, in anticipation of an invasion from France. Forty odd sail of vessels of war were counted from our ship, as the day dawned, that had been cruising in the narrow waters, during the night, to prevent a surprise.

We worked our way up to London, with the tides, and were carried into London dock; where we discharged. This was my first visit to the modern Babylon, of course; but I had little opportunity of seeing much. I had one or two cruises, of a Sunday, in tow of Cooper, who soon became a branch pilot, in those waters, about the parks and west end; but I was too young to learn much, or to observe much. Most of us went to see the monument, St. Paul's, and the lions; and Cooper put himself in charge of a beef-eater, and took a look at the arsenals, jewels and armoury. He had a rum time of it, in his sailor rig, but hoisted in a wonderful deal of gibberish, according to his own account of his cruise.

Captain Johnston now got a freight for the ship, and we hauled into the stream, abreast of the dock-gates, and took in shingle ballast. The Prussian, Dane, second mate, and

3. A common British 18th and early 19th century practice to ensure that the Royal Navy had sufficient hands to man its many ships. A "press gang" would march through a town visiting businesses frequented by sailors, seizing those who could not prove they were already employed at sea. Once pressed, several years might pass before a sailor was discharged. Even then, if the discharge certificate were not at hand, he could suffer reimpressment.

the English cooper, all left us, in London. We got a Philadelphian, a chap from Maine, who had just been discharged from an English man-of-war, and an Irish lad, in their places. In January we sailed, making the best of our way for the straits of Gibraltar. The passage was stormy—the Bay of Biscay, in particular, giving us a touch of its qualities. It was marked by only two incidents, however, out of the usual way. While running down the coast of Portugal, with the land in sight, we made an armed felucca astern,[4] and to windward. This vessel gave chase; and, the captain disliking her appearance, we carried hard, in order to avoid her. The weather was thick, and it blew fresh, occasionally, in squalls. Whenever it lulled, the felucca gained on us, we having, a very little, the advantage in the puffs. At length the felucca began to fire; and, finding that his shot were coming pretty near, Captain Johnston, knowing that he was in ballast, thought it wisest to heave-to. Ten minutes after our maintopsail was aback, the felucca ranged up close under our lee; hailed, and ordered us to send a boat, with our papers, on board her. A more rascally-looking craft never gave such an order to an unarmed merchantman. As our ship rose on a sea, and he fell into the trough, we could look directly down upon his decks, and thus form some notion of what we were to expect, when he got possession of us. His people were in red caps and shirts, and appeared to be composed of the rakings of such places as Gibraltar, Cadiz and Lisbon. He had ten long guns; and pikes, pistols and muskets, were plenty with him. On the end of each latine-yard was a chap on the look-out, who occasionally turned his eyes towards us, as if to anticipate the gleanings. That we should be plundered, every one expected; and it was quite likely we might be ill-treated. As soon as we hove-to, Captain Johnston gave me the best spy-glass, with

4. A type of rig commonly used in Mediterranean waters, with two or three masts and lateen-rigged sails.

orders to hand it to Cooper, to hide. The latter buried it in the shingle ballast. We, in the cabin, concealed a bag of guineas so effectually, that, after all was over, we could not find it ourselves.

The jolly-boat had been stowed in the launch, on account of the rough weather we had expected to meet, and tackles had to be got aloft before we could hoist it out. This consumed some time, during which there was a lull. The felucca, seeing us busy at this work, waited patiently until we had got the boat over the side, and into the water. Cooper, Dan McCoy, Big Dan, and Spanish Joe, then got into her; and the captain had actually passed his writing-desk into the boat, and had his leg on the rail, to go over the side himself, when a squall struck the ship. The men were called out of the boat to clew down the topsails, and a quarter of an hour passed in taking care of the vessel. By this time the squall had passed, and it lightened up a little. There lay the felucca, waiting for the boat; and the men were reluctantly going into the latter again, when the commander of the felucca waved his hand to us, his craft fell off and filled, wing-and-wing, skimming away towards the coast, like a duck. We stood gaping and staring at her, not knowing what to make of this manœuvre, when "bang!" went a heavy gun, a little on our weather quarter. The shot passed our wake, for we had filled our topsail, and it went skipping from sea to sea, after the felucca. Turning our eyes in the direction of the report, we saw a frigate running down upon the felucca, carrying studding-sails on both sides, with the water foaming up to her hawse-holes. As she passed our stern, she showed an English ensign, but took no other notice of us, continuing on after the felucca, and occasionally measuring her distance with a shot. Both vessels soon disappeared in the mist, though we heard guns for some time. As for ourselves, we jogged along on our course, wishing good luck to the Englishman. The felucca showed no ensign, the whole day. Our guineas were found, some weeks later, in a bread-locker, after we had fairly eaten our way down to them.

The other adventure occurred very soon after this escape; for, though the felucca may have had a commission, she was a pirate in appearance, and most probably in her practices. The thick westerly weather continued until we had passed the Straits. The night we were abreast of Cape Trafalgar, the captain came on deck in the middle watch, and, hailing the forecastle, ordered a sharp look-out kept, as we must be running through Lord Collingwood's fleet.[5] The words were hardly out of his mouth, when Spanish Joe sung out, "sail ho!" There she was, sure enough, travelling right down upon us, in a line that threatened to take us between the fore and main masts. The captain ordered our helm hard up, and yelled for Cooper to bring up the cabin lantern. The youngster made one leap down the ladder, just scraping the steps with his heels, and was in the mizzen rigging with the light, in half a minute. That saved us. So near was the stranger, that we plainly heard the officer of the deck call out to his own quarter-master to "port, hard a-port—*hard* a-port, and be d——d to you!" Hard a-port it was, and a two-decker came brushing along on our weather beam—so near, that, when she lifted on the seas, it seemed as if the muzzles of her guns would smash our rails. The *Sterling* did not behave well on this occasion, for, getting a yaw to windward, she seemed disposed to go right into the Englishman, before she would mind her helm. After the man-of-war hailed, and got our answer, her officer quaintly remarked that we were "close on board him." It blew too fresh for boats, and we were suffered to pass without being boarded.

The ship proceeded up to Carthagena, and went in. Here we were put in quarantine for several days. The port was

5. Admiral Cuthbert Collingwood, RN, one of Nelson's "band of brothers." He succeeded to command of the Royal Navy's Mediterranean Squadron after Nelson's death at the Battle of Trafalgar in 1805.

full of heavy ships of war, several of which were three-deckers; and an arrival direct from London made quite a sensation among them. We had divers visits from the officers, though I do not know what it all amounted to. From Carthagena we were sent down the coast to a little place called Aguilas, where we began to take in a cargo of barilla. At night we would discharge our shingle ballast into the water, contrary to law; and, in the day, we took in cargo. So clear was the water, that our night's work might easily be seen next morning, lying beneath the ship. As we lay in a roadstead, it mattered little, few vessels touching at the port. While at this place, there was an alarm of an attack from an English man-of-war that was seen in the offing, and priests enough turned out to defend an ordinary town.

We got about half our freight at this little village, and then came down as low as Almeria, an old Moorish town, just below Cape de Gatte, for the remainder. Here we lay several weeks, finishing stowing our cargo. I went ashore almost every day to market, and had an opportunity of seeing something of the Spaniards. Our ship lay a good distance off, and we landed at a quarantine station, half a mile, at least, from the water-gate, to which we were compelled to walk along the beach.

One of my journeys to the town produced a little adventure. The captain had ordered Cooper to boil some pitch at the galley. By some accident, the pot was capsized, and the ship came near being burned. A fresh pot was now provided, and Cooper and Dan McCoy were sent ashore, at the station, with orders to boil down pitch on the land. There was no wharf, and it was always necessary to get ashore through a surf. The bay is merely an elbow, half the winds blowing in from the open sea. Sometimes, therefore, landing is ticklish work and requires much skill. I went ashore with the pitch, and proceeded into the town on my errands, whilst the two lads lighted their fire and began to boil down. When all was ready, it was seen there was a good deal of swell, and that the breakers looked squally. The orders, however, were to go off, on such occasions, and not to wait, as delay generally made matters worse. We got into the boat, accordingly, and shoved off. For a minute, or more, things went well enough, when a breaker took the bows of the jolly-boat, lifted her nearly on end, and turned her keel uppermost. One scarcely knows how he gets out of such a scrape. We all came ashore, however, heels over head, people, pot, boat, and oars. The experiment was renewed, less the pitch and a pair of new shoes of mine, and it met with exactly the same result. On a third effort, the boat got through the surf and we succeeded in reaching the ship. These are the sorts of scenes that harden lads, and make them fond of risks. I could not swim a stroke, and certainly would have been drowned had not the Mediterranean cast me ashore, as if disdaining to take a life of so little value to anybody but myself.

After lying several weeks at Almeria, the ship got under way for England again. We had fresh westerly gales, and beat to and fro, between Europe and Africa, for some time, when we got a Levanter that shoved us out into the Atlantic at a furious rate.[6] In the Straits we passed a squadron of Portuguese frigates, that was cruising against the Algerines. It was the practice of these ships to lie at the Rock until it blew strong enough from the eastward to carry vessels through the Gut, when they weighed and kept in the offing until the wind shifted. This was blockading the Atlantic against their enemies, and the Mediterranean against their own ships.

We had a long passage and were short of salt provisions. Falling in with an American in the Bay of Biscay, we got a barrel of beef which lasted us in. When near the chops of the channel, with a light southerly wind, we made a sail in our wake, that came up with us hand over hand. She went

6. An easterly gale in the Mediterranean.

nearly two feet to our one, the barilla pressing the *Sterling* down into the water, and making her very dull, more especially in light airs. When the stranger got near enough, we saw that he was pumping, the water running out of his scuppers in a constant stream. He was several hours in sight, the whole time pumping. This ship passed within a cable's-length of us, without taking any more notice of us than if we had been a mile-stone. She was an English two-decker, and we could distinguish the features of her men, as they stood in the waist, apparently taking breath after their trial at the pumps. She dropped a hawse-bucket, and we picked it up, when she was about half a mile ahead of us. It had the broad-arrow on it, and a custom-house officer seeing it, some time after, was disposed to seize it as a prize.

We never knew the name of this ship, but there was something proud and stately in her manner of passing us, in her distress, without so much as a hail. It is true, we could have done her no good, and her object, doubtless, was to get into dock as soon as possible. Some thought she had been in action, and was going home to repair damages that could not be remedied at sea.

Soon after this vessel was seen, we had proof how difficult it is to judge of a ship's size at sea. A vessel was made ahead, standing directly for us. Mr. Irish soon pronounced her a sloop of war. Half an hour later she grew into a frigate, but when she came abeam she showed three tiers of ports, being a ninety. This ship also passed without deigning to take any notice of us.

CHAPTER III

WE MADE THE LAND'S END IN FINE WEATHER, and with a fair wind. Instead of keeping up channel, however, our ship hauled in for the land. Cooper was at the helm, and the captain asked him if he knew of any one on board who had ever been into Falmouth. He was told that Philadelphia Bill had been pointing out the different headlands on the forecastle, and that, by his own account, he had sailed a long time out of the port. This Bill was a man of fifty, steady, trust-worthy, quiet, and respected by every man in the ship. He had taken a great liking to Cooper, whom he used to teach how to knot and splice, and other niceties of the calling, and Cooper often took him ashore with him, and amused him with historical anecdotes of the different places we visited. In short, the intimacy between them was as great as well could be, seeing the difference in their educations and ages. But, even to Cooper, Bill always called himself a Philadelphian. In appearance, indeed, he resembled one of those whom we call Yankees, in America, more than anything else.

Bill was now sent for and questioned. He seemed uneasy, but admitted he could take the ship into Falmouth. There was nothing in the way, but a rock abreast Pendennis Castle, but it was easy to give that a berth. We now learned that the captain had made up his mind to go into this port and ride out the quarantine to which all Mediterranean vessels were subject. Bill took us in very quietly, and the ship was ordered up a few miles above the town, to a bay where vessels rode out their quarantine. The next day a doctor's boat came alongside, and we were ordered to show ourselves, and flourish our limbs, in order to make it evident we were alive and kicking. There were four men in the boat, and, as it turned out, every one of them recognised Bill, who was born within a few miles of the very spot where the ship lay, and had a wife then living a great deal nearer to him than he desired. It was this wife—there happening to be too much of her—that had driven the poor fellow to America, twenty years before, and which rendered him unwilling to live in his native country. By private means, Bill managed to have some communication with the men in the boat, and got their promises not to betray him. This was done by signs altogether, speaking being quite out of the question.

We were near, or quite, a fortnight in quarantine; after which the ship dropped down abreast of the town. This was of a Saturday, and Sunday, a portion of the crew were permitted to go ashore. Bill was of the number, and when he returned he admitted that he had been so much excited at finding himself in the place, that he had been a little indiscreet. That night he was very uncomfortable, but nothing occurred to molest any of us. The next morning all seemed right, and Bill began to be himself again; often wishing, however, that the anchor was a-weigh, and the ship turning out of the harbour. We soon got at work, and began to work down to the mouth of the haven, with a light breeze. The moment we were clear of the points, or headlands, we could make a fair wind of it up channel. The ship was in stays, pretty well down, under Pendennis, and the order had been given to swing the head yards. Bill and Cooper were pulling together at the foretopsail brace, when the report of a musket was heard quite near the ship. Bill let go the brace, turned as white as a sheet, and exclaimed, "I'm gone!" At first, the men near him thought he was shot, but a gesture towards the boat which had fired, explained his meaning. The order was given to belay the head braces, and we waited the result in silence.

The press-gang was soon on board us, and its officer asked to have the crew mustered. This humiliating order was obeyed, and all hands of us were called aft. The officer seemed easily satisfied, until he came to Bill. "What countryman are *you?*" he asked. "An American—a Philadelphian," answered Bill. "You are an Englishman." "No, sir; I was born—" "Over here, across the bay," interrupted the officer, with a cool smile, "where your dear wife is at this moment. Your name is ——— ———, and you are well known in Falmouth. Get your clothes, and be ready to go in the boat."

This settled the matter. Captain Johnston paid Bill his wages, his chest was lowered into the boat, and the poor fellow took an affectionate leave of his ship-mates. He told those around him that his fate was sealed. He was too old to outlive a war that appeared to have no end, and they would never trust *him* on shore. "My foot will never touch the land again," he said to Cooper, as he squeezed his young friend's hand, "and I am to live and die, with a ship for my prison."

The loss of poor Bill made us all sad; but there was no remedy. We got into the offing, and squared away for the river again. When we reached London, the ship discharged down at Limehouse, where she lay in a tier of Americans for some time. We then took in a little ballast, and went up opposite to the dock gates once more. We next docked and cleaned the ship, on the Deptford side, and then hauled into the wet-dock in which we had discharged our flour.

Here the ship lay part of May, all of June, and most of July, taking in freight for Philadelphia, as it offered. This gave our people a good deal of spare time, and we were allowed to go ashore whenever we were not wanted. Cooper now took me in tow, and many a drift I had with him and Dan McCoy up to St. Paul's, the parks, palaces, and the Abbey. A little accident that happened about this time, attached me to Cooper more than common, and made me more desirous than ever to cruise in his company.

I was alone, on deck, one Sunday, when I saw a little dog running about on board a vessel that lay outside of us. Around the neck of this animal, some one had fastened a sixpence, by a bit of riband rove through a hole. I thought this sixpence might be made better use of, in purchasing some cherries, for which I had a strong longing, and I gave chase. In attempting to return to our own ship, with the dog, I fell into the water, between the two vessels. I could not swim a stroke; and I sang out, lustily, for help. As good luck would have it, Cooper came on board at that precise instant; and, hearing my outcry, he sprang down between the ships, and rescued me from drowning. I thought I was gone; and my condition made an impression on me that never will be lost. Had not Cooper accidentally appeared, just as he did, Ned Myers's yarn would have ended with this paragraph. I ought to add, that the sixpence got clear, the dog swimming away with it.

I had another escape from drowning, while we lay in the docks, having fallen overboard from the jolly-boat, while making an attempt at sculling. I forget, now, how I was saved; but then I had the boat and the oar to hold on to. In the end, it will be seen by what a terrific lesson I finally learned to swim.

One Sunday we were drifting up around the palace; and then it was that I told Cooper that the Duke of Kent was my godfather. He tried to persuade me to make a call; saying I could do no less than pay this respect to the prince. I had half a mind to try my hand at a visit; but felt too shy, and too much afraid. Had I done as Cooper so strongly urged me to do, one cannot say what might have been the consequences, or what change might have been brought about in my fortunes.[1]

One day Mr. Irish was in high glee, having received a message from Captain Johnston, to inform him that the latter was pressed! The captain used to dress in a blue long-tog, drab-breeches and top-boots, when he went ashore. "He thought he could pass for a gentleman from the country," said Mr. Irish, laughing, "but them pressgang chaps smelt the tar in his very boots!" Cooper was sent to the rendezvous, with the captain's desk and papers, and the latter was liberated. We all liked the captain, who was kind and considerate in his treatment of all hands; but it was fine fun for us to have "the old fellow" pressed—"*old fellow*" of six or eight-and-twenty, as he was then.

About the last of July, we left London, bound home. Our crew had again undergone some changes. We shipped a second mate, a New-England man. Jim Russel left us. We had lost Bill; and, another Bill, a dull Irish lad, who had gone to Spain, quitted us also. Our crew consisted of only Spanish Joe; Big Dan; Little Dan; Stephen, the Kennebunk man; Cooper; a Swede, shipped in London; a man whose name I have forgotten; and a young man who passed by the name of Davis, but who was, in truth, ——— ———, a son of the pilot who had brought us in, and taken us out, each time we passed up or down the river. This Davis had sailed in a coaster belonging to his father, and had got pressed in Sir Home Popham's South-American squadron. They made him a midshipman; but, disliking the sea, he was determined to go to America. We had to smuggle him out of the country, on account of the pressgang; he making his appearance on board us, suddenly, one night, in the river.

1. I well remember using these arguments to Ned; though less with any expectations of being admitted, than the boy seemed to believe. There was more roguery, than anything else, in my persuasion; though it was mixed with a latent wish to see the interior of the palace.—EDITOR.

The *Sterling* was short-handed this passage, mustering but four hands in a watch. Notwithstanding, we often reefed in the watch, though Cooper and Little Dan were both scarcely more than boys. Our mates used to go aloft, and both were active, powerful men. The cook, too, was a famous fellow at a drag. In these delicate times, when two or three days of watch and watch knock up a set of young men, one looks back with pride to a passage like this, when fourteen men and boys—four of the latter—brought a good sized ship across the ocean, reefing in the watch, weathering many a gale, and thinking nothing of it. I presume half our people, on a pinch, could have brought the *Sterling* in. One of the boys I have mentioned was named John Pugh, a little fellow the captain had taken as an apprentice in London, and who was now at sea for the first time in his life.

We had a long passage. Every inch of the way to the Downs was tide-work. Here we lay several days, waiting for a wind. It blew fresh from the southwest half of that summer, and the captain was not willing to go out with a foul wind. We were surrounded with vessels of war, most of the Channel Fleet being at anchor around us. This made a gay scene, and we had plenty of music, and plenty of saluting. One day all hands turned-to together, and fired starboard and larboard, until we could see nothing but a few mast-heads. What it all meant I never heard, but it made a famous smoke, and a tremendous noise.

A frigate came in, and anchored just ahead of us. She lowered a boat, and sent a reefer alongside to inform us that she was His Majesty's ship ———; that she had lost all her anchors but the stream, and she might strike adrift, and he advised us to get out of her way. The captain held on that day, however, but next morning she came into us, sure enough. The ships did not get clear without some trouble, and we thought it wisest to shift our berth. Once aweigh, the captain thought it best to turn out of the Downs, which we did, working through the Straits, and anchoring under Dungeness, as soon as the flood made. Here we lay until near sun-set, when we got under way to try our hand upon the ebb. I believe the skipper had made up his mind to tide it down to the Land's End, rather than remain idle any longer. There was a sloop of war lying in-shore of us, a mile or so, and just as we stretched out from under the land, she began to telegraph with a signal station ashore. Soon after, she weighed, and came out, also. In the middle watch we passed this ship, on opposite tacks, and learned that an embargo had been laid, and that we had only saved our distance by some ten or fifteen minutes! This embargo was to prevent the intelligence of the Copenhagen expedition from reaching the Danes.[2] That very day, we passed a convoy of transports, carrying a brigade from Pendennis Castle to Yarmouth, in order to join the main fleet. A gun-brig brought us to, and came near pressing the Swede, under the pretence that being allies of his king, England had a right to his services. Had not the man been as obstinate as a bull, and positively refused to go, I do believe we should have lost him. He was ordered into the boat at least half-a-dozen times, but swore he would not budge. Cooper had a little row with this boarding officer, but was silenced by the captain.

After the news received from the sloop of war, it may be supposed we did not venture to anchor anywhere on English ground. Keeping the channel, we passed the Isle of Wight several times, losing on the flood, the distance made on the ebb. At length we got a slant and fetched out into the Atlantic, heading well to the southward, however. Our passage was long, even after we got clear, the winds carrying us down as low as Corvo, which island we made, and then

2. A planned British attack on Denmark, an ally of Napoleonic France, which took place September 2–7, 1807.

taking us well north again. We had one very heavy blow that forced us to scud, the *Sterling* being one of the wettest ships that ever floated, when heading up to the sea.

When near the American coast, we spoke an English brig that gave us an account of the affair between the *Leopard* and the *Chesapeake,* though he made his own countrymen come out second-best.[3] Bitter were the revilings of Mr. Irish when the pilot told us the real state of the case. As was usual with this ship's luck, we tided it up the bay and river, and got safe alongside of the wharf at Philadelphia, at last. Here our crew was broken up, of course, and, with the exception of Jack Pugh, my brother apprentice, and Cooper, I never saw a single soul of them afterwards. Most of them went on to New York, and were swallowed up in the great vortex of seamen. Mr. Irish, I heard, died the next voyage he made, chief mate of an Indiaman. He was a prime fellow, and fit to command a ship.

Such was my first voyage at sea, for I count the passage round from Halifax as nothing. I had been kept in the cabin, it is true, but our work had been of the most active kind. The *Sterling* must have brought up, and been got under way, between fifty and a hundred times; and as for tacking, wearing, chapelling round, and box-hauling, we had so much of it by the channel pilots, that the old barky scarce knew which end was going foremost.[4] In that day, a

3. HMS *Leopard* made an unprovoked attack on the U.S. frigate *Chesapeake* as she was departing the Virginia Capes for the Mediterranean on 22 June 1807. Three American seamen died and eighteen, including Commodore James Barron, were wounded. The British justified the attack on the grounds they suspected *Chesapeake* had among its crew some deserters from the Royal Navy, and that the *Chesapeake*'s captain refused to permit a boarding party to search for the deserters. The outrage that followed very nearly drove the United States to declare war, but President Jefferson preferred to negotiate.

4. Tacking, wearing, chapelling round, and box hauling are technical terms for maneuvering a full-rigged ship through the wind's axis to reach the opposite tack. For excellent composite, illustrated explana-

ship did not get from the Forelands up to London without some trouble, and great was our envy of the large blocks and light cordage of the colliers, which made such easy work for their men. We singled much of our rigging, the second voyage up the river, ourselves, and it was a great relief to the people. A set of grass foresheets, too, that we bought in Spain, got to be great favourites, though, in the end, they cost the ship the life of a very valuable man.

Captain Johnston now determined to send me to Wiscasset, that I might go to school. A Wiscasset schooner, called the *Clarissa,* had come into Philadelphia, with freight from the West Indies, and she was about to sail for home in ballast. I was put on board as a passenger, and we sailed about a week after the ship got in from London. Jack Pugh staid behind, the *Sterling* being about to load for Ireland. On board the *Clarissa* I made the acquaintance of a Philadelphian born, who was an apprentice to the master of the schooner, of the name of Jack Mallet. He was a little older than myself, and we soon became intimate, and, in time, were fated to see many strange things in company.

The *Clarissa* went, by the Vineyard Sound and the Shoals, into Boston. Here she landed a few crates, and then sailed for Wiscasset, where we arrived after a pretty long passage. I was kindly received by the mother and family of Captain Johnston, and immediately sent to school. Shortly after, we heard of the embargo, and, the *Clarissa* being laid up, Jack Mallet became one of my school-mates.[5] We soon learned

---

tions based on contemporary sources, see John Harland, *Seamanship in the Age of Sail; an account of the shiphandling of the sailing man-of-war, 1600–1860, based on contemporary sources* (Naval Institute Press, 1984), pp. 181–202, and Darcy Lever, *The Young Sea Officer's Sheet Anchor, or a Key to the Leading of Rigging and to Practical Seamanship,* 2nd. ed. (reprint, New York, 1963), pp. 76–95, 120.

5. Jefferson's embargo of 1808 prohibited the departure of anything but coastal trade, and even those vessels had to post bond guaranteeing

that the *Sterling* had not been able to get out, and, ere long, Jack Pugh joined our party. A little later, Captain Johnston arrived, to go into the commercial quarantine with the rest of us.

This was the long embargo, as sailors called it, and it did not terminate until Erskine's arrangement was made, in 1809.[6] All this time I remained in Wiscasset, at school, well treated, and, if anything, too much indulged. Captain Johnston remained at home all this time, also, and, having nothing else to do, he set about looking out for a wife. We had, at school, Jack Pugh, Jack Mallet, and Bill Swett, the latter being a lad a little older than myself, and a nephew of the captain's. I was now sixteen, and had nearly gotten my growth.

As soon as the embargo was removed, Captain Johnston, accompanied by Swett, started for Philadelphia, to bring the ship round to New York. From that place he intended to sail for Liverpool, where Jack Pugh and myself were to join him, sailing in a ship called the *Columbia.* This plan was changed, however, and we were sent round by sea to join the *Sterling* again, in the port where I had first found her.

---

that their cargoes would remain in the United States. This act was prompted by British Orders in Council, which condemned vessels trading with any but British ports. The embargo was an attempt at economic coercion, meant to persuade Great Britain to revoke the offending Orders in Council by withholding the benefits of American trade from British manufacturers. See Dumas Malone, *Jefferson the President, Second Term, 1805–1809* (Boston, 1974), pp. 469–90.

6. British diplomat David M. Erskine attempted to negotiate with Americans on the trade question. In 1809, he promised, without authorization, that the Orders in Council of 1807 would be revoked for the United States. On the strength of this, President Madison legalized trade with Great Britain. When the Foreign Office repudiated the agreement and ordered Erskine's return to England, Madison revived the trade restrictions against Britain. See Bradford Perkins, *Prologue to War: England and the United States, 1805–1812,* pp. 212–17.

As this was near three years after I had quitted the Heizer's so unceremoniously, I went to look for them. Their old neighbours told me they had been gone to Martinique, about a twelvemonth. This was the last intelligence I ever heard of them. Bill Swett was now put into the cabin, and Jack Pugh and myself were sent regularly to duty before the mast. We lived in the steerage, and had cabin fare; but, otherwise, had the fortunes of foremast Jacks. Our freight was wheat in the lower hold, flour betwixt decks, and cotton on deck. The ship was very deep. Our crew was good, but both our mates were foreigners.

Nothing occurred until we got near soundings, when it came on to blow very heavy from the southward and westward.[7] The ship was running under a close-reefed main-topsail and foresail, with a tremendous sea on. Just as night set in, one Harry, a Prussian, came on deck from his supper to relieve the wheel, and, fetching a lurch as he went aft, he brought up against the launch, and thence down against our grass fore-sheet, which had been so great a favourite in the London passages. This rope had been stretched above the deck load for a ridge rope, but, being rotten, it gave way when the poor Prussian struck it, and he went into the sea. We could do no more than throw him the sky-light, which was large; but the ship went foaming ahead, leaving the poor fellow to his fate, in the midst of the hissing waters. Some of our people thought they saw poor Harry on the sky-light, but this could not have made much difference in such a raging sea. It was impossible to round-to, and as for a boat's living, it was out of the question.[8] This was the first man I saw lost at sea, and, notwithstanding the severity of the gale, and the danger of the ship herself, the fate of this excellent man made us all melancholy. The captain felt it

7. When a ship arrived near land where the sea bottom shoaled sufficiently for a lead line to reach bottom and enable a depth reading to be taken, the ship was said to be "on soundings."

8. To bring the ship around facing into the wind so as to heave to and stay near the stranded sailor.

bitterly, as was evident from his manner. Still, the thing was unavoidable.

We had begun to shorten sail early in the afternoon, and Harry was lost in the first dog-watch. A little later the larboard fore-sheet went, and the sail was split. All hands were called, and the rags were rolled up, and the gaskets passed. The ship now laboured so awfully that she began to leak. The swell was so high that we did not dare to come by the wind, and the seas would come in, just about the main chains, meet in board and travel out over her bows in a way to threaten everything that could be moved. We lads were lashed at the pumps, and ordered to keep at work; and to make matters worse, the wheat began to work its way into the pump-well. While things were in this state, the main-top-sail split, leaving the ship without a rag of sail on her.

The *Sterling* loved to be under water, even in moderate weather. Many a time have I seen her send the water aft, into the quarter-deck scuppers, and, as for diving, no loon was quicker than she. Now, that she was deep and was rolling her deck-load to the water, it was time to think of lightening her. The cotton was thrown overboard as fast as we could, and what the men could not start the seas did. After a while we eased the ship sensibly, and it was well we did; the wheat choking the pumps so often, that we had little opportunity for getting out the water.

I do not now recollect at what hour of this fearful night, Captain Johnston shouted out to us all to "look out"—and "hold on." The ship was broaching-to. Fortunately she did this at a lucky moment, and, always lying-to well, though wet, we made much better weather on deck. The mizzen-staysail was now set to keep her from falling off into the troughs of the sea. Still the wind blew as hard as ever. First one sail, then another, got loose, and a hard time we had to keep the canvass to the yards. Then the foretopmast went, with a heavy lurch, and soon after the main, carrying with it the mizzen-top-gallant-mast. We owed this to the embargo, in my judgment, the ship's rigging having got damaged lying dry so long. We were all night clearing the wreck, and the men who used the hatchets, told us that the wind would cant their tools so violently that they sometimes struck on the eyes, instead of the edge. The gale fairly seemed like a hard substance.

We passed a fearful night, working at the pumps, and endeavouring to take care of the ship. Next morning it moderated a little, and the vessel was got before the wind, which was perfectly fair. She could carry but little sail; though we got up top-gallant-masts for top-masts, as soon as the sea would permit. About four, I saw the land myself, and pointed it out to the mate. It was Cape Clear, and we were heading for it as straight as we could go. We hauled up to clear it, and ran into the Irish channel. A large fleet of vessels had gathered in and near the chops of the channel, in readiness to run into Liverpool by a particular day, that had been named in the law opening the trade, and great had been the destruction among them. I do not remember the number of the ships we saw, but there must have been more than a hundred. It was afterwards reported, that near fifty vessels were wrecked on the Irish coast. Almost every craft we fell in with was more or less dismasted, and one vessel, a ship called the *Liberty,* was reported to have gone down, with every soul on board her.

The weather becoming moderate, all hands of us went into Liverpool, the best way we could. The *Sterling* had good luck in getting up, though we lay some time in the river before we were able to get into dock. When we got out the cargo, we found it much damaged, particularly the wheat. The last was so hot that we could not bear our feet among it. We got it all out in a few days, when we went into a dry dock, and repaired.

This visit to Liverpool scattered our crew as if it had been so much dust in a squall. Most of our men were pressed, and those that were not, ran.[9] But one man, us boys ex-

9. Deserted the ship.

cepted, stuck by the ship. The chief mate—a foreigner, though of what country I never could discover—lived at a house kept by a handsome landlady. To oblige this lady, he ordered William Swett and myself to carry a bucket-full of salt, each, up to her house. The salt came out of the harness-cask, and we took it ashore openly, but we were stopped on the quay by a custom-house officer, who threatened to seize the ship. Such was the penalty for landing two buckets of Liverpool salt at Liverpool!

Captain Johnston had the matter explained, and he discharged the mate. Next day, the discharged man and the second mate were pressed. We got the last, who was a Swede, clear; and the chief mate, in the end, made his escape, and found his way back to New York. Among those impressed, was Jack Pugh, who having been bound in London, we did not dare show his papers. The captain tried hard to get the boy clear, but without success. I never saw poor Jack after this; though I learn he ran from the market-boat of the guard-ship, made his way back to Wiscasset, where he stayed some time, then shipped, and was lost at sea.

CHAPTER IV

AT LENGTH WE GOT A NEW CREW, and sailed for home. We had several passengers on board, masters of American ships who could go back themselves, but not carry their vessels with them, on account of certain liberties the last had taken with the laws. These persons were called "embargo captains." One of them, a Captain B——, kept Captain Johnston's watch, and got so much into his confidence and favour, that he gave him the vessel in the end. The passage home was stormy and long, but offered nothing remarkable. A non-importation law had been passed during our absence, and our ship was seized in New York in consequence of having a cargo of English salt.[1] We had taken the precaution, however, to have the salt cleared in Liver-

1. A misnamed reference to the Non-Intercourse Act of 15 March 1809. Before leaving office, President Jefferson repealed the embargo and proclaimed non-intercourse as a new policy, by which trade was resumed with all nations except France and Great Britain. The president was authorized to resume trade with either belligerent when that nation ceased to violate America's neutral rights. The actual "Non-Importation Act" was passed in 1806 and then suspended in favor of the embargo, a non-exportation act, in 1807.

pool, and put afloat before the day named in the law, and got clear after a detention of two months. Salt rose so much in the interval, that the seizure turned out to be a good thing for the owners.

While the ship was lying off the Battery, on her return from this voyage, and before she had hauled in, a boat came alongside with a young man in her in naval uniform. This was Cooper, who, in pulling across to go aboard his own vessel, had recognised our mast-heads, and now came to look at us.[2] This was the last time I met him, until the year 1843; or, for thirty-four years.

We now loaded with naval stores, and cleared again for Liverpool. Bill Swett did not make this voyage with us, the cook acting as steward. We had good passages out and home, experiencing no detention or accidents. In the spring of 1810, Captain Johnston gave the ship to Captain B——, who carried us to Liverpool for the third time. Nothing took place this voyage either, worthy of being mentioned, the ship getting back in good season. We now took in a cargo of staves for Limerick. Off the Hook we were brought-to by the *Indian* sloop-of-war, one of the Halifax cruisers, a squadron in company. Several vessels were coming out at the same time, and among them were several of the clippers in the French trade. The *Amiable Matilda* and the *Colt* went to windward of the Englishmen as if the last had been at anchor; but the *Tameahmeah,* when nearest to the English, got her yards locked in stays, and was captured. We saw all this, and felt, as was natural to men who beheld such things enacted at the mouth of their own port. Our passages both ways were pleasant, and nothing occurred out of the usual course. I fell in with a press-gang, however, in Limerick,

2. Midshipman James Fenimore Cooper, at his own request, was assigned to Lieutenant James Lawrence's *Wasp* based in New York harbor. Lawrence assigned Cooper to recruiting duty. See James Franklin Beard, ed., *The Letters and Journals of James Fenimore Cooper,* 4 vols. (Cambridge, Mass., 1960), vol. 1, pp. 15–16, 16*n*.

which would have nabbed me, but for a party of Irishmen, who showed fight and frightened the fellows so much that I got clear. Once before, I had been in the hands of these vermin in Liverpool, but Captain Johnston had got me clear by means of my indentures. I was acting as second-mate this voyage.

On our return home, the ship was ordered to Charleston to get a cargo of yellow pine, under a contract. Captain B—— was still in command, my old master, Captain Johnston, being then at home, occupied in building a new ship. I never saw this kind-hearted and indulgent seaman until the year 1842, when I made a journey to Wiscasset expressly to see him. Captain B—— and myself were never very good friends, and I was getting to be impatient of his authority; but I still stuck by the ship.

We had an ordinary run to Charleston, and began to prepare for the reception of our cargo. At this time, there were two French privateers on the southern coast, that did a great deal of damage to our trade. One went into Savannah, and got burned, for her pains; and the other came into Charleston, and narrowly escaped the same fate. A mob collected—made a fire-raft, and came alongside of our ship, demanding some tar. To own the truth, though then clothed with all the dignity of a "Dicky," [second-mate] I liked the fun, and offered no resistance. Bill Swett had come in, in a ship called the *United States;* and he was on board the *Sterling,* at the time, on a visit to me. We two, off hatches, and whipped a barrel of tar on deck; which we turned over to the raftsmen, with our hearty good wishes for their success. All this was, legally, very wrong; but, I still think, it was not so very far from being morally just; at least, as regards the privateersmen. The attempt failed, however, and those implicated were blamed a great deal more than they would have been, had they burned up the Frenchmen's eye-bolts. It is bad to fail, in a legal undertaking; but success is indispensable for forgiveness, to one that is illegal.

That night, Captain B—— and the chief mate, came down upon me, like a gust, for having parted with the tar. They concluded their lecture, by threatening to work me up. Bill Swett was by, and he got his share of the dose. When we were left to ourselves, we held a council of war, about future proceedings. Our crew had run, to a man, the cook excepted, as usually happens, in Charleston; and we brought in the cook, as a counsellor. This man told me, that he had overheard the captain and mate laying a plan to give me a threshing, as soon as I had turned in. Bill, now, frankly proposed that I should run, as well as himself; for he had already left his ship; and our plan was soon laid. Bill went ashore, and brought a boat down under the bows of the ship, and I passed my dunnage into her, by going through the forecastle; I then left the *Sterling,* for ever, never putting my foot on board of her again. I saw her, once or twice, afterwards, at a distance, and she always looked like a sort of home to me. She was subsequently lost, on the eastern coast, Captain Johnston still owning her, and being actually on board her, though only as a passenger. I had been out in her twelve times, from country to country, besides several short runs, from port to port. She always seemed natural to me; and I had got to know every timber and stick about her. I felt more, in quitting this ship, than I did in quitting Halifax. This desertion was the third great error of my life. The first was, quitting those with whom I had been left by my father; the second, abandoning my good friends, the Heizers; and the third, leaving the *Sterling.* Had Captain Johnston been in the ship, I never should have dreamed of running. He was always kind to me; and, if he failed in justice, it was on the side of indulgence. Had I continued with him, I make no doubt, my career would have been very different from what it has since turned out to be; and, I fear, I must refer one of the very bad habits, that afterwards marred my fortunes, that of drinking too much, to this act. Still, it will be remembered, I was only nineteen, loved adventure, and detested Captain B——.

After this exploit, Swett and I kept housed for a week. He then got into a ship called the *President,* and I into another called the *Tontine,* and both sailed for New York, where we arrived within a few days of each other. We now shipped together in a vessel called the *Jane,* bound to Limerick. This was near the close of the year 1811. Our passage out was tremendously bad, and we met with some serious accidents to our people. We were not far from the mouth of the Irish channel when the ship broached-to, in scudding under the foresail and main-top-sail, Bill Swett being at the helm. The watch below ran on deck and hauled up the foresail, without orders, to prevent the ship from going down stern foremost, the yards being square. As the ship came-to, she took a sea in, on her starboard side, which drove poor Bill to leeward, under some water-casks and boards, beating in two of his ribs. Both mates were injured also, and were off duty in consequence for several weeks. The plank sheer was ripped off the vessel from aft to amidships, as neatly as if it had been done by the carpenters. We could look down among the timbers the same as if the vessel were on the stocks.

The men braced up the after-yards, and then the ship was lying-to under a close-reefed main-top-sail. After this, she did well enough. We now passed the hurt below, and got tarred canvass over the timber-heads, and managed to keep out the water. Next day we made sail for our port. It blowing too fresh to get a pilot, we ran into a roadstead at the mouth of the Shannon, and anchored with both bowers. We rode out the gale, and then went up to Limerick. Here all hands got well, and returned to duty. In due time, we sailed for home in ballast. As we came into the Hook, we were hailed by a gun-boat, and heard of the "Little Embargo."[3]

The question now came up seriously between Bill and

3. A short-term prohibition on exports passed on 4 April 1812, limited to 90 days, this embargo was issued as a warning to American ship captains and owners that war was imminent.

myself, what was best to be done. I was for going to Wiscasset, like two prodigals, own our fault, and endeavour to amend. Bill thought otherwise. Now we were cast ashore, without employment, he thought it more manly to try and shift for ourselves. He had an uncle who was a captain of artillery, and who was then stationed on Governor's Island, and we took him into our councils. This gentleman treated us kindly, and kept us with him on the island for two days. Finding his nephew bent on doing something for himself, he gave us a letter to Lt. Trenchard, of the navy, by whom we were both shipped for the service. Swett got a master's-mate's berth, and I was offered the same, but felt too much afraid of myself to accept it. I entered the navy, then, for the first time, as a common Jack.

This was a very short time before war was declared, and a large flotilla of gun-boats was getting ready for the New York station.[4] Bill was put on board of No. 112, and I was ordered to No. 107, Sailing-Master Costigan. Soon after, we were all employed in fitting the *Essex* for sea; and while thus occupied the Declaration of War actually arrived. On this occasion I got drunk, for the second time in my life. A quantity of whiskey was started into a tub, and all hands drank to the success of the conflict. A little upset me, then, nor would I have drunk anything, but for the persuasions of some of my Wiscasset acquaintances, of whom there were

4. President Thomas Jefferson believed a standing navy might be a provocation to other nations and that the United States would be drawn into a European war by virtue of its existence. Rather than construct 74-gun ships-of-the-line as planned by his predecessor John Adams, Jefferson elected to construct almost 200 small gunboats of various rigs for purely defensive purposes. By the outbreak of the War of 1812, each major port possessed its own flotilla of up to 20 gunboats. For a sympathetic discussion of Jefferson's position, see Julia H. Macleod, "Jefferson and the Navy: A Defense," *Huntington Library Quarterly,* vol. 8 (1944–45), pp. 153–81. An objective account is Craig L. Symonds, *Navalists and Antinavalists: The Naval Policy Debate in the United States, 1785–1827* (Newark, Del., 1980).

several in the ship. I advise all young men, who feel no desire to drink, to follow their own propensities, and not to yield themselves up, body and soul, to the thoughtless persuasions of others. There is no real good-fellowship in swilling rum and whiskey; but the taste, once acquired, is hard to cure. I never drank much, as to quantity, but a little filled me with the love of mischief, and that little served to press me down for all the more valuable years of my life; valuable, as to the advancement of my worldly interests, though I can scarcely say I began really to live, as a creature of God's should live, to honour his name and serve his ends, until the year 1839.

After the *Essex* was fitted out, the flotilla cruised in the Sound, and was kept generally on the look-out, about the waters of New York. Towards the end of the season, our boat, with several others, was lying abreast of the Yard, when orders came off to meet the Yard Commander, Captain Chauncey, on the wharf.[5] Here, this officer addressed us, and said he was about to proceed to Lake Ontario, to take command, and asking who would volunteer to go with him. This was agreeable news to us, for we hated the gunboats, and would go anywhere to be quit of them. Every man and boy volunteered. We got twenty-four hours' liberty, with a few dollars in money, and when this scrape was over every man returned, and we embarked in a sloop for Albany. Our draft contained near 140 men, and was commanded by Mr. Mix, then a sailing-master, but who died a commander a few years since. Messrs. Osgood and Mallaby were also with

5. Captain Isaac Chauncey entered the navy from the merchant service as a lieutenant in 1799. He supervised construction of the frigate *President* and served in her under Captain Thomas Truxtun. Later he served with Commodores Richard Morris and Edward Preble in the Mediterranean, and commanded the brig *Hornet* during her sea trials in 1805. After a two-year furlough and a trading voyage to China, Chauncey returned to the navy and was appointed commandant of the New York Navy Yard at Brooklyn in 1809.

us, and two midshipmen, viz: Messrs. Sands and Livingston. The former of these young gentlemen is now a commander, but I do not know what became of Mr. Livingston. We had also two master's-mates, Messrs. Bogardus and Emory.

On reaching Albany, we paid a visit to the Governor, gave him three cheers, got some good cheer in return, and were all stowed in wagons, a mess in each, before his door. We now took to our land tacks, and a merry time we had of it. Our first day's run was to a place called Schenectady, and here the officers found an empty house, and berthed us all together, fastening the doors. This did not suit our notions of a land cruise, and we began to grumble. There was a regular hard horse of a boatswain's-mate with us, of the name of McNally. This man had been in the service a long time, and was a thorough man-of-war's man. He had collected twenty-four of us, whom he called his 'disciples,' and shamed am I to say, I was one. McNally called all hands on the upper deck, as he called it, that is to say, in the garret, and made us a speech. He said this was no way to treat volunteers, and proposed that we should "unship the awning." We rigged pries, and, first singing out, "stand from under," hove one half of the roof into the street, and the other into the garden. We then gave three cheers at our success. The officers now came down, and gave us a lecture. But we made out so good a case, that they let us run till morning, when every soul was back and mustered in the wagons. In this way we went through the country, cracking our jokes, laughing, and noting all oddities that crossed our course. I believe we were ten or twelve days working our way through the state, to Oswego. At Onondaga Lake we got into boats, and did better than in the wagons. At a village on the lake shore, the people were very bitter against us, and we had some difficulty. The word went among us they were Scotch, from the Canadas, but of this I know nothing. We heard in the morning, however, that most of our officers were in limbo, and we crossed and marched up a hill, intending to burn, sink, and destroy, if they were not liberated. Mischief was prevented by the appearance of Mr. Mix, with the other gentlemen, and we pushed off without coming to blows.

It came on to rain very hard, and we fetched up at a solitary house in the woods, and tried to get quarters. These were denied us, and we were told to shift for ourselves. This we did in a large barn, where we made good stowage until morning. In the night, we caught the owner coming about with a lantern to set fire to the barn, and we carried him down to a boat, and lashed him there until morning, letting the rain wash all the combustible matter out of him. That day we reached Oswego Falls, where a party of us were stationed some time, running boats over, and carrying stores across the portage.

When everything reached Oswego, all hands turned to, to equip some lake craft that had been bought for the service. These were schooners, salt droggers, of about sixty or eighty tons. All we did at Oswego, however, was to load these vessels, some six or eight in all, and put to sea. I went off in one of the first, a vessel called the *Fair American*. Having no armaments, we sailed in the night, to avoid John Bull's cruisers, of which there were several out at the time. As we got in with some islands, at no great distance from Sackett's Harbour, we fell in with the *Oneida*'s launch, which was always kept in the offing at night, rowing, or sailing, guard.[6] Bill Swett was in her, and we then met for the first time on fresh water. I now learned that Jack Mallet was on the station, too, whom I had not fallen in with since

6. A protected port at the extreme eastern end of Lake Ontario, near the mouth of the St. Lawrence River. Commodore Chauncey commanded the Lake Ontario squadron from Sackets Harbor (modern spelling) during the War of 1812. It was also the site of Henry Eckford's energetic shipbuilding during the war, 40 miles from the British naval base at Kingston, Ontario.

we parted at Wiscasset, more than three years before. A fortnight later I found him, acting as boatswain of the *Julia,* Sailing-Master Trant, a craft I have every reason to remember as long as I shall live.

The day after I reached the harbour, I was ordered on board the *Scourge.* This vessel was English-built, and had been captured before the war, and condemned, for violating the revenue laws, under the name of the Lord Nelson, by the *Oneida,* 16, Lt. Com. Woolsey—the only cruiser we then had on the lake.[7] This craft was unfit for her duty, but time pressed, and no better offered. Bulwarks had been raised on her, and she mounted eight sixes, in regular broadside. Her accommodations were bad enough, and she was so tender, that we could do little or nothing with her in a blow. It was often prognosticated that she would prove our coffin. Besides Mr. Osgood, who was put in command of this vessel, we had Mr. Bogardus, and Mr. Livingston, as officers. We must have had about forty-five souls on board, all told. We did not get this schooner out that season, however.

The commodore arriving, and an expedition against Kingston being in the wind, a party of us volunteered from the *Scourge,* to go on board the *Oneida.* This was in November, rather a latish month for active service on those waters. The brig went out in company with the *Conquest, Hamilton, Governor Tompkins, Pert, Julia,* and *Growler,* schooners. These last craft were all merchantmen, mostly without quarters, and scarcely fit for the duty on which they were employed. The *Oneida* was a warm little brig, of sixteen 24

7. Melancthon Woolsey (1780–1838), commander at the Sackets Harbor naval base until Chauncey arrived in 1812. He commanded the brig *Oneida,* and was Chauncey's second-in-command until superseded by Lieutenant Jesse D. Elliott. For a few months, in 1808–1809, Midshipman J. F. Cooper served under Lieutenant Woolsey when supervising construction of *Oneida* at Oswego, New York. Like William B. Shubrick, Woolsey was one of Cooper's lifelong naval friends.

lb. carronades, but as dull as a transport. She had been built to cross the bars of the American harbours, and would not travel to windward.

We went off the False Ducks, where we made the *Royal George,* a ship the English had built expressly to overlay the *Oneida,* two or three years before, and which was big enough to eat us. Her officers, however, did not belong to the Royal Navy; and we made such a show of schooners, that, though she had herself a vessel or two in company, she did not choose to wait for us. We chased her into the Bay of Quinté, and there we lost her in the darkness. Next morning, however, we saw her at anchor in the channel that leads to Kingston.[8] A general chase now commenced, and we ran down into the bay, and engaged the ship and batteries, as close as we could well get. The firing was sharp on both sides, and it lasted a great while. I was stationed at a gun, as her second captain, and was too busy to see much; but I know we kept our piece speaking as fast as we could, for a good bit. We drove the *Royal George* from a second anchorage, quite up to a berth abreast of the town; and it was said that her people actually deserted her, at one time. We gave her nothing but round-shot from our gun, and these we gave her with all our hearts. Whenever we noticed the shore, a stand of grape was added.

I know nothing of the damage done the enemy. We had the best of it, so far as I could see; and I think, if the

8. Commodore Chauncey sortied with the *Oneida* and his armed schooners in November 1812, to capture the *Royal George,* 22 guns, the strongest ship of the Provincial Marine on Lake Ontario. Though unsuccessful in capturing *Royal George,* Chauncey did establish his superiority in guns and ability to blockade Kingston, thereby obtaining control of the lake at the close of the 1812 campaigning season. See Chauncey's reports contained in William S. Dudley, ed., *The Naval War of 1812: A Documentary History* (Washington, 1985), pp. 337–54; for a Canadian perspective, see C. P. Stacey's "Commodore Chauncey's Attack on Kingston Harbour, Nov. 10, 1812," *Canadian Historical Review,* 32 (June 1951), pp. 126–38.

weather had not compelled us to haul off, something serious might have been done. As it was, we beat out with flying colours, and anchored a few miles from the light.

These were the first shot I ever saw fired in anger. Out brig had one man killed and three wounded, and she was somewhat injured aloft. One shot came in not far from my gun, and scattered lots of cat-tails, breaking in the hammock-cloths. This was the nearest chance I ran, that day; and, on the whole, I think we escaped pretty well. On our return to the harbour, the ten Scourges who had volunteered for the cruise, returned to their own schooner. None of us were hurt, though all of us were half frozen, the water freezing as fast as it fell.

Shortly after both sides went into winter quarters, and both sides commenced building. We launched a ship called the *Madison,* about this time, and we laid the keel of another, that was named the *Pike.* What John Bull was about is more than I can say, though the next season showed he had not been idle. The navigation did not absolutely close, notwithstanding, until December.

Our vessels were moored about the harbour, and we were all frozen in, as a matter of course. Around each craft, however, a space was kept cut, to form a sort of ditch, in order to prevent being boarded. Parties were regularly stationed to defend the *Madison,* and, in the days, we worked at her rigging, and at that of the *Pike,* in gangs. Our larboard guns were landed, and placed in a block-house, while the starboard were kept mounted. My station was that of captain of one of the guns that remained.

The winter lasted more than four months, and we made good times of it. We often went after wood, and occasionally we knocked over a deer. We had a target out on the lake, and this we practised on, making ourselves rather expert cannoneers. Now and then they rowsed us out on a false alarm, but I know of no serious attempt's being made by the enemy, to molest us.

The lake was fit to navigate about the middle of April. Somewhere about the 20th[9] the soldiers began to embark, to the number of 1700 men. A company came on board the *Scourge,* and they filled us chock-a-block. It came on to blow, and we were obliged to keep these poor fellows, cramped as we were, most of the time on deck, exposed to rain and storm. On the 25th we got out, rather a showy force altogether, though there was not much service in our small craft. We had a ship, a brig, and twelve schooners, fourteen sail in all. The next morning we were off Little York, having sailed with a fair wind.[10] All hands anchored about a mile from the beach. I volunteered to go in a boat, to carry soldiers ashore. Each of us brought across the lake two of these boats in tow, but we had lost one of ours, dragging her after us in a staggering breeze. I got into the one that was left, and we put half our soldiers in her, and shoved off. We had little or no order in landing, each boat pulling as hard as she could. The English blazed away at us, concealed in a wood, and our men fired back again from the boat. I never was more disappointed in men, than I was in the soldiers. They were mostly tall, pale-looking Yankees, half dead with sickness and the bad weather—so mealy, indeed, that half of them could not take their grog, which, by this time, I had got to think a bad sign. As soon as they got near the enemy, however, they became wide awake, pointed out to each other where to aim, and many of them actually jumped into the water, in order to get the sooner ashore. No men could have behaved better, for I confess

9. 22d—Author

10. A joint operation against the capital of Upper Canada on 27 April 1813. Some 2,000 troops were carried across Lake Ontario in Chauncey's squadron: the ship *Madison,* the brig *Oneida,* and schooners *Hamilton, Scourge, Conquest, Governor Tompkins, Julia, Growler, Ontario, Fair American, Pert, Asp,* and *Lady of the Lake.* For the leading secondary account of the war, see Reginald Horsman, *The War of 1812* (New York, 1969).

frankly I did not like the work at all. It is no fun to pull in under a sharp fire, with one's back to his enemy, and nothing but an oar to amuse himself with. The shot flew pretty thick, and two of our oars were split. This was all done with musketry, no heavy guns being used at this place. I landed twice in this way, but the danger was principally in the first affair. There was fighting up on the bank, but it gave us no trouble. Mr. Livingston commanded the boat.

When we got back to the schooner, we found her lifting her anchors. Several of the smaller craft were now ordered up the bay, to open on the batteries nearer to the town. We were the third from the van, and we all anchored within canister range. We heard a magazine blow up, as we stood in, and this brought three cheers from us. We now had some sharp work with the batteries, keeping up a steady fire. The schooner ahead of us had to cut, and she shifted her berth outside of us. The leading schooner, however, held on. In the midst of it all, we heard cheers down the line, and presently we saw the commodore pulling in among us, in his gig. He came on board us, and we greeted him with three cheers. While he was on the quarter-deck, a hot shot struck the upper part of the after-port, cut all the boarding-pikes adrift from the main-boom, and wounded a man named Lemuel Bryant, who leaped from his quarters and fell at my feet. His clothes were all on fire when he fell, and, after putting them out, the commodore himself ordered me to pass him below. The old man spoke encouragingly to us, and a little thing took place that drew his attention to my crew. Two of the trucks of the gun we were fighting had been carried away, and I determined to shift over its opposite. My crew were five negroes, strapping fellows, and as strong as jackasses. The gun was called the Black Joke. Shoving the disabled gun out of the way, these chaps crossed the deck, unhooked the breechings and gun-tackles, raised the piece from the deck, and placed it in the vacant port. The commodore commended us, and called out, "that is quick work, my lads!" In less than three minutes, I am certain, we were playing on the enemy with the fresh gun.

As for the old man, he pulled through the fire as coolly as if it were only a snow-balling scrape, though many a poor fellow lost the number of his mess in the boats that day. When he left us, we cheered him again. He had not left us long, before we heard an awful explosion on shore. Stones as big as my two fists fell on board of us, though nobody was hurt by them. We cheered, thinking some dire calamity had befallen the enemy. The firing ceased soon after this explosion, though one English gun held on, under the bank, for some little time.

CHAPTER V

WE DID NOT KNOW THE CAUSE OF THE LAST EXPLOSION, until after the firing ceased. I had seen an awful black cloud, and objects in the air that I took for men; but little did we imagine the explosion had cost us so dear. Our schooner lay at no great distance from the common landing, and no sooner were we certain of the success of the day, than Mr. Osgood ordered his boat's crew called away, and he landed. As I belonged to the boat, I had an early opportunity of entering the town.

We found the place deserted. With the exception of our own men, I found but one living being in it. This was an old woman whom I discovered stowed away in a potatoe locker, in the government house. I saw tables set, and eggs in the cups, but no inhabitant. Our orders were of the most severe kind, not to plunder, and we did not touch a morsel of food even. The liquor, however, was too much for our poor natures, and a parcel of us had broke bulk in a better sort of grocery, when some officers came in and stove the casks. I made sail, and got out of the company. The army had gone in pursuit of the enemy, with the exception of a few riflemen, who, being now at liberty, found their way into the place.

I ought to feel ashamed, and do feel ashamed of what occurred that night; but I must relate it, lest I feel more ashamed for concealing the truth. We had spliced the main-brace pretty freely throughout the day, and the pull I got in the grocery just made me ripe for mischief. When we got aboard the schooner again, we found a canoe that had drifted athwart-hawse and had been secured. My gun's crew, the Black Jokers, wished to have some fun in the town, and they proposed to me to take a cruise ashore. We had few officers on board, and the boatswain, a boatswain's mate in fact, consented to let us leave. We all went ashore in this canoe, then, and were soon alongside of a wharf. On landing, we were near a large store, and looking in at a window, we saw a man sitting asleep, with a gun in the hollow of his arm. His head was on the counter, and there was a lamp burning. One of the blacks pitched through the window, and was on him in a moment. The rest followed, and we made him a prisoner. The poor fellow said he had come to look after his property, and he was told no one would hurt him. My blacks now began to look about them, and to help themselves to such articles as they thought they wanted. I confess I helped myself to some tea and sugar, nor will I deny that I was in such a state as to think the whole good fun. We carried off one canoe load, and even returned for a second. Of course such an exploit could not have been effected without letting all in the secret share; and one boat-load of plunder was not enough. The negroes began to drink, however, and I was sober enough to see the consequences, if they were left ashore any longer. Some riflemen came in, too, and I succeeded in getting my jokers away.

The recklessness of sailors may be seen in our conduct. All we received for our plunder was some eight or ten gallons of whiskey, when we got back to the harbour, and this at the risk of being flogged through the fleet![1] It seemed to us to be a scrape, and that was a sufficient excuse for disobeying orders, and for committing a crime. For myself, I was influenced more by the love of mischief, and a weak desire to have it said I was foremost in such an exploit, than from any mercenary motive. Notwithstanding the severity of the orders, and one or two pretty sharp examples of punishment inflicted by the commodore, the Black Jokers were not the only plunderers ashore that night. One master's-mate had the buttons taken off his coat, for stealing a feather bed, besides being obliged to carry it back again. Of course he was a shipped master's-mate.

I was ashore every day while the squadron remained in the port. Our schooner never shifted her berth from the last one she occupied in the battle, and that was pretty well up the bay. I paid a visit to the gun that had troubled us all so much, and which we could not silence, for it was under a bank, near the landing-place. It was a long French eighteen, and did better service, that day, than any other piece of John Bull's. I think it hulled us several times.

I walked over the ground where the explosion took place. It was a dreadful sight; the dead being so mutilated that it was scarcely possible to tell their colour. I saw gun-barrels bent nearly double. I think we saw Sir Roger Sheafe, the British General, galloping across the field, by himself, a few minutes before the explosion. At all events, we saw a mounted officer, and fired at him. He galloped up to the government-house, dismounted, went in, remained a short time, and then galloped out of town. All this I saw; and the

1. A British, not an American, naval practice, severe punishment used here in the figurative sense. The U.S. Navy countenanced the lash or cat-o'-nine-tails but did not "flog through the fleet," by which the culprit is put in a ship's boat, lashed to a grating, and rowed to each vessel of the fleet where the boatswain or other designated warrant of that ship climbs down and gives 36 or more strokes with the "cat."

old woman in the potato-locker told me the general had been in the house a short time before we landed. Her account agreed with the appearance of the officer I saw; though I will not pretend to be certain it was General Sheafe.

I ought to mention the kindness of the commodore to the poor of York. As most of the inhabitants came back to their habitations the next day, the poor were suffering for food. Our men were ordered to roll barrels of salt meat and barrels of bread to their doors, from the government stores that fell into our hands. We captured an immense amount of these stores, a portion of which we carried away. We sunk many guns in the lake; and as for the powder, *that* had taken care of itself. Among other things we took, was the body of an English officer, preserved in rum, which, they said, was General Brock's.[2] I saw it hoisted out of the *Duke of Gloucester,* the man-of-war brig we captured, at Sackett's Harbour, and saw the body put in a fresh cask. I am ashamed to say, that some of our men were inclined to drink the old rum.

We burned a large corvette, that was nearly ready for launching, and otherwise did the enemy a good deal of harm. The inhabitants that returned were very submissive, and thankful for what they received. As for the man of the red store, I never saw him after the night he was plundered, nor was anything ever said of the scrape.

Our troops had lost near three hundred men in the attack, the wounded included; and as a great many of these green soldiers were now sick from exposure, the army was much reduced in force. We took the troops on board on the 1st of

2. Major General Isaac Brock, who commanded British forces in Upper Canada in 1812. It is untrue that the "body of an English officer, preserved in rum" to which Ned refers, was that of General Brock. He died eight months before, in the battle of Queenston Heights (13 October 1812) on the Niagara River. His body was buried in the bastion at Fort George after the American withdrawal. It was later reinterred in the family plot at Hamilton, Ontario, in 1856.

May, but could not sail, on account of a gale, until the 8th, which made the matter worse. Then we got under way, and crossed the lake, landing the soldiers a few miles to the eastward of Fort Niagara. Our schooner now went to the Harbour, along with the commodore, though some of the craft remained near the head of the lake. Here we took in another lot of soldiers, placed two more large batteaux in tow, and sailed for the army again. We had good passages both ways, and this duty was done within a few days. While at the Harbour, I got a message to go and visit Bill Swett, but the poor fellow died without my being able to see him. I heard he was hurt at York, but never could come at the truth.

On the 27th May, the army got into the batteaux, formed in two divisions, and commenced pulling towards the mouth of the Niagara. The morning was foggy, with a light wind, and the vessels getting under way, kept company with the boats, a little outside of them. The schooners were closest in, and some of them opened on Fort George, while others kept along the coast, scouring the shore with grape and canister as they moved ahead.[3] The *Scourge* came to an anchor a short distance above the place selected for the landing, and sprung her broadside to the shore.[4] We now kept up a steady fire with grape and canister, until the boats had got in-shore and were engaged with the enemy, when we

3. On 27 May, one month to the day after the capture of York, an American force made an amphibious attack on Fort George, a British fortification at the mouth of the Niagara River. The attack was under the command of General Henry Dearborn, whose troops landed from barges protected by Chauncey's squadron. Master Commandant Oliver H. Perry, in charge of the U.S. squadron on Lake Erie, assisted Chauncey during the attack, directing the cannon fire of the supporting schooners.

4. To counter the unsteadying effects of wind and surf, American gunboats had to anchor bow and stern, parallel to the beach, in order to fire at the British defenders and protect the attacking force led by Colonel Winfield Scott.

threw round-shot, over the heads of our own men, upon the English. As soon as Colonel Scott was ashore, we sprung our broadside upon a two-gun battery that had been pretty busy, and we silenced that among us. This affair, for our craft, was nothing like that of York, though I was told the vessels nearer the river had warmer berths of it. We had no one hurt, though we were hulled once or twice. A little rigging was cut; but we set this down as light work compared to what the old Black Joke had seen that day month. There was a little sharp fighting ashore, but our men were too strong for the enemy, when they could fairly get their feet on solid ground.

Just after we had anchored, Mr. Bogardus was sent aloft to ascertain if any enemy were to be seen. At first he found nobody; but, after a little while, he called out to have my gun fired at a little thicket of brushwood that lay on an inclined plain, near the water. Mr. Osgood came and elevated the gun, and I touched it off. We had been looking out for the blink of muskets, which was one certain guide to find a soldier; and the moment we sent this grist of grape and canister into those bushes, the place lighted up as if a thousand muskets were there. We then gave the chaps the remainder of our broadside. We peppered that wood well, and did a good deal of harm to the troops stationed at the place.

The wind blew on shore, and began to increase; and the commodore now threw out a signal for the boats to land, to take care of the batteaux that were thumping on the beach, and then for their crews to assist in taking care of the wounded. Of course I went in my own boat, Mr. Bogardus having charge of her. We left the schooner, just as we quitted our guns, black with powder, in our shirts and trowsers, though we took the precaution to carry our boarding-belts, with a brace of pistols each, and a cutlass. On landing, we first hauled up the boats, taking some dead and wounded men out of them, and laying them on the beach.

We were now ordered to divide ourselves into groups of three, and go over the ground, pick up the wounded, and carry them to a large house that had been selected as a hospital. My party consisted of Bill Southard, Simeon Grant, and myself, we being messmates. The first man we fell in with, was a young English soldier, who was seated on the bank, quite near the lake. He was badly hurt, and sat leaning his head on his hands. He begged for water, and I took his cap down to the lake and filled it, giving him a drink; then washing his face. This revived him, and he offered us his canteen, in which was some excellent Jamaica. To us chaps, who got nothing better than whiskey, this was a rare treat, and we emptied the remainder of his half pint, at a pull a-piece. After tapping this rum, we carried the poor lad up to the house, and turned him over to the doctors. We found the rooms filled with wounded already, and the American and English doctors hard at work on them.

As we left the hospital, we agreed to get a canteen a-piece, and go round among the dead, and fill them with Jamaica. When our canteens were about a third full, we came upon a young American rifleman, who was lying under an apple-tree. He was hit in the head, and was in a very bad way. We were all three much struck with the appearance of this young man, and I now remember him as one of the handsomest youths I had ever seen. His wound did not bleed, though I thought the brains were oozing out, and I felt so much sympathy for him, that I washed his hurt with the rum. I fear I did him harm, but my motive was good. Bill Southard ran to find a surgeon, of whom several were operating out on the field. The young man kept saying "no use," and he mentioned "father and mother," "Vermont." He even gave me the names of his parents, but I was too much in the wind, from the use of rum, to remember them. We might have been half an hour with this young rifleman, busy on him most of the time, when he murmured a few words, gave me one of the sweetest smiles I ever saw on a man's face, and made no more signs of life. I kept at work, notwithstanding, until Bill got back with the doctor. The latter cast an eye on the rifleman, pronounced him dead, and coolly walked away.

There was a bridge, in a sort of a swamp, that we had fired on for some time, and we now moved down to it, just to see what we had done. We found a good many dead, and several horses in the mire, but no wounded. We kept emptying canteens, as we went along, until our own would hold no more. On our return from the bridge, we went to a brook in order to mix some grog, and then we got a full view of the offing. Not a craft was to be seen! Everything had weighed and disappeared. This discovery knocked us all a-back, and we were quite at a loss how to proceed. We agreed, however, to pass through a bit of woods, and get into the town, it being now quite late in the day. There we knew we should find the army, and might get tidings of the fleet. The battle-ground was now nearly deserted, and to own the truth we were, all three, at least two sheets in the wind. Still I remember everything, for my stomach would never allow me to get beastly drunk; it rejecting any very great quantity of liquor. As we went through the wood, open pine trees, we came across an officer lying dead, with one leg over his horse, which was dead also. I went up to the body, turned it over, and examined it for a canteen, but found none. We made a few idle remarks, and proceeded.

In quitting the place, I led the party; and, as we went through a little thicket, I heard female voices. This startled me a little; and, on looking round, I saw a white female dress, belonging to a person who was evidently endeavouring to conceal herself from us. I was now alone, and walked up to the women, when I found two; one, a lady, in dress and manner, and the other a person that I have always supposed was her servant. The first was in white; the last in a dark calico. They were both under thirty, judging from their looks; and the lady was exceedingly well-looking.

They were much alarmed; and, as I came up, the lady asked me if I would hurt her. I told her no; and that no person should harm her, while she remained with us. This relieved her, and she was able to give an account of her errand on the field of battle. Our looks, half intoxicated, and begrimed with the smoke of a battle, as we were, certainly were enough to alarm her; but I do not think one of the three would have hesitated about fighting for a female, that they thus found weeping, in this manner, in the open field. The maid was crying also. Simeon Grant, and Southard, did make use of some improper language, at first; but I brought them up, and they said they were sorry, and would go all lengths, with me, to protect the women. The fact was, these men supposed we had fallen in with common camp followers; but I had seen too much of officers' wives, in my boyhood, not to know that this was one.

The lady then told her story. She had just come from Kingston, to join her husband; having arrived but a few hours before. She did not see her husband, but she had heard he was left wounded on the field; and she had come out in the hope of finding him. She then described him, as an officer mounted, with a particular dress, and inquired if we had met with any such person, on the field. We told her of the horseman we had just left; and led her back to the spot. The moment the lady saw the body, she threw herself on it, and began to weep and mourn over it, in a very touching manner. The maid, too, was almost as bad as the mistress. We were all so much affected, in spite of the rum, that, I believe, all three of us shed tears. We said all we could, to console her, and swore we would stand by her, until she was safe back among her friends.

It was a good bit before we could persuade the lady to quit her husband's body. She took a miniature from his neck, and I drew his purse and watch from him and handed them to her. She wanted me to keep the purse, but this we all three refused, up and down. We had hauled our manly tacks aboard, and had no thoughts of plunder. Even the maid urged us to keep the money, but we would have nothing to do with it. I shall freely own my faults; I hope I shall be believed when I relate facts that show I am not altogether without proper feelings.

The officer had been hit somewhere about the hip, and the horse must have been killed by another grape-shot, fired from the same gun. We laid the body of the first over in such a manner as to get a good look at him, but we did not draw the leg from under the horse.[5]

When we succeeded in persuading the lady to quit her husband's body, we shaped our course for the light-house. Glad were we three tars to see the mast-heads of the shipping in the river, as we came near the banks of the Niagara. The house at the light was empty; but, on my hailing, a woman's voice answered from the cellar. It was an old

5. When Myers related this circumstance, I remembered that a Lieutenant-Colonel Meyers had been killed in the affair at Fort George, something in the way here mentioned. On consulting the American official account, I found that my recollection was just, so far as this—a Lieutenant-Colonel Meyers was reported as wounded and taken prisoner. I then recollected to have been present at a conversation between Major-General Lewis and Major Baker, his adjutant-general, shortly after the battle, in which the question arose whether the same shot had killed Colonel Meyers that killed his horse. General Lewis thought not; Major Baker thought it had. On my referring to the official account as reporting this gentleman to have been only *wounded,* I was told it was a mistake, he having been *killed.* Now for the probabilities. Both Ned and his sister understand that their father was slain in battle, about this time. Ned thought this occurred at Waterloo, but the sister thinks not. Neither knew anything of the object of my inquiry. The sister says letters were received from *Quebec* in relation to the father's personal effects. It would be a strange thing, if Ned had actually found his own father's body on the field, in this extraordinary manner! I pretend not to say it is so; but it must be allowed it looks very much like it. The lady may have been a wife, married between the years 1796 and 1813, when Mr. Meyers had got higher rank. This occurrence was related by Ned without the slightest notion of the inference that I have here drawn.—EDITOR.

woman who had taken shelter from shot down in the hold, the rest of the family having slipped and run. We now got some milk for the lady, who continued in tears most of the time. Sometimes she would knock off crying for a bit, when she seemed to have some distrust of us; but, on the whole, we made very good weather in company. After staying about half an hour at the light-house, we left it for the town, my advice to the lady being to put herself under the protection of some of our officers. I told her if the news of what had happened reached the commodore, she might depend on her husband's being buried with the honours of war, and said such other things to comfort her as came to the mind of a man who had been sailing so near the wind.

I forgot to relate one part of the adventure. Before we had got fairly clear of the woods, we fell in with four of Forsyth's men, notoriously the wickedest corps in the army.[6] These fellows began to crack their jokes at the expense of the two females, and we came near having a brush with them. When we spoke of our pistols, and of our determination to use them, before we would let our convoy come to harm, these chaps laughed at our pop-guns, and told us they had such things as 'rifles.' This was true enough, and had we come to broadsides, I make no doubt they would have knocked us over like so many snipes. I began to reason with them, on the impropriety of offending respectable females; and one of the fellows, who was a kind of a corporal, or something of that sort, shook my hand, said I was right, and offered to be friends. So we spliced the main-brace, and parted. Glad enough was the lady to be rid of them so easily. In these squalls she would bring up in her tears, and then when all went smooth again, she would break out afresh.

After quitting the light, we made the best of our way for the town. Just as we reached it, we fell in with a party of

6. Captain Benjamin Forsyth's company of riflemen, who had been garrisoned near Ogdensburg in northern New York, served as part of the invading force under Colonel Scott.

soldier-officers, and we turned the lady and her woman over to their care. These gentlemen said a good word in our favour, and here we parted company with our convoy, I never hearing, or seeing, anything of either afterwards.

By this time it was near dark, and Bill Southard and I began to look out for the *Scourge*. She was anchored in the river, with the rest of the fleet, and we went down upon a wharf to make a signal for a boat. On the way we saw a woman crying before a watch-maker's shop, and a party of Forsyth's close by. On enquiry, we learned these fellows had threatened to rob her shop. We had been such defenders of the sex, that we could not think of deserting this woman, and we swore we would stand by her, too. We should have had a skirmish here, I do believe, had not one or two rifle officers hove in sight, when the whole party made sail from us. We turned the woman over to these gentlemen, who said, "ay, there are some of our vagabonds, again." One of them said it would be better to call in their parties, and before we reached the water we heard the bugle sounding the recall.

They had given us up on board the schooner. A report of some Indians being out had reached her, and we three were set down as scalped. Thank God, I've got all the hair on my head yet, and battered as my old hulk has got to be, and shattered as are my timbers, it is as black as a raven's wing at this moment. This, my old ship-mate, who is logging this yarn, says he thinks is a proof my mother was a French Canadian, though such is not the fact, as it has been told to me.

Those riflemen were regular scamps. Just before we went down to the wharf, we saw one walking sentinel before the door of a sort of barracks. On drawing near and asking what was going on inside, we were told we had nothing to do with their fun ashore, that we might look in at a window, however, but should not go in. We took him at his word; a merry scene it was inside. The English officers' dunnage had been broken into, and there was a party of the corps strutting about in uniform coats and feathers. We thought it best to give these dare-devils a berth, and so we left them. One was never safe with them on the field of battle, friend or enemy.

We met a large party of marines on the wharf, marching up under Major Smith.[7] They were going to protect the people of the town from further mischief. Mr. Osgood was glad enough to see us, and we got plenty of praise for what we had done with the women. As for the canteens, we had to empty them, after treating the crew of the boat that was sent to take us off. I did not enter the town after that night.

We lay some time in the Niagara, the commodore going to the harbour to get the *Pike* ready.[8] Captain Crane took the rest of us off Kingston, where we were joined by the commodore, and made sail again for the Niagara.[9] Here Colonel Scott embarked with a body of troops, and we went

7. Major Richard Smith was the commander of the U.S. Marines of Chauncey's squadron. Marines were not used as assault troops in the early 19th century. Rather, they reinforced discipline on board U.S. naval vessels, posted guard at naval depots, and served as marksmen and boarders during battles at sea.

8. The ship *General Pike,* named in honor of Brigadier General Zebulon Pike, recently killed by the magazine explosion at York. Commodore Chauncey returned hastily to Sackets Harbor when he learned of an unsuccessful British attack led by Commodore Sir James Lucas Yeo and Governor-General George Prevost. Defenders of Sackets Harbor, although successful, had prematurely set fire to the *General Pike,* fearing she would be captured. Though the damage was repaired and the ship launched, Chauncey became very cautious about leaving his base without naval defense. Theodore Roosevelt, *The Naval War of 1812* (New York, 1882), pp. 233–35.

9. Master Commandant William M. Crane, former commander of U.S. brig *Nautilus,* the first U.S. Navy vessel captured by the British during the War of 1812. Made prisoner in July 1812, Crane was paroled, exchanged, and returned to Boston. When the lake squadrons were enlarged in 1813, the Navy Department sent Crane to Sackets Harbor, where Chauncey made him flag captain in the 24-gun corvette *Madison.*

to Burlington Bay to carry the heights. They were found to be too strong; and the men, after landing, returned to the vessels. We then went to York, again, and took possession of the place a second time. Here we destroyed several boats, and stores, set fire to the barracks, and did the enemy a good deal of damage otherwise; after which we left the place. Two or three days later we crossed the lake and landed the soldiers, again, at Fort Niagara.

Early in August, while we were still in the river, Sir James Yeo hove in sight with two ships, two brigs, and two schooners.[10] We had thirteen sail in all, such as they were, and immediately got under way, and manœuvred for the weather-gauge. All the enemy's vessels had regular quarters, and the ships were stout craft.[11] Our squadron sailed very unequally, some being pretty fast, and others as dull as droggers. Nor were we more than half fitted out. On board the *Scourge* the only square-sail we had, was made out of an English marquée we had laid our hands on at York, the first time we were there. I ought to say, too, that we got two small brass guns at York, four-pounders, I believe, which Mr. Osgood clapped into our two spare ports forward.[12] This gave us ten guns in all, sixes and fours. I remember that Jack Mallet laughed at us heartily for the fuss we made with our pop-guns, as he called them, while we were working upon the English batteries, saying we might just as well have spared our powder, as for any good we did. He be-

10. Commodore Yeo's squadron consisted of the ships *Wolfe* and *Royal George,* brigs *Melville* and *Moira,* and schooners *Sydney Smith* and *Beresford.* C. Winton-Clare [R. C. Anderson], "A Ship-builders War," in Morris Zaslow, ed., *The Defended Border: Upper Canada and the War of 1812* (Toronto: Macmillan Company of Canada, 1964), pp. 165–73.

11. The British vessels were purpose-built for war, having bulwarks to protect the crew serving the guns and other seamen working the ships during a battle. While *Scourge* had raised bulwarks, they were lacking in most of the converted schooners under Chauncey's command.

12. Weight refers to the weight of shot thrown by the cannon, not the cannon itself, which would weigh many times as much.

longed to the *Julia,* which had a long thirty-two, forward, which they called the "Old Sow," and one smart eighteen aft. She had two sixes in her waist, also; but *they* disdained to use *them*.

While we were up at the harbour, the last time, Mr. Mix, who had married a sister of Mr. Osgood, took a party of us in a boat, and we went up Black River, shooting. The two gentlemen landed, and as we were coming down the river, we saw something swimming, which proved to be a bear. We had no arms, but we pulled over the beast, and had a regular squaw-fight with him. We were an hour at work with this animal, the fellow coming very near mastering us. I struck at his nose with an iron tiller fifty times, but he warded the blow like a boxer. He broke our boat-hook, and once or twice, he came near boarding us. At length a wood-boat gave us an axe, and with this we killed him. Mr. Osgood had this bear skinned, and said he should send the skin to his family. If he did, it must have been one of the last memorials it ever got from him.

CHAPTER VI

I LEFT THE TWO FLEETS MANOEUVRING FOR THE WIND, in the last chapter. About nine o'clock, the *Pike* got abeam of the *Wolfe,* Sir James Yeo's own ship, hoisted her ensign, and fired a few guns to try the range of her shot. The distance was too great to engage. At this time our sternmost vessels were two leagues off, and the commodore wore round, and hauled up on the other tack.[1] The enemy did the same; but, perceiving that our leading ships were likely to weather on him, he tacked, and hauled off to the northward. We stood on in pursuit, tacking too; but the wind soon fell, and about sunset it was quite calm.

Throughout the day, the *Scourge* had as much as she could do to keep anywhere near her station. As for the old *Oneida,* she could not be kept within a long distance of her proper berth. We were sweeping, at odd times, for hours that day.[2] Towards evening, all the light craft were doing the same, to close with the commodore. Our object was to get together,

1. One league equalled about 3 nautical miles or 6,000 yards.
2. A sweep is a colloquial term for oar; in this era "sweeping" meant rowing.

lest the enemy should cut off some of our small vessels during the night.

Before dark the whole line was formed again, with the exception of the *Oneida,* which was still astern, towing.[3] She ought to have been near the commodore, but could not get there. A little before sunset, Mr. Osgood ordered us to pull in our sweeps, and to take a spell. It was a lovely evening, not a cloud visible, and the lake being as smooth as a looking-glass. The English fleet was but a short distance to the northward of us; so near, indeed, that we could almost count their ports. They were becalmed, like ourselves, and a little scattered.

We took in our sweeps as ordered, laying them athwart the deck, in readiness to be used when wanted. The vessels ahead and astern of us were, generally, within speaking distance. Just as the sun went below the horizon, George Turnblatt, a Swede, who was our gunner, came to me, and said he thought we ought to secure our guns; for we had been cleared for action all day, and the crew at quarters. We were still at quarters, in name; but the petty officers were allowed to move about, and as much license was given to the people as was wanted. I answered that I would gladly secure mine if he would get an order for it; but as we were still at quarters, and there lay John Bull, we might get a slap at him in the night. On this the gunner said he would go aft, and speak to Mr. Osgood on the subject. He did so, but met the captain (as we always called Mr. Osgood) at the break of the quarter-deck. When George had told his errand, the captain looked at the heavens, and remarked that the night was so calm, there could be no great use in securing the guns, and the English were so near we should certainly engage, if

3. Commodore Chauncey usually had his slow sailing schooners towed by the faster square-rigged ships because the schooners served as platforms for his heavy, long-range cannon. Even though the brig *Oneida* was herself a slow sailer, she was used as a towing vessel on this day.

there came a breeze; that the men would sleep at their quarters, of course, and would be ready to take care of their guns; but that he might catch a turn with the side-tackle-falls around the pommelions of the guns, which would be sufficient.[4] He then ordered the boatswain to call all hands aft, to the break of the quarter-deck.

As soon as the people had collected, Mr. Osgood said—"You must be pretty well fagged out, men; I think we may have a hard night's work, yet, and I wish you to get your suppers, and then catch as much sleep as you can, at your guns." He then ordered the purser's steward to splice the main-brace. These were the last words I ever heard from Mr. Osgood. As soon as he gave the order, he went below, leaving the deck in charge of Mr. Bogardus. All our old crew were on board but Mr. Livingston, who had left us, and Simeon Grant, one of my companions in the cruise over the battle-ground at Fort George. Grant had cut his hand off, in a saw-mill, while we were last at the Harbour, and had been left behind in the hospital. There was a pilot on board, who used to keep a look-out occasionally, and sometimes the boatswain had the watch.

The schooner, at this time, was under her mainsail, jib, and fore-top-sail. The foresail was brailed, and the foot stopped, and the flying-jib was stowed. None of the halyards were racked, nor sheets stoppered. This was a precaution we always took, on account of the craft's being so tender.

4. Shipborne cannon normally were carried on carriages that were fastened to the deck by means of hooks attached to ropes rove through heavy blocks, which provided a mechanical advantage. Thus, the gun, having recoiled after firing, could be hauled back into position at the gun port and reloaded for another firing. By securing the ropes of the side tackles around the large knob at the end of the cannon's breech, one could provide a temporary stop in case the ship should roll. Were the cannon not secured, it could fly unimpeded to the opposite side of the vessel, injuring men and damaging bulwarks or weapons, the origin of the term "loose cannon."

We first spliced the main-brace and then got our suppers, eating between the guns, where we generally messed, indeed.[5] One of my messmates, Tom Goldsmith, was captain of the gun next to me, and as we sat there finishing our suppers, I says to him, "Tom, bring up that rug that you pinned at Little York, and that will do for both of us to stow ourselves away under." Tom went down and got the rug, which was an article for the camp that he had laid hands on, and it made us a capital bed-quilt. As all hands were pretty well tired, we lay down, with our heads on shot-boxes, and soon went to sleep.

In speaking of the canvass that was set, I ought to have said something of the state of our decks. The guns had the side-tackles fastened as I have mentioned. There was a box of canister, and another of grape, at each gun, besides extra stands of both, under the shot-racks.[6] There was also one grummet of round-shot at every gun, besides the racks being filled. Each gun's crew slept at the gun and its opposite, thus dividing the people pretty equally on both sides of the deck. Those who were stationed below, slept below. I think it probable that, as the night grew cool, as it always does on the fresh waters, some of the men stole below to get warmer berths. This was easily done in that craft, as we had but two regular officers on board, the acting boatswain and gunner being little more than two of ourselves.

I was soon asleep, as sound as if lying in the bed of a king. How long my nap lasted, or what took place in the

5. Sailor's language for having a drink of liquor. The actual meaning is to splice or weave together parts of the principal rope being used to control the yardarms. The expression is described as a fictional command, but "splicing the main brace" was common nautical phraseology in several European languages when all hands were called for an extra ration of rum or grog after completing a particularly arduous task. Harland, *Seamanship in the Age of Sail,* pp. 296–97.

6. Types of anti-personnel ammunition used at this period both at sea and ashore.

interval, I cannot say. I awoke, however, in consequence of large drops of rain falling on my face. Tom Goldsmith awoke at the same moment. When I opened my eyes, it was so dark I could not see the length of the deck. I arose and spoke to Tom, telling him it was about to rain, and that I meant to go down and get a nip, out of a little stuff we kept in our mess-chest, and that I would bring up the bottle if he wanted a taste. Tom answered, "this is nothing; we're neither pepper nor salt." One of the black men spoke, and asked me to bring up the bottle, and give him a nip, too. All this took half a minute, perhaps. I now remember to have heard a strange rushing noise to windward as I went towards the forward hatch, though it made no impression on me at the time. We had been lying between the starboard guns, which was the weather side of the vessel, if there were any weather side to it, there not being a breath of air, and no motion to the water, and I passed round to the larboard side, in order to find the ladder, which led up in that direction. The hatch was so small that two men could not pass at a time, and I felt my way to it, in no haste. One hand was on the bitts, and a foot was on the ladder, when a flash of lightning almost blinded me. The thunder came at the next instant, and with it a rushing of winds that fairly smothered the clap.

The instant I was aware there was a squall, I sprang for the jib-sheet. Being captain of the forecastle, I knew where to find it, and throw it loose at a jerk. In doing this, I jumped on a man named Leonard Lewis, and called on him to lend me a hand. I next let fly the larboard, or lee topsail-sheet, got hold of the clew-line, and, assisted by Lewis, got the clew half up. All this time I kept shouting to the man at the wheel to put his helm "hard down." The water was now up to my breast, and I knew the schooner must go over. Lewis had not said a word, but I called out to him to shift for himself, and belaying the clew-line, in hauling myself forward of the foremast, I received a blow from the jib-sheet that came near breaking my left arm. I did not feel the effect of this blow at the time, though the arm has since been operated on, to extract a tumour produced by this very injury.

All this occupied less than a minute. The flashes of lightning were incessant, and nearly blinded me. Our decks seemed on fire, and yet I could see nothing. I heard no hail, no order, no call; but the schooner was filled with the shrieks and cries of the men to leeward, who were lying jammed under the guns, shot-boxes, shot, and other heavy things that had gone down as the vessel fell over. The starboard second gun, from forward, had capsized, and come down directly over the forward hatch, and I caught a glimpse of a man struggling to get past it. Apprehension of this gun had induced me to drag myself forward of the mast, where I received the blow mentioned.

I succeeded in hauling myself up to windward, and in getting into the schooner's fore-channels. Here I met William Deer, the boatswain, and a black boy of the name of Philips, who was the powder-boy of our gun. "Deer, she's gone!" I said. The boatswain made no answer, but walked out on the fore-rigging, towards the mast-head. He probably had some vague notion that the schooner's masts would be out of water if she went down, and took this course as the safest. The boy was in the chains the last I saw of him.

I now crawled aft, on the upper side of the bulwarks, amid a most awful and infernal din of thunder, and shrieks, and dazzling flashes of lightning; the wind blowing all the while like a tornado. When I reached the port of my own gun, I put a foot in, thinking to step on the muzzle of the piece; but it had gone to leeward with all the rest, and I fell through the port, until I brought up with my arms. I struggled up again, and continued working my way aft. As I got abreast of the main-mast, I saw some one had let run the halyards. I soon reached the beckets of the sweeps, and found four in them.[7] I could not swim a stroke, and it crossed my mind to get one of the sweeps to keep me afloat. In striving to jerk the becket clear, it parted, and the forward ends of the four sweeps rolled down the schooner's side into the water. This caused the other ends to slide, and all the sweeps got away from me. I then crawled quite aft, as far as the fashion-piece. The water was pouring down the cabin companion-way like a sluice; and as I stood, for an instant, on the fashion-piece, I saw Mr. Osgood, with his head and part of his shoulders through one of the cabin windows, struggling to get out. He must have been within six feet of me. I saw him but a moment, by means of a flash of lightning, and I think he must have seen me. At the same time, there was a man visible on the end of the main-boom, holding on by the clew of the sail. I do not know who it was. This man probably saw me, and that I was about to spring; for he called out, "Don't jump overboard!—don't jump overboard! The schooner is righting."

I was not in a state of mind to reflect much on anything. I do not think more than three or four minutes, if as many, had passed since the squall struck us, and there I was standing on the vessel's quarter, led by Providence more than by any discretion of my own. It now came across me that if the schooner should right she was filled, and must go down, and that she might carry me with her in the suction. I made a spring, therefore, and fell into the water several feet from the place where I had stood. It is my opinion the schooner sunk as I left her. I went down some distance myself, and when I came up to the surface, I began to swim vigorously for the first time in my life. I think I swam several yards, but of course will not pretend to be certain of such a thing, at such a moment, until I felt my hand hit something hard. I made another stroke, and felt my hand pass down the side

7. Beckets, the restraining cords with an eye at one end and a knot at the other, holding a cluster of oars together.

of an object that I knew at once was a clincher-built boat.[8] I belonged to this boat, and I now recollected that she had been towing astern. Until that instant I had not thought of her, but thus was I led in the dark to the best possible means of saving my life. I made a grab at the gunwale, and caught it in the stern-sheets. Had I swum another yard, I should have passed the boat, and missed her altogether! I got in without any difficulty, being all alive and much excited.

My first look was for the schooner. She had disappeared, and I supposed she was just settling under water. It rained as if the flood-gates of heaven were opened, and it lightened awfully. It did not seem to me that there was a breath of air, and the water was unruffled, the effects of the rain excepted. All this I saw, as it might be, at a glance. But my chief concern was to preserve my own life. I was cockswain of this very boat, and had made it fast to the taffrail that same afternoon, with a round turn and two half-hitches, by its best painter. Of course I expected the vessel would drag the boat down with her, for I had no knife to cut the painter. There was a gang-board in the boat, however, which lay fore and aft, and I thought this might keep me afloat until some of the fleet should pick me up. To clear this gang-board, then, and get it into the water, was my first object. I ran forward to throw off the lazy-painter that was coiled on its end, and in doing this I caught the boat's painter in my hand, by accident.[9] A pull satisfied me that it was all clear! Some one on board must have cast off this painter, and then lost his chance of getting into the boat by an accident. At all events, I was safe, and I now dared to look about me.

My only chance of seeing, was during the flashes; and these left me almost blind. I had thrown the gang-board into the water, and I now called out to encourage the men,

8. A ship's boat built with boards overlapped so as to make a firm seal and prevent leakage. Sometimes referred to as "lapstrake" design, similar to clapboard siding in appearance.

9. A line attached to the bow of a small boat, used to secure the boat to a pier or to another vessel.

telling them I was in the boat. I could hear many around me, and, occasionally, I saw the heads of men, struggling in the lake. There being no proper place to scull in, I got an oar in the after rullock, and made out to scull a little, in that fashion. I now saw a man quite near the boat; and, hauling in the oar, made a spring amidships, catching this poor fellow by the collar. He was very near gone; and I had a great deal of difficulty in getting him in over the gunwale. Our joint weight brought the boat down, so low, that she shipped a good deal of water. This turned out to be Leonard Lewis, the young man who had helped me to clew up the fore-topsail. He could not stand, and spoke with difficulty. I asked him to crawl aft, out of the water; which he did, lying down in the stern-sheets.

I now looked about me, and heard another; leaning over the gunwale, I got a glimpse of a man, struggling, quite near the boat. I caught him by the collar, too; and had to drag him in very much in the way I had done with Lewis. This proved to be Lemuel Bryant, the man who had been wounded by a hot shot, at York, as already mentioned, while the commodore was on board us.[10] His wound had not yet healed, but he was less exhausted than Lewis. He could not help me, however, lying down in the bottom of the boat, the instant he was able.

For a few moments, I now heard no more in the water; and I began to scull again. By my calculation, I moved a few yards, and must have got over the spot where the schooner went down. Here, in the flashes, I saw many heads, the men swimming in confusion, and at random. By this time, little was said, the whole scene being one of fearful struggling and frightful silence. It still rained; but the flashes were less frequent, and less fierce. They told me, afterwards, in the squadron, that it thundered awfully; but I cannot say I heard a clap, after I struck the water. The

10. Metal round shot heated red-hot before firing at an enemy ship or fortification so that its heat would cause the target to burst into flames if penetrated.

next man caught the boat himself. It was a mulatto, from Martinique, who was Mr. Osgood's steward; and I helped him in. He was much exhausted, though an excellent swimmer; but alarm nearly deprived him of his strength. He kept saying, "Oh! Masser Ned—Oh! Masser Ned!" and lay down in the bottom of the boat, like the two others; I taking care to shove him over to the larboard side, so as to trim our small craft.

I kept calling out, to encourage the swimmers, and presently I heard a voice, saying, "Ned, I'm here, close by you." This was Tom Goldsmith, a messmate, and the very man under whose rug I had been sleeping, at quarters. He did not want much help, getting in, pretty much, by himself. I asked him, if he were able to help me. "Yes, Ned," he answered, "I'll stand by you to the last; what shall I do?" I told him to take his tarpaulin, and to bail the boat, which, by this time, was a third full of water. This he did, while I sculled a little ahead. "Ned," says Tom, "she's gone down with her colours flying, for her pennant came near getting a round turn about my body, and carrying me down with her. Davy has made a good haul, and he gave us a close shave; but he didn't get you and me."[11] In this manner did this thoughtless sailor express himself, as soon as rescued from the grasp of death! Seeing something on the water, I asked Tom to take my oar, while I sprang to the gunwale, and caught Mr. Bogardus, the master's mate, who was clinging to one of the sweeps. I hauled him in, and he told me, he thought, some one had hold of the other end of the sweep. It was so dark, however, we could not see even that distance. I hauled the sweep along, until I found Ebenezer Duffy, a mulatto, and the ship's cook. He could not swim a stroke; and was nearly gone. I got him in, alone, Tom bailing, lest the boat, which was quite small, should swamp with us.

11. "Davy Jones," a mythical character who collects drowned seamen and stows them in his "locker."

As the boat drifted along, she reached another man, whom I caught also by the collar. I was afraid to haul this person in amidships, the boat being now so deep and so small, and so I dragged him ahead, and hauled him in over the bows. This was the pilot, whose name I never knew. He was a lake-man, and had been aboard us the whole summer. The poor fellow was almost gone, and like all the rest, with the exception of Tom, he lay down and said not a word.

We had now as many in the boat as it would carry, and Tom and myself thought it would not do to take in any more. It is true, we saw no more, everything around us appearing still as death, the pattering of the rain excepted. Tom began to bail again, and I commenced hallooing. I sculled about several minutes, thinking of giving others a tow, or of even hauling in one or two more, after we got the water out of the boat; but we found no one else. I think it probable I sculled away from the spot, as there was nothing to guide me. I suppose, however, that by this time, all the Scourges had gone down, for no more were ever heard from.

Tom Goldsmith and myself now put our heads together as to what was best to be done. We were both afraid of falling into the enemy's hands, for, they might have bore up in the squall, and run down near us. On the whole, however, we thought the distance between the two squadrons was too great for this; at all events, something must be done at once. So we began to row, in what direction even we did not know. It still rained as hard as it could pour, though there was not a breath of wind. The lightning came now at considerable intervals, and the gust was evidently passing away towards the broader parts of the lake. While we were rowing and talking about our chance of falling in with the enemy, Tom cried out to me to "avast pulling."[12] He had seen a vessel, by a flash, and he thought she was English, from her size. As he said she was a schooner, however, I

12. Sailors' language, derived from the German "Houd Vast" (Hold Fast) or the Italian "basta" for "stop rowing."

thought it must be one of our own craft, and got her direction from him. At the next flash I saw her, and felt satisfied she belonged to us. Before we began to pull, however, we were hailed "boat ahoy!" I answered. "If you pull another stroke, I'll fire into you"—came back—"what boat's that? Lay on your oars, or I'll fire into you." It was clear we were mistaken ourselves for an enemy, and I called out to know what schooner it was. No answer was given, though the threat to fire was repeated, if we pulled another stroke. I now turned to Tom and said, "I know that voice—that is old Trant." Tom thought "we were in the wrong shop." I now sung out, "This is the *Scourge*'s boat—our schooner has gone down, and we want to come alongside." A voice next called from the schooner—"Is that you, Ned?" This I knew was my old ship-mate and school-fellow, Jack Mallet, who was acting as boatswain of the *Julia,* the schooner commanded by sailing-master James Trant, one of the oddities of the service, and a man with whom the blow often came as soon as the word.[13] I had known Mr. Trant's voice, and felt more afraid he would fire into us, than I had done of anything which had occurred that fearful night. Mr. Trant, himself, now called out—"Oh-ho; give way, boys, and come alongside." This we did, and a very few strokes took us up to the *Julia,* where we were received with the utmost kindness. The men were passed out of the boat, while I gave Mr. Trant an account of all that had happened. This took but a minute or two.

13. Ned Myers [Cooper] claims that Trant had been in the American navy since the Revolution. "Perhaps no man in the navy was more generally known." Actually, Trant joined the U.S. Navy as of 10 April 1799, served in the USS *Adams* during the Quasi-War with France, resigned on 31 March 1802, was reinstated on 16 May 1804, served in the frigate *Essex* in the Mediterranean during the Barbary Wars, 1804–1806, and took furlough for service in a merchantman in 1807. See *Register of Officer Personnel, United States Navy and Marine Corps and Ships' Data, 1801–1807* (Washington, 1945).

Mr. Trant now inquired in what direction the *Scourge* had gone down, and, as soon as I had told him, in the best manner I could, he called out to Jack Mallet—"Oh-ho, Mallet—take four hands, and go in the boat and see what you can do—take a lantern, and I will show a light on the water's edge, so you may know me." Mallet did as ordered, and was off in less than three minutes after we got alongside. Mr. Trant, who was much humoured, had no officer in the *Julia,* unless Mallet could be called one. He was an Irishman by birth, but had been in the American navy ever since the revolution, dying a lieutenant, a few years after this war. Perhaps no man in the navy was more generally known, or excited more amusement by his oddities, or more respect for his courage. He had come on the lake with the commodore, with whom he was a great pet, and had been active in all the fights and affairs that had yet taken place. His religion was to hate an Englishman.

Mr. Trant now called the Scourges aft, and asked more of the particulars. He then gave us a glass of grog all round, and made his own crew splice the main-brace.[14] The Julias now offered us dry clothes. I got a change from Jack Reilly, who had been an old messmate, and with whom I had always been on good terms. It knocked off raining, but we shifted ourselves at the galley fire below. I then went on deck, and presently we heard the boat pulling back. It soon came alongside, bringing in it four more men that had been found floating about on sweeps and gratings. On inquiry, it turned out that these men belonged to the *Hamilton,* Lt. Winter—a schooner that had gone down in the same squall that carried us over. These men were very much exhausted, too, and we all went below, and were told to turn in.

I had been so much excited during the scenes through which I had just passed, and had been so much stimulated by grog, that, as yet, I had not felt much of the depression

14. Rum diluted with water.

natural to such events. I even slept soundly that night, nor did I turn out until six the next morning.

When I got on deck, there was a fine breeze; it was a lovely day, and the lake was perfectly smooth. Our fleet was in a good line, in pretty close order, with the exception of the *Governor Tompkins,* Lieutenant Tom Brown, which was a little to leeward, but carrying a press of sail to close with the commodore. Mr. Trant perceiving that the *Tompkins* wished to speak us in passing, brailed his foresail and let her luff up close under our lee. "Two of the schooners, the *Hamilton* and the *Scourge,* have gone down in the night," called out Mr. Brown; "for I have picked up four of the *Hamilton*'s." "Oh-ho!"—answered Mr. Trant—"That's no news at all! for I have picked up *twelve;* eight of the *Scourge*'s, and four of the *Hamilton*'s—aft fore-sheet."

These were all that were ever saved from the two schooners, which must have had near a hundred souls on board them. The two commanders, Lieutenant Winter and Mr. Osgood were both lost, and with Mr. Winter went down I believe, one or two young gentlemen. The squadron could not have moved much between the time when the accidents happened and that when I came on deck, or we must have come round and gone over the same ground again, for we now passed many relics of the scene, floating about in the water. I saw spunges, gratings, sweeps, hats, &c., scattered about, and in passing ahead we saw one of the latter that we tried to catch; Mr. Trant ordering it done, as he said it must have been Lieutenant Winter's. We did not succeed, however; nor was any article taken on board. A good look-out was kept for men, from aloft, but none were seen from any of the vessels. The lake had swallowed up the rest of the two crews; and the *Scourge,* as had been often predicted, had literally become a coffin to a large portion of her people.[15]

15. The converted schooners of Commodore Chauncey's squadron were unstable, for they were not designed to carry armament on deck. In doing so, their center of gravity was raised to a dangerous level. Lake

There was a good deal of manœuvring between the two fleets this day, and some efforts were made to engage; but, to own the truth, I felt so melancholy about the loss of so many ship-mates, that I did not take much notice of what passed. All my Black Jokers were drowned, and nothing remained of the craft and people with which and whom I had been associated all summer. Bill Southard, too, was among the lost, as indeed were all my messmates but Tom Goldsmith and Lemuel Bryant. I had very serious and proper impressions for the moment; but my new shipmates, some of whom had been old shipmates in other crafts, managed to cheer me up with grog. The effect was not durable, and in a short time I ceased to think of what had happened. I have probably reflected more on the merciful manner in which my life was spared, amid a scene so terrific, within the last five years, than I did in the twenty-five that immediately followed the accidents.

The fleet went in, off the Niagara, and anchored. Mr. Trant now mustered the remaining Scourges, and told us he wanted just our number of hands, and that he meant to get an order to keep us in the *Julia*. In the meantime, he should station and quarter us. I was stationed at the braces, and quartered at the long thirty-two as second loader.[16] The *Julia* mounted a long thirty-two, and an eighteen on pivots, besides two sixes in the waist.[17] The last were little used, as I have already mentioned. She was a small, but a fast

---

schooners had shallow draft compared to those designed for ocean navigation and were very tender in heavy winds. If they heeled too far over because of excessive weight on deck, they would capsize, the water pouring through deck hatches and other openings. This only decreased the vessels' buoyancy and made sinking inevitable.

16. Ned's assignment (station) under normal cruising conditions was to man the ropes that controlled the schooner's topsail yardarm. In battle, Ned was assigned ("quartered") to assist loading the schooner's largest gun.

17. The *Julia* carried a 32-pounder long gun as main armament, a long 18-pounder that swiveled on the main deck and could be fired

schooner, and had about forty souls on board. She was altogether a better craft than the *Scourge,* though destitute of any quarters, but a low rail with wash-boards, and carrying fewer guns.

---

over either side, and two 6-pounders located amidships between her masts.

CHAPTER VII

I NEVER KNEW WHAT BECAME OF THE FOUR HAMILTONS that were picked up by the *Julia*'s boat, though I suppose they were put in some other vessel along with their shipmates; nor did I ever learn the particulars of the loss of this schooner, beyond the fact that her topsail-sheets were stoppered, and her halyards racked.[1] This much I learned from the men who were brought on board the *Julia,* who said that their craft was ready, in all respects, for action. Some seamen have thought this wrong, and some right; but, in my opinion, it made but little difference in such a gust as that which passed over us. What was remarkable, the *Julia,* which could not have been far from the *Scourge* when we

1. The *Hamilton,* like the other schooners, had one square sail on the foremast, above the fore-and-aft sail. The topsail was trimmed taut or loose by means of sheets, light lines that were knotted at certain positions. The lines that hauled the sail up and down the mast (halyards) were secured around belaying pins located at the foot of the mast. Since the sheets were stoppered and the halyards racked, the sail could not quickly be loosened or hauled down in a sudden gust. This helps to explain why the *Hamilton* capsized so quickly.

went over, felt no great matter of wind, just luffing up, and shaking her sails, to be rid of it!

We lay only one night off the mouth of the Niagara. The next morning the squadron weighed, and stood out in pursuit of the English. The weather was very variable, and we could not get within reach of Sir James all that day. This was the 9th of August. The *Scourge* had gone down on the night of the 7th, or the morning of the 8th, I never knew which. On the morning of the 10th, however, we were under the north shore, and to windward of John Bull. The Commodore now took the *Asp,* the *Madison* and the *Fair American,* in tow, and we all kept away, expecting certainly a general action.[2] But the wind shifted, bringing the English to windward. The afternoon was calm; or had variable airs. Towards sunset, the enemy was becalmed under the American shore, and we got a breeze from the southward. We now closed, and at 6 formed our line for engaging. We continued to close until 7, when the wind came out fresh at S.W., putting John again to windward.

I can hardly tell what followed, there was so much manœuvring and shifting of berths. Both squadrons were standing across the lake, the enemy being to windward, and a little astern of us. We now passed within hail of the commodore, who gave us orders to form a new line of battle, which we did in the following manner. One line, composed of the smallest schooners, was formed to windward, while the ships, brig, and two heaviest schooners, formed another line to leeward. We had the weathermost line, having the *Growler,* Lieutenant Deacon, for the vessel next astern of us.

2. Chauncey's flagship, the *General Pike,* had been on the lake only since 21 July, less than a month. The corvette *Madison,* Chauncey's former flagship, once commanded by Lieutenant Jesse Elliott, now sailed under Master Commandant William Crane. Elliott had departed Niagara with Perry, heading for Lake Erie after the attack on Fort George. As usual, the slower lake schooners were towed to make sure their long guns could be brought to action when needed.

This much I could see, though I did not understand the object. I now learn the plan was for the weather line to engage the enemy, and then, by edging away, draw them down upon the lee line, which line contained our principal force. According to the orders, we ought to have rather edged off, as soon as the English began to fire, in order to draw them down upon the commodore; but it will be seen that our schooner pursued a very different course.

It must have been near midnight, when the enemy began to fire at the *Fair American,* the sternmost vessel of our weather line. We were a long bit ahead of her, and did not engage for some time. The firing became pretty smart astern, but we stood on, without engaging, the enemy not yet being far enough ahead for us. After a while, the four sternmost schooners of our line kept off, according to orders, but the *Julia* and *Growler* still stood on. I suppose the English kept off, too, at the same time, as the commodore had expected. At any rate, we found ourselves so well up with the enemy, that, instead of bearing up, Mr. Trant tacked in the *Julia,* and the *Growler* came round after us. We now began to fire on the headmost ships of the enemy, which were coming on towards us. We were able to lay past the enemy on this tack, and fairly got to windward of them. When we were a little on John Bull's weather bow, we brailed the foresail, and gave him several rounds, within a pretty fair distance. The enemy answered us, and, from that moment, he seemed to give up all thoughts of the vessels to leeward of him, turning his whole attention on the *Julia* and *Growler.*

The English fleet stood on the same tack, until it had got between us and our own line, when it went about in chase of us. We now began to make short tacks to windward; the enemy separating so as to spread a wide clew, in order that they might prevent our getting past, by turning their line and running to leeward. As for keeping to windward, we had no difficulty—occasionally brailing our foresail, and even edging off, now and then, to be certain that our shot would tell.[3] In moderate weather, the *Julia* was the fastest vessel in the American squadron, the *Lady of the Lake* excepted; and the *Growler* was far from being dull. Had there been room, I make no doubt we might have kept clear of John Bull, with the greatest ease; touching him up with our long, heavy guns, from time to time, as it suited us. I have often thought that Mr. Trant forgot we were between the enemy and the land, and that he fancied himself out at sea. It was a hazy, moonlight morning, and we did not see anything of the main, though it turned out to be nearer to us than we wished.[4]

All hands were now turning to windward; the two schooners still edging off, occasionally, and firing. The enemy's shot went far beyond us, and did us some mischief, though nothing that was not immediately repaired. The main throat-halyards, on board the *Julia,* were shot away, as was the clew of the mainsail. It is probable the enemy did not keep his luff, towards the last, on account of the land.

Our two schooners kept quite near each other, sometimes one being to windward, sometimes the other. It happened that the *Growler* was a short distance to windward of us, when we first became aware of the nature of our critical situation. She up helm, and, running down within hail, Lieutenant Deacon informed Mr. Trant he had just sounded in two fathoms, and that he could see lights ashore.[5] He

3. Brailing, a temporary gathering up of the sail on the foremast to allow the unimpeded working of the deck guns.

4. "Main" refers to the mainland—that is, the north shore of the lake.

5. The wind was coming from the north. The American schooners had discovered that they were in danger of running aground, since they were in only 12 feet (two fathoms) of water. The British squadron had carefully cut them off from the support of the rest of Chauncey's squadron. To "up helm" was to push the tiller toward the wind, the rudder turning the vessel away (running down) with the wind astern, in the direction of the British pursuers, who were awaiting this eventuality.

thought there must be Indians, in great numbers, in this vicinity, and that we must, at all events, avoid the land. "What do you think we had best do?" asked Lieutenant Deacon. "Run the gauntlet," called out Mr. Trant. "Very well, sir: which shall lead?" "I'll lead the van," answered Mr. Trant, and then all was settled.

We now up helm, and steered for a vacancy among the British vessels. The enemy seemed to expect us, for they formed in two lines, leaving us room to enter between them. When we bore up, even in these critical circumstances, it was under our mainsail, fore-top-sail, jib, flying-jib, and fore-sail. So insufficient were the equipments of these small craft, that we had neither square-sail nor studding-sails on board us. I never saw a studding-sail in any of the schooners, the *Scourge* excepted.

The *Julia* and *Growler* now ran down, the former leading, half a cable's-length apart. When we entered between the two lines of the enemy, we were within short canister-range, and got it smartly on both tacks. The two English ships were to leeward, each leading a line; and we had a brig, and three large, regular man-of-war schooners, to get past, with the certainty of meeting the *Wolfe* and *Royal George,* should we succeed in clearing these four craft. Both of us kept up a heavy fire, swivelling our guns round, so as not to neglect any one. As we drew near the ships, however, we paid them the compliment of throwing all the heavy shot at them, as was due to their rank and size.

For a few minutes we fared pretty well; but we were no sooner well entered between the lines, than we got it, hot and hard.[6] Our rigging began to come down about our ears, and one shot passed a few feet above our heads, cutting both topsail-sheets, and scooping a bit of wood as big as a thirty-two pound shot, out of the foremast. I went up on one side,

6. Ned's narrative is the best explanation of the loss of the *Julia* and *Growler* that we have. The official reports explain only *that* it happened, not *how* it happened.

myself, to knot one of these sheets, and, while aloft, discovered the injury that had been done to the spar. Soon after, the tack of the mainsail caught fire,[7] from a wad of one of the Englishmen; for, by this time, we were close at it. I think, indeed, that the nearness of the enemy alone prevented our decks from being entirely swept. The grape and canister were passing just above our heads like hail, and the foresail was literally in ribands. The halyards being gone, the mainsail came down by the run, and the jib settled as low as it could. The topsail-yard was on the cap, and the schooner now came up into the wind.

All this time, we kept working the guns. The old man went from one gun to the other, pointing each himself, as it was ready. He was at the eighteen when things were getting near the worst, and, as he left her, he called out to her crew to "fill her—fill her to the muzzle!" He then came to our gun, which was already loaded with one round, a stand of grape, and a case of canister shot. This I know, for I put them all in with my own hands. At this time, the *Melville,* a brig of the enemy's, was close up with us, firing upon our decks from her fore-top. She was coming up on our larboard quarter, while a large schooner was nearing us fast on the starboard. Mr. Trant directed our gun to be elevated so as to sweep the brig's forecastle, and then he called out, "Now's the time, lads—fire at the b——s! fire away at 'em!" But no match was to be found! Some one had thrown both overboard. By this time the brig's jib-boom was over our quarter, and the English were actually coming on board of us. The enemy were now all round us. The *Wolfe,* herself, was within hail, and still firing. The last I saw of any of our people, was Mallet passing forward, and I sat down on the slide of the thirty-two, myself, sullen as a bear. Two or three of the English passed me, without saying anything. Even at this instant, a volley of bullets came out of the brig's fore-

7. That part of the mainsail attached to the boom nearest the mast.

top, and struck all around me; some hitting the deck, and others the gun itself. Just then, an English officer came up, and said—"What are you doing here, you Yankee?" I felt exceedingly savage, and answered, "Looking at your fools firing upon their own men." "Take that for your sauce," he said, giving me a thrust with his sword, as he spoke. The point of the cutlass just passed my hip-bone, and gave me a smart flesh-wound. The hurt was not dangerous, though it bled freely, and was some weeks in healing. I now rose to go below, and heard a hail from one of the ships—the *Wolfe,* as I took her to be. "Have you struck?" demanded some one. The officer who had hurt me now called out, "Don't fire into us, sir, for I'm on board, and have got possession." The officer from the ship next asked, "Is there anybody alive on board her?" To which the prize-officer answered, "I don't know, sir; I've seen but one man, as yet."

I now went down below. First, I got a bandage on my wound, to stop the bleeding, and then I had an opportunity to look about me. A party of English was below, and some of our men having joined them, the heads were knocked out of two barrels of whiskey. The kids and bread-bags were procured, and all hands, without distinction of country, sat down to enjoy themselves. Some even began to sing, and, as for good-fellowship, it was just as marked, as it would have been in a jollification ashore.

In a few minutes the officer who had hurt me jumped down among us. The instant he saw what we were at, he sang out—"Halloo! here's high life below stairs!" Then he called to another officer to bear a hand down and see the fun. Some one sung out from among ourselves to "dowse the glim." The lights were put out, and then the two officers capsized the whiskey. While this was doing, most of the Englishmen ran up the forward hatch. We Julias all remained below.

In less than an hour we were sent on board the enemy's vessels. I was carried to the *Royal George,* but Mr. Trant was taken on board the *Wolfe.* The *Growler* had lost her bowsprit, and was otherwise damaged, and had been forced to strike also. She had a man killed, and I believe one or two wounded.[8] On board of us, not a man, besides myself, had been touched! We seemed to have been preserved by a miracle, for every one of the enemy had a slap at us, and, for some time, we were within pistol-shot. Then we had no quarters at all, being perfectly exposed to grape and canister. The enemy must have fired too high, for nothing else could have saved us.

In July, while I still belonged to the *Scourge,* I had been sent with a boat's crew, under Mr. Bogardus, on board an English flag of truce that had come into the Harbour. While in this vessel, our boat's crew were "hail-fellows-well-met" with the Englishmen, and we had agreed among us to take care of each other, should either side happen to be taken. I had been on board the *Royal George* but a short time, when two of these very men came up to me with some grog and some grub; and next morning they brought me my bitters. I saw no more of them, however, except when they came to shake hands with us at the gang-way, as we were leaving the ship.

After breakfast, next morning, we were all called aft to the ward-room, one at a time. I was pumped as to the force of the Americans, the names of the vessels, the numbers of the crews, and the names of the commanders. I answered a little saucily, and was ordered out of the wardroom. As I was quitting the place, I was called back by one of the lieutenants, whose appearance I did not like from the first. Although it was now eight years since I left Halifax, and we had both so much altered, I took this gentleman for Mr. Bowen, the very midshipman of the *Cleopatra,* who had been

8. It is supposed that Capt. Deacon died, a few years since, in consequence of an injury he received on board the *Growler,* this night. A shot struck her main-boom, within a short distance of one of his ears, and he ever after complained of its effects. At his death this side of his head was much swollen and affected.—EDITOR.

my schoolmate, and whom I had known on board the prize-brig I have mentioned.

This officer asked me where I was born. I told him New York. He said he knew better, and asked my name. I told him it was what he found it on the muster-roll, and that by which I had been called. He said I knew better, and that I should hear more of this, hereafter. If this were my old schoolfellow, he knew that I was always called Edward Robert Meyers, whereas I had dropped the middle name, and now called myself Myers. He may not, however, have been the person I took him for, and might have mistaken me for some one else; for I never had an opportunity of ascertaining any more about him.

We got into Little York, and were sent ashore that evening. I can say nothing of our squadron, having been kept below the whole time I was on board the *Royal George.* I could not find out whether we did the enemy any harm, or not, the night we were taken; though I remember that a sixty-eight pound carronade, that stood near the gang-way of the *Royal George,* was dismounted, the night I passed into her. It looked to me as if the trucks were gone. This I know, that the ship was more than usually screened off; though for what reason I will not pretend to say.

At York, we were put in the gaol, where we were kept three weeks. Our treatment was every way bad, with the exception that we were not crowded. As to food, we were kept "six upon four" the whole time I was prisoner.[9] The bread was bad, and the pork little better. While in this gaol, a party of drunken Indians gave us a volley, in passing; but luckily it did us no harm.

At the end of three weeks, we received a haversack apiece, and two days' allowance. Our clothes were taken from us, and the men were told they would get them below; a thing

9. By this, Ned means six men had to subsist on the usual allowance of four men; a distinction that was made between men on duty and men off. Prisoners, too, are commonly allowed to help themselves in a variety of ways.—EDITOR.

that happened to very few of us, I believe. As for myself, I was luckily without anything to lose; my effects having gone down in the *Scourge.* All I had on earth was a shirt and two handkerchiefs, and an old slouched hat, that I had got in exchange for a Scotch cap that had been given to me in the *Julia.* I was without shoes, and so continued until I reached Halifax. All this gave me little concern; my spirits being elastic, and my disposition gay. My great trouble was the apprehension of being known, through the recollections of the officer I have mentioned.

We now commenced our march for Kingston, under the guard of a company of the Glengarians and a party of Indians. The last kept on our flanks, and it was understood they would shoot and scalp any man who left the ranks. We marched two and two, being something like eighty prisoners. It was hard work for the first day or two, the road being nothing but an Indian trail, and our lodging-places the open air. My feet became very sore, and, as for food, we had to eat our pork raw, there being nothing to cook in. The soldiers fared no better than ourselves, however, with the exception of being on full allowance. It seems that our provisions were sent by water, and left for us at particular places; for every eight-and-forty hours we touched the lake shore, and found them ready for us. They were left on the beach without any guard, or any one near them. In this way we picked up our supplies the whole distance.

At the dépôt, Mr. Bogardus and the pilot found a boat, and managed to get into her, and put out into the lake. After being absent a day and night, they were driven in by rough weather, and fell into the hands of a party of dragoons who were escorting Sir George Prevost along the lake shore. We found them at a sort of tavern, where were the English Governor and his escort at the time. They were sent back among us, with two American army officers, who had fallen into the hands of the Indians, and had been most foully treated. One of these officers was wounded in the arm.

The night of the day we fell in with Sir George Prevost, we passed through a hamlet, and slept just without it. As we entered the village the guard played Yankee Doodle, winding up with the Rogue's March. As we went through the place, I got leave to go to a house and ask for a drink of milk. The woman of this house said they had been expecting us for two days, and that they had been saving their milk expressly to give us. I got as much as I wanted, and a small loaf of bread in the bargain, as did several others with me. These people seemed to me to be all well affected to the Americans, and much disposed to treat us kindly. We slept on a barn floor that night.

We were much provoked at the insult of playing the Rogue's March. Jack Reilly and I laid a plan to have our revenge, should it be repeated. Two or three days later we had the same tune, at another village, and I caught up a couple of large stones, ran ahead, and dashed them through both ends of the drum, before the boy, who was beating it, knew what I was about. Jack snatched the fife out of the other boy's hand, and it was passed from one to another among us, until it reached one who threw it over the railing of a bridge. After this, we had no more music, good or bad. Not a word was said to any of us about this affair, and I really think the officers were ashamed of themselves.

After a march of several days we came to a hamlet, not a great distance from Kingston. I saw a good many geese about, and took a fancy to have one for supper. I told Mallet if he would cook a goose, I would tip one over. The matter was arranged between us, and picking up a club I made a dash at a flock, and knocked a bird over. I caught up the goose and ran, when my fellow-prisoners called out to me to dodge, which I did, behind a stump, not knowing from what quarter the danger might come. It was well I did, for two Indians fired at me, one hitting the stump, and the other ball passing just over my head. A militia officer now gallopped up, and drove back the Indians who were running up to me, to look after the scalp, I suppose. This officer remonstrated with me, but spoke mildly and even kindly. I told him I was hungry, and that I wanted a warm mess. "But you are committing a robbery," he said. "If I am, I'm robbing an enemy." "You do not know but it may be a friend," was his significant answer. "Well, if I am, *he*'ll not grudge me the goose," says I. On hearing this, the officer laughed, and asked me how I meant to cook the goose. I told him that one of my messmates had promised to do this for me. He then bade me carry the goose into the ranks, and to come to him when we halted at night. I did this, and he gave us a pan, some potatoes, onions, &c., out of which we made the only good mess we got on our march. I may say this was the last hearty and really palatable meal I made until I reached Halifax, a period of several weeks.

While Jack Mallet was cooking the goose, I went in behind a pile of boards, attended by a soldier to watch me, and, while there, I saw an ivory rule lying on the boards, with fifteen pence alongside of it. These I pinned, as a lawful prize, being in an enemy's country. The money served to buy us some bread. The rule was bartered for half a gallon of rum. This made us a merry night, taking all things together.

We made no halt at Kingston, though the Indians left us. We now marched through a settled country, with some militia for our guards. Our treatment was much better than it had been, the people of the country treating us kindly. When we were abreast of the Thousand Islands, Mr. Bogardus and the pilot made another attempt to escape, and got fairly off. These were the only two who did succeed. How they effected it I cannot say, but I know they escaped. I never saw either afterwards.

At the Long Sault, we were all put in boats, with a Canadian pilot in each end. The militia staid behind, and down we went; they say at the rate of nine miles in fifteen minutes. We found a new guard at the foot of the rapids.

This was done, beyond a doubt, to save us and themselves, though we thought hard of it at the time, for it appeared to us, as if they thrust us into a danger they did not like to run themselves. I have since heard that even ladies travelling, used to go down these formidable rapids in the same way; and that, with skilful pilots, there is little or no danger.

When we reached Montreal we were confined in a gaol, where we remained three weeks. There was an American lady confined in this building, though she had more liberty than we, and from her we received much aid. She sent us soap, and she gave me bandages &c., for my hurt. Occasionally she gave us little things to eat. I never knew her name, but heard she had two sons in the American army, and that she had been detected in corresponding with them.

We remained at Montreal two or three weeks, and then were sent down to Quebec, where we were put on board of prison-ships. I was sent to the *Lord Cathcart,* and most of the *Julia*'s men with me. Our provisions were very bad, and the mortality among us was great. The bread was intolerably bad. Mr. Trant came to see us, privately, and he brought some salt with him, which was a great relief to us. Jack Mallet asked him whether some of us might not go to work on board a transport, that lay just astern of us, in order to get something better to eat. Mr. Trant said yes, and eight of us went on board this craft, every day, getting provisions and grog for our pay. At sunset, we returned regularly to the *Cathcart.* I got a second shirt and a pair of trowsers in this way.

About a fortnight after this arrangement, the *Surprise,* 32, and a sloop-of-war, came in, anchoring some distance below the town. These ships sent their boats up to the prison-ships to examine them for men. After going through those vessels, they came on board the transport, and finding us fresh, clean, fed and tolerably clad, they pronounced us all Englishmen, and carried us on board the frigate. We were not permitted even to go and take leave of our shipmates. Of the eight men thus taken, five were native Americans, one was from Mozambique, one I suppose to have been an English subject born, but long settled in America; and, as for me, the reader knows as much of my origin as I know myself.

We were asked if we would go to duty on board the *Surprise,* and we all refused. We were then put in close confinement, on the berth-deck, under the charge of a sentry. In a day or two, the ship sailed; and off Cape Breton we met with a heavy gale, in which the people suffered severely with snow and cold. The ship was kept off the land, with great difficulty. After all, we prisoners saved the ship, though I think it likely the injury originally came from some of us. The breechings of two of the guns had been cut, and the guns broke adrift in the height of the gale. All the crew were on deck, and the sentinel permitting it, we went up and smothered the guns with hammocks. We were now allowed to go about deck, but this lasted a short time, the whole of us being sent below, again, as soon as the gale abated.

On reaching Halifax, we were all put on board of the *Regulus* transport, bound to Bermuda. Here we eight were thrown into irons, under the accusation of being British subjects. At the end of twenty-four hours, however, the captain came to us, and offered to let us out of irons, and to give us ship's treatment, if we would help in working the vessel to Bermuda. I have since thought we were ironed merely to extort this arrangement from us. We consulted together; and, thinking a chance might offer to get possession of the *Regulus,* which had only a few Canadians in her, and was to be convoyed by the *Pictou* schooner, we consented. We were now turned up to duty, and I got the first pair of shoes that had been on my feet since the *Scourge* sunk from under me.

The reader will imagine I had not been in the harbour of Halifax, without a strong desire to ascertain something about those I had left behind me, in that town. I was nervously afraid of being discovered, and yet had a feverish wish to go ashore. The manner in which I gratified this wish, and the consequences to which it led, will be seen in the sequel.

CHAPTER VIII

JACK MALLET HAD LONG KNOWN MY HISTORY. He was my confidant, and entered into all my feelings. The night we went to duty on board the transport, a boat was lying alongside of the ship, and the weather being thick, it afforded a good opportunity for gratifying my longing. Jack and myself got in, after putting our heads together, and stole off undetected. I pulled directly up to the wharf of Mr. Marchinton, and at once found myself at home. I will not pretend to describe my sensations, but they were a strange mixture of apprehension, disquiet, hope, and natural attachment. I wished much to see my sister, but was afraid to venture on that.

There was a family, however, of the name of Fraser, that lived near the shore, with which I had been well acquainted, and in whose members I had great confidence. They were respectable in position, its head being called a judge, and they were all intimate with the Marchintons. To the Frasers, then, I went; Jack keeping me company. I was afraid, if I knocked, the servant would not let me in, appearing, as I did, in the dress of a common sailor; so I opened the street-door without any ceremony, and went directly to that of the parlour, which I entered before there was time to stop me. Jack brought up the entry.

Mrs. Fraser and her daughter were seated together, on a settee, and the judge was reading at a table. My sudden apparition astonished them, and all three gazed at me in silence. Mr. Fraser then said, "In the name of heaven, where did you come from, Edward!" I told him I had been in the American service, but that I now belonged to an English transport that was to sail in the morning, and that I had just come ashore to inquire how all hands did; particularly my sister. He told me that my sister was living, a married woman, in Halifax; that Mr. Marchinton was dead, and had grieved very much at my disappearance; that I was supposed to be dead. He then gave me much advice as to my future course, and reminded me how much I had lost by my early mistakes. He was particularly anxious I should quit my adopted country, and wished me to remain in Halifax. He offered to send a servant with me to find my sister, but I was afraid to let my presence be known to so many. I begged my visit might be kept a secret, as I felt ashamed of being seen in so humble circumstances. I was well treated, as was Jack Mallet, both of us receiving wine and cake, &c. Mr. Fraser also gave me a guinea, and as I went away, Mrs. Fraser slipped a pound note into my hand. The latter said to me, in a whisper—"I know what you are afraid of, but I shall tell Harriet of your visit; she will be secret."

I staid about an hour, receiving every mark of kindness from these excellent and respectable people, leaving them to believe we were to sail in the morning. When we got back to the transport no one knew of our absence, and nothing was ever said of our taking the boat. The *Regulus* did not sail for twenty hours after this, but I had no more communication with the shore. We got to sea, at last, two transports, under the convoy of the *Pictou*.

During the whole passage, we eight prisoners kept a

sharp look-out for a chance to get possession of the ship. We were closely watched, there being a lieutenant and his boat's crew on board, besides the Canadians, the master, mate, &c. All the arms were secreted, and nothing was left at hand, that we could use in a rising.

About mid passage, it blowing fresh, with the ship under double-reefed topsails, I was at the weather, with one of the Canadians at the lee, wheel. Mallet was at work in the larboard, or weather, mizen chains, ready to lend me a hand. At this moment the *Pictou* came up under our lee, to speak us in relation to carrying a light during the night. Her masts swung so she could not carry one herself, and her commander wished us to carry our top-light, he keeping near it, instead of our keeping near him. The schooner came very close to us, it blowing heavily, and Mallet called out, "Ned, now is your time. Up helm and into him. A couple of seas will send him down." This was said loud enough to be heard, though all on deck were attending to the schooner; and, as for the Canadian, he did not understand English. I managed to get the helm hard up, and Mallet jumped inboard. The ship fell off fast; but the lieutenant, who was on board as an agent, was standing in the companion-way with his wife, and, the instant he saw what I had done, he ran aft, struck me a sharp blow, and put the helm hard down with his own hands. This saved the *Pictou,* though there was a great outcry on board her. The lieutenant's wife screamed, and there was a pretty uproar for a minute, in every direction. As the *Regulus* luffed-to, her jib-boom-end just cleared the *Pictou*'s forward rigging, and a man might almost have jumped from the ship to the schooner, as we got alongside of each other. Another minute, and we should have travelled over His Majesty's schooner, like a rail-road car going over a squash.

The lieutenant now denounced us, and we prisoners were all put in irons. I am merely relating facts. How far we were right, I leave others to decide; but it must be remembered that Jack had, in that day, a mortal enmity to a British man-of-war, which was a little too apt to lay hands on all that she fell in with, on the high seas. Perhaps severe moralists might say that we had entered into a bargain with the captain of the *Regulus,* not to make war on him during the passage; in answer to which, we can reply that we were not attacking *him,* but the *Pictou.* Our intention, it must be confessed, however, was to seize the *Regulus* in the confusion. Had we been better treated as prisoners, our tempers might not have been so savage. But we got no good treatment, except for our own work; and, being hedged in in this manner, common sailors reason very much as they feel. We were not permitted to go at large again, in the *Regulus,* in which the English were very right, as Jack Mallet, in particular, was a man to put his shipmates up to almost any enterprise.

The anchor was hardly down, at Bermuda, before a signal was made to the *Goliah,* razée, for a boat, and we were sent on board that ship. This was a cruising vessel, and she went to sea next morning. We were distributed about the ship, and ordered to go to work. The intention, evidently, was to swallow us all in the enormous maw of the British navy. We refused to do duty, however, to a man; most of our fellows being pretty bold, as native Americans. We were a fortnight in this situation, the greater part of the time playing green, with our tin pots slung round our necks. We did so much of this, that the people began to laugh at us, as real Johnny Raws, though the old salts knew better. The last even helped us along, some giving us clothes, extra grog, and otherwise being very kind to us. The officers treated us pretty well, too, all things considered. None of us got flogged, nor were we even threatened with the gangway. At length the plan was changed. The boatswain was asked if he got anything out of us, and, making a bad report, we were sent down to the lower gun-deck, under a sentry's charge, and put at "six upon four," again. Here we remained until the ship went into Bermuda, after a six weeks' cruise. This vessel, an old seventy-four cut down, did not answer, for she was soon after sent to England. I overheard her officers, from our berth near the bulkhead, wishing to fall in with the *President,* Commodore Rodgers—a vessel they fancied they could easily handle.[1] I cannot say they could not, but one day an elderly man among them spoke very rationally on the subject, saying, they *might,* or they might *not,* get the best of it in such a fight. For his part, he did not wish to see any such craft, with the miserable crew they had in the *Goliah.*

We found the *Ramilies,* Sir Thomas Hardy, lying in Bermuda Roads.[2] This ship sent a boat, which took us on board the *Ardent,* 64, which was then used as a prison-ship. About a week before we reached this vessel an American midshipman got hold of a boat, and effected his escape, actually making the passage between Bermuda and Cape Henry all alone, by himself.[3] In consequence of this unusual occurrence, a bright look out was kept on all the boats, thus defeating one of our plans, which was to get off in the same way. When we reached the *Ardent,* we found but four Americans in her. After we had been on board her about a week, three men joined us, who had given themselves up on board English men-of-war, as native Americans. One of these men, whose name was Baily, had been fourteen years in the English service, into which he had been pressed, his protection having been torn up before his face. He was a Connecticut man, and had given himself up at the commencement

1. A U.S. Navy frigate, in 1813 under the command of Commodore John Rodgers, mentioned by British officers as a ship they would like to fight.

2. Rear Admiral Hardy's flagship *Ramilies,* at Bermuda when Ned saw her, had done blockade duty during the summer of 1813 in Long Island Sound and was primarily responsible for keeping Decatur from going to sea.

3. The name of this young officer was King. He is now dead, having been lost in the Lynx, Lt. Madison.—EDITOR.

of the war, getting three dozen for his pains. He was then sent on the Halifax station, where he gave himself up again. He received three dozen more, then had his shirt thrown over his back and was sent to us. I saw the back and the shirt, myself, and Baily said he would keep the last to be buried with him. Bradbury and Patrick were served very much in the same manner. I saw all their backs, and give the remainder of the story, as they gave it to me. Baily and Bradbury got off in season to join the *Constitution,* and to make the last cruise in her during this war. I afterwards fell in with Bradbury, who mentioned this circumstance to me.

It is good to have these things known, for I do believe the English nation would be averse to men's receiving such treatment, could they fairly be made to understand it. It surely is bad enough to be compelled to fight the battles of a foreign country, without being flogged for not fighting them when they happen to be against one's own people. For myself, I was born, of German parents, in the English territory, it is true; but America was, and ever has been, the country of my choice, and, while yet a child, I may say, I decided for myself to sail under the American flag; and, if my father had a right to make an Englishman of me, by taking service under the English crown, I think I had a right to make myself what I pleased, when he had left me to get on as I could, without his counsel and advice.

After being about three weeks in the *Ardent,* we eight prisoners were sent on board the *Ramilies,* to be tried as Englishmen who had been fighting against their king. The trial took place on board the *Asia,* 74, a flag-ship; but we lived in the *Ramilies,* during the time the investigation was going on. Sir Thomas Hardy held several conversations with me, on the quarter-deck, in which he manifested great kindness of feeling. He inquired whether I was really an American; but I evaded any direct answer. I told him, however, that I had been an apprentice, in New York, in the employment of Jacob Barker; which was true, in one sense, as Mr. Barker was the consignee of the *Sterling,* and knew of my indentures. I mentioned him, as a person more likely to be known than Captain Johnston. Sir Thomas said he had some knowledge of Mr. Barker; and, I think, I have heard that they were, in some way, connected. This was laying an anchor to-windward, as it turned out, in the end.

We were all on board the *Asia,* for trial, or investigation, two days, before I was sent for into the cabin. I was very much frightened; and scarce knew what I said, or did. It is a cruel thing to leave sailors without counsel, on such occasions; though the officers behaved very kindly and considerately to me; and, I believe, to all of us. There were several officers seated round a table; and all were in swabs. They said, the gentleman who presided, was a Sir Borlase Warren, the admiral on the station.[4] This gentleman, whoever he was, probably saw that I was frightened. He slewed himself round, in his chair, and said to me; "My man, you need not be alarmed; we know *who* you are, and *what* you are; but your apprenticeship will be of great service to you." This was not said, however, until Sir Thomas Hardy had got out the story of my being an apprentice in Jacob Barker's employ, again, before them all, in the cabin. I was told to send for a copy of my indentures, by one of the white-washed Swedes, that sailed between Bermuda and New York. This I did, that very day. I was in the cabin of the *Asia,* half an hour, perhaps; and I felt greatly relieved, when I got out of it. It was decided, in my presence, to send me back among the prisoners, on board the *Ardent.* The same decision was made, as to the whole eight of us, that had come on in the *Regulus.*

When we got back to the *Ramilies,* Sir Thomas Hardy had some more conversation with me. I have thought, ever since, that he knew something about my birth, and of my

4. If this be true, this could hardly have been a court, but must have been a mere investigation; as Sir John Borlase Warren was commander-in-chief, and would scarcely sit in a court of his own ordering.—EDITOR.

being the prince's godson. He wished me to join the British service, seemingly, very much, and encouraged me with the hope of being promoted. But, it is due to myself, to say, I held out against it all. I do not believe America had a truer heart, in her service, than mine; and I do not think an English commission would have bought me. I have nothing to hope, from saying this, for I am now old, and a cripple; but, as I have sat down to relate the truth, let the truth be told, whether it tell for, or against me.

We were now sent back to the *Ardent;* where we remained three weeks, or a month, longer. During this time we got our papers from New York; I receiving a copy of my indentures, together with the sum of ten dollars; which reached me through Sir Thomas Hardy, as I understood. Nothing more was ever said, to any of the eight, about their being Englishmen; the whole of us being treated as prisoners of war. Prisoners arrived fast, until we had four hundred in the *Ardent.* The old *Ruby,* a forty-four, on two decks, was obliged to receive some of them. Most of these prisoners were privateersmen; though there were a few soldiers, and some citizens that had been picked up in Chesapeake Bay. Before we left Bermuda, the crew of a French frigate was put into the *Ardent,* to the number of near four hundred men. In the whole, we must have had eight hundred souls, and all on one deck. This was close stowage, and I was heartily glad when I quitted the ship.

Soon after the French arrived, four hundred of us Americans were put on board transports, and we sailed for Halifax, under the convoy of the *Ramilies.* A day or two after we got out, we fell in with an American privateer, which continued hovering around us for several days. As this was a bold fellow, frequently coming within gun-shot, and sporting his sticks and canvass in all sorts of ways, Sir Thomas Hardy felt afraid he would get one of the four transports, and he took all us prisoners into the *Ramilies.* We staid in the ship the rest of the passage, and when we went into

Halifax it was all alone, the four transports having disappeared. Two of them subsequently got in; but I think the other two were actually taken by that saucy fellow.

The prisoners, at first, had great liberty allowed them, on board the *Ramilies*. On all occasions, Sir Thomas Hardy treated the Americans well. A party of marines was stationed on the poop, and another on the forecastle, and the ship's people had arms; but this was all the precaution that was used. The opportunity tempted some of our men to plan a rising, with a view to seize the ship. Privateer officers were at the head of this scheme, which was communicated to me, among others, soon after the plot was laid. Most of the prisoners knew of the intention, and everybody seemed to enter into the affair with hearty good-will. Our design was to rise at the end of the second dog-watch, overcome the crew, and carry the ship upon our own coast. If unable to pass the blockading squadrons, we intended to run her ashore. The people of the *Ramilies* outnumbered us by near one-half, and they had arms, it is true; but we trusted to the effect of a surprise, and something to the disposition of most English sailors to get quit of their own service. Had the attempt been made, from what I saw of the crew, I think our main trouble would have been with the officers and the marines. We were prevented from trying the experiment, however, in consequence of having been betrayed by some one who was in the secret, the whole of us being suddenly sent into the cable tiers and amongst the water casks, under the vigilant care of sentinels posted in the wings. After that, we were allowed to come on deck singly, only, and then under a sentinel's charge. When Sir Thomas spoke to us concerning this change of treatment, he did not abuse us for our plan, but was mild and reasonable, while he reminded us of the necessity of what he was doing. I have no idea he would have been in the least injured, had we got possession of the ship; for, to the last, our people praised him, and the treatment they received, while under his orders.

Before we were sent below, Sir Thomas spoke to me again, on the subject of my joining the English service. He was quite earnest about it, and reasoned with me like a father; but I was determined not to yield. I did not like England, and I did like America. My birth in Quebec was a thing I could not help; but having chosen to serve under the American flag, and having done so now for years, I did not choose to go over to the enemy.

At Halifax, fifteen or twenty of us were sent on board the old *Centurion,* 44, Lord Anson's ship, as retaliation-men. We eight were of the number. We found something like thirty more in the ship, all retaliation-men, like ourselves. Those we found in the *Centurion* did not appear to me to be foremast Jacks, but struck me as being citizens from ashore. We were well treated, however, suffering no other confinement that that of the ship. We were on "six upon four," it is true, like other prisoners, but our own country gave us small stores, and extra bread and beef. In the way of grub, we fared like sailor kings. At the end of three weeks, we eight lakesmen were sent to Melville Island, among the great herd of prisoners.[5] I cannot explain the reason of all these changes; but I know that when the gate was shut on us, the turnkey said we had gone into a home that would last as long as the war lasted.

Melville is an island of more than a mile in circumference, with low, rocky shores. It lies about three miles from the town of Halifax, but not in sight. It is connected with the main by a bridge that is thrown across a narrow passage of something like a quarter of a mile in width. In the centre of the island is an eminence, which was occupied by the garrison, and had some artillery. This eminence commanded the whole island. Another post on the main, also, com-

5. Melville Island is located in Halifax harbor, three miles from the city. Ned estimated that 1,200 American prisoners were confined there, along with a few French.

manded the prisoners' barracks. These barracks were ordinary wooden buildings, enclosed on the side of the island with a strong stone wall, and on the side of the post on the main, by high, open palisades. Of course, a sufficient guard was maintained.

It was said there were about twelve hundred Americans on the island, when I passed the gate. Among them were a few French, some of whom were a part of the crew of the *Ville de Milan,* the ship that had been taken before I first left Halifax; or more than eight years previously to this time. This did, indeed, look like the place's being a home to a poor fellow, and I did not relish the circumstance at all. Among our people were soldiers, sailors, and 'long-shoremen. There was no difference in the treatment, which, for a prison, was good. We got only "six upon four" from the English, of course; but our own country made up the difference here, as on board the *Centurion.* They had a prison dress, with one leg of the trowsers yellow and the other blue, &c.; but we would not stand that. Our agent managed the matter so that we got regular jackets and trowsers of the true old colour. The poor Frenchmen looked like peacocks in their dress, but we did not envy them their finery.

I had been on the island about a fortnight, when I was told by Jack Mallet that a woman, whom he thought to be my sister, was at the gate. Jack knew my whole history, and came to his opinion from a resemblance that he saw between me and the person who had inquired for me. I refused to go to the gate, however, to see who it was, and Jack was sent back to tell the woman that I had been left behind at Bermuda. He was directed to throw in a few hints about the expediency of her not coming back to look for me, and that it would be better if she never named me. All this was done, I getting a berth from which I could see the female. I knew her in a moment, although she was married, and had a son with her, and my heart was very near giving way, especially when I saw her shedding tears. She went away from the gate, however, going up on the ramparts, from which she could look down into the prison-yard. There she remained an hour, as if she wished to satisfy her own eyes as to the truth of Jack's story; but I took good care to keep out of her sight.

As I knew there was little hope of an exchange of prisoners, I now began to think of the means of making my escape. Jack Mallet dared not attempt to swim, on account of the rheumatism and cramps, having narrowly escaped drowning at Bermuda, and he could not join in our schemes. As for myself, I have been able to swim ever since danger taught me the important lesson, the night the *Scourge* went down. Money would be necessary to aid me in escaping, and Jack and I put our heads together, in order to raise some. I had still the ten dollars given me by Sir Thomas Hardy, and I commenced operations by purchasing shares in a dice-board, a *vingt et un* table, and a quino table.[6] Jack Mallet and I, also, set up a shop, on a capital of three dollars. We sold smoked herring, pipes, tobacco, segars, spruce beer, and, as chances of smuggling it in offered, now and then a little Jamaica. All this time, the number of the prisoners increased, until, in the end, we got to have a full prison, when they began to send them to England. Only one of the Julias was sent away, however, all the rest remaining at Melville Island, from some cause I cannot explain.

I cannot say we made money very fast. On every shilling won at dice, we received a penny; at *vingt et un,* the commission was the same; as it was also at the other games. New cards, however, brought a little higher rate. All this was wrong I *now* know, but *then* it gave me very little trouble. I hope I would not do the same thing over again, even to make my escape from Melville Island, but one never knows to what distress may drive him.

6. Ned means Loto, probably.—EDITOR.

Some person among the American prisoners—a soldier it was said—commenced counterfeiting Spanish dollars. I am afraid most of us helped to circulate them. We thought it no harm to cheat the people of the canteens, for we knew they were doing all they could to cheat us. This was prison morality, in war-time, and I say nothing in its favour; though, for myself, I will own I felt more of the consciousness of wrong-doing in holding the shares in the gambling establishments, than in giving bad dollars for poor rum. The counterfeiting business was destroyed by one of the dollars happening to break, as some of the officers were pitching them; when, on examination, it turned out that most of the money in the prison was bad. It was said the people of the canteens had about four hundred of the dollars, when they came to overhaul their lockers. A good many found their way into Halifax.

My trade lasted all winter—(that of 1813–14,) and by March I had gained the sum of eighty French crowns. Dollars I was afraid to hold on account of the base money. The ice now began to give way, and a few of us, who had been discussing the matter all winter, set about forming serious plans to escape. My confederates were a man of the name of Johnson, who had been taken in the *Snapdragon* privateer, and an Irishman of the name of Littlefield.[7] Barnet, the Mozambique man, joined us also, making four in all. It was quite early in the month, when we made the attempt. Our windows were long, and had perpendicular bars of wrought iron to secure them, but no cross-bars. There was no glass; but outside shutters, that we could open at our pleasure. Outside of the windows were sentinels, and there were two rows of pickets between us and the shore.

7. A privateer schooner, 6 guns, out of Wilmington, North Carolina, that captured 10 vessels in all during 1813–1814. See Edgar S. Maclay, *A History of The American Privateers* (New York, 1924), pp. 321–22.

I put my crowns in a belt around my waist. Another belt, or skin, was filled with rum, for the double purpose of buoying me in the water, and of comforting me when ashore. At that day, I found rum one of the great blessings of life; now I look upon it as one of the greatest evils. My companions made similar provisions of money and rum, though neither was as rich as myself. I left Mallet and Leonard Lewis my heirs at law if I escaped, and my trustees should I be caught. Lewis was a young man of better origin than most in the prison, and I have always thought some calamity drove him to the seas. He was in ill health, and did not appear to be destined to a long life. He would have joined us, heart and hand, but was not strong enough to endure the fatigue which we well knew we must undergo, before we could get clear.

The night selected for the attempt was so cold, dark, and dismal, as to drive all the sentinels into their boxes. It rained hard, in the bargain. About eight, or as soon as the lights were out, we got the lanyards of our hammocks around two of the window bars, and using a bit of fire-wood for a heaver, we easily brought them together. This left room for our bodies to pass out, without any difficulty. Jack Mallet, and those we left behind, hove the bars straight again, so that the keepers were at a loss to know how we had got off. We met with no obstacle between the prison and the water. The pickets we removed, having cut them in the day-time. In a word, all four of us reached the shore of the Island in two or three minutes after we had taken leave of our messmates. The difficulty lay before us. We entered into the water, at once, and began to swim. When I was a few rods from the place of landing, which was quite near the guard-house, on the main, Johnson began to sing out that he was drowning. I told him to be quiet, but it was of no use. The guard on the main heard him, and commenced firing, and of course we swam all the harder. Three of us were soon ashore, and, knowing the roads well, I led them in a direction to avoid the soldiers. By running into the woods, we got clear, though poor Johnson fell again into the hands of the enemy. He deserved it for bawling as he did; it being the duty of a man in such circumstances to die with a shut mouth.

CHAPTER IX

THE THREE WHO HAD ESCAPED RAN, for a quarter of a mile, in the woods, when we brought up, and took a drink. Hearing no more firing, or any further alarm, we now consulted as to our future course. There were some mills at the head of the bay, about four miles from the guard-house, and I led the party thither. We reached the place towards morning, and found a berth in them before any one was stirring. We hid ourselves in an old granary; but no person appeared near the place throughout the next day. We had put a little bread and a few herrings in our hats, and on these we subsisted. The rum cheered us up, and, if rum ever did good, I think it was to us on that occasion. We slept soundly, with one man on the look-out; a rule we observed the whole time we were out. It stopped raining in the course of the day, though the weather was bitter cold.

Next night we got under way, and walked in a direction which led us within three miles of the town. In doing this, we passed the Prince's Lodge, a place where I had often been, and the sight of which reminded me of home, and of my childish days. There was no use in regrets, however, and we pushed ahead. The men saw my melancholy, and they questioned me; but I evaded the answer, pretending that nothing ailed me. There was a tavern about a league from the town, kept by a man of the name of Grant, and Littlefield ventured into it. He bought a small cheese and a loaf of bread; getting off clear, though not unsuspected. This helped us along famously, and we pushed on as fast as we could. Before morning we came near a bridge, on which there was a sentinel posted, with a guard-house near its end. To avoid this danger, we turned the guard-house, striking the river above the bridge. Here we met two Indians, and fell into discourse with them. Our rum now served us a better turn than ever, buying the Indians in a minute. We told these chaps we were deserters from the *Bulwark,* 74, and begged them to help us along. At first, they thought we were Yankess, whom they evidently disliked, and that right heartily; but the story of the desertion took, and made them disposed to serve us.

These two Indians led us down to the bed of the river, and actually carried us beneath the bridge, on the side of the river next the guard, where we found a party of about thirty of these red-skins, men, women and children. Here we stayed no less than three days; faring extremely well, having fish, bread, butter, and other common food. The weather was very bad, and we did not like to turn out in it, besides, thinking the search for us might be less keen after a short delay. All this time, we were within a few rods of the guard, hearing the sentinels cry "all's well," from half-hour to half-hour. We were free with our rum, and, as much as we dared to be, with our money. These people never betrayed us.

The third night we left the bridge, guided by a young Indian. He led us about two miles up the river, passing through the Maroon town in the night, after which he left us. We wished him to keep on with us for some distance further, but he refused. He quitted us near morning, and we turned into a deserted log-house, on the banks of the river, where we passed the day. The country was thinly populated, and the houses we saw were poor and mean. We must now have been about five-and-twenty miles from Halifax.

Our object was to cross the neck of land between the Atlantic and the Bay of Fundy, and to get to Annapolis Royal, where we expected to be able to procure a boat, by fair means if we could, by stealth if necessary, and cross over to the American shore. We had still a long road before us, and had some little difficulty to find the way. The Indians, however, gave us directions that greatly assisted us; and we travelled a long bit, and pretty fast all that night. In the morning, the country had more the appearance of being peopled and cultivated, and I suspected we were getting into the vicinity of Horton, a place through which it would be indispensable to pass. The weather became bad again, and it was necessary to make a halt. Coming near a log-house, we sent Littlefield ahead to make some inquiries of a woman who appeared to be in it alone. On his return, he reported well of the woman. He had told her we were deserters from the *Bulwark,* and had promised to pay her if she would let us stay about her premises that day, and get us something to eat. The woman had consented to our occupying an out-house, and had agreed to buy the provisions. We now took possession of the out-house, where the woman visited us, and getting some money, she left us in quest of food. We were uneasy during her absence, but she came back with some meat, eggs, bread, and butter, at the end of an hour, and all seemed right. We made two comfortable meals in this out-house, where we remained until near evening. I had the look-out about noon, and I saw a man hanging about the house, and took the alarm. The man did not stay long, however, and I got a nap as soon as he disappeared. About four we were all up, and one of us taking a look, saw this same man, and two others, go into the house. The woman had already told us that a party of soldiers had gone ahead, in pursuit of three Yankee runaways; that four had broken prison, but one had been retaken, and the rest were still out. This left little doubt that she knew who we were; and we thought it best to steal away, at once, lest the men in the house should be consulting with her, at that very moment, about selling us for the reward, which we know was always four pounds ahead. The out-house was near the river, and there was a good deal of brush growing along the banks, and we succeeded in getting away unseen.

We went down to the margin, under the bank, and pursued our way along the stream. Before it was dark we came in sight of the bridge, for which we had been travelling ever since we left the other bridge, and were sorry to see a sentry-box on it. We now halted for a council, and came to a determination to wait until dark, and then advance. This we did, getting under this bridge, as we had done with the other. We had no Indians, however, to comfort and feed us.

I had known a good deal of this part of the country when a boy, from the circumstance that Mr. Marchinton had a large farm, near a place called Cornwallis, on the Bay, where I had even spent whole summers with the family. This bridge I recollected well; and I remembered there was a ford a little on one side of it, when the tide was out. The tides are tremendous in this part of the world, and we did not dare to steal a boat here, lest we should be caught in one of the bores, as they are called, when the tide came in. It was now half ebb, and we resolved to wait, and try the ford.

It was quite dark when we left the bridge, and we had a delicate bit of work before us. The naked flats were very wide, and we sallied out, with the bridge as our guide. I was up to my middle in mud, at times, but the water was not very deep. We must have been near an hour in the mud, for we were not exactly on the proper ford, of course, and made bad navigation of it in the dark. But we were afraid to lose sight of the bridge, lest we should get all adrift.

At length we reached the firm ground, covered with mud and chilled with cold. We found the road, and the village of Horton, and skirted the last, until all was clear. Then we took to the road, and carried sail hard all night. Whenever we saw any one, we hid ourselves, but we met few while travelling. Next morning we walked until we came to a deserted saw-mill, which I also remembered, and here we halted for the day. No one troubled us, nor did I see any one; but Littlefield said that a man drove a herd of cattle past, during his watch on deck.

I told my companions that night, if they would be busy, we might reach Cornwallis, where I should be at home. We were pretty well fagged, and wanted rest, for Jack is no great traveller ashore; and I promised the lads a good snug berth at Mr. Marchinton's farm. We pushed ahead briskly, in consequence, and I led the party up to the farm, just as day was dawning. A Newfoundland dog, named Hunter, met us with some ferocity; but, on my calling him by name, he was pacified, and began to leap on me, and to caress me. I have always thought that dog knew me, after an absence of so many years. There was no time to waste with dogs, however, and we took the way to the barn. We had wit enough not to get on the hay, but to throw ourselves on a mow filled with straw, as the first was probably in use. Here we went to sleep, with one man on the look-out. This was the warmest and most comfortable rest we had got since quitting the island, from which we had now been absent eight or nine days.

We remained one night and two days in this barn. The workmen entered it often, and even stayed some time on the barn-floor; but no one seemed to think of ascending our mow. The dog kept much about the place, and I was greatly afraid he would be the means of betraying us. Our provisions were getting low, and, the night we were at the farm, I sallied out, accompanied by Barnet, and we made our way into the dairy. Here we found a pan of bread, milk, cheese, butter, eggs, and codfish. Of course, we took our fill of milk; but Barnet got hold of a vessel of sour cream, and came near hallowing out, when he had taken a good pull at it. As we returned to the barn, the geese set up an outcry, and glad enough was I to find myself safe on the mow again, without being discovered. Next day, however, we overheard the men in the barn speaking of the robbery, and a complaining, in particular, of the uselessness of the dog. I did not know any of these persons, although a young man appeared among them, this day, who I fancied had been a playfellow of mine, when a boy. I could not trust him, or any one else there; and all the advantage we got from the farm, was through my knowledge of the localities, and of the habits of the place.

I had never been further on the road between Halifax and Annapolis, than to Cornwallis. The rest of the distance was unknown to me, though I was familiar with the route which went out of Cornwallis, and which was called the Annapolis road. It was a fine star-light evening, and we made good headway. We all felt refreshed, and journeyed on full stomachs. We did not meet a soul, though we travelled through a well-settled country. The next morning we halted in a wood, the weather being warm and pleasant. Here we slept and rested as usual, and were off again at night. Littlefield pinned three fowls as we went along, declaring that he intended to have a warm mess next day, and he got off without discovery. About four o'clock in the morning, we fell in with a river, and left the highway, following the banks of the stream for a short distance. It now came on to blow and rain, with the wind on shore, and we saw it would not do to get a boat and go out in such a time. There was a rising ground, in a thick wood, near us, and we went up the hill to pass the day. We had seen two men pulling ashore in a good-looking boat, and it was our determination to get this boat, and shape our course down stream to the Bay, as soon as it moderated. From the hill, we could overlook the river, and the adjacent country. We saw the fishermen land, take their sail and oars out of the boat, haul the latter up, turn her over, and stow their sails and oars beneath her. They had a breaker of fresh water, too, and everything seemed fitted for our purposes. We liked the craft, and, what is more, we liked the cruise.

We could not see the town of Annapolis, which turned out to be up-stream from us, though we afterwards ascertained that we were within a mile or two of it. The fishermen walked in the direction of the town, and disappeared. All we wanted now was tolerably good weather, with a fair wind, or, at least, with less wind. The blow had driven in the fishermen, and we thought it wise to be governed by their experience. Nothing occurred in the course of the day, the weather remaining the same, and we being exposed to the rain, with no other cover than trees without leaves. There were many pines, however, and they gave us a little shelter.

At dusk, Littlefield lighted a fire, and began to cook his fowls. The supper was soon ready, and we eat it with a good relish. We then went to sleep, leaving Barnet on the look-out. I had just got into a good sleep, when I was awoke by the tramp of horses, and the shouting of men. On springing up, I found that a party of five horsemen were upon us. One called out—"Here they are—we've found them at last." This left me no doubt of their errand, and we were all re-taken. Our arms were tied, and we were made to mount behind the horsemen, when they rode off with us, taking the road by which we had come. We went but a few miles that night, when we halted.

We were taken the whole distance to Halifax, in this manner, riding on great-coats, without stirrups, the horses on a smart walk. We did not go by Cornwallis, which, it seems, was not the nearest road; but we passed through Horton, and crossed the bridge, beneath which we had waded through the mud. At Horton we passed a night. We were confined in a sort of a prison, that was covered with mud. We did not like our berths; and, finding that the logs, of which the building was made, were rotten, we actually worked our way through them, and got fairly out. Littlefield, who was as reckless an Irishman as ever lived, swore he would set fire to the place; which he did, by returning through the hole we had made, and getting up into a loft, that was dry and combustible. But for this silly act, we might have escaped; and, as it was, we did get off for the rest of the night, being caught, next morning, nearly down, again, by the bridge at Windsor.

This time, our treatment was a good deal worse, than at first. A sharp look-out was kept, and they got us back to Halifax, without any more adventures. We were pretty well fagged; though we had to taper off with the black hole, and bread and water, for the next ten days; the regular punishment for such misdemeanors as ours. At the end of the ten days, we were let out, and came together again. Our return brought about a great deal of discussion; and, not a little criticism, as to the prudence of our course. To hear the chaps talk, one would think every man among them could have got off, had he been in our situation; though none of them did any better; several having got off the island, in our absence, and been retaken, within the first day or two. While I was in prison, however, I remember but one man who got entirely clear. This was a privateersman, from Marblehead; who did get fairly off; though he was back again, in six weeks, having been taken once more, a few days out.

We adventurers were pretty savage, about our failure; and, the moment we were out of the black hole, we began to lay our heads together for a new trial. My idea was, to steer a different course, in the new attempt; making the best of our way towards Liverpool, which lay to the southward, coastwise. This would leave us on the Atlantic, it was true; but our notion was, to ship in a small privateer, called the *Liverpool,* and then run our chance of getting off from her;

as she was constantly crossing over to the American coast.[1] As this craft was quite small, and often had but few hands in her, we did not know but we might get hold of the schooner itself. Then there was some probability of being put in a coaster; which we might run away with. At all events, any chance seemed better to us, than that of remaining in prison, until the end of a war that might last years, or until we got to be grey-headed. I remembered, when the *Ville de Milan* was brought into Halifax; this was a year, or two, before I went to sea; and yet here were some of her people still, on Melville Island!

I renewed my trade as soon as out of the Black Hole, but did not give up the idea of escaping. Leonard Lewis and Jack Mallet were the only men we let into the secret. They both declined joining us; Mallet on account of his dread of the water, and Lewis, because certain he could not outlive the fatigue; but they wished us good luck, and aided us all they could. With Johnson we would have no further concern.

The keepers did not ascertain the means by which we had left the barracks, though they had seen the cut pickets of course. We did not attempt, therefore, to cut through again, but resolved to climb. The English had strengthened the pickets with cross-pieces, which were a great assistance to *us,* and I now desire to express my thanks for the same. We waited for a warm, but dark and rainy night in May, before we commenced our new movement. We had still plenty of money, I having brought back with me to prison forty crowns, and having driven a thriving trade in the interval. We got out through the bars, precisely as we had done before, and at the very same window. This was a small job. After climbing the pickets, either Littlefield or Barnet dropped on the outside, a little too carelessly, and was overheard. This sentinel immediately called for the corporal of

1. The *Liverpool Packet,* a Halifax privateer noted for taking prizes off Cape Cod and in Long Island Sound during 1812 and 1813.

the guard, but we were in the water, swimming quite near the bridge, and some little distance from the guardhouse on the main. There was a stir on the island, while we were in the water, but we all got ashore, safe and unseen.

We took to the same woods as before, but turned south instead of west. Our route brought us along by the waterside, and we travelled hard all that night. Littlefield pretended to be our guide, but we got lost, and remained two days and nights in the woods, without food, and completely at fault as to which way to steer. At length we ventured out into a high-way, by open day-light, and good luck threw an old Irish seaman, who then lived by fishing, in our way. After a little conversation, we told this old man we were deserters from a vessel of war, and he seemed to like us all the better for it. He had served himself, and had a son impressed, and seemed to like the English navy little better than we did ourselves. He took us to a hut on the beach, and fed us with fish, potatoes, and bread, giving us a very comfortable and hearty meal. We remained in this hut until sunset, receiving a great deal of useful advice from the old man, and then we left him. We used some precaution in travelling, sleeping in the woods; but we kept moving by day as well as by night, and halting only when tired, and a good place offered. We were not very well off for food, though we brought a little from the fisherman's hut, and found quantities of winter-berries by the way-side.

We entered Liverpool about eight at night, and went immediately to the rendezvous of the privateer, giving a little girl a shilling to be our guide. The keeper of the rendezvous received us gladly, and we shipped immediately. Of course we were lodged and fed, in waiting for the schooner to come in. Each of us got four pounds bounty, and both parties seemed delighted with the bargain. To own the truth, we now began to drink, and the next day was pretty much a blank with us all. The second day, after breakfast, the landlord rushed into our room with a newspaper in his hand, and broke out upon us, with a pretty string of names, denouncing us for having told him we were deserters, when we were only runaway Yankees! The twelve pounds troubled him, and he demanded it back. We laughed at him, and advised him to be quiet and put us aboard the privateer. He then told us the guard was after us, hot-foot, and that it was too late. This proved to be true enough, for, in less than an hour an officer and a platoon of men had us in custody. We had some fun in hearing the officer give it to the landlord, who still kept talking about his twelve pounds. The officer told him plainly that he was rightly served, for attempting to smuggle off deserters, and I suppose this was the reason no one endeavoured to get the money away from us, except by words. We kept the twelve pounds, right or wrong.

We were now put in a coaster, and sent to Halifax by water. We were in irons, but otherwise were well enough treated. We were kept in the Navy-yard guard-house, at Halifax, several hours, and were visited by a great many officers. These gentlemen were curious to hear our story, and we let them have it, very frankly. They laughed, and said, generally, we were not to be blamed for trying to get off, if their own look-outs were so bad as to let us. We did not tell them, however, by what means we passed out of the prison-barracks. Among the officers who came and spoke to us, was an admiral, Sir Isaac Coffin.[2] This gentleman was a native American, and was then in Halifax to assist the Nantucket men, whom he managed to get exchanged. His own nephew was said to be among them; but him he would not serve, as

2. A Boston-born admiral of the Royal Navy who had come to Halifax to assist the Nantucket men, despite his having fought against his countrymen in the American Revolution. A rough-hewn, salty individual, he was subject to discrimination by British officers because of his American birth. He eventually rose to become Admiral of the Blue. Though resident in England, he continued to express a lifelong interest in America. The prize money he had earned, increased through investment, was eventually dispersed in philanthropy, notably in the Coffin School in Nantucket in 1827.

he had been captured in a privateer. Had he been captured in a man-of-war, or a merchant-man, he would have done all he could for him; but, as it was, he let him go to Dartmoor—at least, this was the story in the prison. The old gentleman spoke very mildly to us, and said he could not blame us for attempting to escape. I do not think he had ever heard of the twelve pounds; though none of the navy officers were sorry that the privateer's-men should be punished. As for us, we considered them all enemies alike, on whom it was fair enough to live in a time of war.

We were sent back to the island, and were quarantined again; though it was for twenty days, this time. When we got pratique, we learned that some one had told of the manner in which we got out of prison, and cross-bars had been placed in all the windows, making them so many "nine of diamonds." This was blocking the channel, and there was no more chance for getting off in that way.

A grand conspiracy was now formed, which was worthy of the men in prison. The plan was to get possession of Halifax itself, and go off in triumph. We were eighteen hundred prisoners in all; though not very well off for officers. About fifty of us entered into the plan, at first; nor did we let in any recruits for something like six weeks. A Mr. Crowninshield, of Salem, was the head man among us, he having been an officer in a privateer.[3] There were a good many privateer officers in the prison, but they were berthed over-head, and were intended to be separated from us at night. The floor was lifted between us, however, and we held our communications by these means. The officers came down at night, and lent us a hand with the work.

3. John Crowninshield of Salem, Massachusetts, commander of the privateer *Diomede* that was captured on 25 June 1814. He participated in the plan to escape from prison on Melville Island. When the plot was discovered, the British sent some 600 Americans to Dartmoor prison in Devonshire, England. John Crowinshield was interned at Dartmoor and survived the massacre of March 1815.

The scheme was very simple, though I do not think it was at all difficult of execution. The black-hole cells were beneath the prison, and we broke through the floor, into one of them, from our bay. A large mess-chest concealed the process, in the day-time. We worked in gangs of six, digging and passing up the dirt into the night-tubs. These tubs we were permitted to empty, every morning, in a tide's way, and thus we got rid of the dirt. At the end of two months we had dug a passage, wide enough for two abreast, some twenty or thirty yards, and were nearly ready to come up to the surface. We now began to recruit, swearing in each man. On the whole, we had got about four hundred names, when the project was defeated, by that great enemy which destroys so many similar schemes, treachery. We were betrayed, as was supposed by one of our own numbers.

Had we got out, the plan was to seize the heights of the island, and get possession of the guns. This effected, it would have been easy to subdue the guard. We then would have pushed for Citadel Hill, which commanded Halifax. Had we succeeded there, we should have given John Bull a great deal of trouble, though no one could say what would have been the result. Hundreds would probably have got off, in different craft, even had the great plan failed. We were not permitted to try the experiment, however, for one day we were all turned out, and a party of English officers, army and navy, entered the barracks, removed the mess-chest, and surveyed our mine at their leisure. A draft of six hundred was sent from the prison that day, and was shipped for Dartmoor; and, by the end of the week, our whole number was reduced to some three or four hundred souls. One of the Julias went in this draft, but all the rest of us were kept at Halifax. For some reason or other, the English seemed to keep their eyes on us.

I never gave up the hope of escaping, and the excitement of the hope was beneficial to both body and mind. We were too well watched, however, and conversation at night was even forbidden. Most of the officers were gone, and this threw me pretty much on my own resources. I have forgotten to say that Lemuel Bryant, the man who fell at the breech of my gun, at Little York, and whom I afterwards hauled into the *Scourge*'s boat, got off, very early after our arrival at Halifax. He made two that got quite clear, instead of the one I have already mentioned. Bryant's escape was so clever, as to deserve notice.

One day a party of some thirty soldiers was called out for exchange, under a capitulation. Among the names was that of Lemuel Bryant, but the man happened to be dead. Our Bryant had found this out, beforehand, and he rigged himself soldier-fashion, and answered to the name. It is probable he ascertained the fact, by means of some relationship, which brought him in contact with the soldier previously to his death. He met with no difficulty, and I have never seen him since. I have heard he is still living, and that he receives a pension for the hurt he received at York. Well does he deserve it, for no man ever had a narrower chance for his life.

Nothing new, worthy of notice, occurred for several months, until one evening in March, 1815, we heard a great rejoicing in Halifax; and, presently, a turnkey appeared on the walls, and called out that England and America had made peace![4] We gave three cheers, and passed the night happy enough. We had a bit of a row with the turnkeys about locking us in again, for we were fierce for liberty; but we were forced to submit for another night.

4. News of the ratification of the Treaty of Ghent had reached Halifax approximately three months after the signing of the treaty on 24 December 1815.

CHAPTER X

THE FOLLOWING MORNING, eight of the names that stood first on the prison-roll were called off, to know if the men would consent to work a liberated Swedish brig to New York. I was one of the eight, as was Jack Mallet and Barnet. Wilcox, one of those who had gone with us to Bermuda, had died, and the rest were left on the island. I never fell in with Leonard Lewis, Littlefield, or any of the rest of those chaps, after I quitted the prison. Lewis, I think, could not have lived long; and as for Littlefield, I heard of him, afterwards, as belonging to the *Washington,* 74.

The Swede, whose name was the *Venus,* was lying at the end of Marchinton's wharf, a place that had been so familiar to me in boyhood. We all went on board, and I was not sorry to find that we were to haul into the stream immediately. I had an extraordinary aversion to Halifax, which my late confinement had not diminished, and had no wish to see a living soul in it. Jack Mallet, however, took on himself the office of paying my sister a visit, and of telling her where I was to be found. This he did contrary to my wishes, and without my knowledge; though I think he meant to do me a favour. The very day we hauled into the stream, a boat came alongside us, and I saw, at a glance, that Harriet was in it. I said a few words to her, requesting her not to come on board, but promising to visit her that evening, which I did.

I stayed several hours with my sister, whom I found living with her husband. She did not mention my father's name to me, at all; and I learned nothing of my other friends, if I ever had any, or of my family. Her husband was a tailor, and they gave me a good outfit of clothes, and treated me with great kindness. It struck me that the unaccountable silence of my father about us children, had brought my sister down in the world a little, but it was no affair of mine; and, as for myself, I cared for no one. After passing the evening with the family, I went on board again, without turning to the right or left to see a single soul more. Even the Frasers were not visited, so strong was my dislike to have anything to do with Halifax.

The *Venus* took on board several passengers, among whom were three or four officers of the navy. Lieutenant Rapp, and a midshipman Randolph were among them, and there were also several merchant-masters of the party. We sailed two days after I joined the brig, and had a ten or twelve days' passage. The moment the *Venus* was alongside the wharf, at New York, we all left, and found ourselves free men once more. I had been a prisoner nineteen months, and that was quite enough for me for the remainder of my life.

We United States' men reported ourselves, the next day, to Captain Evans, the commandant of the Brooklyn Yard, and, after giving in our names, we were advised to go on board the *Epervier,* which was then fitting out for the Mediterranean, under the command of Captain Downes.[1] To

1. Captain Samuel Evans, commanding officer of the USS *Chesapeake* in 1812–1813, who requested reassignment in April 1813 because of the festering of an old wound. Captain James Lawrence was his replacement.

this we objected, however, as we wanted a cruise ashore, before we took to the water again. This was a lucky decision of ours, though scarcely to be defended as to our views: the *Epervier* being lost, and all hands perishing, a few months later, on her return passage from the Straits.

Captain Evans then directed us to report ourselves daily, which we did. But the press of business at Washington prevented our cases from being attended to; and being destitute of money, while wages were high, we determined, with Captain Evans' approbation, to make a voyage, each, in the merchant service, and to get our accounts settled on our return. Jack Mallet, Barnet and I, shipped, therefore, in another brig called the *Venus,* that was bound on a sealing voyage, as was thought, in some part of the world where seals were said to be plenty. We were ignorant of the work, or we might have discovered there was a deception intended, from the outfit of the vessel. She had no salt even, while she had plenty of cross-cut saws, iron dogs, chains, &c. The brig sailed, however, and stood across the Atlantic, as if in good earnest. When near the Cape de Verdes, the captain called us aft, and told us he thought the season too far advanced for sealing, and that, if we would consent, he would run down to St. Domingo, and make an arrangement with some one there to cut mahogany on shares, with fustick and lignum-vitæ. The secret was now out; but what could we poor salts do? The work we were asked to do turned out to be extremely laborious; and I suppose we had been deceived on account of the difficulty of getting men, just at that time, for such a voyage. There we were, in the midst of the ocean, and we agreed to the proposal, pretty much as a matter of course.

The brig now bore up, and stood for St. Domingo. She first went in to the city of St. Domingo, where the arrangements were made, and Spaniards were got to help to cut the wood, when we sailed for a bay, of which I have forgotten the name, and anchored near the shore. The trees were sawed down, about ten miles up a river, and floated to its bar, across which they had to be hauled by studding-sail halyards, through the surf; one man hauling two logs at a time, made into a sort of raft. Sharks abounded, and we had to keep a bright look-out, lest they got a leg while we were busy with the logs. I had a narrow escape from two while we lay at St. Domingo. A man fell overboard, and I went after him, succeeding in catching the poor fellow. A boat was dropped astern to pick us up, and, as we hauled the man in, two large sharks came up close alongside. This affair had set us drinking, and I got a good deal of punch aboard. The idea of remaining in the brig was unpleasant to me, and I had thought of quitting her for some days. A small schooner bound to America, and short of hands, lay near us; and I had told the captain I would come and join him that night. Jack Mallet and the rest tried to persuade me not to go, but I had too much punch and grog in me to listen to reason. When all hands aft were asleep, therefore, I let myself down into the water, and swam quite a cable's-length to the schooner. One of the men was looking out for me. He heard me in the water, and stood ready to receive me. As I drew near the schooner, this man threw me a rope, and helped me up the side, but, as soon as I was on the deck, he told me to look behind me. I did so, and there I saw an enormous shark swimming about, a fellow that was sixteen or eighteen feet long. This shark, I was told, had kept company with me as long as I had been in sight from the schooner. I cannot well describe the effect that was produced on me by this discovery. When I entered the water, I was under the influence of liquor, but this escape sobered me in a minute; so much so, indeed, that I insisted on being put in a boat, and sent back to the brig, which was done. I was a little influenced in this, however, by some reluctance that was manifested to keep me on board the schooner. I got on board the *Venus* without being discovered, and came to a resolution to stick by the craft until the voyage was up.

We filled up with mahogany, and took in a heavy deck-load, in the course of four months, which was a most laborious process. When ready, the brig sailed for New York. We encountered a heavy gale, about a week out, which swept away our deck-load, bulwarks, &c. At this time, the master, supercargo, mate, cook, and three of the crew, were down with the fever; leaving Mallet, Barnet and myself, to take care of the brig. We three brought the vessel up as far as Barnegat, where we procured assistance, and she arrived safe at the quarantine ground.

As soon as we got pratique, Mallet, Barnet and myself, went up to town to look after our affairs, leaving the brig below. The owners gave us thirty dollars each, to begin upon. We ascertained that our landlord had received our wages from government, and held it ready for us, sailor fashion. I also sold my share in the *Venus*' voyage for one hundred and twenty dollars. This gave me, in all, about five hundred dollars, which money lasted me between five and six weeks! How true it is, that "sailors make their money like horses, and spend it like asses!" I cannot say this prodigal waste of my means afforded me any substantial gratification. I have experienced more real pleasure from one day passed in a way of which my conscience could approve, than from all the loose and thoughtless follies, in which I was then in the habit of indulging when ashore, of a whole life. The manner in which this hard-earned gold was thrown away, may serve to warn some brother tar of the dangers that beset me; and let the reader understand the real wants of so large a body of his fellow-creatures.

On turning out in the morning, I felt an approach to that which seamen call the "horrors," and continued in this state, until I had swallowed several glasses of rum. I had no appetite for breakfast, and life was sustained principally by drink. Half of the time I ate no dinner, and when I did, it was almost drowned in grog. Occasionally I drove out in a coach, or a gig, and generally had something extra to pay for damages. One of these cruises cost me forty dollars, and I shall always think I was given a horse that sailed crab-fashion, on purpose to do me out of the money. At night, I generally went to the play, and felt bound to treat the landlord and his family to tickets and refreshments. We always had a coach to go in, and it was a reasonable night that cost me only ten dollars. At first I was a sort of "king among beggars;" but as the money went, Ned's importance went with it, until, one day, the virtuous landlord intimated to me that it would be well, as I happened to be sober, to overhaul our accounts. He then began to read from his books, ten dollars for this, twenty dollars for that, and thirty for the other, until I was soon tired, and wanted to know how much was left. I had still fifty dollars, even according to his account of the matter; and as that might last a week, with good management, I wanted to hear no more about the items.

All this time, I was separated from my old shipmates, being left comparatively among strangers. Jack Mallet had gone to join his friends in Philadelphia, and Barnet went south, whither I cannot say. I never fell in with either of them again, it being the fate of seamen to encounter the greatest risks and hardships in company, and then to cut adrift from each other, with little ceremony, never to meet again. I was still young, being scarcely two-and-twenty and might, even then, have hauled in my oars, and come to be an officer and a man.

As I knew I must go to sea, as soon as the accounts were balanced, I began to think a little seriously of my prospects. Dissipation had wearied me, and I wanted to go a voyage of a length that would prevent my falling soon into the same course of folly and vice. I had often bitter thoughts as to my conduct, nor was I entirely free from reflection on the subject of my peculiar situation. I might be said to be without a friend, or relative, in the world. "When my hat was on, my house was thatched." Of my father, I knew nothing; I have since ascertained he must then have been dead. My sister was little to me, and I never expected to see her again. The separation from all my old lakers, too, gave me some trouble, for I never met with one of them after parting from Barnet and Mallet, with the exception of Tom Goldsmith and Jack Reilly. Tom and I fell in with each other, on my return from St. Domingo, in the streets of New York, and had a yarn of two hours, about old times. This was all I ever saw of Tom. He had suffered a good deal with the English, who kept him in Kingston, Upper Canada, until the peace, when they let him go with the rest. As for Reilly, we have been in harbour together, in our old age, and I may speak of him again.

Under the feelings I have mentioned, as soon as the looks of my landlord let me know that there were no more shot in the locker, I shipped in a South Sea whaler, named the *Edward,* that was expected to be absent between two and three years. She was a small vessel, and carried only three boats. I got a pretty good outfit from my landlord, though most of the articles were second-hald. We parted good friends, however, and I came back to him, and played the same silly game more than once. He was not a bad *landlord,* as landlords then went, and I make no doubt he took better care of my money than I should have done myself. On the whole, this class of men are not as bad as they seem, though there are precious rascals among them. The respectable sailor landlord is quite as good, in his way, as one could expect, all things considered.

The voyage I made in the *Edward* was one of very little interest, the ship being exceedingly successful. The usage and living were good, and the whaling must have been good too, or we never should have been back again, as soon as we were. We went round the Horn, and took our first whale between the coast of South America and that of New Holland. I must have been present at the striking of thirty fish, but never met with any accident. I pulled a mid-ship oar, being a new hand at the business, and had little else to do, but keep clear of the line, and look out for my paddle. The voyage is now so common, and the mode of taking whales is so well known, that I shall say little about either. We went off the coast of Japan, as it is called, though a long bit from the land, and we made New Holland, though without touching. The return passage was by the Cape of Good Hope and St. Helena. We let go our anchor but once the whole voyage, and that was at Puna, at the mouth of the Guayaquil river, on the coast of Chili. We lay there a week, but, with this exception, the *Edward* was actually under her canvass the whole voyage, or eighteen months. We did intend to anchor at St. Helena, but were forbidden on account of Bonaparte, who was then a prisoner on the Island. As we stood in, we were met by a man-of-war brig, that kept close to us until we had sunk the heights, on our passage off again. We were not permitted even to send a boat in, for fresh grub.

I sold my voyage in the *Edward* for two hundred and fifty dollars, and went back to my landlord, in Water street. Of course, everybody was glad to see me, a sailor's importance in such places being estimated by the length of his voyage. In Wall street they used to call a man "a hundred thousand dollar man," and in Water, "an eighteen months, or a two years' voyage man." As none but whalers, Indiamen, and Statesmen could hold out so long, we were all A. No. 1, for a fortnight or three weeks. The man-of-war's-man is generally most esteemed, his cruise lasting three years; the *lucky* whaler comes next, and the Canton-man third. The *Edward* had been a lucky ship, and, insomuch, I had been a lucky fellow. I behaved far better this time, however, than I had done on my return from St. Domingo. I kept sober more, did not spend my money as foolishly or as fast, and did not wait to be kicked out of doors, before I thought of getting some more. When I shipped anew, I actually left a hundred dollars behind me in my landlord's hands; a very extraordinary thing for Jack, and what is equally worthy of notice, I got it all again, on my next return from sea.

My steadiness was owing, in a great measure, to the following circumstances. I fell in with two old acquaintances, who had been in prison with me, of the names of Tibbets and Wilson. This Tibbets was not the man who had been sent to Bermuda with me, but another of the same name. These men had belonged to the *Gov. Tompkins* privateer, and had received a considerable sum in prize-money, on returning home.[2] They had used their money discreetly, having purchased an English prize-brig, at a low price, and fitted her out. On board the *Tompkins,* both had been foremost hands, and in prison they had messed in our bay, so that we had been hail-fellows-well-met, on Melville Island. After getting this brig ready, they had been to the West Indies in her, and were now about to sail for Ireland. They wished me to go with them, and gave me so much good advice, on the subject of taking care of my money, that it produced the effect I have just mentioned.

The name of the prize-brig was the *Susan,* though I forget from what small eastern port she hailed. She was of about two hundred tons burthen, but must have been old and rotten. Tibbets was master, and Wilson was chief-mate. I shipped as a sort of second-mate, keeping a watch, though I lived forward at my own request. We must have sailed about January, 1818, bound to Belfast. There were fourteen of us, altogether, on board, most of us down-easters. Our run off the coast was with a strong north-west gale, which compelled us to heave-to, the sea being too high for scudding. Finding that the vessel laboured very much, however, and leaked badly, we kept off again, and scudded for the rest of the blow. On the whole, we got out of this difficulty

2. A highly successful privateer schooner of 14 guns, named for Daniel Tompkins, governor of New York during the War of 1812. She was under the command of Nathaniel Shaler and later J. Skinner, based in New York but owned by Baltimore investors.

pretty well. We got but two observations the whole passage, but in the afternoon of the twenty-third day out, we made the coast of Ireland, close aboard, in thick weather; the wind directly on shore, blowing a gale. The brig was under close-reefed topsails, running free, at the time, and we found it necessary to haul up. We now discovered the defects of old canvass and old rigging, splitting the fore-topsail, foresail, and fore-topmast-staysail, besides carrying away sheets, &c. We succeeded in hauling up the foresail, however, and I went upon the yard and mended it, after a fashion. It was now nearly night, and it blew in a way "to need two men to hold one man's hair on his head." I cannot say I thought much of our situation, my principal concern being to get below, with some warm, dry clothes on. We saw nothing of the land after the first half-hour, but at midnight we wore ship, and came up on the larboard tack. The brig had hardly got round before the fore-tack went, and the foresail split into ribands. We let the sail blow from the yard. By this time, things began to look very serious, though, for some reason, I felt no great alarm. The case was different with Tibbets and Wilson, who were uneasy about Cape Clear. I had had a bit of a spat with them about waring, believing, myself, that we should have gone clear of the Cape, or the starboard track. This prevented them saying much to me, and we had little communication with each other that night. To own the truth, I was sorry I had shipped in such a craft. Her owners were too poor to give a sea-going vessel a proper outfit, and they were too near my own level to create respect.

The fore-topsail had been mended as well as the foresail, and was set anew. The sheets went, however, about two in the morning, and the sail flew from the reef-band like a bit of muslin torn by a shop-boy. The brig now had nothing set but a close-reefed main-topsail, and this I expected, every minute, would follow the other canvass. It rained, blew tremendously, and the sea was making constant breaches over us. Most of the men were fagged out, some going below, while others, who remained on deck, did, or *could* do, nothing. At the same time, it was so dark that we could not see the length of the vessel.

I now went aft to speak to Tibbets, telling him I thought it was all over with us. He had still some hope, as the bay was deep, and he thought light might return before we got to the bottom of it. I was of a different opinion, believing the brig then to be within the influence of the ground-swell, though not absolutely within the breakers. All this time the people were quiet, and there was no drinking. Indeed, I hardly saw any one moving about. It was an hour after the conversation with Tibbets, that I was standing, holding on by the weather-main-clew-garnet, when I got a glimpse of breakers directly under our lee. I sung out, "there's breakers, and everybody must shift for himself." At the next instant, the brig rose on a sea, settled in the trough, and struck. The blow threw me off my feet, though I held on to the clew-garnet. Then I heard the crash of the fore-mast as it went down to leeward. The brig rolled over on her beam-ends, but righted at the next sea, drove in some distance, and down she came again, with a force that threatened to break her up. I bethought me of the main-mast, and managed to get forward as far as the bitts, in order to be out of its way. It was well I did, as I felt a movement as if her upper works were parting from the bottom. I was near no one, and the last person I saw, or spoke to on board, was Tibetts, who was then standing in the companion-way. This was an hour before the brig struck.

There might have been an interval of half a minute between the time I reached the windlass, and that in which I saw a tremendous white foaming sea rolling down upon the vessel. At this ominous sight, I instinctively seized the bitts for protection. I can remember the rushing of the water down upon me, and have some faint impressions of passing through a mass of rigging, but this is all. When I came to my senses, it was in an Irish mud-cabin, with an old woman and her daughter taking care of me. My head was bandaged, and most of the hair had been cut off in front. I was stiff and sore all over me. Fortunately, none of my bones were broken.

The account given me of what had passed, was this. I was found by the old man, who lived in the hut, a fisherman and the husband of my nurse, with some other persons, lying on my face, between two shelves of rock. There was nothing very near me, not even a bit of wood, or a rope. Two lads that belonged to the brig were found not far from me, both alive, though both badly hurt, one of them having had his thigh broken. Of the rest of the fourteen souls on board the *Susan,* there were no traces. I never heard that even their bodies were found. Tibbets and Wilson had gone with their old prize, and anything but a prize did she prove to me. I lost a good outfit, and, after belonging to her about three weeks, here was I left naked on the shores of Ireland. I am sorry to say, my feelings were those of repining, rather than of gratitude. Of religion I had hardly a notion, and I am afraid that all which had been driven into me in childhood, was already lost. In this state of mind, I naturally felt more of the hardships I had endured, than of the mercy that had been shown me. I look back with shame at the hardness of heart which rendered me insensible to the many mercies I had received, in escaping so often from the perils of my calling.

It was three days after the wreck, before I left my bed. Nothing could have been kinder than the treatment I received from those poor Irish people. Certainly no reward was before them, but that which Heaven gives the merciful; and yet I could not have been more cared for, had I been their own son. They fed me, nursed me, and warmed me, without receiving any other return from me than my thanks. I staid with them three weeks, doing nothing on account of the bruises I had received. The *Susan*'s had been a thorough wreck. Not enough of her could be found, of which to build a launch. Her cargo was as effectually destroyed as her hull, and, to say the truth, it took but little to break her up. As for the two lads, I could not get as far as the cabin in which they had been put. It was two or three miles along the coast, and, having no shoes, I could not walk that distance over the sharp stones. Several messages passed between us, but I never saw a single soul that belonged to the brig, after the last look I had of Tibetts in the companion-way.

A coaster passing near the cabin, and it falling calm, the fisherman went off to her, told my story, and got a passage for me to Liverpool. I now took my leave of these honest people, giving them all I had—my sincere thanks—and went on board the sloop. Here I was well treated, nor did any one expect me to work. We reached Liverpool the second day, and I went and hunted up Molly Hutson, the landlady with whom the crew of the *Sterling* had lodged, when Captain B—— had her. The old woman helped me to some clothes, received me well, and seemed sorry for my misfortunes. As it would not do to remain idle, however, I shipped on board the *Robert Burns,* and sailed for New York within the week. I got no wages, but met with excellent treatment, and had a very short winter passage. In less than three months after I left him, I was back again with my old landlord, who gave me my hundred dollars without any difficulty. I had sailed with him in the *Sterling,* and he always seemed to think of me a little differently from what landlords generally think of Jack.

A good deal was said among my associates, now, about the advantages of making a voyage to the coast of Ireland for the purpose of smuggling tobacco, and I determined to try my hand at one. Of the morality of smuggling I have nothing to say. I would not make such a voyage now, if I know myself; but poor sailors are not taught to make just distinctions in such things, and the merchants must take their share of the shame. I fear there are few merchants, and fewer seamen, man-of-war officers excepted, who will not smuggle.[3]

I laid out most of my hundred dollars, in getting a new outfit, and then shipped in a small pilot-boat-built schooner, called the *M'Donough,* bound to Ireland, to supply such honest fellows as my old fisherman with good tobacco, cheap. Our cargo was in small bales, being the raw material, intended to be passed by hand. We had seventeen hands before the mast, but carried no armament, pistols, &c., excepted. The schooner sailed like a witch, carrying only two gaff-topsails. We made the land in fourteen days after we left the Hook, our port being Tory Island, off the northwest coast of Ireland. We arrived in the day-time, and showed a signal, which was answered in the course of the day, by a smoke on some rocks. A large boat then came off to us, and we filled her with tobacco the same evening. In the course of the night, we had despatched four or five more boats, loaded with the same cargo; but, as day approached, we hauled our wind, and stood off the land. Next night we went in, again, and met more boats, and the succeeding morning we hauled off, as before. When we saw a boat, we hailed and asked "if they were outward bound." If the answer was satisfactory, we brailed the foresail and permitted the boat to come alongside. In this manner we continued shoving cargo ashore, for quite a week, sometimes falling in with only one boat of a night, and, at others, with three or four; just as it might happen. We had got about two-thirds of the tobacco out, and a boat had just left us, on the morning of the sixth or seventh day, when we saw a man-of-war

3. Ned might have added "few duchesses." The ambassadors' bags, in Europe, might tell many a tale of *foulards, &c.,* sent from one court to another. The writer believes that the higher class of American gentlemen and ladies smuggle less than those of any other country. It should be remembered, too, that no seaman goes in a smuggler, that is not sent by traders ashore.—EDITOR.

brig coming round Tory Island, in chase. At this sight, we hauled up close on a wind, it blowing very fresh. As the English never employed any but the fastest cruisers for this station, we had a scratching time of it. The brig sailed very fast, and out-carried us; but our little schooner held on well. For two days and one night we had it, tack and tack, with her. The brig certainly gained on us, our craft carrying a balanced reef-mainsail, bonnet off the foresail and one reef in, and bonnet off the jib. The flying-jib was inboard. At sunset, on the second night, the brig was so near us, we could see her people, and it was blowing fresher than ever. This was just her play, while ours was in more moderate weather. Our skipper got uneasy, now, and determined to try a trick. It set in dark and rainy; and, as soon as we lost sight of the brig, we tacked, stood on a short distance, lowered everything, and extinguished all our lights. We lay in this situation three hours, when we stuck the craft down again for Tory Island, as straight as we could go. I never knew what became of the brig, which may be chasing us yet, for aught I know, for I saw no more of her. Next day we had the signal flying again, and the smoke came up from the same rock, as before. It took us three days longer to get all the tobacco ashore, in consequence of some trouble on the island; but it all went in the end, and went clear, as I was told, one or two boat-loads excepted. The cargo was no sooner out, than we made sail for New York, where we arrived in another short passage. We were absent but little more than two months, and my wages and presents came to near one hundred dollars. I never tried the tobacco trade again.

CHAPTER XI

I NOW STAYED ASHORE TWO MONTHS. I had determined to study navigation, and to try to get off the forecastle, in which wise course I was encouraged by several discreet friends. I had fallen in with a young woman of respectable character and agreeable person, and, to own the truth, was completely in irons with her. I believe a mother is a good deal more on the look-out than a father, in such matters; for I was overhauled by the old woman, and questioned as to my intentions about Sarah, whereas the old man was somewhat more moderate. I confessed my wish to marry her daughter; but the old woman thought I was too wild, which was not Sarah's opinion, I believe. Had we been left to ourselves, we should have got married; though I was really desirous of going out once as an officer, before I took so important a step. I have sometimes suspected that Sarah's parents had a hand in getting me shipped, again, as they were intimate with the captain who now proposed to take me with him as his second-mate. I consented to go, with some reluctance; but, on the whole, thought it was the best thing I could do. My reluctance proceeded from a desire to remain with Sarah, when the time came; though the berth was exactly the thing I wanted, whenever I reasoned coolly on the subject.

I shipped, accordingly, in a vessel of the Costers', called the *William and Jane,* bound to Holland and Canton, as her second-mate. My leave-taking with Sarah was very tender; and I believe we both felt much grieved at the necessity of parting. Nothing occurred on the passage out worth mentioning. I got along with my duty well enough, for I had been broken-in on board the *Sterling,* and one or two other vessels. We went to the Texel, but found some difficulty in procuring dollars, which caused us to return to New York, after getting only twenty thousand.[1] We had no other return cargo, with the exception of a little gin. We were absent five months; and I found Sarah as pretty, and as true, as ever. I did not quit the vessel, however; but, finding my knowledge of the lunars too limited, I was obliged to go backward a little—becoming third-mate. We were a month in New York, and it was pretty hard work to keep from eloping with Sarah; but I clawed off the breakers as well as I could. I gave her a silver thimble, and told her to take it to a smith; and get our joint names cut on it, which she did. The consequences of this act will be seen in the end.

We had a little breeze on board the ship before we could get off; the people refusing to sail with a new first-mate that had joined her. It ended by getting another mate, when we went to sea. I believe that no other vessel ever went out with such articles as our crew insisted on. The men stipulated for three quarts of water a day, and the forenoon's watch below. All this was put in black and white, and it gave us some trouble before we got to our destination.

1. A protected roadstead known locally as the Texel Stroom between the West Frisian Island of Texel and North Holland province inside the entrance to the Wadden Zee. It was to this sheltered anchorage that Commodore John Paul Jones brought his prize HMS *Serapis* after it struck to his Continental Navy ship *Bonhomme Richard.*

Our passage out was a very long one, lasting two hundred and ten days. When we got into the trades, we stripped one mast after the other, to a girt-line, overhauling everything, and actually getting new gangs of rigging up over the lower-mast-heads. We were a long time about it, but lost little or nothing in distance, as the ship was going before the wind the whole time, with everything packed on the masts that were rigged. Before overhauling the rigging, we fell in with an English ship, called the *General Blucher,* and kept company with her for quite a fortnight. While the two ships were together, we were chased by a strange brig, that kept in sight three or four days, evidently watching us, and both vessels suspected him of being a pirate. As we had six guns, and thirty-one souls, and the *Blucher* was, at least, as strong, the two captains thought, by standing by each other, they might beat the fellow off, should he attack us. The brig frequently came near enough to get a good look at us, and then dropped astern. He continued this game several days, until he suddenly hauled his wind, and left us. Our ship would have been a famous prize; having, it was said, no less than two hundred and fifty thousand Spanish dollars on board.

We parted company with the *Blucher,* in a heavy gale; our ship bearing up for Rio. After getting rid of some of our ballast, however, and changing the cargo of pig-lead, our vessel was easier, and did not go in. Nothing further occurred, worth mentioning, until we got off Van Diemen's Land. Two days after seeing the land, a boy fell from the fore-top-gallant yard, while reeving the studding-sail halyards. I had just turned in, after eating my dinner, having the watch below, when I heard the cry of "a man overboard!" Running on deck, as I was, I jumped into a quarter-boat, followed by four men, and we were immediately lowered down. The ship was rounded-to, and I heard the poor fellow calling out to me by name, to save him. I saw him, astern, very plainly, while on the ship's quarter; but lost sight of him, as soon as the boat was in the water. The skylight-hood had been thrown overboard, and was floating in the ship's wake. We steered for that; but could neither see nor hear anything more of the poor fellow. We got his hat, and we picked up the hood of the skylight, but could not find the boy. He had, unquestionably, gone down before we reached the spot where he had been floating, as his hat must have pointed out the place. We got the hat first; and then, seeing nothing of the lad, we pulled back to take in the hood; which was quite large. While employed in taking it in, a squall passed over the boat; which nearly blew it away from us. Being very busy in securing the hood, no one had leisure to look about; but the duty was no sooner done, than one of the men called out, that he could not see the ship! Sure enough, the *William and Jane* had disappeared! and there we were, left in the middle of the ocean, in a six-oared pinnace, without a morsel of food, and I, myself, without hat, shoes, jacket or trowsers. In a word, I had nothing on me but my drawers and a flannel shirt. Fortunately, the captain kept a breaker of fresh water in each boat, and we had a small supply of this great requisite;—enough, perhaps, to last five men two or three days.

All our boats had sails; but those of the pinnace had been spread on the quarter-deck, to dry; and we had nothing but the ash to depend on. At first, we pulled to leeward; but the weather was so thick, we could not see a cable's-length; and our search for the vessel, in that direction, proved useless. At the end of an hour or two, we ceased rowing, and held a consultation. I proposed to pull in the direction of the land; which was pulling to windward. If the ship should search for us, it would certainly be in that quarter; and if we should miss her, altogether, our only chance was in reaching the shore. There, we might find something to eat; of which there was little hope, out on the ocean. The men did not relish the idea of quitting the spot; but, after some talk, they came into my plan.

It remained thick weather all that afternoon, night, and succeeding day, until about noon. We were without a compass, and steered by the direction of the wind and sea. Occasionally it lightened up a little, so as to show us a star or two, or during the day to permit us to see a few miles around the boat; but we got no glimpse of the ship. It blew so heavily that we made no great progress, in my judgment doing very little more than keeping the boat head to sea. Could we have pulled four oars, this might not have been the case, but we took it watch and watch, two men pulling, while two tried to get a little rest, under the shelter of the hood. I steered as long as I could, but was compelled to row part of the time to keep myself warm. In this manner were passed about six-and-twenty of the most unpleasant hours of my life, when some of us thought they heard the report of a distant gun. I did not believe it; but, after listening attentively some ten or fifteen minutes, another report was heard, beyond all dispute, dead to leeward of us!

This signal produced a wonderful effect on us all. The four oars were manned, and away we went before the wind and sea, as fast as we could pull, I steering for the reports as they came heavily up to windward at intervals of about a quarter of an hour. Three or four of these guns were heard, each report sounding nearer than the other, to our great joy, until I got a glimpse of the ship, about two miles distant from us. She was on the starboard tack, close hauled, a proof she was in search of us, with top-gallant-sails set over single-reefed topsails. She was drawing ahead of us fast, however, and had we not seen her as we did, we should have crossed her wake, and been lost without a hope, by running to leeward. We altered our course the instant she was seen; but what could a boat do in such a sea, pulling after a fast ship under such canvass? Perhaps we felt more keen anxiety, after we saw the ship, than we did before, since we beheld all the risk we ran. Never shall I forget the sensations with which I saw her start her main-tack and haul up the sail! The foresail and top-gallant-sail followed, and then the main-yard came round, and laid the topsail aback! Everything seemed to fly on board her, and we knew we were safe. In a few minutes we were alongside. The boat was at the davits, the helm was up, and the old barky squared away for China.

We in the boat were all pretty well fagged out with hunger, toil, and exposure. I was the worst off, having so little clothing in cool weather, and I think another day would have destroyed us all, unless we had taken refuge in the well-known dreadful alternative of seamen. The captain was delighted to see us, as indeed were all hands. They had determined to turn to windward, on short tacks, until they made the land, the best thing that could have been done, and the course that actually saved us.

When we got into the latitude of Port Jackson, the crew was put on two quarts of water a man, three quarts having been stipulated for in the articles. This produced a mutiny, the men refusing duty. This was awkward enough, in that distant sea. The captain took advantage of the men's going below, however, to secure the scuttle and keep them there. He then mustered us, who lived aft, six men and three boys, and laid the question before us, *whether we would take the ship into Canton,* or go into Port Jackson, and get some water. He admitted we were about seventy-five days' run from Canton, but he himself leaned to the plan of continuing on our course. We saw all the difficulties before us, and told him of them.

There were twenty men below, and to carry them eight or ten thousand miles in that situation, would have been troublesome, to say the least, and might have caused the death of some among them. We were armed, and had no apprehensions of the people, but we did not like to work a ship of five hundred tons with so few hands, one-third of whom were boys, so great a distance. The crew, moreover, had a good deal of right on their side, the articles stipulating that they should have the water, and this water was to be had a short distance to windward.

The captain yielded to our reasoning, and we beat up to Port Jackson, where we arrived in three or four days. The people were then sent to prison, as mutineers, and we watered the ship. We were in port a fortnight, thus occupied. All this time the men were in gaol. No men were to be had, and then arose the question about trusting the old crew. There was no choice, and, the ship being ready to sail, we received the people on board again, and turned them all to duty. We had no further trouble with them, however, the fellows behaving perfectly well, as men commonly will, who have been once put down. No mutiny is dangerous when the officers are apprised of its existence, and are fairly ready to meet it. The king's name is a tower of strength.

We arrived at Canton in due time, and found our cargo ready for us. We took it in, and sailed again, for the Texel, in three weeks. Our passage to Europe was two hundred and eleven days, but we met with no accident. At the Texel I found two letters from New York, one being from Sarah, and the other from a female friend. Sarah was married to the very silversmith who had engraven our names on the thimble! This man saw her for the first time, when she carried that miserable thimble to him, fell in love with her, and, being in good circumstances, her friends prevailed on her to have him. Her letter to me admitted her error, and confessed her unhappiness; but there was no remedy. I did not like the idea of returning to New York, under the circumstances, and resolved to quit the ship. I got my discharge, therefore, from the *William and Jane,* and left her, never seeing the vessel afterwards.

There was a small Baltimore ship, called the *Wabash,* at the Texel, getting ready for Canton, and I entered on board her, as a foremast Jack, again. My plan was to quit her in China, and to remain beyond the Capes for ever. The disappointment in my matrimonial plans had soured me, and I wanted to get as far from America as I could. This was the turning point of my life, and was to settle my position in my calling. I was now twenty-seven, and when a man gets stern-way on him, at that age, he must sail a good craft ever to work his way into his proper berth again.

The *Wabash* had a good passage out, without any unusual occurrence. On her arrival at Canton, I told the captain my views, and he allowed me to go. I was now adrift in the Imperial Empire, with a couple of hundred dollars in my pocket, and a chest full of good clothes. So far all was well, and I began to look about me for a berth. We had found an English country ship lying at Whampao, smuggling opium, and I got on board of her, as third-mate, a few days after I quitted the *Wabash.* This was the first and only time I ever sailed under the English flag, for I do not call my other passages in English vessels, sailing *under* the flag, though it was waving over my head. My new ship was the *Hope,* of Calcutta, commanded by Captain Kid, or Kyd, I forget which. The vessel was built of teak, and had been a frigate in the Portuguese service. She was so old no one knew exactly when she was built, but sailed like a witch. Her crew consisted principally of Lascars, with a few Europeans and negroes, as is usual in those craft.[2] My wages did not amount to much in dollars, but everything was so cheap, they counted up in the long run. I had perquisites, too, which amounted to something handsome. They kept a very good table.

The *Hope* had a good deal of opium, when I joined her, and it was all to be smuggled before we sailed. As this trade has made a great deal of noise, latterly, I will relate the manner in which we disposed of the drug. Of the morality of this species of commerce, I have no more to say in its defence, than I had of the tobacco voyage, unless it be to aver that were I compelled, now, to embark in one of the

2. East Indian sailors.

two, it should be to give the countrymen of my honest fisherman cheap tobacco, in preference to making the Chinese drunk on opium.

Our opium was packed in wooden boxes of forty cylinders, weighing about ten pounds each cylinder. Of course each box weighed about four hundred pounds. The main cargo was cotton, and salt-petre, and ebony; but there were four hundred boxes of this opium.

The sales of the article were made by the captain, up at the factory. They seldom exceeded six or eight boxes at a time, and were oftener two or three. The purchaser then brought, or sent, an order on board the ship, for the delivery of the opium. He also provided bags. The custom-house officers did not remain in the ship, as in other countries, but were on board a large armed boat, hanging astern. These crafts are called Hoppoo boats. This arrangement left us tolerably free to do as we pleased, on board. If an officer happened to come on board, however, we had early notice of it, of course. As third-mate, it was my duty to see the boxes taken out of the hold, and the opium delivered. The box was opened, and the cylinders counted off, and stowed in the bags, which were of sizes convenient to handle. All this was done on the gun-deck, the purchaser receiving possession of his opium, on board us. It was his loss, if anything failed afterwards.

As soon as the buyer had his opium in the bags, he placed the latter near two or three open ports, amidships, and hung out a signal to the shore. This signal was soon answered, and then it was look out for the smuggling boats! These smuggling boats are long, swift craft, that have double-banked paddles, frequently to the number of sixty men. They are armed, and are swift as arrows. When all is ready, they appear suddenly on the water, and dash alongside of the vessel for which they are bound, and find the labourers of the purchaser standing at the ports, with the bags of cylinders ready. These bags are thrown into the boat, the purchaser and his men tumble after them, and away she paddles, like a racer. The whole operation occupies but a minute or two.

As soon as the Hoppoo boat sees what is going on, it begins to blow conches. This gives the alarm, and then follows a chase from an armed custom-house boat, of which there are many constantly plying about. It always appeared to me that the custom-house people were either afraid of the smugglers, or that they were paid for not doing their duty. I never saw any fight, or seizure, though I am told such sometimes happen. I suppose it is in China, as it is in other parts of the world; that men occasionally do their whole duty, but that they oftener do not. If the connivance of custom-house officers will justify smuggling in China, it will justify smuggling in London, and possibly in New York.

We not only smuggled cargo out, but we smuggled cargo in. The favourite prohibited article was a species of metal, that came in plates, like tin, or copper, of which we took in large quantities. It was brought to us by the smuggling-boats, and thrown on board, very much as the opium was taken out, and we stowed it away in the hold. All this was done in the day-time, but I never heard of any one's following the article into the ship. Once there, it appeared to be considered safe. Then we got sycee silver, which was prohibited for exportation. All came on board in the same manner. For every box of opium sold, the mate got a china dollar as a perquisite. Of course my share on four hundred boxes came to one hundred and thirty-three of these dollars, or about one hundred and sixteen of our own. I am ashamed to say there was a great deal of cheating all round, each party evidently regarding the other as rogues, and, instead of "doing as they *would* be done by," doing as they *thought* they *were* done by.

The *Hope* sailed as soon as the opium was sold, about a month, and had a quick passage to Calcutta. I now began to pick up a little Bengalee, and, before I left the trade, could work a ship very well in the language. The Lascars were more like monkeys than men aloft, though they wanted strength. A topsail, that six of our common men would furl, would employ twenty of them. This was partly from habit, perhaps, though they actually want physical force. They eat little besides rice, and are small in frame. We had a curious mode of punishing them, when slack, aloft. Our standing rigging was of grass, and wiry enough to cut even hands that were used to it. The ratlines were not seized to the forward and after shrouds, by means of eyes, as is done in our vessels, but were made fast by a round turn, and stopping back the ends. We used to take down all the ratlines, and make the darkies go up without them. In doing this, they took the rigging between the great and second toe, and walked up, instead of shinning it, like Christians. This soon gave them sore toes, and they would beg hard to have the ratlines replaced. On the whole, they were easily managed, and were respectful and obedient. We had near a hundred of these fellows in the *Hope,* and kept them at work by means of a boatswain and four mates, all countrymen of their own. In addition, we had about thirty more souls, including the Europeans—Christians, as we were called!

At Calcutta we loaded with cotton, and returned to Canton, having another short passage. We had no opium in the ship, this time, it being out of season; but we smuggled cargo in, as before. We lay at Whampao a few weeks, and returned to Calcutta. By this time the *Hope* was dying of old age, and Captain Kyd began to think, if he did not bury her, she might bury him. Her beams actually dropped, as we removed the cotton at Canton, though she still remained tight. But it would have been dangerous to encounter heavy weather in her.

A new ship, called the *Hopping Castle,* had been built by Captain Kyd's father-in-law, expressly for him. She was a stout, large vessel, and promised to sail well. The officers were all transferred to her; but most of the old Lascars refused to ship, on account of a quarrel with the boatswain. This compelled us to ship a new set of these men, most of whom were strangers to us.

By a law of Calcutta, if anything happens to a vessel before she gets to sea, the people retain the two months' advance it is customary to give them. This rule brought us into difficulty. The *Hopping Castle* cleared for Bombay, with a light cargo. We had dropped down the river, discharged the pilot, and made sail on our course, when a fire suddenly broke up out of the fore-hatch. A quantity of grass junk, and two or three cables of the same material, were in that part of the ship, and they all burnt like tinder. I went with the other officers and threw overboard the powder, but it was useless to attempt extinguishing the flames. Luckily, there were two pilot brigs still near us, and they came alongside and received all hands. The *Hopping Castle* burnt to the water's edge, and we saw her wreck go down. This was a short career for so fine a ship, and it gave us all great pain; all but the rascals of Lascars. I lost everything I had in the world in her, but a few clothes I saved in a small trunk. I had little or no money, Calcutta being no place for economy. In a country in which it is a distinction to be a white man, and *called* a Christian, one must maintain his dignity by a little extravagance.

Captain Kyd felt satisfied that the Lascars had set his ship on fire, and he had us all landed on Tiger Island. Here the serang, or boatswain, took the matter in hand, and attempted to find out the facts. I was present at the proceeding, and witnessed it all. It was so remarkable as to deserve being mentioned. The men were drawn up in rings, of twenty or thirty each, and the boatswain stood in the centre. He then put a little white powder into each man's hand, and ordered him to spit in it. The idea was that the innocent men would spit without any difficulty, while the mouths of the guilty would become too dry and husky to allow them to comply. At any rate, the serang picked out ten men as guilty, and they were sent to Calcutta to be tried. I was told, afterwards, that all these ten men admitted their guilt, criminated two more, and that the whole twelve were subsequently hanged in chains, near Castle William. Of the legal trial and execution I know nothing, unless by report; but the trial by spittle, I saw with my own eyes; and it was evident the Lascars looked upon it as a very serious matter. I never saw criminals in court betray more uneasiness, than these fellows, while the serang was busy with them.

I was now out of employment. Captain Kyd wished me to go on an indigo plantation, offering me high wages. I never drank at sea, and had behaved in a way to gain his confidence, I believe, so that he urged me a good deal to accept his offers. I would not consent, however, being afraid of death. There was a Philadelphia ship, called the *Benjamin Rush,* at Calcutta, and I determined to join her. By this time, I felt less on the subject of my disappointment, and had a desire to see home, again. I shipped, accordingly, in the vessel mentioned, as a foremast hand. We sailed soon after, and had a pleasant passage to the Capes of the Delaware, which I now entered, again, for the first time since I had done so on my return from my original voyage in the *Sterling.*

As soon as paid off, I proceeded to New York. I was short of cash; and, my old landlord being dead, I had to look about me for a new ship. This time, I went in a brig, called the *Boxer,* a clipper, belonging to John Jacob Astor, bound to Canton. This proved to be a pleasant and successful voyage, so far as the vessel was concerned, at least; the brig being back at New York, again, eight months after we sailed. I went in her before the mast.

My money was soon gone; and I was obliged to ship again. I now went as second-made, in the *Trio;* an old English prize-ship, belonging to David Dunham. We were bound to Batavia, and sailed in January. After being a short time at sea, we found all our water gone, with the exception of one cask. The remainder had been lost by the bursting of the hoops, in consequence of the water's having frozen. We went on a short allowance; and suffered a good deal by the privation. Our supercargo, a young gentleman of the name of Croes, came near dying. We went on, however, intending to go into one of the Cape de Verdes. We got up our casks, and repaired them, in the meanwhile. Off the Island of Fuego, we hove to, and found we could get no water. We got a few goats, and a little fruit; but were compelled to proceed. Luckily, it came on to rain very hard, and we stopped all the scuppers, filling every cask we had, in this easy manner. We began about eight at night, and were through before morning. Capital water it proved; and it lasted us to Batavia. There, indeed, it would even have brought a premium; being so much better than anything to be had in that port. It changed; but sweetened itself very soon.

We first went into Batavia, and entered the ship; after which, we sailed for a roadstead, called Terragall, to take in rice. The vessel was in ballast, and had brought money to make her purchases with. We got our cargo off in boats, and sailed for Batavia, to clear; all within a few weeks. The second night out, the ship struck, in fair weather, and a moderate sea, on a mud-bank; and brought up all standing. We first endeavoured to force the vessel over the bank; but this did not succeed; and, the tide leaving her, the ship fell over on her bilge; bringing her gunwales under water. Luckily, she lay quiet; though a good deal strained. The captain now took a boat, and four men, and pulled ashore, to get prows, to lighten the vessel. We had but eight men before the mast, and six aft. This, of course, left only nine souls on board. That night nothing occurred; but, in the morning early, two piratical prows approached, and showed a disposition to board us. Mr. Croes was the person who saved the ship. He stuck up handspikes, and other objects, about deck; putting hats and caps on them, so as to make us appear very strong-handed. At the same time, we got a couple of sixes to bear on the prows; and succeeded in keeping them at a safe distance. They hovered about until sunset, when they left us; pulling ashore. Just as they were quitting us, twenty-seven boats hove in sight; and we made a signal to them, which was not answered. We set them down as enemies, too; but, as they came nearer, we perceived our own boat among them, and felt certain it was the captain.

We discharged everything betwixt decks into the boats, that night, and got the ship afloat before morning. We now hove clear of the bank, restowed the cargo, and made sail for Batavia. The ship leaked badly, and kept us hard at the pumps. As there were no means for repairing the vessel where we were, it was resolved to take in extra hands, ship two box-pumps, and carry the vessel to the Isle of France, in order to repair her. I did not like the prospect of such a passage, and confess I played "old soldier" to get rid of it. I contrived to get, on a sick ticket, into the hospital, and the ship sailed without me. At the Isle of France, the *Trio* was condemned; her hulk being, in truth, much worse than my own, docked though I was.

CHAPTER XII

AS SOON AS THE *TRIO* WAS OFF, I GOT WELL. Little did I then think of the great risk I ran in going ashore; for it was almost certain death for an European to land, for any length of time, at that season. Still less did I, or *could* I, anticipate what was to happen to myself, in this very hospital, a few years later; or how long I was to be one of its truly suffering, and, I hope, repentant inmates. The consul was frank enough to tell me that I had been shamming Abraham; and I so far imitated his sincerity as distinctly to state, it was quite true. I thought the old *Trio* ought to have been left on the bank, where Providence had placed her; but, it being the pleasure of her captain and the supercargo to take her bones to the Isle of France for burial, I did not choose to go so far, weeping through the pumps, to attend her funeral.

As the consul held my wages, and refused to give me any money, I was compelled to get on board some vessel as soon as I could. Batavia was not a place for an American constitution, and I was glad to be off. I shipped, before the mast, in the *Clyde,* of Salem, a good little ship, with good living and good treatment. We sailed immediately, but not soon enough to escape the Batavia fever. Two of the crew died, about a week out, and were buried in the Straits of Banca. The day we lost sight of Java Head, it came on to blow fresh, and we had to take in the jib, and double-reef the topsails. A man of the name of Day went down on the bowsprit shrouds to clear the jib-sheets, when the ship made a heavy pitch, and washed him away. The second mate and myself got into the boat, and were lowered as soon as the ship was rounded-to. There was a very heavy sea on, but we succeeded in finding the poor fellow, who was swimming with great apparent strength. His face was towards the boat, and, as we came near, I rose, and threw the blade of my oar towards him, calling out to him to be of good cheer. At this instant, Day seemed to spring nearly his length out of water, and immediately sunk. What caused this extraordinary effort, and sudden failure, was never known. I have sometimes thought a shark must have struck him, though I saw neither blood nor fish. The man was hopelessly lost, and we returned to the ship, feeling as seamen always feel on such occasions.

A few days later, another man died of the fever. This left but five of us in the forecastle, with the ship a long way to the eastward of the Cape of Good Hope. Before we got up with the Cape, another foremast hand went crazy, and, instead of helping us, became a cause of much trouble for the rest of the passage. In the end, he died, mad. We had now only three men in a watch, the officers included; and of course, it was trick and trick at the helm. Notwithstanding all this, we did very well, having a good run, until we got on the coast, which we reached in the month of January. A north-wester drove us off, and we had a pretty tough week of it, but brought the ship up to the Hook, at the end of that time, and anchored her safely in the East River. The *Clyde* must have been a ship of about three hundred tons, and, including every one on board, nine of us sailed her from the eastward of the Cape to her port, without any serious difficulty.

I did not stay long ashore, for the money went like smoke, but shipped in a brig called the *Margaret,* bound to Belfast. This vessel struck in the Irish channel, but she was backed off with little difficulty, and got safe into her port. The return passage was pleasant, and without any accident.

Such a voyage left little to spend, and I was soon on the look-out for a fresh berth. I shipped this time as mate, in a brig called the *William Henry,* bound on a smuggling voyage to the coast of Spain. We took in tobacco, segars, &c. &c., and the brig dropped down to Staten Island. Here I quarrelled with the captain about some cotton wick, and I threw up my situation. I knew there were more ships than parish churches, and felt no concern about finding a place in one, up at town. The balance of my advance was paid back, and I left the smuggling trade, like an honest man. I only wish this change of purpose had proceeded from a better motive.

My next windfall was Jack's berth on board a beautiful little schooner called the *Ida,* that was to sail for Curaçoa, in the hope of being purchased by the governor of the island for a yacht. I expected to find my way to the Spanish main, after the craft was sold. We got out without any accident, going into port of a Sunday morning. The same morning, an English frigate and a sloop-of-war came in and anchored. That afternoon these vessels commenced giving liberty to their men. We were alongside of a wharf, and, in the afternoon, our crew took a drift in some public gardens in the suburbs of the town. Here an incident occurred that is sufficiently singular to be mentioned.

I was by myself in the garden, ruminating on the past, and, I suppose, looking melancholy and in the market, when I perceived an English man-of-war's-man eyeing me pretty closely. After a while, he came up, and fell into discourse with me. Something that fell from him made me distrust him from the first, and I acted with great caution.

After sounding me for some time, he inquired if I had any berth. I told him, no. He then went on, little by little, until he got such answers as gave him confidence, when he let me into the secret of his real object. He said he belonged to the frigate, and had liberty until next morning—that he and four of his shipmates who were ashore, had determined to get possession of the pretty little Yankee schooner that was lying alongside of the *Telegraph,* at the wharf, and carry her down to Laguayra. All this was to be done that night, and he wished me to join the party. By what fell from this man, I made no doubt his design was to turn pirate, after he had sold the flour then in the *Ida.* I encouraged him to go on, and we drank together, until he let me into his whole plan. The scheme was to come on board the schooner, after the crew had turned in, to fasten all hands below, set the foresail and jib, and run out with the land-breeze; a thing that was feasible enough, considering there is never any watch kept in merchant-vessels that lie at wharves.

After a long talk, I consented to join the enterprise, and agreed to be, at nine o'clock, on board the *Telegraph,* a Philadelphia ship, outside of which our schooner lay. This vessel had a crew of blacks, and, as most of them were then ashore, it was supposed many would not return to her that night. My conspirator observed—"the Yankees that belong to the schooner are up yonder in the garden, and will be half drunk, so they will all be sound asleep, and can give us little trouble." I remember he professed to have no intention of hurting any of us, but merely to run away with us, and sell the craft from under us. We parted with a clear understanding of the manner in which everything was to be done.

I know no other reason why this man chose to select me for his companion in such an adventure, than the circumstance that I happened to be alone, and perhaps I may have looked a little under the weather. He was no sooner gone, however, than I managed to get near my shipmates, and to call them out of the garden, one by one. As we went away,

I told them all that had happened, and we laid our counter-plot. When we reached the *Telegraph,* it was near night, and finding only two of the blacks on board her, we let them into the secret, and they joined us, heart and hand. We got something to drink, as a matter of course, and tried to pass the time as well as we could, until the hour for springing the mine should arrive.

Pretty punctually to the hour, we heard footsteps on the quay, and then a gang of men stopped alongside of the ship. We stowed ourselves under the bulwarks, and presently the gentlemen came on board, one by one. The negroes were too impatient, however, springing out upon their prey a little too soon. We secured three of the rascals, but two escaped us, by jumping down upon the quay and running. Considering we were all captains, this was doing pretty well.

Our three chaps were Englishmen, and I make no doubt belonged to the frigate, as stated. As soon as they were fairly pinned, and they understood there was no officer among us, they began to beg. They said their lives would be forfeited if we gave them up, and they entreated us to let them go. We kept them about half an hour, and finally yielded to their solicitations, giving them their liberty again. They were very thankful for their escape, especially as I told them what had passed between myself and the man in the garden. This fellow was one of the two that escaped, and had the appearance of a man who might very well become a leader among pirates.

The next day the two men-of-war went to sea, and I make no doubt carried off the intended pirates in them. As for us seamen, we never told our own officers anything about the affair, for I was not quite satisfied with myself, after letting the scoundrels go. One scarcely knows what to do in such a case, as one does not like to be the means of getting a fellow-creature hanged, or of letting a rogue escape. A pirate, of all scoundrels, deserves no mercy, and yet Jack does not relish the idea of being a sort of Jack Ketch, neither. If the thing were to be done over again, I think I should hold on to my prisoners.

We discharged our cargo of flour, and failing in the attempt to sell the schooner, we took in dye-wood, and returned to New York. I now made a serious attempt to alter my mode of living, and to try to get up a few rounds of the great ladder of life. Hitherto, I had felt a singular indifference whether I went to sea as an officer, or as a foremast Jack, with the exception of the time I had a marriage with Sarah in view. But I was now drawing near to thirty, and if anything was to be done, it must be done at once. Looking about me, I found a brig called the *Hippomenes,* bound to Gibraltar, and back. I shipped before the mast, but kept a reckoning, and did all I could to qualify myself to become an officer. We had a winter passage out, but a pleasant one home. Nothing worthy of being recorded, however, occurred. I still continued to be tolerably correct, and after a short stay on shore, I shipped in the *Belle Savage,* commanded by one of the liberated Halifax prisoners, who had come home in the *Swede,* at the time of my own return. This person agreed to take me as chief mate, and I shipped accordingly. The *Belle Savage* was a regular Curaçoa trader, and we sailed ten or twelve days after the *Hippomenes* got in. Our passages both ways were pleasant and safe, and I stuck by the craft, endeavouring to be less thoughtless and careless about myself. I cannot say, however, I had any very serious plans for making provision for old age, my maxim being to live as I went along.

Our second passage out to Curaçoa, in the *Belle Savage,* was pleasant, and brought about nothing worthy of being mentioned. At Curaçoa we took in mahogany, and in so doing a particularly large log got away from us, and slid, end on, against the side of the vessel. We saw no consequences at the time, and went on to fill up, with different articles, principally dye-woods, coffee, cocoa, &c. We got some passengers, among whom was a Jew merchant, who had a considerable amount of money on board. When ready, we sailed, being thirty souls in all, crew and passengers included.

The *Belle Savage* had cleared the islands, and was standing on her course, one day, with a fair wind and a five or six knot breeze, under a fore-top-mast studding-sail, everything looking bright and prosperous. The brig must have been about a day's run to the southward of Bermuda. It was my watch below, but having just breakfasted, I was on deck, and looking about me carelessly, I was struck with the appearance of the vessel's being deeper than common. I had a little conversation about it, with a man in the forechains, who thought the same thing. This man leaned over, in order to get a better look, when he called out that he could see that we had started a butt! I went over, immediately, and got a look at this serious injury. A butt had started, sure enough, just under the chains, but so low down as to be quite out of our reach. The plank had started quite an inch, and it was loosened as much as two feet, forward and aft. We sounded the pumps, as soon as possible, and found the brig was half full of water!

All hands were now called to get both the boats afloat, and there was certainly no time to be lost. The water rose over the cabin-floor while we were doing it. We did not stand to get up tackles, but cut away the rail and launched the long-boat by hand. We got the passengers, men, women, children, and servants into her, as fast as possible, and followed ourselves. Fortunately, there had been a brig in company for some time, and she was now less than two leagues ahead of us, outsailing the *Belle Savage* a little. We had hoisted our ensign, union down, as a signal of distress, and well knew she must see that our craft had sunk, after it happened, if she did not observe our ensign. She perceived the signal, however, and could not fail to notice the manner in which the brig was all adrift, as soon as we deserted the helm. The strange brig had hauled up for us, even before we got out the launch. This rendered any supply of food or water unnecessary, and we were soon ready to shove off. I was in the small boat, with three men. We pulled off a little distance, and lay looking at our sinking craft with saddened eyes. Even the gold, that precious dust which lures so many souls to eternal perdition, was abandoned in the hurry to save the remnants of lives to be passed on earth. The *Belle Savage* settled quite slowly into the ocean, one sail disappearing after another, her main-royal being the last thing that went out of sight, looking like the lug of a man-of-war's boat on the water. It is a solemn thing to see a craft thus swallowed up in the great vortex of the ocean.

The brig in sight proved to be the *Mary,* of New York, from St. Thomas, bound home. She received us kindly, and six days later landed us all at no great distance from Fulton Market. When my foot touched the wharf, my whole estate was under my hat, and my pockets were as empty as a vessel with a swept hold. On the wharf, itself, I saw a man who had been second-mate of the *Tontine,* the little ship in which I had sailed when I first ran from the *Sterling.* He was now master of a brig called the *Mechanic,* that was loading near by, for Trinidad de Cuba. He heard my story, and shipped me on the spot, at nine dollars a month, as a forward hand. I began to think I was born to bad luck, and being almost naked, was in nowise particular what became of me. I had not the means of getting a mate's outfit, though I might possibly have got credit; but at no period of my life did I run in debt. Here, then, my craft got stern-way on her again, and I had a long bit of rough water to go over.

The *Mechanic* sailed four or five days after the *Mary* arrived, and I travelled the old road over again. Nothing happened until we got to the southward of Cuba. But my bad luck had thrown me into the West India trade at the very moment when piracy was coming to its height in those seas, though I never thought on the subject at all. Off the Isle of Pines, one morning, we made a schooner and a sloop, in-shore of us, and both bore up in chase. We knew them to be pirates, and crowded sail dead before the wind to get clear. The captain determined, if necessary, to run down as far as Jamaica, where he expected to fall in with some of the English cruisers. The schooner sailed very fast, and was for coming up with us, but they made the mistake of setting a flying-topsail on board her, and from that moment we dropped her. It was thought in our brig, that the little craft buried too much, with such a pressure aloft. The chase lasted all day, a Sunday, and a part of the night; but the following morning nothing was to be seen of either of our pursuers. Our captain, whose name was Ray, thought he knew who commanded the schooner, a man who had been his enemy, and it was believed the pirates knew our brig, as she was a regular trader to Trinidad. This made our captain more ticklish, and was the reason he was off so soon.

When we found the coast clear, we hauled up, again, and made our port without further molestation. The chase was so common a thing, that little was said about the affair. We discharged, took in a new cargo, and sailed for home in due time. Care was had in sailing at an early hour, and we sent a boat out to look if the coast were clear, before we put to sea. We met with no interruption, however, reaching New York in due time.

Captain Ray was desirous I should stick by the brig; but, for some reason I cannot explain, I felt averse to returning to Trinidad. I liked the vessel well enough, was fond of the captain, and thought little of the pirates; and yet I felt an unaccountable reluctance to re-shipping in the craft. It was well I had this feeling, for, I have since heard, this very schooner got the brig the next passage out, murdered all hands, and burnt the vessel, in sight of the port! I set this escape down, as one of the many unmerited favours I have received from Providence.

My next berth was that of second-mate on board a new ship, in the Charleston trade, called the *Franklin.* I made the voyage, and, for a novelty, did not run in the southern port, which was a rare circumstance in that place.

I got but twelve dollars, as dickey, in the *Franklin,* and left her to get twenty, with the same berth, on board a ship called the *Foster,* commanded by the same master as had commanded the *Jane,* in my former voyage to Ireland. The *Foster* was bound to Belfast, which port we reached without any accident. We took in salt, and a few boxes of linens, for Norfolk; arrived safe, discharged, and went up the James river to City Point, after a cargo of tobacco. Thence we sailed for Rotterdam. The ship brought back a quantity of gin to New York, and this gin caused me some trouble. We had a tremendous passage home—one of the worst I ever experienced at sea. The ship's rudder got loose, and was secured with difficulty. We had to reef all three of our top-masts, also, to save the spars; after which we could only carry double-reefed topsails. It was in the dead of winter, and the winds hung to the westward for a long time. The cook, a surly negro, was slack in duty, and refused to make scouse for us, though there were plenty of potatoes on board.[1] All the people but five were off duty, and it came hard on those who kept watch. We determined, at length, to bring the black to his senses, and I had him seized to the windlass. Everybody but the captain took three clips at him; the fellow being regularly cobbed, according to sea usage. This was lawful punishment for a cook.

We got our scouse after this, but the negro logged the whole transaction, as one may suppose. He was particularly

1. A Dutch seamen's stew of meat, vegetables, hardtack, and other ingredients.

set against me, as I had been ringleader in the cobbing. The weather continued bad, the watches were much fagged, and the ship gave no grog. At length I could stand it no longer, or thought I could not; and I led down betwixt decks, tapped a cask of gin, introduced the stem of a clean pipe and took a nip at the bowl. All my watch smoked this pipe, pretty regularly, first at one cask and then at another, until we got into port. The larboard watch did the same, and I do think the strong liquor helped us along that time. As bad luck would have it, the cook's wood was stowed among the casks, and, one morning, just as the last of us had knocked off smoking, we saw the wool of this gentleman heaving in sight, through the hatch by which we went down. Still, nothing was said until we came to be paid off, when the darky came out with his yarn. I owned it all, and insisted we never could have brought the ship in, unless we had got the gin. I do believe both captain and owner were sorry we had been complained of, but they could not overlook the matter. I was mulcted five-and-twenty dollars, and left the ship. I know I did wrong, and I know that the owners did what was right; but I cannot help thinking, bad as gin is on a long pull, that this did us good. I was not driven from the ship; on the contrary, both master and owners wished me to remain; but I felt a little savage, and quitted their employment.

That I did not carry a very bad character away with me, is to be proved by the fact that I shipped, the same day, on board the *Washington,* a vessel bound to London, and which lay directly alongside of the *Foster.* I had the same berth as that I had just left, with the advantage of getting better wages. This voyage carried me to London for the first time since I left it in the *Sterling.* Too many years had elapsed, in the interval, for me to find any old acquaintances; and I had grown from a boy to a man. Here I got a little insight into the business of carrying passengers, our ship bringing more or less, each passage. I stuck by the *Washington* a year, making no less than three voyages in her; the last, as her chief mate. Nothing occurred worth mentioning in the four first passages across the Atlantic; but the fifth produced a little more variety.

The *Washington* had proved to be a leaky ship, every passage I made in her. We had docked her twice in London, and it had done her good. The first week out, on the fifth passage, the ship proved tight, but the weather was moderate. It came on to blow heavily, however, when we got to the eastward of the Banks, and the vessel, which was scudding under her close-reefed main-topsail and foresail, laboured so much, that I became uneasy. I knew she was overloaded, and was afraid of the effects of a gale. It was my practice to keep one pump ready for sounding the wells, and I never neglected this duty in my watch. When the gale was at the height, in my forenoon's watch below, I felt so uncomfortable, that I turned out and went on deck, in nothing but my trowsers, to sound, although I had sounded less than two hours before, and found the water at the sucking-height, only. To my surprise, it was now three feet!

This change was so great and so sudden, all of us thought there must be some mistake. I carried the rod below, to dry it, and covered the lower part with ashes. I could not have been busy in drying the rod more than ten or fifteen minutes, when it was lowered again. The water had risen several inches in that short period!

All this looked very serious; and I began to think a third craft was to founder under me. After a short consultation, it was determined to lighten the ship. The foresail was hauled up, the men got into the rigging to keep clear of the seas, and the vessel was rounded-to. We then knocked away the wash-boards in the wake of the two hatches, and began to tumble the barrels of turpentine on deck. I never felt so strong in my life, nor did so much work in so short a time. During the labour I went below to splice the mainbrace, and, after putting a second-mate's nip of brandy into my glass, filled it, as I supposed, with water, drinking it all down without stopping to breathe. It turned out that my water was high-proof gin; yet this draught had no more effect on me than if it had been so much cold water. In ordinary times, it would have made me roaring drunk.

We tumbled up all the cargo from betwixt decks, landing it on deck, where it rolled into the sea of itself, and were about to begin upon the lower hold, when the captain called out avast, as the pumps gained fast. Half an hour later, they sucked. This was joyful news, indeed, for I had begun to think we should be driven to the boats. Among the cargo were some pickled calf-skins. In the height of the danger I caught the cook knocking the head out of a cask, and stowing some of the skins in a tub. Asking the reason why he did this, he told me he wanted to take some of those fine skins home with him! It was a pity they should be lost!

As soon as the pumps sucked, the ship was kept away to her course, and she proved to be as tight as a bottle. Eight or ten days later, while running on our course under studding-sails, we made a large vessel ahead, going before the wind like ourselves, but carrying reefed topsails, with topgallant-sails over them, and her ensign whipped. Of course we neared her fast, and as we came up with her, saw that she was full of men, and that her crew were pumping and bailing. We knew how to pity the poor fellows, and running alongside, demanded the news. We were answered first with three cheers, after which we heard their story.

The vessel was an English bark, full of soldiers, bound to New Brunswick. She had sprung a leak, like ourselves, and was only kept afloat by constant pumping and bailing. She had put back for England on account of the wind and the distance. Our captain was asked to keep near the transport, and we shortened sail accordingly. For three days and nights the two vessels ran side by side, within hail; our passengers and officers drinking to theirs, and *vice versâ,* at dinner. On the fourth day, the weather being fine, the wind fair, and our reckoning making us near the channel, we told the Englishman we would run ahead, make the land, and heave-to. We stood in so far that the poor fellows owned afterwards they thought we had left them. This was not our intention, however, for we no sooner made the land than we hauled up, and brought them the joyful news of its vicinity. They cheered us again, as we closed with them, and both ships jogged on in company.

Next morning, being well in with the land, and many vessels in sight, the Englishmen desired us to make sail, as they could carry their bark into Falmouth. We did so, and reached London, in due time. On our return to New York, the *Washington* was sold, and I lost my preferment in that employment, though I went with a character to another vessel, and got the same berth.

CHAPTER XIII

MY NEXT CRAFT WAS THE *CAMILLUS,* a ship that was bound to Greenock, via Charleston. We got to the latter port without accident, and took in a cargo of cotton. The ship was all ready for sailing of a Saturday, and the captain had gone ashore, telling me he would be on board early in the morning, when we could haul out and go to sea, should the wind be favourable. I gave the people their Saturday's night, and went into the cabin to freshen the nip, myself. I took a glass or two, and certainly had more in me than is good for a man, though I was far from being downright drunk. In a word, I had too much, though I could have carried a good deal more, on a pinch. The steward had gone ashore, and there being no second-mate, I was all alone.

In this state of things, I heard a noise, and went on deck to inquire what was the matter. My old ship, the *Franklin,* was shifting her berth, and her jib-boom had come foul of our taffrail. After some hailing, I got on the taffrail to shove our neighbour off, when, by some carelessness of my own, I fell head-foremost, hitting the gunwale of the boat, which was hanging, about half way up to the davits, into the water. The tide set me away, and carried me between the wharf and the ship astern of us, which happened to be the *William Thompson,* Captain Thompson, owner Thompson, mate Thompson, and all Thompson, as Mathews used to have it. Captain Thompson was reading near the cabin windows, and he luckily heard me groan. Giving the alarm, a boat was got round, and I taken in. As the night was dark, and I lost all consciousness after the fall, I consider this escape as standing second only to that from the shark in the West Indies, and old Trant's gun, the night the *Scourge* went down. I did not recover my recollection for several hours. This was not the effect of liquor, but of the fall, as I remember everything distinctly that occurred before I went from the taffrail. Still I confess that liquor did all the mischief, as I had drunk just enough to make me careless.

In the morning, I found myself disabled in the left arm, and I went to a doctor. This gentlemen said he never told a fellow what ailed him until he got his whack. I gave him a dollar, and he then let me into the secret. My collar-bone was broken. "And, now," says he, "for another dollar I'll patch you up." I turned out the other Spaniard, when he was as good as his word. Going in the ship, however, was out of the question, and I was obliged to get a young man to go on board the *Camillus* in my place; thus losing the voyage and my berth.

I was now ashore, with two or three months of drift before me. Since the time I joined the *Washington,* I had been going regularly ahead, and I do think had I been able to stick by the *Camillus,* I might have brought up a master. I had laid up money, and being employed while in port, I was gradually losing my taste for sailor amusements, and getting more respect for myself. That fall from the taffrail was a sad drawback for me, and I never recovered the lee-way it brought about.

I was more than two months ashore, behaving myself rationally on account of my arm. At the end of that time, I went on board the *Sally,* a ship also bound to Greenock, as her second-mate. This vessel belonged to Charleston, and it was intended she should return to her own port. The voyage turned out well, and my arm got as strong as ever. On reaching Charleston, I left the craft, which was laid up, and shipped in a schooner of the same name, bound to St. Domingo, as her chief mate. This was no great craft, certainly, though she proved a tight, wholesome sea-boat. We went out without any accident, arriving in safety at Cape Henry. After discharging cargo, and smuggling on board a quantity of doubloons—four hundred and eighty, it was said—we got under way for the island of Cuba. We intended to go into Matanzas, and kept along the coast. After crossing the Windward Passage, we reached Cuba; and were standing on, with a light wind, under our squaresail, the morning of the third day out, when we saw a large boat, carrying two sails, standing out from the shore, evidently in chase of the schooner. We had on board eight souls, viz. the owner, a Frenchman, who had been a dragoon in the service of his own country, but who was now between seventy and eighty; the captain, myself, a boy, the cook, and four men forward. We could see that there were nine men in the boat. We had no arms in the schooner, not even a pistol, and the men in the boat had muskets. We did not ascertain this last fact, however, for some time. I thought the strangers pirates the moment I saw them come out from under the land, but the captain maintained that they were turtle-men. The boat was rowing, and came up with us, hand over hand. When near, they commenced firing muskets at us, to drive us below. All the crew forward, with the cook, ran down into the forecastle, leaving no one on deck but the captain, the old Frenchman, and myself. The boy got into the companion-way.

What the others did on deck, as these gentry came alongside, amusing themselves with keeping up a smart fire of musketry, I do not know; but my own occupation was to dodge behind the foremast. It was not long, however, before they came tumbling in, and immediately got possession of the schooner. One or two came forward and secured the forecastle hatch, to keep the people down. Then they probably felt that they were masters. One chap drew a fearful-looking knife, long, slender, sharp and glittering, and he cut the halyards of the square-sail. All the men I saw in the schooner struck me as Americans, or English, affecting to be Spaniards. There is such a difference in the height, complexion, and general appearance of the people of Spain, and those of the two other countries, without reference to the manner of speaking, that I do not think I could be mistaken. I saw but one man among these pirates, whom I took for a real Spaniard. It is true their faces were all blacked to disguise them, but one could get enough glimpses of the skin to judge of the true colour. There was no negro among them.

The chap who cut away the square-sail halyards, I felt certain was no Spaniard. The sail was no sooner down, than he ran his knife along the head, below the bolt-rope, as if to cut away the cloth with the least trouble to himself. I was standing near, and asked him why he destroyed the sail; if he wanted it, why he did not take it whole? At this, he turned short round upon me, raised his arm, and struck a heavy blow at me with his fearful-looking knife. The point of the deadly weapon struck square on my breastbone! I fell, partly through the force of the blow, and partly from policy; for I thought it safest to be lying on my back. I got several hearty kicks, in addition to this fierce attack, together with sundry curses in broken Spanish. I spoke in English, of course; and that the man understood me was clear enough by the expression of his countenance, and his act. The wound was slight, though it bled a good deal, covering my shirt and trowsers with blood, as much as if I had been run through the heart. An inch or two, either way, in the direction of the knife, would certainly have killed me.

I do not know what might have been the end of this affair, had not one of the pirates come forward, at this critical instant, and checked my assailant by shaking a finger at him. This man, I feel very certain, I knew. I will not mention his name, as there is a doubt; but I cannot think I was mistaken. If I am right, he was a young man from Connecticut, who sailed one voyage to Liverpool with me in the *Sterling*. With that young man I had been very intimate, and was oftener with him ashore than with any other of the crew. His face was blackened, like those of all his companions, but this did not conceal his air, manner, size, eyes and voice. When he spoke, it was in a jargon of broken English and broken Spanish, such as no man accustomed to either language from infancy would have used. The same was true as to all the rest I heard speak, with the exception of an old fellow in the boat, whom I shall presently have occasion to mention, again.

The man I took to be my old shipmate, also seemed to know me. I was but a lad when I quitted the *Sterling,* it is true; but they tell me I have not altered a great deal in general appearance. My hair is still black; and then, when I was in the very prime of life, it must have been easy to recognize me. So strongly was I impressed, at the time, that I saw an old acquaintance, I was about to call him by name, when, luckily, it crossed my mind this might be dangerous. The pirates wished clearly to be unknown, and it was wisest to let them think they were so. My supposed shipmate, however, proved my friend, and I received no more personal ill treatment after he had spoken to his companion. I sometimes think he was the means, indeed, of saving all our lives. He asked me if there was any money, and, on my denying it, he told me they knew better: the schooner was in ballast, and must have got something for her outward cargo. I refused to tell, and he ordered me into their boat, whither the captain had been sent before me. In doing all this, his manner wore an appearance, to me, of assumed severity.

The poor old Frenchman fared worse. They seemed to know he was owner, and probably thought he could give the best account of the money. At any rate, he was unmercifully flogged, though he held out to the last, refusing to betray his doubloons. The boy was next attacked with threats of throwing him overboard. This extracted the secret, and the doubloons were soon discovered.

The captain and myself had been stowed under a half-deck, in the boat, but as soon as the money was found, the old Spaniard, who stood sentinel over us, was told to let us out, that we might see the fun. There were the eight scoundrels, paraded around the trunk of the schooner, dividing the doubloons. As soon as this was done, we were told to come alongside with our boat, which had been used to carry us to the piratical craft. The captain got on board the *Sally* and I was ordered to scull the rogues, in one gang, back to their own craft. The scamps were in high spirits, seeming much pleased with their haul. They cracked a good many jokes at our expense, but were so well satisfied with their gold, that they left the square-sail behind them. They had robbed the cabin, however, carrying off, for me, a quadrant, a watch, and a large portion of my clothes. The forecastle had not been entered, though the men had four hundred dollars lying under a pile of dirt and old junk, to keep them out of sight.

My supposed ship-mate bore me in mind to the last. When we reached his craft, he poured out a glass of brandy and offered it to me. I was afraid to drink, thinking it might be poisoned. He seemed to understand me, and swallowed it himself, in a significant manner. This gave me courage, and I took the next nip without hesitation. He then told me to shove off, which I did without waiting for a second order. The pirates pulled away at the same time.

We were a melancholy party, as soon as we found ourselves left to ourselves. The old Frenchman was sad enough, and all of us pitied him. He made no complaint of the boy, notwithstanding, and little was said among us about the robbery. My wound proved trifling, though the old man was so bruised and beaten that he could scarcely walk.

As soon as a breeze came, we went into Charleston, having no means to buy the cargo we had intended to get at Matanzas. This was the first time I was ever actually boarded by a pirate, although I had had several narrow escapes before. The first was in the *Sterling,* off the coast of Portugal; the next was in the *William and Jane,* outward bound to Canton; the third was on the bank, in the *Trio,* off the coast of Java; and the fourth, in the *Mechanic,* on the other side of Cuba. It was not the last of my affairs with them, however, as will be seen in the sequel.

I went out in the *Sally* again, making a voyage to Matanzas and back, without any accident, or incident, worth mentioning. I still intended to remain in this schooner, the captain and I agreeing perfectly well, had I not been driven out of her by one of those unlucky accidents, of which so many have laid me athwart-hawse.

We were discharging sugar at Charleston, in very heavy casks. The tide being in, the vessel's rail was higher than the wharf, and we landed the casks on the rail, from which they were rolled down some planks to the shore. Two negroes were stationed on the wharf to receive the casks, and to ease them down. One of these fellows was in the practice of running up the planks, instead of standing at their side and holding on to the end of the hogsheads. I remonstrated with him several times about the danger he ran, but he paid no attention to what I said. At length my words came true; a cask got away from the men, and rolled directly over this negro, flattening him like a bit of dough.

This was clearly an accident, and no one thought of accusing me of any connection with it. But the owner of the black looked upon him as one would look upon a hack-horse that had been lamed, or killed; and he came down to the schooner, on hearing that his man was done for, swearing I should pay for him! As for paying the price of an athletic "nigger," it was even more impossible for me, than it would seem it is for the great State of Pennsylvania to pay the interest on its debt; and, disliking a lawsuit, I carried my dunnage on board another vessel that same afternoon, and agreed to work my passage to New York, as her secondmate.

The vessel I now went on board of was the *Commodore Rodgers,* a regular liner between the two ports. We sailed next morning, and I paid for the poor "nigger" with the fore-topsail. The ship's husband was on board as we hauled out, a man who was much in the habit of abusing the mates. On this occasion he was particularly abusive to our chief mate; so much so, indeed, that I remonstrated with the latter on his forbearance. Nothing came of it, however, though I could not forget the character of the man who had used such language. When we reached New York, our chief mate left us, and I was offered the berth. It was a little hazardous to go back to Charleston, but wages were low, and business dull, the yellow fever being in New York; and I thought, by a little management, I might give my "nigger owner" a sufficient berth. I accordingly agreed to go.

When we got back to Charleston, our ship lay at her own wharf, and I saw nothing of my chap. He worked up town, and we lay low down. But another misfortune befel me, that led even to worse consequences. The ship's husband, who was so foul-mouthed, was as busy as ever, blackguarding right and left, and finding fault with everything. Our cargo was nearly out, and this man and I had a row about some kegs of white lead. In the course of the dialogue, he called me "a saucy son of a b——h." This was too much for my temper, and I seized him and sent him down the hatchway. The fall was not great, and some hemp lay in the wake of the hatch; but the chap's collar-bone went. He sung out like a singing-master, but I did not stop to chime in. Throwing my slate on deck in a high passion, I left the ship and went ashore. I fell in with the captain on the wharf, told him my story, got a promise from him to send me my clothes, and vanished. In an hour or two, half the constables in Charleston were in chase of me. I kept so close they could not find me, lying snug for a couple of days.

This state of things could not last for ever. The constables were not half so ferocious as they seemed; for one of them managed to get me off, on board a coaster, called the *Gov. Russel;* where I engaged, I may say, as chief mate and all hands. The *Gov. Russel* was a Buford trader, making trips about fifteen or twenty leagues long. This was the smallest navigation, and the smallest craft, a gun-boat excepted, with which I ever had anything to do. The crew consisted of two negroes, both slaves to the owner; while the captain and myself were aft. Whether she would have held so many, or not, I never knew, as the captain did not join, while I belonged to her. The schooner lay three miles below the town; and, in so much, was a good craft for me; as no one would think of following an old Canton trader into such a long-shore-looking thing. We busied ourselves in painting her, and in overhauling her rigging; while the ship's husband, and his myrmidons, amused themselves in searching for me up in town.

I had been on board the *Gov. Russel* three days, when it came on to blow from the southward and westward, in true southern style. The gale came on butt-end foremost; and was thought to be as severe, as anything seen in the port for many a year. Most of the shipping broke adrift from the wharves; and everything that was anchored, a man-of-war and a revenue-cutter excepted, struck adrift, or dragged. As for ourselves, we were lying at single anchor; and soon began to walk down towards the bar. I let go the spare anchor; but she snapped her cables, as if they had been pack-thread; and away she went to leeward. Making sail was out of the question, had any been bent, as ours were not; and I had to let her travel her own road.

All this happened at night; when it was so dark, one could not see, between the spray, the storm and the hour, the length of the craft. I knew we were going towards the ocean; and my great cause of apprehension was the bar. Looking for the channel, was out of the question; I did not know it, in the first place; and, had I been a branch-pilot, I could not find it in the dark. I never was more completely adrift, in my life, ashore or afloat. We passed a most anxious hour, or two; the schooner driving, broadside-to, I knew not whither, or to what fate. The two blacks were frightened out of their wits; and were of no assistance to me.

At length, I felt the keel come down upon the sands; and then I knew we were on the bar. This happened amid a whirlwind of spray; with nothing visible but the white foam of the waters, and the breakers around us. The first blow threw both masts out of the steps; ripping up the decks to a considerable extent. The next minute we were on our beam-ends; the sea making a clear breach over us. All we could do, was to hold on; and this we did with difficulty. I and the two blacks got on the weather-quarter of the schooner, where we lashed ourselves with the main-sheet. As this was a stout rope, something must part, before we could be washed away. The craft made but two raps on the bar, when she drifted clear.

I now knew we were at sea, and were drifting directly off the coast. As we got into deep water, the sea did not make such terrible surges over us; though they continued to break over our quarter. The masts were thumping away; but for this I cared little, the hold being full of water already. Sink we could not, having a swept hold, and being built, in a great measure, of pine. The schooner floated with about five feet of her quarter-deck above water. Her bows had settled the most; and this gave us rather a better chance aft.

Fortunately, we got the worst of this blow at the first go off. The wind began to lessen in strength soon after we passed the bar, and by daylight it only blew a stiff breeze. No land was in sight, though I knew, by the colour of the water, that we could not be a very great distance from the coast. We had come out on an ebb-tibe, and this had set us off the land, but all that southern coast is so low, that it was not to be seen from the surface of the ocean at any great distance.

The day that succeeded was sad and dreary enough. The weather was fine, the sun coming out even hot upon us, but the wind continued to blow fresh off the land, and we were drifting further out, every instant, upon the bosom of the ocean. Our only hope was in falling in with some coaster, and I began to dread drifting outside of their track. We were without food or water, and were partly seated on the rail, and partly supported by the main-sheet. Neither of us attempted to change his berth that day. Little was said between us, though I occasionally encouraged the negroes to hold on, as something would yet pick us up. I had a feeling of security on this head that was unreasonable, perhaps; but a sanguine temperament has ever made me a little too indifferent to consequences.

Night brought no change, unless it was to diminish the force of the wind. A short time before the sun set, one of the negroes said to me, "Masser Ned, John gone." I was forward of the two blacks, and was not looking at them at the time; I suppose I may have been dozing; but, on looking up, I found that one of the negroes had, indeed, disappeared. How this happened I cannot say, as he appeared to be well lashed; but I suppose he worked himself free, and being exhausted, he fell into the water, and sunk before I could get a glimpse of him. There was nothing to be done, however, and the loss of this man had a tendency to make me think our situation worse than it had before seemed to be. Some persons, all good Christians I should suppose, will feel some curiosity to know whether a man in my situation had no disposition to take a religious view of his case, and whether his conscience did not apprise him of the chances of perdition that seemed to stare him in the face. In answer to this, I am compelled to say that no such thoughts came over me. In all my risks and emergencies, I am not sensible of having given a thought to my Maker. I had a sense of fear, an apprehension of death, and an instinctive desire to save my life, but no consciousness of the necessity of calling on any being to save my soul. Notwithstanding all the lessons I had received in childhood, I was pretty nearly in the situation of one who had never heard the name of the Saviour mentioned. The extent of my reflections on such subjects, was the self-delusion of believing that I was to save myself—I had done no great harm, according to the notions of sailors; had not robbed; had not murdered; and had observed the mariner's code of morals, so far as I understood them; and this gave me a sort of *claim* on the mercy of God. In a word, the future condition of my soul gave me no trouble whatever.

I dare say my two companions on this little wreck had the same indifference on this subject, as I felt myself. I heard no prayer, no appeal to God for mercy, nothing indeed from any of us, to show that we thought at all on the subject. Hunger gave me a little trouble, and during the second night I would fall into a doze, and wake myself up by dreaming of eating meals that were peculiarly grateful to me. I have had the same thing happen on other occasions, when on short allowance of food. Neither of the blacks said anything on the subject of animal suffering, and the one that was lost, went out, as it might be, like a candle.

The sun rose on the morning of the second day bright and clear. The wind shifted about this time, to a gentle breeze from the southward and eastward. This was a little encouraging, as it was setting the schooner in-shore again, but I could discover nothing in sight. There was still a good deal of sea going, and we were so low in the water, that our range of sight was very limited.

It was late in the forenoon, when the negro called out, suddenly, "Massa Ned, dere a vessel!" Almost at the same instant, I heard voices calling out; and, looking round, I saw a small coasting schooner, almost upon us. She was coming down before the wind, had evidently seen us some time before we saw her, and now ranged up under our lee, and hove-to. The schooner down boat, and took us on board without any delay. We moved with difficulty, and I found ny limbs so stiff as to be scarcely manageable. The black vas in a much worse state than I was myself, and I think welve hours longer would have destroyed both of us.

The schooner that picked us up was manned entirely with lacks, and was bound into Charleston. At the time she fell n with us, we must have been twenty miles from the bar, t taking us all the afternoon, with a fair wind, to reach it. We went below, and as soon as I got in the cabin, I discovered a kettle of boiled rice, on which I pounced like a hawk. The negroes wished to get it away from me, thinking I hould injure myself; but I would not part with it. The weetest meal I ever had in my life, was this rice, a fair ortion of which, however, I gave to my companion. We ad not fasted long enough materially to weaken our stomachs, and no ill consequences followed from the indulgence. After eating heartily, we both lay down on the cabin floor, nd went to sleep. We reached the wharf about eight in the vening. Just within the bar, the schooner was spoken by a raft that was going out in search of the *Gov. Russel.* The lacks told her people where the wreck was to be found, and he craft stood out to sea.

I was strong enough to walk up to my boarding-house, where I went again into quarantine. The *Gov. Russel* was ound, towed into port, was repaired, and went about her usiness, as usual, in the Buford trade. I never saw her or er captain again, however. I parted with the negro that was aved with me, on the wharf, and never heard anything bout him afterwards, either. Such is the life of a sailor!

I was still afraid of the constables. So much damage had een done to more important shipping, and so many lives ost, however, that little was said of the escape of the *Gov. Russel.* Then I was not known in this schooner by my surname. When I threw the ship's husband down the hold, I was Mr. Myers; when wrecked in the coaster, only Ned.

CHAPTER XIV

NOTWITHSTANDING MY COMPARATIVE INSIGNIFICANCE, there was no real security in remaining long in Charleston, and it was my strong desire to quit the place. As "beggars cannot be choosers," I was glad to get on board the schooner *Carpenter,* bound to St. Mary's and Philadelphia, for, and with, ship-timber, as a foremast hand. I got on board undetected, and we sailed the same day. Nothing occurred until after we left St. Mary's, when we met with a singular accident. A few days out, it blowing heavy at the time, our deck-load pressed so hard upon the beams as to loosen them, and the schooner filled as far as her cargo—yellow pine—would allow. This calamity proceeded from the fact, that the negroes who stowed the craft neglected to wedge up the beams; a precaution that should never be forgotten, with a heavy weight on deck. No very serious consequences followed, however, as we managed to drive the craft ahead, and finally got her into Phildelphia, with all her cargo on board. We did not lose a stick, which showed that our captain was game, and did not like to let go when he had once got hold. This person was a down-easter, and was well acquainted with the Johnstons and Wiscasset. He tried hard to persuade me to continue in the schooner as mate, with a view to carrying me back to my old friends; but I turned a deaf ear to his advice. To own the truth, I was afraid to go back to Wiscassett. My own desertion could not well be excused, and then I was apprehensive the family might attribute to me the desertion and death of young Swett. He had been my senior, it is true, and was as able to influence me as I was to influence him; but conscience is a thing so sensitive, that, when we do wrong, it is apt to throw the whole error into our faces.

Quitting the *Carpenter* in Philadelphia, therefore, I went to live in a respectable boarding-house, and engaged to go out in a brig called the *Margaret,* working on board as a rigger and stevedore, until she should be ready to sail. My berth was to be that of mate. The owner of this brig was as notorious, in his way, as the ship's husband in Charleston. I had heard his character, and was determined, if he attempted to ride me, as he was said to do many of his mates, and even captains, he should find himself mounted on a hard-going animal. One day, things came to a crisis. The owner was on the wharf, with me, and such a string of abuse as he launched out upon me, I never before listened to. A crowd collected, and my blood got up. I seized the man, and dropped him off the wharf into the water, alongside of some hoop-poles, that I knew must prevent any accident. In this last respect, I was sufficiently careful, though the ducking was very thorough. The crowd gave three cheers, which I considered as a proof I was not so very wrong. Nothing was said of any suit on this occasion; but I walked off, and went directly on board a ship called the *Coromandel,* on which I had had an eye, as a lee, for several days. In this vessel I shipped as second-mate; carrying with me all the better character for the ducking given to the notorious——— ———.

The *Coromandel* was bound to Cadiz, and thence round the Horn. The outward bound cargo was flour, but to which ports we were going in South America, I was ignorant. Our crew were all blacks, the officers excepted. We had a good passage, until we got off Cape Trafalgar, when it came on to blow heavily, directly on end. We lay-to off the Cape two days, and then ran into Gibraltar, and anchored. Here we lay about a fortnight, when there came on a gale from the south-west, which sent a tremendous sea in from the Atlantic. This gale commenced in the afternoon, and blew very heavily all that night. The force of the wind increased, little by little, until it began to tell seriously among the shipping, of which a great number were lying in front of the Rock. The second day of the gale, our ship was pitching bows under, sending the water aft to the taffrail, while many other craft struck adrift, or foundered at their anchors. The *Coromandel* had one chain cable, and this was out. It was the only cable we used for the first twenty-four hours. As the gale increased, however, it was thought necessary to let go the sheet-anchor, which had a hempen cable bent to it. Our chain, indeed, was said to be the first that was ever used out of Philadelphia, though it had then been in the ship for some time, and had proved itself a faithful servant the voyage before. Unfortunately, most of the chain was out before we let go of the sheet-anchor, and there was no possibility of getting out a scope of the hempen cable. Dragging on shore, where we lay, was pretty much out of the question, as the bottom shelved inward, and the anchor, to come home, must have gone up hill.[1]

In this manner the *Coromandel* rode for two nights and two days, the sea getting worse and worse, and the wind, if anything, rather increasing. We took the weight of the last

1. A friend, who was then American Consul at Gibraltar, and an old navy officer, tells me Ned is mistaken as to the nature of the anchorage. The ship was a little too far out for the best holding ground. The same friend adds that the character of this gale is not at all overcharged, the vessels actually lost, including small craft of every description, amounting to the every way extraordinary number of just three hundred and sixty-five.—EDITOR.

in squalls, some of which were terrific. By this time the bay was well cleared of craft, nearly everything having sunk, or gone ashore. An English packet lay directly ahead of us, rather more than a cable's length distant, and she held on like ourselves. The *Governor Brooks,* of Boston, lay over nearer to Algeciras, where the sea and wind were a little broken, and, of course, she made better weather than ourselves.

About eight o'clock, the third night, I was in the cabin, when the men on deck sung out that the chain had gone. At this time the ship had been pitching her spritsail-yard under water, and it blew a little hurricane. We were on deck in a moment, all hands paying out sheet. We brought the ship up with this cable, but not until she got it nearly to the bitter end. Unfortunately, we had got into shoal water, or what became shoal water by the depth of the troughs. It was said, afterwards, we were in five fathoms water at this time, but for this I will not vouch. It seems too much water for what happened. Our anchor, however, did actually lie in sixteen fathoms.

We had hardly paid out the cable, before the ship came down upon the bottom, on an even keel, apparently, with a force that almost threw those on deck off their feet. These blows were repeated, from time to time, at intervals of several minutes, some of the thumps being much heavier than others. The English packet must have struck adrift at the same time with ourselves, for she came down upon us, letting go an anchor in a way to overlay our cable. I suppose the rocks and this sawing together, parted our hempen cable, and away we went towards the shore, broadside-to. As the ship drifted in, she continued to thump; but, luckily for us, the sea made no breaches over her. The old *Coromandel* was a very strong ship, and she continued working her way in-shore, until she lay in a good substantial berth, without any motion. We manned the pumps, and kept the ship tolerably free of water, though she lay over considerably. The English packet followed us in, going ashore more towards the Spanish lines. This vessel bilged, and lost some of her crew. As for ourselves, we had a comfortable berth, considering the manner in which we had got into it. No apprehension was felt for our personal safety, and perfect order was observed on board. The men worked as usual, nor was there any extra liquor drunk.

That night the gale broke, and before morning it had materially moderated. Lighters were brought alongside, and we began to discharge our flour into them. The cargo was all discharged, and all in good order, so far as the water was concerned; though several of the keelson bolts were driven into the ground tier of barrels. I am almost afraid to tell this story, but I know it to be true, as I released the barrels with my own hands. As soon as clear, the ship was hove off into deep water, on the top of a high tide, and was found to leak so much as to need a shore-gang at the pumps to keep her afloat. She was accordingly sold for the benefit of the underwriters. She was subsequently docked and sent to sea.

Of course, this broke up our voyage. The captain advised me to take a second-mate's berth in the *Governor Brooks,* the only American that escaped the gale, and I did so. This vessel was a brig, bound round the Horn, also, and a large, new craft. I know of no other vessel, that lay in front of the Rock that rode out this gale; and she did it with two hempen cables out, partly protected, however, by a good berth. There was a Swede that came back next day to her anchorage, which was said to have got back-strapped, behind the Rock, by some legerdemain, and so escaped also. I do not know how many lives were lost on this occasion; but the destruction of property must have been very great.

Three weeks after the gale, the *Governor Brooks* sailed. We had a hard time in doubling the Cape, being a fortnight knocking about between Falkland and the Main. We were one hundred and forty-four days out, touching nowhere, until we anchored at Callao. We found flour, of which our cargo was composed, at seven dollars a barrel, with seven dollars duty. The *Franklin,* 74, was lying here, with the *Aurora,* English frigate, the castle being at war with the people inland. Our flour was landed, and what became of it is more than I can tell.

We now took in ballast, and ran down to Guayaquil. Here an affair occurred that might very well have given me the most serious cause of regret, all the days of my life. Our steward was a Portuguese negro, of the most vicious and surly temper. Most of the people and officers were really afraid of him. One evening, the captain and chief mate being both ashore, I was sitting on deck, idle, and I took a fancy to a glass of grog. I ordered the steward, accordingly, to pour me out one, and bring it up. The man pretended that the captain had carried off the keys, and no rum was to be had. I thought this a little extraordinary; and, as one would be very apt to be, felt much hurt at the circumstance. I had never been drunk in the craft, and was not a drunkard in one sense of the term, at all; seldom drinking so as to affect me, except when on a frolic, ashore.

As I sat brooding over this fancied insult, however, I smelt rum; and looking down the sky-light, saw this same steward passing forward with a pot filled with the liquor. I was fairly blinded with passion. Running down, I met the fellow, just as he was coming out of the cabin, and brought him up all standing. The man carried a knife along his leg, a weapon that had caused a good deal of uneasiness in the brig, and he now reached down to get it. Seeing there was no time to parley, I raised him from the floor, and threw him down with a great force, his head coming under. There he lay like a log, and all my efforts with vinegar and water had no visible effect.

I now thought the man dead. He gave no sign of life that I could detect, and fear of the consequences came over me. The devil put it into my head to throw the body overboard, as the most effectual means of concealing what I had done.

The steward had threatened to run, by swimming, more than once, and I believe had been detected in making such an attempt; and I fancied if I could get the body through one of the cabin-windows, it would seem as if he had been drowned in carrying his project into execution. I tried all I could first to restore the steward to life; but failing of this, I actually began to drag him aft, in order to force his body out of a cabin-window. The transom was high, and the man very heavy; so I was a good while in dragging the load up to the necessary height. Just as I got it there, the fellow gave a groan, and I felt a relief that I had never before experienced. It seemed to me like a reprieve from the gallows.

I now took the steward down, upon one of the lower transoms, where he sat rubbing his head a few minutes, I watching him closely the whole time. At length he got up, and staggered out of the cabin. He went and turned in, and I saw no more of him until next day. As it turned out, good instead of harm, resulted from this affair; the black being ever afterwards greatly afraid of me. If I did not break his neck, I broke his temper; and the captain used to threaten to set me at him, whenever he behaved amiss. I owned the whole affair to the captain and mate, both of whom laughed heartily at what had happened, though I rejoiced, in my inmost heart, that it was no worse.

The brig loaded with cocoa, in bulk, at Guayaquil, and sailed for Cadiz. The passage was a fine one, as we doubled the Horn at midsummer. On this occasion we beat round the cape, under top-gallant-sails. The weather was so fine, we stood close in to get the benefit of the currents, after tacking, as it seemed to me, within a league of the land. Our passage to Cadiz lasted one hundred and forty-one, or two, days, being nearly the same length as that out, though much smoother.

The French had just got possession of Cadiz, as we got in, and we found the white flag flying. We lay here a month, and then went round to the Rock. After passing a week at Gibraltar, to take in some dollars, we sailed for New Orleans, in ballast. As I had been on twenty-two dollars a month, there was a pretty good whack coming to me, as soon as we reached an American port, and I felt a desire to spend it, before I went to sea again. They wished me to stick by the brig, which was going the very same voyage over; but I could not make up my mind to travel so long a road, with a pocket full of money. I had passed so many years at sea, that a short land cruise was getting to be grateful, as a novelty.

The only craft I could get on board of, to come round into my own latitude, in order to enjoy myself in the old way, was an eastern schooner, called the *James*. On board this vessel I shipped as mate, bound to Philadelphia. She was the most meagre craft, in the way of outfit, I ever put to sea in. Her boat would not swim, and she had not a spare spar on board her. In this style, we went jogging along north, until we were met by a north-west gale, between Bermuda and Cape Hatteras, which forced us to heave-to. During this gale, I had a proof of the truth that "where the treasure is, there will the heart be also."

I was standing leaning on the rail, and looking over the schooner's quarter, when I saw what I supposed to be a plank come up alongside! The idea of sailing in a craft of which the bottom was literally dropping out, was not very pleasant, and I thought all was lost. I cannot explain the folly of my conduct, except by supposing that my many escapes at sea, had brought me to imagine I was to be saved, myself, let what would happen to all the rest on board. Without stopping to reflect, I ran below and secured my dollars. Tearing up a blanket, I made a belt, and lashed about twenty-five pounds weight of silver to my body, with the prospect before me of swimming two or three hundred miles with it, before I could get ashore. As for boat, or spars, the former would not float, and of the last there was not one. I now look back on my acts of this day with wonder, for I had forgotten all my habitual knowledge of vessels, in the desire to save the paltry dollars. For the first and only time in my life I felt avaricious, and lost sight of everything in money!

It was my duty to sound the pumps, but this I did not deem necessary. No sooner were the dollars secure, or, rather, ready to anchor me in the bottom of the ocean, than I remembered the captain. He was asleep, and waking him up, I told him what had happened. The old man, a dry, drawling, cool, downeaster, laughed in my face for my pains, telling me I had seen one of the sheeting-boards, with which he had had the bottom of the schooner covered, to protect it from the worms, at Campeachy, and that I need be under no concern about the schooner's bottom. This was the simple truth, and I cast off the dollars, again, with a sneaking consciousness of not having done my duty. I suppose all men have moments when they are not exactly themselves, in which they act very differently from what it has been their practice to act. On this occasion, I was not alarmed for myself, but I thought the course I took was necessary to save that dross which lures so many to perdition. Avarice blinded me to the secrets of my own trade.

I had come all the way from New Orleans to Philadelphia, to spend my four hundred dollars to my satisfaction. For two months I lived respectably, and actually began to go to church. I did not live in a boarding-house, but in a private family. My landlady was a pious woman, and a member of the Dutch Reformed Church, but her husband was a Universalist. I must say, I liked the doctrine of the last the best, as it made smooth water for the whole cruise. I usually went with the man to church of a morning, which was falling among shoals, as a poor fellow was striving to get into port. I received a great deal of good advice from my landlady, however, and it made so much impression on me as to influence my conduct; though I cannot say it really touched my heart. I became more considerate, and better mannered, if I were not truly repentant for my sins. These two months were passed more rationally than any time of mine on shore, since the hour when I ran from the *Sterling*.

The *James* was still lying in Philadelphia, undergoing repairs, and waiting for freight; but being now ready for sea, I shipped in her again, on a voyage to St. Thomas, with a cargo of flour. When we sailed, I left near a hundred dollars behind me, besides carrying some money to sea; the good effects of good company. At St. Thomas we discharged, and took in ballast for Turk's Island, where we got a cargo of salt, returning with it to Philadelphia. My conduct had been such on board this schooner, that her commander, who was her owner, and very old, having determined to knock off going to sea, tried to persuade me to stick by the craft, promising to make me her captain as soon as he could carry her down east, where she belonged. I now think I made a great mistake in not accepting this offer, though I was honestly diffident about my knowledge of navigation. I never had a clear understanding of the lunars, though I worked hard to master them. It is true, chronometers were coming into general use, in large vessels, and I could work the time; but a chronometer was a thing never heard of on board the *James*. Attachment to the larger towns, and a dislike for little voyages, had as much influence on me as anything else. I delined the offer; the only direct one ever made me to command any sort of craft, and remained what I am. I had a little contempt, too, for vessels of such a rig and outfit, which probably had its influence. I liked rich owners.

On my return to Philadelphia, I found the family in which I had last lived much deranged by illness. I got my money, but was obliged to look for new lodgings. The respectable people with whom I had been before, did not keep lodgers, I being their only boarder; but I now went to a regular sailor's boarding-house. There was a little aristocracy, it is true, in my new lodgings, to which none but mates, dickies, and thorough salts came; but this was getting into the hurricane latitudes as to morals. I returned to all my old habits, throwing the dollars right and left, and forgetting all about even a Universalist church.

A month cleaned me out, in such company. I spent every cent I had, with the exception of about fifteen dollars, that I had laid by as nest-eggs. I then shipped as second-mate, in the *Rebecca Simms,* a ship bound to St. Jago de Cuba, with flour. The voyage lasted four months; producing nothing of moment, but a little affair that was personal to myself, and which cost me nearly all my wages. The steward was a saucy black; and, on one occasion, in bad weather, he neglected to give me anything warm for breakfast. I took an opportunity to give him a taste of the end of the main-clew-garnet, as an admonisher; and there the matter ended, so long as I remained in the ship. It seemed quite right, to all on board, but the steward. He bore the matter in mind, and set a whole pack of quakers on me, as soon as we got in. The suit was tried; and it cost me sixty dollars, in damages, beside legal charges. I dare say it was all right, according to law and evidence; but I feel certain, just such a rubbing down, once a week, would have been very useful to that same steward. Well-meaning men often do quite as much harm, in this world, as the evil-disposed. Philanthropists of this school should not forget, that, if colour is no sufficient reason why a man should be always wrong, it is no sufficient reason why he should be always right.

The lawsuit drove me to sea, again, in a very short time. Finding no better berth, and feeling very savage at the blindness of justice, I shipped before the mast, in the *Superior,* an Indiaman, of quite eight hundred tons, bound to Canton. This was the pleasantest voyage I ever made to sea, in a merchantman, so far as the weather, and, I may say, usage, were concerned. We lost our top-gallant-masts, homeward bound; but this was the only accident that occurred. The ship was gone nine months; the passage from Whampao to the capes having been made in ninety-four days. When we got in, the owners had failed, and there was no money forthcoming, at the moment. To remain, and libel the ship, was dull business; so, leaving a power of attorney behind me, I went on board a schooner, called the *Sophia,* bound to Vera Cruz, as foremast Jack.

The *Sophia* was a clipper; and made the run out in a few days. We went into Vera Cruz; but found it nearly deserted. Our cargo went ashore a little irregularly; sometimes by day, and sometimes by night; being assorted, and suited to all classes of customers. As soon as ready, we sailed for Philadelphia, again; where we arrived, after an absence of only two months.

I now got my wages for the Canton voyage; but they lasted me only a fortnight! It was necessary to go to sea, again; and I went on board the *Caledonia;* once more bound to Canton. This voyage lasted eleven months; but, like most China voyages, produced no event of importance. We lost our top-gallant-masts, this time, too; but that is nothing unusual, off Good Hope. I can say but little, in favour of the ship, or the treatment.

On getting back to Philadelphia, the money went in the old way. I occasionally walked round to see my good religious friends, with whom I had once lived, but they ceased to have any great influence over my conduct. As soon as necessary, I shipped in the *Delaware,* a vessel bound to Savannah and Liverpool. Southern fashion, I ran from this vessel in Savannah, owing her nothing, however, but was obliged to leave my protection behind, as it was in the captain's hands. I cannot give any reason but caprice for quitting this ship. The usage was excellent, and the wages high; yet run I did. As long as the *Delaware* remained in port, I kept stowed away; but, as soon as she sailed, I came out into the world, and walked about the wharves as big as an owner.

I now went on board a ship called the *Tobacco Plant,* bound to Liverpool and Philadelphia, for two dollars a month less wages, worse treatment, and no grog. So much for following the fashion. The voyage produced nothing to be mentioned.

On my return to Philadelphia, I resolved to shift my ground, and try a new tack. I was now thirty-four, and began to give up all thoughts of getting a lift in my profession. I had got so many stern-boards on me, every time I was going ahead, and was so completely alone in the world, that I had become indifferent, and had made up my mind to take things as they offered. As for money, my rule had come to be, to spend it as I got it, and go to sea for more. "If I tumbled overboard," I said to myself, "there is none to cry over me;" therefore let things jog on their own course. All the disposition to morality that had been aroused within me, at Philadelphia, was completely gone, and I thought as little of church and of religion, as ever. It is true I had bought a Bible on board the *Superior,* and I was in the practice of reading in it, from time to time, though it was only the narratives, such as those of Sampson and Goliath, that formed any interest for me. The history of Jonah and the whale, I read at least twenty times. I cannot remember that the morality, or thought, or devotion of a single passage ever struck me on these occasions. In word, I read this sacred book for amusement, and not for light.

I now wanted change, and began to think of going back to the navy, by way of novelty. I had been round the world once, had been to Canton five timas, doubling the Cape, round the Horn twice, to Batavia once, the West-Indies, on the Spanish main, and had crossed the Atlantic so often, that I thought I knew all the mile-stones. I had seen but little of the Mediterranean, and fancied a man-of-war's cruise would show me those seas. Most of the Tobacco Plants had shipped in Philadelphia, and I determined to go with them, to go in the navy. There is a fashion in all things, and just then it was the fashion to enter in the service.

I was shipped by Lieutenant M'Kean, now Commander M'Kean, a grandson of the old Governor of Pennsylvania, as they tell me. All hands of us were sent on board the *Cyane,* an English prize twenty-gun ship, where we remained about six weeks. A draft was then made, and more than a hundred of us were sent round to Norfolk, in a sloop, to join the *Delaware,* 80, then fitting out for the Mediterranean. We found the ship lying alongside the Navy-yard wharf, and after passing one night in the receiving-ship, were sent on board the two-decker. The *Delaware* soon hauled out, and was turned over to Captain Downes, the very officer who had almost persuaded me to go in that ill-fated brig, the *Epervier.*

I was stationed on the *Delaware*'s forecastle, and was soon ordered to do second captain's duty. We had for lieutenants on board, Mr. Ramage, first, Messrs. Williamson, Ten Eick, Shubrick, Byrne, Chauncey, Harris, and several whose names I have forgotten. Mr. Ramage has since been cashiered, I understand; and Messrs. Ten Eick, Shubrick, Chauncey, Harris, and Byrne, are now all commanders.

The ship sailed in the winter of 1828, in the month of January I think, having on board the Prince of Musignano, and his family, who were going to Italy. This gentleman was Charles Bonaparte, eldest son of Lucien, Prince of Canino, they tell me, and is now Prince of Canino himself. He had been living some time in America, and got a passage in our ship, on account of the difficulty of travelling in Europe, for one of his name and family. He was the first, and only Prince I ever had for a shipmate.

CHAPTER XV

OUR PASSAGE OUT IN THE *DELAWARE* WAS VERY ROUGH, the ship rolling heavily.[1] It was the first time she had been at sea, and it required some little time to get her trim and sailing. She turned out, however, to be a good vessel; sailing fairly, steering well, and proving an excellent sea-boat. We went into Algeciras, where we lay only twenty-four hours. We then sailed for Mahon, but were met by orders off the port, to proceed to Leghorn and land our passengers. I have been told this was done on account of the Princess of Musignano's being a daughter of the ex-King of Spain, and it was not thought delicate to bring her within

1. A 74-gun ship-of-the-line constructed at Norfolk and launched in 1820. Myers signed for a three-year (1827–1829) cruise in the flagship of Commodore William M. Crane, who also served with Chauncey on Lake Ontario. Myers does not mention Crane's role on Lake Ontario, where he commanded the corvette *Madison* and later the *General Pike,* but does mention Mervine Mix, formerly a sailing master on the lakes, who was First Lieutenant of the *Delaware.* Myers's comment on this cruise was typical of his attitude toward naval service. "The treatment on board this ship was excellent. The happiest time I ever spent at sea was in the *Delaware.*"

the territory of the reigning king. I have even heard that the commodore was offered an order of knighthood for the delicacy he manifested on this occasion, which offer he declined accepting, as a matter of course.

The ship had a good run from off Mahon to Leghorn, where we anchored in the outer roads. We landed the passengers the afternoon of the day we arrived. That very night it came on to blow heavily from the northward and eastward, or a little off shore, according to the best of my recollection. This was the first time I ever saw preparations made to send down lower yards, and to house top-masts—merchantmen not being strong-handed enough to cut such capers with their sticks. We had three anchors ahead, if not four, the ship labouring a good deal. We lost one man from the starboard forechains, by his getting caught in the buoy-rope, as we let go a sheet-anchor. The poor fellow could not be picked up, on account of the sea and the darkness of the night, though an attempt was made to save him.

The next day the weather moderated a little, and we got under way for Mahon. Our passage down was pleasant, and this time we went in. Captain Downes now left us, and Commodore Crane hoisted his broad-pennant on board us. The ship now lay a long time in port. The commodore went aloft in one of the sloops, and was absent several months. I was told he was employed in making a treaty with the Turks, but us poor Jacks knew little of such matters. On his return, there was a regular blow-up with the first-lieutenant, who left the ship, to nobody's regret, so far as I know. Mr. Mix, who had led our party to the lakes in 1812, and was with us in all my lake service, and who was Mr. Osgood's brother-in-law, now joined us as first-lieutenant. I had got to be first-captain of the forecastle, a berth I held to the end of the cruise.

The treatment on board this ship was excellent. The happiest time I ever spent at sea, was in the *Delaware*. After Mr. Mix took Mr. Ramage's place, everybody seemed contented, and I never knew a better satisifed ship's company. The third year out, we had a long cruise off Cape de Gatte, keeping the ship under her canvass quite three months. We took in supplies at sea, the object being to keep us from getting rusty. On the fourth of July we had regular holiday. At four in the morning, the ship was close in under the north shore, and we were off the land. Sail was then shortened. After this, we had music, and more saluting and grog. The day was passed merrily, and I do not remember a fight, or a black eye, in the ship.

I volunteered to go one cruise in the *Warren,* under Mr. Byrne. The present Commodore Kearny commanded this ship, and he took us down to the Rock. The reason of our volunteering was this. The men-of-war of the Dutch and the French, rendezvoused at Mahon, as well as ourselves. The French and our people had several rows ashore. Which was right and which wrong, I cannot say, as it was the *Java*'s men, and not the *Delaware*'s, that were engaged in them, on our side. One of the Javas was run through the body, and a French officer got killed. It was said the French suspected us of a design of sending away the man who killed their officer, and meant to stop the *Warren,* which was bound to the Rock on duty. All I know is, that two French brigs anchored at the mouth of the harbour, and some of us were called on to volunteer. Forty-five of us did so, and went on board the sloop.

After the *Warren* got under way, we went to quarters, manning both batteries. In this manner we stood down between the two French brigs, with top-gallant-sails furled and the courses in the brails. We passed directly between the two brigs, keeping a broadside trained upon each; but nothing was said, or done, to us. We anchored first at the Rock, but next day crossed over to the Spanish coast. In a short time we returned to Mahon, and we volunteers went back to the *Delaware.* The two brigs had gone, but there was still a considerable French force in port. Nothing came of the difficulty, however, so far as I could see or hear.

In the season of 1830, the *Constellation,* Commodore Biddle, came out, and our ship and commodore were relieved. We had a run up as far as Sicily, however, before this took place, and went off Tripoli. There I saw a wreck, lying across the bay, that they told me was the bones of the *Philadelphia* frigate. We were also at Leghorn, several weeks, the commodore going to some baths in the neighbourhood, for his health.

Among other ports, the *Delaware* visited Carthagena, Malta, and Syracuse. At the latter place, the ship lay six weeks, I should think. This was the season of our arrival out. Here we underwent a course of severe exercise, that brought the crew up to a high state of discipline. At four in the morning, we would turn out, and commence our work. All the manœuvres of unmooring, making sail, reefing, furling, and packaging on her again, were gone through, until the people got so much accustomed to work together, the great secret of the efficiency of a man-of-war, that the officer of the deck was forced to sing out "belay!" before the yards were up by a foot, lest the men should spring the spars. When we got through this drill, the commodore told us we would do, and that he was not ashamed to show us alongside of anything that floated. I do not pretend to give our movements in the order in which they occurred, however, nor am I quite certain what year it was the commodore went up to Smyrna. On reflection, it may have been later than I have stated.

Our cruise off Cape de Gatte was one of the last things we did; and when we came back to Mahon, we took in supplies for America. We made the southern passage home, and anchored in Hampton Roads, in the winter of 1831. I believe the whole crew of the *Delaware* was sorry when the cruise was up. There are always a certain number of 'longshore chaps in a man-of-war, who are never satisfied with discipline, and the wholesome restraints of a ship; but as for us old salts, I never heard one give the *Delaware* a bad name. We had heard an awful report of the commodore, who was called a "burster," and expected sharp times under him; and his manner of taking possession was of a nature to alarm us. All hands had been called to receive him, and the first words he said were "Call all hands to witness punishment." A pin might have been heard falling among us, for this sounded ominous. It was to clear the brig, only, Captain Downes having left three men in it, whom he would not release on quitting the vessel. The offences were serious, and could not be overlooked. These three chaps got it; but there was only one other man brought regularly to the gangway while I was in the ship, and he was under the sentence of a court, and belonged to the *Warren.* As soon as the brig was cleared, the commodore told us we should be treated as we treated others, and then turned away among the officers. The next day we found we were to live under a just rule, and that satisfied us. One of the great causes of the contentment that reigned in the ship, was the method, and the regularity of the hours observed. The men knew on what they could calculate, in ordinary times, and this left them their own masters within certain hours. I repeat, she was the happiest ship I ever served in, though I have always found good treatment in the navy.

I can say conscientiously, that were my life to be passed over again, without the hope of commanding a vessel, it should be passed in the navy. The food is better, the service is lighter, the treatment is better, if a man behave himself at all well, he is better cared for, has a port under his lee in case of accidents, and gets good, steady, wages, with the certainty of being paid. If his ship is lost, his wages are safe; and if he gets hurt, he is pensioned. Then he is pretty certain of having gentlemen over him, and that is a great deal for any man. He has good quarters below; and if he serve in a ship as large as a frigate, he has a cover over his head, half the time, at least, in bad weather. This is the honest opinion of one who has served in all sorts of crafts, liners, Indiamen, coasters, smugglers, whalers, and transient ships. I have been in a ship of the line, two frigates, three sloops of war, and several smaller craft; and such is the result of all my experience in Uncle Sam's navy. No man can go to sea and always meet with fair weather, but he will get as little of foul in one of our vessels of war, as in any craft that floats, if a man only behave himself. I think the American merchantmen give better wages than are to be found in other services; and I think the American men-of-war, as a rule, give better treatment than the American merchantman. God bless the flag, I say, and this, too, without the fear of being hanged!

The *Delaware* lay two or three weeks in the Roads before she went up to the Yard. At the latter place we began to strip the ship. While thus employed, we were told that seventy-five of us, whose times were not quite out, were to be drafted for the *Brandywine,* 44, then fitting out at New York, for a short cruise in the Gulf. This was bad news, for Jack likes a swing ashore after a long service abroad. Go we must, and did, however. We were sent round to New York in a schooner, and found the frigate still lying at the Yard. We were hulked on board the *Hudson* until she was ready to receive us, when we were sent to our new vessel. Captain Ballard commanded the *Brandywine,* and among her lieutenants, Mr. M'Kenny was the first. This is a fine ship, and she got her name from the battle in which La Fayette was wounded in this country, having been first fitted out to carry him to France, after his last visit to America. She is a first-class frigate, mounting thirty long thirty-two's on her gun-deck; and I conceive it to be some honour to a sailor to have it in his power to say he has been captain of the forecastle in such a ship, for I was rated in this frigate the same as I had been rated in the *Delaware;* with this difference, that, for my service in the *Brandywine,* I received my regular eighteen dollars a month as a petty officer; whereas, though actually captain of the *Delaware*'s forecastle for quite two years, and second-captain nearly all the rest of the time I was in the ship, I never got more than seaman's wages, or twelve dollars a month. I do not know how this happened, though I supposed it to have arisen from some mistake connected with the circumstance that I was paid off for my services in the *Delaware,* by the purser of the frigate. This was in consequence of the transfer.

The *Brandywine* sailed in March for the Gulf. Our cruise lasted about five months, during which time we went to Vera Cruz, Pensacola, and the Havana. We appeared to me to be a single ship, as we were never in squadron, and saw no broad-pennant. No accident happened, the cruise being altogether pleasant. The ship returned to Norfolk, and twenty-five of us, principally old Delawares, were discharged, our times being out. We all of us intended to return to the frigate, after a cruise ashore, and we chartered a schooner to carry us to Philadelphia in a body, determining not to part company.

The morning the schooner sailed, I was leading the whole party along one of the streets of Norfolk, when I saw something white lying in the middle of the carriage-way. It turned out to be an old messmate, Jack Dove, who had been discharged three days before, and had left us to go to Philadelphia, but had been brought up by King Grog. While we were overhauling the poor fellow, who could not speak, his landlady came out to us, and told us that he had eat nothing for three days, and did nothing but drink. She begged us to take care of him, as he disregarded all she said. This honest woman gave us Jack's wages to a cent, for I knew what they had come to; and we made a collection of ten dollars for her, calculating that Jack must have swallowed that much in three days. Jack we took with us, bag and hammock; but he would eat nothing on the passage, calling out constantly for drink. We gave him liquor, thinking it would do him good; but he grew worse, and, when we reached Philadelphia, he was sent to the hospital. Here, in the course of a few days, he died.

Never, in all my folly and excesses, did I give myself so much up to drink, as when I reached Philadelphia this time. I was not quite as bad as Jack Dove, but I soon lost my appetite, living principally on liquor. When we heard of Jack's death, we proposed among ourselves to give him a sailor's funeral. We turned out, accordingly, to the number of a hundred, or more, in blue jackets and white trowsers, and marched up to the hospital in a body. I was one of the leaders in this arrangement, and felt much interest in it, as Jack had been my messmate; but, the instant I saw his coffin, a fit of the "horrors" came over me, and I actually left the place, running down street towards the river, as if pursued by devils. Luckily, I stopped to rest on the stoop of a druggist. The worthy man took me in, gave me some soda water, and some good advice. When a little strengthened, I made my way home, but gave up at the door. Then followed a severe indisposition, which kept me in bed for a fortnight, during which I suffered the torments of the damned.

I have had two or three visits from the "horrors," in the course of my life, but nothing to equal this attack. I came near following Jack Dove to the grave, but God, in His mercy, spared me from such an end. It is not possible for one who has never experienced the effects of his excesses, in this particular form, to get any correct notions of the sufferings I endured. Among other conceits, I thought the colour which the tar usually leaves on seamen's nails, was the sign that I had the yellow fever. This idea haunted me for days, and gave me great uneasiness. In short, I was like a man suspended over a yawning chasm, expecting, every instant, to fall and be dashed to pieces, and yet, who could not die.

For some time after my recovery, I could not bear the smell of liquor; but evil companions lured me back to my old habits. I was soon in a bad way again, and it was only owing to the necessity of going to sea, that I had not a return of the dreadful malady. When I shipped in the *Delaware,* I had left my watch, quadrant, and good clothes, to the value of near two hundred dollars, with my present landlord, and he now restored them all to me, safe and sound. I made considerable additions to the stock of clothes, and when I again went to sea, left the whole, and more, with the same landlord.

Our plan of going back to the *Brandywine* was altered by circumstances; and a party of us shipped in the *Monongahela,* a Liverpool liner, out of Philadelphia. The cabin of this vessel was taken by two gentlemen, going to visit Europe, viz.: Mr. Hare Powell and Mr. Edward Burd; and getting these passengers, with their families, on board, the ship sailed. By this time, I had pretty much given up the hope of preferment, and did not trouble myself whether I lived forward or aft. I joined the *Monongahela* as a forward hand, therefore, quite as well satisfied as if her chief mate.

We left the Delaware in the month of August, and, a short time out, encountered one of the heaviest gales of wind I ever witnessed at sea. It came on from the eastward, and would have driven us ashore, had not the wind suddenly shifted to south-west. The ship was lying-to, under bare poles, pressed down upon the water in such a way that she lay almost as steady as if in a river; nor did the force of the wind allow the sea to get up. A part of the time, our lee lower yard-arms were nearly in the water. We had everything aloft, but sending them down was quite out of the question. It was not possible, at one time, for a man to go aloft at all. I tried it myself, and could with difficulty keep my feet on the ratlines. I make no doubt I should have been blown out of the top, could I have reached it, did I let go my hold to do any work.

We had sailed in company with the *Kensington,* a corvette belonging to the Emperor of Russia, and saw a ship, during the gale, that was said to be she. The *Kensington* was dismasted, and had to return to refit, but we did not part a rope-yarn. When the wind shifted, we were on soundings; and, it still continuing to blow a gale, we set the main-top-sail close-reefed, and the fore-sail, and shoved the vessel off the land at the rate of a steam-boat. After this, the wind favoured us, and our passage out was very short. We stayed but a few days in Liverpool; took in passengers, and got back to Philadelphia, after an absence of a little more than two months. The *Kensington*'s report of the gale, and of our situation, had caused much uneasiness in Philadelphia, but our two passages were so short, that we brought the news of our safety.

I now inquired for the *Brandywine,* but found she had sailed for the Mediterranean. It was my intention to have gone on board her, but missing this ship, and a set of officers that I knew, I looked out for a merchantman. I found a brig called the *Amelia,* bound to Bordeaux, and shipped in her before the mast.

The *Amelia* had a bad passage out. It was in the autumn, and the brig leaked badly. This kept us a great deal at the pumps, an occupation that a sailor does anything but delight in. I am of opinion that pumping a leaky ship is the most detestable work in the world. Nothing but the dread of drowning ought to make a man do it, although some men will pump to save their property. As for myself, I am not certain I would take twenty-four hours of hard pumping to save any sum I shall probably ever own, or ever did own.

After a long passage, we made the Cordovan, but, the wind blowing heavy off the land, we could not get in for near a fortnight. Not a pilot would come out, and if they had, it would have done us no good. After a while, the wind shifted, and we got into the river, and up to the town. We took in a return cargo of brandy, and sailed for Philadelphia. Our homeward-bound passage was long and stormy, but we made the capes, at last. Here we were boarded by a pilot, who told us we were too late; the Delaware had frozen up, and we had to keep away, with a south-east wind, for New York. We had a bad time of it, as soon as night came on. The gale increased, blowing directly into the bight, and we had to haul up under close-reefed topsails and reefed fore-sail, to claw off the land. The weather was very thick, and the night dark, and all we could do was to get round, when the land gave us a hint it was time. This we generally did in five fathoms water. We had to ware, for the brig would not tack under such short canvss, and, of course, lost much ground in so doing. About three in the morning we knew that it was nearly up with us. The soundings gave warning of this, and we got round, on what I supposed would be the *Amelia*'s last leg. But Providence took care of us, when we could not help ourselves. The wind came out at north-west, as it might be by word of command; the mist cleared up, and we saw the lights, for the first time, close aboard us. The brig was taken aback, but we got her round, shortened sail, and hove her to, under a close-reefed main-topsail. We now got it from the northwest, making very bad weather. The gale must have set us a long way to leeward, as we did not get in for a fortnight. We shipped a heavy sea, that stove our boat, and almost swept the decks. We were out of pork and beef, and our fire-wood was nearly gone. The binnacle was also gone. As good luck would have it, we killed a porpoise, soon after the wind shifted, and on this we lived, in a great measure, for more than a week, sometimes cooking it, but oftener eating it raw. At length the wind shifted, and we got in.

I was no sooner out of this difficulty, than a hasty temper got me into another. While still in the stream, an Irish boatman called me a "Yankee son of a ———," and I lent him a clip. The fellow sued me, and, contriving to catch me before I left the vessel, I was sent to jail, for the first and only time in my life. This turned out to be a new and very revolting school for me. I was sent among as precious a set of rascals as New York could furnish. Their conversation was very edifying. One would tell how he cut the hoses of the engines at fires, with razor-blades fastened to his shoes; another, how many pocket-books he and his associates had taken at this or that fire; and a third, the manner of breaking open stores, and the best mode of disposing of stolen goods. The cool, open, impudent manner in which these fellows spoke of such transactions, fairly astounded me. They must have thought I was in jail for some crime similar to their own, or they would not have talked so freely before a stranger. These chaps seemed to value a man by the enormity and number of his crimes.

At length the captain and my landlord found out where I had been sent, and I was immediately bailed. Glad enough was I to get out of prison, and still more so to get out of the company I found in it. Such association is enough to undermine the morals of a saint, in a week or two. And yet these fellows were well dressed, and well enough looking, and might very well pass for a sort of gentlemen, with those who had seen but little of men of the true quality.

I had got enough of law, and wished to push the matter no farther. The Irishman was sent for, and I compromised with him on the spot. The whole affair cost me my entire wages, and I was bound over to keep the peace, for, I do not know how long. This scrape compelled me to weigh my anchor at a short notice, as there is no living in New York without money. I went on board the *Sully,* therefore—a Havre liner—a day or two after getting out of the atmosphere of the City Hall. They may talk of Batavia, if they please; but, in my judgment, it is the healthiest place of the two.

Our passages, out and home, produced nothing worth mentioning, and I left the ship in New York. My wages went in the old way, and then I shipped in a schooner called the *Susan and Mary,* that was about to sail for Buenos Aires, in the expectation that she would be sold there. The craft was a good one, though our passage out was very long. On reaching our port, I took my discharge, under the impression the vessel would be sold. A notion now came over me, that I would join the Buenos Airean navy, in order to see what sort of a service it was. I knew it was a mixed American and English affair, and, by this time, I had become very reckless as to my own fate. I wished to do nothing very wrong, but was incapable of doing anything that was very right.

My windfall carried me on board a schooner, of eight or ten guns, called the *Suradaha*. I did not ship, making an arrangement by which I was to be left to decide for myself, whether I would remain in her, or not. Although a pretty good craft, I soon got enough of this service. In one week I was thoroughly disgusted, and left the schooner. It is well I did, as there was a "*revolution*" on board of her, a few days later, and she was carried up the river, and, as I was told, was there sunk. With her, sunk all my laurels in that service.

The *Susan and Mary* was not sold, but took in hides for New York. I returned to her, therefore, and we sailed for home in due time. The passage proved long, but mild, and we were compelled to run in, off Point Petre, Guadaloupe, where we took in some provisions. After this, nothing occurred until we reached New York.

I now shifted the name of my craft, end for end, joining a half-rigged brig, called the *Mary and Susan*. I gained little by the change, this vessel being just the worst-looking hooker I did ever sail in. Still she was tight, strong enough, and not a very bad sailing vessel. But, for some reason or other, externals were not regarded, and we made anything but a holiday appearance on the water. I had seen the time when I would disdain to go chief-mate of such a looking craft; but I now shipped in her as a common hand.

We sailed for Para, in Brazil, a port nearly under the line, having gunpowder, dry-goods, &c. Our passage, until we came near the coast of South America, was good, and nothing occurred to mention. When under the line, however, we made a rakish-looking schooner, carrying two top-sails, one forenoon. We made no effort to escape, knowing it to be useless. The schooner set a Spanish ensign, and brought us to. We were ordered to lower our boat and to go on board the schooner, which were done. I happened to be at the helm, and remained in the *Mary and Susan.* The strangers ordered our people out of the boat, and sent an armed party in her, on board us. These men rummaged about for a short time, and then were hailed from their vessel to know if we promised well. Our looks deceived the head man of the boarders, who answered that we were *very* poor. On receiving this information, the captain of the schooner ordered his boarding party to quit us. Our boat came back, but was ordered to return and bring another gang of the strangers. This time we were questioned about canvass, but got off by concealing the truth. We had thirty bolts on board, but produced only one. The bolt shown did not happen to suit, and the strangers again left us. We were told not to make sail until we received notice by signal, and the schooner hauled her wind. After standing on some time, however, these gentry seemed indisposed to quit us, for they came down again, and rounded to on our weather-beam. We were now questioned about our longitude, and whether we had a chronometer. We gave the former, but had nothing like the latter on board. Telling us once more not to make sail without the signal, the schooner left us, standing on until fairly out of sight. We waited until she sunk her topsails, and then went on our course.

None of us doubted that this fellow was a pirate. The men on board us were an ill-looking set of rascals, of all countries. They spoke Spanish, but we gave them credit for being a mixture. Our escape was probably owing to our appearance, which promised anything but a rich booty. Our dry-goods and powder were concealed in casks under the ballast, and I suppose the papers were not particularly minute. At any rate, when we got into Para, most of the cargo went out of our schooner privately, being landed from lighters. We had a passenger, who passed for some revolutionary man, who also landed secretly. This gentleman was in a good deal of concern about the pirates, keeping himself hid while they were near us.

CHAPTER XVI

OUR PASSAGE FROM PARA WAS GOOD until the brig reached the latitude of Bermuda. Here, one morning, for the first time in this craft, Sundays excepted, we got a forenoon watch below. I was profiting by the opportunity to do a little work for myself, when the mate, an inexperienced young man, who was connected with the owners, came and ordered us up to help jibe ship. It was easy enough to do this in the watch, but he thought differently. As an old seaman, I do not hesitate to say that the order was both inconsiderate and unnecessary; though I do not wish to appear even to justify my own conduct, on the occasion. A hasty temper is one of my besetting weaknesses, and, at that time, I was in no degree influenced by any considerations of a moral nature, as connected with language. Exceedingly exasperated at this interference with our comfort, I did not hesitate to tell the mate my opinion of his order. Warming with my own complaints, I soon became fearfully profane and denunciatory. I called down curses on the brig, and all that belonged to her, not hesitating about wishing that she might founder at sea, and carry all hands of us to the bottom of the ocean. In a word, I indulged in all that looseness and profanity of the tongue, which is common enough with those who feel no restraints on the subject, and who are highly exasperated.

I do think the extent to which I carried my curses and wishes, on this occasion, frightened the officers. They said nothing, but let me curse myself out, to my heart's content. A man soon wearies of so bootless a task, and the storm passed off, like one in the heavens, with a low rumbling. I gave myself no concern about the matter afterwards, but things took their course until noon. While the people were at dinner, the mate came forward again, however, and called all hands to shorten sail. Going on deck, I saw a very menacing black cloud astern, and went to work, with a will, to discharge a duty that everybody could see was necessary.

We gathered in the canvass as fast as we could; but, before we could get through, and while I was lending a hand to furl the foresail, the squall struck the brig. I call it a squall, but it was more like the tail of a hurricane. Most of our canvass blew from the gaskets, the cloth going in ribands. The foresail and fore-topsail we managed to save, but all our light canvass went. I was still aloft when the brig broached-to. As she came up to the wind, the fore-topmast went over to leeward, being carried away at the cap. All the hamper came down, and began to thresh against the larboard side of the lower rigging. Just at this instant, a sea seemed to strike the brig under her bilge, and fairly throw her on her beam-ends.

All this appeared to me to be the work of only a minute. I had scrambled to windward, to get out of the way of the wreck, and stood with one foot on the upper side of the bitts, holding on, to steady myself, by some of the running rigging. This was being in a very different attitude, but on the precise spot, where, two or three hours before, I had called on the Almighty to pour out his vials of wrath upon the vessel, myself, and all she contained! At that fearful instant, conscience pricked me, and I felt both shame and dread, at my recent language. It seemed to me as if I had been heard, and that my impious prayers were about to be granted. In the bitterness of my heart, I vowed, should my life be spared, never to be guilty of such gross profanity, again.

These feelings, however, occupied me but a moment. I was too much of a real sea-dog to be standing idle at a time like that. There was but one man before the mast on whom I could call for anything in such a strait, and that was a New Yorker, of the name of Jack Neal. This man was near me, and I suggested to him the plan of getting the fore-top-mast staysail loose, notwithstanding the mast was gone, in the hope it might blow open, and help the brig's bows round. Jack was a fellow to act, and he succeeded in loosening the sail, which did blow out in a way greatly to help us, as I think. I then proposed we should clamber aft, and try to get the helm up. This we did, also; though I question if the rudder could have had much power, in the position in which the brig lay.

Either owing to the fore-top mast staysail, or to some providential sea, the vessel did fall off, however, and presently she righted, coming up with great force, with a heavy roll to windward. The staysail helped us, I feel persuaded, as the stay had got taut in the wreck, and the wind had blown out the hanks. The brig's helm being hard up, as soon as she got way, the craft flew round like a top, coming up on the other tack, in spite of us, and throwing her nearly over again. She did not come fairly down, however, though I thought she was gone, for an instant.

Finding it possible to move, I now ran forward, and succeeded in stopping the wreck into the rigging and bitts. At this time the brig minded her helm, and fell off, coming under command. To help us, the head of the spencer got loose, from the throat-brail up, and, blowing out against the wreck, the whole formed, together, a body of hamper, that acted as a sort of sail, which helped the brig to keep clear of the seas.[1] By close attention to the helm, we were enabled to prevent the vessel from broaching-to again, and, of course, managed to sail her on her bottom. About sunset, it moderated, and, next morning, the weather was fine. We then went to work, and rigged jury-masts; reaching New York a few days later.

Had this accident occurred to our vessel in the night, as did that to the *Scourge,* our fate would probably have been decided in a few minutes. As it was, half an hour, in the sort of sea that was going, would have finished her. As for my repentance, if I can use the term on such an occasion, and for such a feeling, it was more lasting than thorough. I have never been so fearfully profane since; and often, when I have felt the disposition to give way to passion in this revolting form, my feelings, as I stood by those bitts, have recurred to my mind—my vow has been remembered, and I hope, together, they did some good, until I was made to see the general errors of my life, and the necessity of throwing all my sins on the merciful interposition of my Saviour.

I was not as reckless and extravagant, this time, in port, as I had usually been, of late years. I shipped, before my money was all gone, on board the *Henry Kneeland,* for Liverpool, viâ New Orleans. On reaching the latter port, all hands of us were beset by the land-sharks, in the shape of landlords, who told us how much better we should be off by running, than by sticking by the ship. We listened to these tales, and went in a body. What made the matter worse, and our conduct the less excusable, was the fact, that we got good wages and good treatment in the *Henry Kneeland.* The landlords came with two boats, in the night; we passed our dunnage down to them, and away we went, leaving only one man on board. The very next day we all shipped on board the *Marian,* United States' Revenue Cut-

1. Spanker, a fore-and-aft gaff-headed sail hoisted on the mizzen.

ter, where I was rated a quarter-mate, at fifteen dollars a month; leaving seventeen to obtain this preferment!

We got a good craft for our money, however. She was a large comfortable schooner, that mounted a few light guns, and our duty was far from heavy. The treatment turned out to be good, also, as some relief to our folly. One of our Henry Kneelands died of the "horrors" before we got to sea, and we buried him at the watering-place, near the lower bar. I must have been about four months in the *Marian,* during which time we visited the different keys, and went into Key West. At this place, our crew became sickly, and I was landed among others, and sent to a boarding-house. It was near a month before we could get the crew together again, when we sailed for Norfolk. At Norfolk, six of us had relapses, and were sent to the hospital; the cutter sailing without us. I never saw the craft afterwards.

I was but a fortnight in the hospital, the disease being only the fever and ague. Just as I came out, the *Alert,* the New York cutter, came in, and I was sent on board her. This separated me from all the Henry Kneelands but one old man. The *Alert* was bound south, on duty connected with the nullification troubles; and, soon after I joined her, she sailed for Charleston, South Carolina.[2] Here a little fleet of

2. On 24 November 1832, a convention created by the South Carolina legislature authorized the state to enact all laws necessary to enforce nullification. This would free South Carolina from having to obey the Tariff of 1832 enacted by the U.S. Congress. South Carolina declared it had the right to nullify acts of Congress that exceeded the grant of authority supposedly delegated by the states in the Constitution. President Jackson acted to prevent South Carolina from disregarding the laws of the United States, sending Commodore Jesse D. Elliott in the sloop-of-war *Natchez,* and the schooner *Experiment* to join the cutters. The crisis ended, thanks to a Henry Clay compromise tariff bill signed on 2 March 1833, giving the President power to collect the South Carolina customs while at the same time gradually reducing the tariff. South Carolina repealed its nullification ordinance on 15 March. With the threat of violence at an end, the navy allowed those sailors at Charleston who wished discharges to have them.

cutters soon collected; no less than seven of us being at anchor in the waters of South Carolina, to prevent any breach of the tariff laws. When I had been on board the *Alert* about a month, a new cutter called the *Jackson,* came in from New York, and being the finest craft on the station, our officers and crew were transferred to her in a body; our captain being the senior of all the revenue captains present.

I must have been at least six months in the waters of South Carolina, thus employed. We never went to sea, but occasionally dropped down as far as Rebellion Roads. We were not allowed to go ashore, except on rare occasions, and towards the last, matters got to be so serious, that we almost looked upon ourselves as in an enemy's country. Commodore Elliott joined the station in the *Natchez* sloop-of-war, and the *Experiment,* man-of-war schooner, also arrived and remained. After the arrival of the *Natchez,* the Commodore took command of all hands of us afloat, and we were kept in a state of high preparation for service. We were occasionally at quarters, nights, though I never exactly knew the reasons. It was said attacks on us were anticipated. General Scott was in the fort, and matters looked very warlike, for several weeks.

At length we got the joyful news that nullification had been thrown overboard, and that no more was to be apprehended. It seems that the crews of the different cutters had been increased for this particular service; but, now it was over, there were more men employed than Government had needed. We were told, in consequence, that those among us who wished our discharges, might have them on application.

I had been long enough in this 'long-shore service, and applied to be discharged, under this provision. My time was so near out, however, that I should have got away soon, in regular course.

I now went ashore at Charleston, and had my swig, as long as the money lasted. I gave myself no trouble about the ship's husband, whose collar-bone I had broken; nor do

I now know whether he was then living, or dead. In a word, I thought only of the present time; the past and the future being equally indifferent to me. My old landlord was dead; and I fell altogether into the hands of a new set. I never took the precaution to change my name, at any period of my life, with the exception, that I dropped the Robert, in signing shipping-articles. I also wrote my name Myers, instead of Meyers, as, I have been informed by my sister, was the true spelling. But this proceeded from ignorance, and not from intention. In all times, and seasons, and weathers, and services, I have sailed as Ned Myers; and as nothing else.

It soon became necessary to ship again; and I went on board the *Harriet and Jesse,* which was bound to Havre de Grace. This proved to be a pleasant, easy voyage; the ship coming back to New York filled with passengers, who were called Swiss; but most of whom, as I understand, came from Wurtemberg, Alsace, and the countries on the Rhine. On reaching New York, I went on to Philadelphia, to obtain the effects I had left there, when I went out in the *Amelia.* But my landlord was dead; his family was scattered; and my property had disappeared. I never knew who got it; but a quadrant, watch, and some entirely new clothes, went in the wreck. I suppose I lost, at least, two hundred dollars, in this way. What odds did it make to me? it would have gone in grog, if it had not gone in this manner.

I staid but a short time in Philadelphia, joining a brig, called the *Topaz,* bound to Havana. We arrived out, after a short passage; and here I was exposed to as strong a temptation to commit crime, as a poor fellow need encounter. A beautiful American-built brig, was lying in port, bound to Africa, for slaves. She was the loveliest craft I ever laid eyes on; and the very sight of her gave me a longing to go in her. She offered forty dollars a month, with the privilege of a slave and a half. I went so far as to try to get on board her; but met with some difficulty, in having my things seized.

The captain found it out; and, by pointing out to me the danger I ran, succeeded in changing my mind.

I will not deny, that I knew the trade was immoral; but so is smuggling; and I viewed them pretty much as the same thing, in this sense. I am now told, that the law of this country pronounces the American citizen, who goes in a slaver, a pirate; and treats him as such; which, to me, seems very extraordinary. I do not understand, how a Spaniard can do that, and be no pirate, which makes an American a pirate, if he be guilty of it. I feel certain, that very few sailors know in what light the law views slaving. Now, piracy is robbing, on the high seas, and has always been contrary to law; but slaving was encouraged by all nations, a short time since; and we poor tars look upon the change, as nothing but a change in policy. As for myself, I should have gone in that brig, in utter ignorance of the risks I ran, and believing myself to be about as guilty, in a moral sense, as I was when I smuggled tobacco, on the coast of Ireland, or opium in Canton.[3]

3. This is the reasoning of Ned. I have always looked upon the American law as erroneous in principle, and too severe in its penalties. Erroneous in principle, as piracy is a crime against the law of nations, and it is not legal for any one community to widen, or narrow, the action of international law. It is peculiarly the policy of this country, rigidly to observe this principle, since she has so many interests dependent on its existence. The punishment of death is too severe, when we consider that nabobs are among us, who laid the foundations of their wealth, as slaving *merchants,* when slaving *was* legal. Sudden mutations in morals, are not to be made by a dash of the pen; and even public sentiment can hardly be made to consider slaving much of a crime, in a slave-holding community. But, even the punishment of death might be inflicted, without arrogating to Congress a power to say what is, and what is not, piracy.

It will probably be said, the error is merely one of language; the jurisdiction being clearly legal. Is this true? Can Congress, legally or constitutionally, legislate for American citizens, when undeniably within the jurisdiction of foreign states? Admit this as a principle, and what is to prevent Congress from punishing acts, that it may be the

As the *Topaz* was coming out of the port of Havana, homeward bound, and just as she was abreast of the Moro, the brig carried away her bobstay. I was busy in helping to unreeve the stay, when I was seized with sudden and violent cramps. This attack proved to be the cholera, which came near carrying me off. The captain had me taken aft, where I was attended with the greatest care. God be praised for his mercy! I got well, though scarcely able to do any more duty before we got in.

A short voyage gives short commons; and I was soon obliged to look out for another craft. This time I shipped in the *Erie,* Captain Funk, a Havre liner, and sailed soon after. This was a noble ship, with the best of usage. Both our passages were pleasant, and give me nothing to relate. While I was at work in the hold, at Havre, a poor female passenger, who came to look at the ship, fell though the

---

policy of foreign countries to exact from even casual residents. If Congress can punish me, as a pirate, for slaving under a foreign flag, and in foreign countries, it can punish me for carrying arms against all American allies; and yet military service may be exacted of even an American citizen, resident in a foreign state, under particular circumstances. The same difficulty, in principle, may be extended to the whole catalogue of legal crime.

Congress exists only for specified purposes. It can *punish* piracy, but it cannot declare what shall, or shall not, be piracy; as this would be invading the authority of international law. Under the general power to pass laws, that are necessary to carry out the system, it can derive no authority; since there can be no legal necessity for any such double legislation, under the comity of nations. Suppose, for instance, England should legalize slaving, again. Could the United States claim the American citizen, who had engaged in slaving, under the English flag, and from a British port, under the renowned Ashburton treaty? Would England give such a man up? No more than she will now give up the slaves that run from the American vessel, which is driven in by stress of weather. One of the vices of philanthropy is to overreach its own policy, by losing sight of all collateral principles and interests. —EDITOR.

hatch, and was so much injured as to be left behind. I mention the circumstance merely to show how near I was to a meeting with my old shipmate, who is writing these pages, and yet missed him. On comparing notes, I find he was on deck when this accident happened, having come to see after some effects he was then shipping to New York. These very effects I handled, and supposed them to belong to a passenger who was to come home in the ship; but, as they were addressed to another name, I could not recognise them. Mr. Cooper did not come home in the *Erie,* but passed over to England, and embarked at London, and so I failed to see him.

In these liners, the captains wish to keep the good men of their crews as long as they can. We liked the *Erie* and her captain so much, that eight or ten of us stuck by the ship, and went out in her again. This time our luck was not so good. The passage out was well enough, but homeward-bound we had a hard time of it. While in Havre, too, we had a narrow escape. Christmas night, a fire broke out in the cabin, and came near smothering us all, forward, before we knew anything about it. Our chief mate, whose name was Everdy,[4] saved the vessel by his caution and exertions; the captain not getting on board until the fire had come to a head. We kept everything closed until an engine was ready, then cut away the deck, and sent down the hose. This expedient, with a free use of water, saved the ship. It is not known how the fire originated. A good deal of damage was done, and some property was lost.

Notwithstanding this accident, we had the ship ready for sea early in January, 1834. For the first week out, we met with head winds and heavy weather; so heavy, indeed, as to render it difficult to get rid of the pilot. The ship beat down channel with him on board, as low as the Eddystone. Here we saw the *Sully,* outward bound, running up channel be-

4. Ned's pronunciation.

fore the wind. Signals were exchanged, and our ship, which was then well off the land, ran in and spoke the *Sully.* We put our pilot on board this ship, which was doing a good turn all around. The afternoon proving fair, and the wind moderating, Captain Funk filled and stood in near to the coast, as his best tack. Towards night, however, the gale freshened, and blew into the bay, between the Start Point and the Lizard, in a heavy, steady manner.

The first thing was to ware off shore; after which, we were compelled to take in nearly all our canvass. The gale continued to increase, and the night set in dark. There were plenty of ports to leeward, but it was ticklish work to lose a foot of ground, unless one knew exactly where he was going. We had no pilot, and the captain decided to hold on. I have seldom known it to blow harder than it did that night; and, for hours, everything depended on our main-topsail's standing, which sail we had set, close-reefed. I did not see anything to guide us, but the compass, until about ten o'clock, when I caught a view of a light close on our lee bow. This was the Eddystone, which stands pretty nearly in a line between the Start and the Lizard, and rather more than three leagues from the land. As we headed, we might lay past, should everything stand; but, if our topsail went, we should have been pretty certain of fetching up on those famous rocks, where a three-decker would have gone to pieces in an hour's time in such a gale.

I suppose we passed the Eddystone at a safe distance, or the captain would not have attempted going to windward of it; but, to me, it appeared that we were fearfully near. The sea was breaking over the light tremendously, and could be plainly seen, as it flashed up near the lantern. We went by, however, surging slowly ahead, though our drift must have been very material.

The Start, and the point to the westward of it, were still to be cleared. They were a good way off, and but a little to leeward, as the ship headed. In smooth water, and with a whole-sail breeze, it would have been easy enough to lay past the Start, when at the Eddystone, with a south-west wind; but, in a gale, it is a serious matter, especially on a flood-tide. I know all hands of us, forward and aft, looked upon our situation as very grave. We passed several uneasy hours, after we lost sight of the Eddystone, before we got a view of the land near the Start. When I saw it, the heights appeared like a dark cloud hanging over us, and I certainly thought the ship was gone. At this time, the captain and mate consulted together, and the latter came to us, in a very calm, steady manner, and said—"Come, boys; we may as well go ashore without masts as with them, and our only hope is in getting more canvass to stand. We must turn-to, and make sail on the ship."

Everybody was in motion on this hint, and the first thing we did was to board fore-tack. The clews of that sail came down as if so many giants had hold of the tack and sheet. We set it, double-reefed, which made it but a rag of a sail, and yet the ship felt it directly. We next tried the fore-topsail, close-reefed, and this stood. It was well we did, for I feel certain the ship was now in the ground-swell. That black hill seemed ready to fall on our heads. We tried the mizzen-topsail, but we found it would not do, and we furled it again, not without great difficulty. Things still looked serious, the land drawing nearer and nearer; and we tried to get the mainsail, double-reefed, on the ship. Everybody mustered at the tack and sheet, and we dragged down that bit of cloth as if it had been muslin. The good ship now quivered like a horse that is over-ridden, but in those liners everything is strong, and everything stood. I never saw spray thrown from a ship's bows, as it was thrown from the *Erie*'s that night. We had a breathless quarter of an hour after the mainsail was set, everybody looking to see what would go first. Every rope and bolt in the craft was tried to the utmost, but all stood! At the most critical moment, we caught a glimpse of a light in a house that was known to stand near the Start; and the mate came among us, pointed it out, and said, if we weathered *that,* we should go clear. After hearing this, my eyes were never off that light, and glad was I to see it slowly drawing more astern, and more under our lee. At last we got it on our quarter, and knew that we had gone clear! The gloomy-looking land disappeared to leeward, in a deep, broad bay, giving us plenty of sea-room.

We now took in canvass, to ease the ship. The mainsail and fore-topsail were furled, leaving her to jog along under the main-topsail, foresail, and fore-topmast staysail. I look upon this as one of my narrowest escapes from shipwreck; and I consider the escape, under the mercy of God, to have been owing to the steadiness of our officers, and the goodness of the ship and her outfit. It was like pushing a horse to the trial of every nerve and sinew, and only winning the race under whip and spur. Wood, and iron, and cordage, and canvass, can do no more than they did that night.

Next morning, at breakfast, the crew talked the matter over. We had a hard set in this ship, the men being prime seamen, but of reckless habits and characters. Some of the most thoughtless among them admitted that they had prayed secretly for succour, and, for myself, I am most thankful that *I* did. These confessions were made half-jestingly, but I believe them to have been true, judging from my own case. It may sound bravely in the ears of the thoughtless and foolish, to boast of indifference on such occasions; but, few men can face death under circumstances like those in which we were placed, without admitting to themselves, however reluctantly, that there is a Power above, on which they must lean for personal safety, as well as for spiritual support. More than usual care was had for the future welfare of sailors among the Havre liners, there being a mariners' church at Havre, at which our captain always attended, as well as his mates; and efforts were made to make us go also. The effect was good, the men being better behaved, and more sober, in consequence.

The wind shifted a day or two after this escape, giving us a slant that carried us past Scilly, fairly out into the Atlantic. A fortnight or so after our interview with the Eddystone we carried away the pintals of the rudder, which was saved only by the modern invention that prevents the head from dropping, by means of the deck. To prevent the strain, and to get some service from the rudder, however, we found it necessary to sling the latter, and to breast it into the stern-post by means of purchases. A spar was laid athwart the coach-house, directly over the rudder, and we rove a chain through the tiller-hole, and passed it over this spar. For this purpose the smallest chain-cable was used, the rudder being raised from the deck by means of sheers. We then got a set of chain-topsail sheets, parcelled them well, and took a clove hitch with them around the rudder, about half-way up. One end was brought into each main-chain, and set up by tackles. In this manner the wheel did tolerably well, though we had to let the ship lie-to in heavy weather.

The chain sheets held on near a month, and then gave way. On examination, it was found that the parcelling had gone under the ship's counter, and that the copper had nearly destroyed the iron. After this, we mustered all the chains of the ship, of proper size, parcelled them very thoroughly, got another clove hitch around the rudder as before, and brought the ends to the hawse-holes, letting the bights fall, one on each side of the ship's keel. The ends were next brought to the windlass and hove taut. This answered pretty well, and stood until we got the ship into New York. Our whole passage was stormy, and lasted seventy days, as near as I can recollect. The ship was almost given up when we got in, and great was the joy at our arrival.

As the *Erie* lost her turn, in consequence of wanting repairs, most of us went on board the *Henry IVth,* in the same line. This voyage was comfortable, and successful, a fine ship and good usage. On our return to New York most of us went back to the *Erie,* liking both vessel and captain, as well as her other officers. I went twice more to Havre and back in this ship, making four voyages in her in all. At the end of the fourth voyage our old mate left us, to do business ashore, and we took a dislike to his successor, though it was without trying him. The mate we lost had been a great favourite, and we seemed to think if he went we must go too. At any rate, nearly all hands went to the *Silvie de Grasse,* where we got another good ship, good officers, and good treatment. In fact, all these Havre liners were very much alike in these respects, the *Silvie de Grasse* being the fourth in which I had then sailed, and to me they all seemed as if they belonged to the same family. I went twice to Havre in this ship also, when I left her for the *Normandy,* in the same line. I made this change in consequence of an affair about some segars in Havre, in which I had no other concern than to father another man's fault. The captain treated me very handsomely, but my temperament is such that I am apt to fly off in a tangent when anything goes up stream. It was caprice that took me from the *Silvie de Grasse,* and put me in her sisterliner.

I liked the *Normandy* as well as the rest of these liners, except that the vessel steered badly. I made only one voyage in her, however, as will be seen in the next chapter.

CHAPTER XVII

I HAD NOW BEEN NO LESS THAN EIGHT VOYAGES in the Havre trade, without intermission. So regular had my occupation become, that I began to think I was a part of a liner myself. I liked the treatment, the food, the ships, and the officers. Whenever we got home, I worked in the ship, at day's work, until paid off; after which, no more was seen of Ned until it was time to go on board to sail. When I got in, in the *Normandy,* it happened as usual, though I took a short swing only. Mr. Everdy, our old mate in the *Erie,* was working gangs of stevedores, riggers, &c., ashore; and when I went and reported myself to him, as ready for work in the *Normandy* again, he observed that her gang was full, but that, by going up-town next morning, to the screw-dock, I should find an excellent job on board a brig. The following day, accordingly, I took my dinner in a pail, and started off for the dock, as directed. On my way, I fell in with an old shipmate in the navy, a boatswain's-mate, of the name of Benson. This man asked me where I was bound with my pail, and I told him. "What's the use," says he, "of dragging your soul out in these liners, when you have a man-of-war under your lee!" Then he told me he meant to ship, and advised me to do the same. I drank with him two or three times, and felt half persuaded to enter; but, recollecting the brig, I left him, and pushed on to the dock. When I got there, it was so late that the vessel had got off the dock, and was already under way in the stream.

My day's work was now up, and I determined to make a full holiday of it. As I went back, I fell in with Captain Mix, the officer with whom I had first gone on the lakes, and my old first-lieutenant in the *Delaware,* and had a bit of navy talk with him; after which I drifted along as far as the rendezvous. The officer in charge was Mr. M'Kenny, my old first-lieutenant in the *Brandywine,* and, before I quitted the house, my name was down, again, for one of Uncle Sam's sailor-men. In this accidental manner have I floated about the world, most of my life—not dreaming in the morning, what would fetch me up before night.

When it was time to go off, I was ready, and was sent on board the *Hudson,* which vessel Captain Mix then commanded. I have the consolation of knowing that I never ran, or thought of running, from either of the eleven men-of-war on board of which I have served, counting big and little, service of days and service of years. I had so long a pull in the receiving-ship, as to get heartily tired of her; and, when an opportunity offered, I put my name down for the *Constellation,* 38, which was then fitting out for the West India station, in Norfolk. A draft of us was sent round to that ship accordingly, and we found she had hauled off from the yard, and was lying between the forts. When I got on board, I ascertained that something like fifty of my old liners were in this very ship, some common motive inducing them to take service in the navy, all at the same time. As for myself, it happened just as I have related, though I always liked the navy, and was ever ready to join a ship of war, for a pleasant cruise.

Commodore Dallas's pennant was flying in the *Constellation* when I joined her. A short time afterwards, the ship sailed for the West Indies. As there was nothing material occurred in the cruise, it is unnecessary to relate things in the order in which they took place. The ship went to Havana, Trinidad, Curaçoa, Laguayra, Santa Cruz, Vera Cruz, Campeachy, Tampico, Key West, &c. We lay more or less time at all these ports, and in Santa Cruz we had a great ball on board. After passing several months in this manner, we went to Pensacola. The *St. Louis* was with us most of this time, though she did not sail from America in company. The next season the whole squadron went to Vera Cruz in company, seven or eight sail of us in all, giving the Mexicans some alarm, I believe.

But the Florida war gave us the most occupation. I was out in all sorts of ways, on expeditions, and can say I never saw an Indian, except those who came to give themselves up. I was in steamboats, cutters, launches, and on shore, marching like a soldier, with a gun on my shoulder, and precious duty it was for a sailor.

The *St. Louis* being short of hands, I was also drafted for a cruise in her; going the rounds much as we had done in the frigate. This was a fine ship, and was then commanded by Captain Rousseau, an officer much respected and liked, by us all. Mr. Byrne, my old shipmate in the *Delaware,* went out with us as first-lieutenant of the *Constellation,* but he did not remain out the whole cruise.

Altogether I was out on the West India station three years, but got into the hospital, for several months of the time, in consequence of a broken bone. While in the hospital, the frigate made a cruise, leaving me ashore. On her return, I was invalided home, in the *Levant,* Captain Paulding, another solid, excellent officer. In a word, I was lucky in my officers, generally; the treatment on board the frigate being just and good. The duty in the *Constellation* was very hard, being a sort of soldier duty, which may be very well for those that are trained to it, but makes bad weather for us blue-jackets. Captain Mix, the officer with whom I went to the lakes, was out on the station in command of the

Concord, sloop of war, and, for some time, was in charge of our ship, during the absence of Commodore Dallas, in his own vessel. In this manner are old shipmates often thrown together, after years of separation.

In the hospital I was rated as porter, Captain Bolton and Captain Latimer being my commanding officers; the first being in charge of the yard, and the second his next in rank. From these two gentlemen I received so many favours, that it would be ungrateful in me not to mention them. Dr. Terrill, the surgeon of the hospital, too, was also exceedingly kind to me, during the time I was under his care.

As I had much leisure time in the hospital, I took charge of a garden, and got to be somewhat of a gardener. It was said I had the best garden about Pensacola, which is quite likely true, as I never saw but one other.

The most important thing, however, that occurred to me while in the hospital, was a disposition that suddenly arose in my mind, to reflect on my future state, and to look at religious things with serious eyes. Dr. Terrill had some blacks in his service, who were in the habit of holding little Methodist meetings, where they sang hymns, and conversed together seriously. I never joined these people, being too white for that, down at Pensacola, but I could overhear them from my own little room. A Roman Catholic in the hospital had a prayer-book in English, which he lent to me, and I got into the habit of reading a prayer in it, daily, as a sort of worshipping of the Almighty. This was the first act of mine, that approached private worship, since the day I left Mr. Marchinton's; if I except the few hasty mental petitions put up in moments of danger.

After a time, I began to think it would never do for me, a Protestant born and baptised, to be studying a Romish prayerbook; and I hunted up one that was Protestant, and which had been written expressly for seamen. This I took to my room, and used in place of the Romish book. Dr. Terrill had a number of bibles under his charge, and I obtained one of these, also, and I actually got into the practice of reading a chapter every night, as well as of reading a prayer. I also knocked off from drink, and ceased to swear. My reading in the bible, now, was not for the stories, but seriously to improve my mind and morals.

I must have been several months getting to be more and more in earnest on the subject of morality, if not of vital religion, when I formed an acquaintance with a new steward, who had just joined the hospital. This man was ready enough to converse with me about the bible, but he turned out to be a Deist. Notwithstanding my own disposition to think more seriously of my true situation, I had many misgivings on the subject of the Saviour's being the Son of God. It seemed improbable to me, and I was falling into the danger which is so apt to beset the new beginner—that of self-sufficiency, and the substituting of human wisdom for faith. The steward was not slow in discovering this; and he produced some of Tom Paine's works, by way of strengthening me in the unbelief. I now read Tom Paine, instead of the bible, and soon had practical evidence of the bad effects of his miserable system. I soon got stern-way on me in morals; began to drink, as before, though seldom intoxicated, and grew indifferent to my bible and prayerbook, as well as careless of the future. I began to think that the things of this world were to be enjoyed, and he was the wisest who made the most of his time.

I must confess, also, that the bad examples which I saw set by men professing to be Christians, had a strong tendency to disgust me with religion. The great mistake I made was, in supposing I had undergone any real change of heart. Circumstances disposed me to reflect, and reflection brought me to be serious, on subjects that I had hitherto treated with levity; but the grace of God was still, in a great degree, withheld from me, leaving me a prey to such arguments as those of the steward, and his great prophet and master, Mr. Paine.

In the hospital, and that, too, at a place like Pensacola, there was little opportunity for me to break out into my old excesses; though I found liquor, on one or two occasions, even there, and got myself into some disgrace in consequence. On the whole, however, the discipline, my situation, and my own resolution, kept me tolerably correct. It is the restraint of a ship that alone prevents sailors from dying much sooner than they do; for it is certain no man could hold out long who passed three or four months every year in the sort of indulgencies into which I myself have often run, after returning from long voyages. This is one advantage of the navy; two or three days of riotous living being all a fellow *can* very well get in a three years' cruise. Any man who has ever been in a vessel of war, particularly in old times, can see the effect produced by the system, and regular living of a ship. When the crew first came on board, the men were listless, almost lifeless, with recent dissipation; some suffering with the "horrors," perhaps; but a few weeks of regular living would bring them all round; and, by the end of the cruise, most of the people would come into port, and be paid off, with renovated constitutions. It is a little different, now, to be sure, as the men ship for general service, and commonly serve a short apprenticeship in a receiving vessel, before they are turned over to the sea-going craft. This brings them on board the last in a little better condition than used to be the case; but, even now, six months in a man-of-war is a new lease for a seaman's life.

I say I got myself into disgrace in the hospital of Pensacola, in consequence of my habit of drinking. The facts were as follows, for I have no desire to conceal, or to parade before the world, my own delinquencies; but, I confess them with the hope that the pictures they present, may have some salutary influence on the conduct of others. The doctor, who was steadily my friend, and often gave me excellent advice, went north, in order to bring his wife to Pensacola. I was considered entitled to a pension for the hurt which had brought me into the hospital, and the doctor had promised to see something about it, while at Washington. This was not done, in consequence of his not passing through Washington, as had been expected. Now, nature has so formed me, that any disgust, or disappointment, makes me reckless, and awakens a desire to revenge myself, on myself, as I may say. It was this feeling which first carried me from Halifax; it was this feeling that made me run from the *Sterling;* and which has often changed, and sometimes marred my prospects, as I have passed through life. As soon as I learned that nothing had been said about my pension, this same feeling came over me, and I became reckless. I had not drawn my grog for months, and, indeed, had left off drinking entirely; but I now determined to have my fill, at the first good opportunity. I meant to make the officers sorry, by doing something that was very wrong, and for which I should be sorry myself.

I kept the keys of the liquor of the hospital. The first thing was to find a confederate, which I did in the person of a Baltimore chap, who entered into my plan from pure love of liquor. I then got a stock of the wine, and we went to work on it, in my room. The liquor was sherry, and it took nine bottles of it to lay us both up. Even this did not make me beastly drunk, but it made me desperate and impudent. I abused the doctor, and came very near putting my foot into it, with Captain Latimer, who is an officer that it will not do, always, to trifle with. Still, these gentlemen, with Captain Bolton, had more consideration for me, than I had for myself, and I escaped with only a good reprimand. It was owing to this frolic, however, that I was invalided home—as they call it out there, no one seeming to consider Pensacola as being in the United States.

When landed from the *Levant,* I was sent to the Navy Yard Hospital, Brooklyn. After staying two or three days here, I determined to go to the seat of government, and take a look at the great guns stationed there, Uncle Sam and all. I was paid off from the *Levant,* accordingly, and leaving the balance with the purser of the yard, I set off on my journey, with fifty dollars in my pockets, which they tell me is about a member of Congress' mileage, for the distance I had to go. Of course this was enough, as a member of Congress would naturally take care and give himself as much as he wanted.

When I got on board the South-Amboy boat, I found a party of Indians there, going to head-quarters, like myself. The sight of these chaps set up all my rigging, and I felt ripe for fun. I treated them to a breakfast each, and gave them as much to drink as they could swallow. We all got merry, and had our own coarse fun, in the usual thoughtless manner of seamen. This was a bad beginning, and, by the time we reached a tavern, I was ready to anchor. Where this was, is more than I know; for I was not in a state to keep a ship's reckoning. Whether any of my money was stolen or not, I cannot say, but I know that some of my clothes were. Next day I got to Philadelphia, where I had another frolic. After this, I went on to Washington, keeping it up, the whole distance. I fell in with a soldier chap, who was out of cash, and who was going to Washington to get a pension, too; and so we lived in common. When we reached Washington, my cash was diminished to three dollars and a half, and all was the consequences of brandy and folly. I had actually spent forty-six dollars and a half, in a journey that might have been made with ten, respectably!

I got my travelling companion to recommend a boarding-house, which he did. I felt miserable from my excesses, and went to bed. In the morning, the three dollars and a half were gone. I felt too ill to go to the Department that day, but kept on drinking—eating nothing. Next day, my landlord took the trouble to inquire into the state of my pocket, and I told him the truth. This brought about a pretty free explanation between us, in which I was given to understand that my time was up in that place. I afterwards found out I had got into a regular soldier-house, and it was no wonder they did not know how to treat an old salt.

Captain Mix had given me a letter to Commodore Chauncey, who was then living, and one of the Commissioners. I felt pretty certain the old gentleman would not let one of the Scourges founder at head-quarters, and so I crawled up to the Department, and got admission to him. The commodore seemed glad to see me; questioned me a good deal about the loss of the schooner, and finally gave me directions how to proceed. I then discovered that my pension ticket had actually reached Washington, but had been sent back to Pensacola, to get some informality corrected. This would compel me to remain some time at Washington. I felt unwell, and got back to my boarding-house with these tidings. The gentlemen who kept the house was far from being satisfied with this, and he gave me a hint that at once put the door between us. This was the first time I ever had a door shut upon me, and I am thankful it happened at a soldier rendezvous. I gave the man all my spare clothes in pawn, and walked away from his house.

I had undoubtedly brought on myself a fit of the "horrors," by my recent excesses. As I went along the streets, I thought every one was sneering at me; and, though burning with thirst, I felt ashamed to enter any house to ask even for water. A black gave me the direction of the Navy Yard, and I shaped my course for it, feeling more like lying down to die, than anything else. When about half-way across the bit of vacant land between the Capitol and the Yard, I sat down under a high picket-fence, and the devil put it into my head, that it would be well to terminate sufferings that seemed too hard to be borne, by hanging myself on that very fence. I took the handkerchief from my neck, made a running bow-line, and got so far as to be at work at a standing bow-line, to hitch over the top of one of the poles of the fence.

I now stood up, and began to look for a proper picket to make fast to, when, in gazing about, I caught sight of the mast-heads of the shipping at the yard, and of the ensign under which I had so long served! These came over me, as a lighthouse comes over a mariner in distress at sea, and I thought there must be friends for me in that quarter. The sight gave me courage and strength, and I determined no old shipmate should hear of a blue-jacket's hanging himself on a picket, in a fit of the horrors. Casting off the bowlines, I replaced the handkerchief on my neck, and made the best of my way towards those blessed mast-heads, which, under God's mercy, were the means of preventing me from committing suicide.

As I came up to the gate of the yard, the marine on post sung out to me, "Halloo, Myers, where are you come from? You look as if you had been dragged though h——, and beaten with a soot-bag!" This man, the first I met at the Navy Yard, had been with me three years in the *Delaware,* and knew me in spite of my miserable appearance. He advised me to go on board the *Fulton,* then lying at the Yard, where he said I should find several more old Delawares, who would take good care of me. I did as he directed, and, on getting on board, I fell in with lots of acquaintances. Some brought me tea, and some brought me grog. I told my yarn, and the chaps around me laid a plan to get ashore on liberty that night, and razée the house from which I had been turned away. But I persuaded them out of the notion, and the landlord went clear.

After a while, I got a direction to a boarding-house near the Yard, and went to it, with a message from my old shipmates that they would be responsible for the pay. But to this the man would not listen; he took me in on my own account, saying that no blue-jacket should be turned from *his* door, in distress. Here I staid and got a comfortable night's rest. Next day I was a new man, holy-stoned the decks, and went a second time to the Department.

All the gentlemen in the office showed a desire to serve and advise me. The Pension Clerk gave me a letter to Mr. Boyle, the Chief Clerk, who gave me another letter to Commodore Patterson, the commandant of the Navy-Yard. It seems that government provides a boarding-house for us pensioners to stay in, while at Washington, looking after our rights. This letter of Mr. Boyle's got me a berth in that house, where I was supplied with everything, even to washing and mending, for six weeks. Through the purser, I drew a stock of money from the purser at New York, and now began, again, to live soberly and respectably, considering all things.

The house in which I lived was a sort of half-hospital, and may have had six or eight of us in it, altogether. Several of us were cripples from wounds and hurts, and, among others, was one Reuben James, a thorough old man-of-war's man, who had been in the service ever since he was a youth. This man had the credit of saving Decatur's life before Tripoli; but he owned to me that he was not the person who did it.[1] He was in the fight, and boarded with Decatur, but did not save his commander's life. He had been often wounded, and had just had a leg amputated for an old wound, received in the war of 1812, I believe. Liquor brought him to that.

The reader will remember that the night the *Scourge* went down I received a severe blow from her jib-sheet blocks. A lump soon formed on the spot where the injury had been inflicted, and it had continued to increase until it was now as large as my fist, or even larger. I showed this lump to James, one day, and he mentioned it to Dr. Foltz, the surgeon who attended the house. The doctor took a look at my arm, and recommended an operation, as the lump would continue to increase, and was already so large as to be inconvenient. I cannot say that it hurt me any, though it was an awkward sort of swab to be carrying on a fellow's shoulder. I had no great relish for being carved, and think I

1. One of the oldest myths in U.S. naval history had Seaman Reuben James virtually sacrificing his life for that of Lieutenant Stephen Decatur during the American attack on Tripoli on 3 August 1804. The virtue of Ned's story is that he actually met James and heard him deny the fable. The credit for the sacrificial act should go to Seaman Daniel Frazier.

should have refused to submit to the operation, were it not for James, who told me he would not be carrying Bunker Hill about on *his* arm, and would show me his own stump by way of encouragement. This man seemed to think an old sailor ought to have a wooden leg, or something of the sort, after he had reached a certain time of life. At all events, he persuaded me to let the doctor go to work, and I am now glad I did, as everything turned out well. Doctor Foltz operated, after I had been about a week under medicine, doing the job as neatly as man could wish. He told me the lump he removed weighed a pound and three quarters, and of course I was so much the lighter. I was about a month, after this, under his care, when he pronounced me to be seaworthy again.

I now got things straight as regards my pension, for the hurt received on board the *Constellation*. It was no great matter, only three dollars a month, being one of the small pensions; and the clerks, when they came to hear about the hurt, for which Dr. Foltz had operated, advised me to get evidence and procure a pension for *that*. I saw the Secretary, Mr. Paulding, on this subject, and the gentlemen were so kind as to overhaul their papers, in order to ascertain who could be found as a witness. They wrote to Captain Deacon, the officer who commanded the *Growler;* but he knew nothing of me, as I never was on board his schooner. This gentleman, however, wrote me a letter, himself, inviting me to come and see him, which I had it not in my power to do. I understand he is now dead. Mr. Trant had been dead many years, and, as for Mr. Bogardus, I never knew what became of him. He was not in the line of promotion, and probably left the navy at the peace. In overhauling the books, however, the pension-clerk came across the name of Lemuel Bryant. This man received a pension for the wound he got at Little York, and was one of those I had hauled into the boat when the *Scourge* went down. He was then living at Portland, in Maine, his native State. Mr. Paulding advised me to get his certificate, for all hands in the Department seemed anxious I should not go away without something better than the three dollars a month. I promised to go on, and see Lemuel Bryant, and obtain his testimony.[2]

Quitting Washington, I went to Alexandria and got on board a brig, called the *Isabella,* bound to New York, at which port we arrived in due time. Here I obtained the rest of my money, and kept myself pretty steady, more on account of my wounds, I fear, than anything else. Still I drank too much; and by way of putting a check on myself, I went to the Sailor's Retreat, Staten Island, and of course got out of the reach of liquor.[3] Here I staid eight or ten days, until my wounds healed. While at the Retreat, the last day I remained there indeed, which was a Sunday, the physician came in, and told me that a clergyman of the Dutch Reformed Church, of the name of Miller, was about to have service down stairs, and that I had better go down and be present. To this request, not only civilly but kindly made, I answered that I had seen enough of the acts of religious men to satisfy me, and that I believed a story I was then

2. Clerks in the Navy Department urged Ned to get a pension for the wound received on board the *Scourge.* Ned testifies that Secretary of the Navy James Paulding himself suggested that he write to commanders on the lakes who were still living. In this way, Cooper allows us to follow up and find what happened to some of the men. But the only one still alive who might know Ned was Lemuel Bryant, who had been given a pension for a wound received at York. Paulding urged Ned to write Bryant at Portland, Maine, to have him certify the wound. Ned promised he would write, but there is no record that he ever did. His widow, however, later obtained the services of James Ottinger, a Philadelphia resident, who assisted her in making a successful claim. See National Archives and Records Administration, Military Service Branch, Pension Records; Beard, *Letters and Journals,* vol. 5, and Egan, "Gentlemen-Sailors," p. 155.

3. There are many other references to Ned's religious attitudes in this work. Churchmen had awakened to the thousands of seamen living outside the reach of the Church. Several denominations saw them as a special target for proselytization during the early 19th century. For further information on missionary work among sailors, see Kverndal, *Seamen's Missions.*

reading in a Magazine, would do me as much good as a sermon. The physician said a little in the way of reproof and admonition, and left me. As soon as his back was turned, some of my companions began to applaud the spirit I had shown, and the answer I had given the doctor. But I was not satisfied with myself. I had more secret respect for such things than I was willing to own, and conscience upbraided me for the manner in which I had slighted so well-meaning a request. Suddenly telling those around me that my mind was changed, and that I *would* go below and hear what was said, I put this new resolution in effect immediately.

I had no recollection of the text from which Mr. Miller preached; it is possible I did not attend to it, at the moment it was given out; but, during the whole discourse, I fancied the clergyman was addressing himself particularly to me, and that his eyes were never off me. That he touched my conscience I know, for the effect produced by this sermon, though not uninterruptedly lasting, is remembered to the present hour. I made many excellent resolutions, and secretly resolved to reform, and to lead a better life. My thoughts were occupied the whole night with what I had heard, and my conscience was keenly active.

The next morning I quitted the Retreat, and saw no more of Mr. Miller, at that time; but I carried away with me many resolutions that would have been very admirable, had they only been adhered to. How short-lived they were, and how completely I was the slave of a vicious habit, will be seen, when I confess that I landed in New York a good deal the worse for having treated some militia-men who were in the steamer, to nearly a dozen glasses of hot-stuff, in crossing the bay. I had plenty of money, and a sailor's disposition to get rid of it, carelessly, and what I thought generously. It was Evacuation-Day, and severely cold, and the hot-stuff pleased everybody, on such an occasion. Nor was this all. In passing Whitehall slip, I saw the Ohio's first-cutter lying there, and it happened that I not only knew the officer of the boat, who had been one of the midshipmen of the *Con-*

stellation, but that I knew most of its crew. I was hailed, of course, and then I asked leave to treat the men. The permission was obtained, and this second act of liberality reduced me to the necessity of going into port, under a pilot's charge. Still I had not absolutely forgotten the sermon, nor all my good resolutions.

At the boarding-house I found a Prussian, named Godfrey, a steady, sedate man, and I agreed with him to go to Savannah, to engage in the shad-fishery, for the winter, and to come north together in the spring. My landlord was not only ill and poor, but he had many children to support, and it is some proof that all my good resolutions were not forgotten, that I was ready to go south before my money was gone, and willing it should do some good, in the interval of my absence. A check for fifty dollars still remained untouched, and I gave it to this man, with the understanding he was to draw the money, use it for his own wants, and return it to me, if he could, when I got back. The money was drawn, but the man died, and I saw no more of it.

Godfrey and I were shipped in a vessel called the *William Taylor,* a regular Savannah packet. It was our intention to quit her as soon as she got in—by running, if necessary. We had a bad passage, and barely missed shipwreck on Hatteras, saving the brig by getting a sudden view of the light, in heavy, thick weather. We got round, under close-reefed topsails, and that was all we did. After this, we had a quick run to Savannah. Godfrey had been taken with the small-pox before we arrived, and was sent to a hospital as soon as possible. In order to prevent running, I feigned illness, too, and went to another. Here the captain paid me several visits, but my conscience was too much hardened by the practices of seamen, to let me hesitate about continuing to be ill. The brig was obliged to sail without me, and the same day I got well, as suddenly as I had fallen ill.

I was not long in making a bargain with a fisherman to aid in catching shad. All this time, I lived at a sailor boarding-house, and was surrounded by men who, like myself, had quitted the vessels in which they had arrived. One night the captain of a ship, called the *Hope,* came to the house to look for a crew. He was bound to Rotterdam, and his ship lay down at the second bar, all ready for sea. After some talk, one man signed the articles; then another, and another, and another, until his crew was complete to one man. I was now called on to ship, and was ridiculed for wishing to turn shad-man. My pride was touched, and I agreed to go, leaving my fisherman in the lurch.

The *Hope* turned out to be a regular down-east craft, and I had been in so many flyers and crack ships as to be saucy enough to laugh at the economical outfit, and staid ways of the vessel. I went on board half drunk, and made myself conspicuous for such sort of strictures from the first hour. The captain treated me mildly, even kindly; but I stuck to my remarks during most of the passage. I was a seaman, and did my duty; but this satisfied me. I had taken a disgust to the ship; and though I had never blasphemed since the hour of the accident in the way I did the day the *Susan and Mary* was thrown on her beam-ends, I may be said to have crossed the Atlantic in the *Hope,* grumbling and swearing at the ship. Still, our living and our treatment were both good.

At Rotterdam, we got a little money, with liberty. When he last was up, I asked for more, and the captain refused it. This brought on an explosion, and I swore I would quit the ship. After a time, the captain consentend, as well as he could, leaving my wages on the cabin-table, where I found them, and telling me I should repent of what I was then doing. Little did I then think he would prove so true a prophet.

CHAPTER XVIII

I HAD LEFT THE *HOPE* in a fit of the sulks. The vessel never pleased me, and yet I can now look back, and acknowledge that both her master and her mate were respectable, considerate men, who had my own good in view more than I had myself. There was an American ship, called the *Plato,* in port, and I had half a mind to try my luck in her. The master of this vessel was said to be a tartar, however, and a set of us had doubts about the expediency of trusting ourselves with such a commander. When we came to sound around him, we discovered he would have nothing to do with us, as he intended to get a crew of regular Dutchmen. This ship had just arrived from Batavia, and was bound to New York. How he did this legally, or whether he did it at all, is more than I know, for I only tell what I was told myself, on this subject.

There was a heavy Dutch Indiaman, then fitting out for Java, lying at Rotterdam. The name of this vessel was the *Stadtdeel*—so pronounced; how spelt, I have no idea—and I began to think I would try a voyage in her. As is common with those who have great reason to find fault with themselves, I was angry with the whole world. I began to think myself a sort of outcast, forgetting that I had deserted my natural relatives, run from my master, and thrown off many friends who were disposed to serve me in everything in which I could be served. I have a cheerful temperament by nature, and I make no doubt that the sombre view I now began to take of things, was the effects of drink. It was necessary for me to get to sea, for there I was shut out from all excesses, by discipline and necessity.

After looking around us, and debating the matter among ourselves, a party of five of us shipped in the *Stadtdeel.* What the others contemplated I do not know, but it was my intention to double Good Hope, and never to return. Chances enough would offer on the other side, to make a man comfortable, and I was no stranger to the ways of that quarter of the world. I could find enough to do between Bombay and Canton; and, if I could not, there were the islands and all of the Pacific before me. I could do a seaman's whole duty, was now in tolerable health and strength, and knew that such men were always wanted. Wherever a ship goes, Jack must go with her, and ships, dollars and hogs, are now to be met with all over the globe.

The *Stadtdeel* lay at Dort, and we went to that place to join her. She was not ready for sea, and as things moved Dutchman fashion, slow and sure, we were about six weeks at Dort before she sailed. This ship was a vessel of the size of a frigate, and carried twelve guns. She had a crew of about forty souls, which was being very short-handed. The ship's company was a strange mixture of seamen, though most of them came from the north of Europe. Among us were Russians, Danes, Swedes, Prussians, English, Americans, and but a very few Dutch. One of the mates, and two of the petty officers, could speak a little English. This made us eight who could converse in that language. We had to learn Dutch as well as we could, and made out tolerably well. Before the ship sailed, I could understand the common orders, without much difficulty. Indeed, the language is nothing but English a little flattened down.

So long as we remained at Dort, the treatment on board this vessel was well enough. We were never well fed, though we got enough food, such as it was. The work was hard, and the weather cold; but these did not frighten me. The wages were eight dollars a month;—I had abandoned eighteen, and an American ship, for this preferment! A wayward temper had done me this service.

The *Stadtdeel* no sooner got into the stream, than there was a great change in the treatment. We were put on an allowance of food and water, in sight of our place of departure; and the rope's-end began to fly round among the crew, we five excepted. For some reason, that I cannot explain, neither of us was ever struck. We got plenty of curses, in Low Dutch, as we supposed; and we gave them back, with interest, in high English. The expression of our faces let the parties into the secret of what was going on.

It is scarcely necessary to add, that we English and Americans soon repented of the step we had taken. I heartily wished myself on board the *Hope,* again, and the master's prophecy became true, much sooner, perhaps, than he had himself anticipated. This time, I conceive that my disgust was fully justified; though I deserved the punishment I was receiving, for entering so blindly into a service every way so inferior to that to which I properly belonged. The bread in this ship was wholesome, I do suppose, but it was nearly black, and such as I was altogether unused to. Inferior as it was, we got but five pounds, each, per week. In our navy, a man gets, per week, seven pounds of such bread as might be put on a gentleman's table. The meat was little better than the bread in quality, and quite as scant in quantity. We got one good dish in the *Stadtdeel,* and that we got every morning. It was a dish of boiled barley, of which I became very fond, and which, indeed, supplied me with the strength necessary for my duty. It was one of the best dishes

I ever fell in with at sea; and I think it might be introduced, to advantage, in our service. Good food produces good work.

As all our movements were of the slow and easy order, the ship lay three weeks at the Helvoetsluys, waiting for passengers. During this time, our party, three English and two Americans, came to a determination to abandon the ship. Our plan was to seize a boat, as we passed down channel, and get ashore in England. We were willing to run all the risks of such a step, in preference of going so long a voyage under such treatment and food. By this time, our discontent amounted to disgust.

At length we got all our passengers on board. These consisted of a family, of which the head was said to be, or to have been, an admiral in the Dutch navy. This gentleman was going to Java to remain; and he took with him his wife, several children, servants, and a lady, who seemed to be a companion to his wife. As soon as this party was on board, the wind coming fair, we sailed. The *Plato* went to sea in company with us, and little did I then think, while wishing myself on board her, how soon I should be thrown into this very ship—the last craft in which I ever was at sea. I was heaving the lead as we passed her; our ship, Dutchman or not, having a fleet pair of heels. The *Stadtdeel,* whatever might be her usage, or her food, sailed and worked well, and was capitally found in everything that related to the safety of the vessel. This was her first voyage, and she was said to be the largest ship out of Rotterdam.

The *Stadtdeel* must have sailed from Helvoetsluys in May, 1839, or about thirty-three years after I sailed from New York, on my first voyage, in the *Sterling.* During all this time I had been toiling at sea, like a dog, risking my health and life, in a variety of ways; and this ship, with my station on board her, was nearly all I had to show for it! God be praised! This voyage, which promised so little, in its commencement, proved, in the end, the most fortunate of any in which I embarked.

There was no opportunity for us to put our plans in execution, in going down channel. The wind was fair, and it blew so fresh, it would not have been easy to get a boat into the water; and we passed the Straits of Dover, by day-light, the very day we sailed. The wind held in the same quarter, until we reached the north-east trades, giving us a quick run as low down as the calm latitudes. All this time, the treatment was as bad as ever, or, if anything, worse; and our discontent increased daily. There were but one or two native Hollanders in the forecastle, boys excepted; but among them was a man who had shipped as an ordinary seaman. He had been a soldier, I believe; at all events, he had a medal, received in consequence of having been in one of the late affairs between his country and Belgium. It is probable this man may not have been very expert in a seaman's duty, and it is possible he may have been drinking, though to me he appeared sober, at the time the thing occurred which I am about to relate. One day the captain fell foul of him, and beat him with a rope severely. The ladies interfered, and got the poor fellow out of the scrape; the captain letting him go, and telling him to go forward. As the man complied, he fell in with the chief mate, who attacked him afresh, and beat him very severely. The man now went below, and was about to turn in, as the captain had ordered,—which renders it probable he had been drinking,—when the second mate, possibly ignorant of what had occurred, missing him from his duty, went below, and beat him up on deck again. These different assaults seem to have made the poor fellow desperate. He ran and jumped into the sea, just forward of the starboard lower-studding-sail-boom. The ship was then in the north-east trades, and had eight or nine knots way on her; notwithstanding, she was rounded to, and a boat was lowered—but the man was never found.

There is something appalling in seeing a fellow-creature driven to such acts of madness; and the effect produced on all of us, by what we witnessed, was profound and sombre.

I shall not pretend to say that this man did not deserve chastisement, or that the two mates were not ignorant of what had happened; but brutal treatment was so much in use on board this ship, that the occurrence made us five nearly desperate. I make no doubt a crew of Americans, who were thus treated, would have secured the officers, and brought the ship in. It is true, that flogging seems necessary to some natures, and I will not say that such a crew as ours could very well get along without it. But we might sometimes be treated as men, and no harm follow.

As I have said, the loss of this man produced a great impression in the ship, generally. The passengers appeared much affected by it, and I thought the captain, in particular, regretted it greatly. He might not have been in the least to blame, for the chastisement he inflicted was such as masters of ships often bestow on their men, but the crew felt very indignant against the mates; one of whom was particularly obnoxious to us all. As for my party, we now began to plot, again, in order to get quit of the ship. After a great deal of discussion, we came to the following resolution:

About a dozen of us entered into the conspiracy. We contemplated no piracy, no act of violence, that should not be rendered necessary in self-defence, nor any robbery, beyond what we conceived indispensable to our object. As the ship passed the Straits of Sunda, we intended to lower as many boats as should be necessary, arm ourselves, place provisions and water in the boats, and abandon the ship. We felt confident that if most of the men did not go with us, they would not oppose us. I can now see that this was a desperate and unjustifiable scheme; but, for myself, I was getting desperate on board the ship, and preferred risking my life to remaining. I will not deny that I was a ringleader in this affair, though I know I had no other motive than escape.

This was a clear case of mutiny, and the only one in which I was ever implicated. I have a thousand times seen reason to rejoice that the attempt was never made, since, so deep was the hostility of the crew to the officers,—the mates, in particular,—that I feel persuaded a horrible scene of bloodshed must have followed. I did not think of this at the time, making sure of getting off unresisted; but, if we had, what would have been the fate of a parcel of seamen who came into an English port in ship's boats? Tried for piracy, probably, and the execution of some, if not all of us.

The ship had passed the island of St. Pauls, and we were impatiently waiting for her entrance into the Straits of Sunda, when an accident occurred that put a stop to the contemplated mutiny, and changed the whole current, as I devoutly hope, of all my subsequent life. At the calling of the middle watch, one stormy night, the ship being under close-reefed topsails at the time, with the mainsail furled, I went on deck as usual, to my duty. In stepping across the deck, between the launch and the galley, I had to cross some spars that were lashed there. While on the pile of spars, the ship lurched suddenly, and I lost my blance, falling my whole length on deck, upon my left side. Nothing broke the fall, my arms being raised to seize a hold above my head, and I came down upon deck with my entire weight, the hip taking the principal force of the fall. The anguish I suffered was acute, and it was some time before I would allow my shipmates even to touch me.

After a time, I was carried down into the steerage, where it was found necessary to sling me on a grating, instead of a hammock. We had a doctor on board, but he could do nothing for me. My clothes could not be taken off, and there I lay wet, and suffering to a degree that I should find difficult to describe, hours and hours.

I was now really on the stool of repentance. In body, I was perfectly helpless, though my mind seemed more active than it had ever been before. I overhauled my whole life, beginning with the hour when I first got drunk, as a boy, on board the *Sterling,* and underrunning every scrape I have mentioned in this sketch of my life, with many of which I have not spoken; and all with a fidelity and truth that satisfy me that man can keep no log-book that is as accurate as his own conscience. I saw that I had been my own worst enemy, and how many excellent opportunities of getting ahead in the world, I had wantonly disregarded. Liquor lay at the root of all my calamities and misconduct, enticing me into bad company, undermining my health and strength, and blasting my hopes. I tried to pray, but did not know how; and, it appeared to me, as if I were lost, body and soul, without a hope of mercy.

My shipmates visited me by stealth, and I pointed out to them, as clearly as in my power, the folly, as well as the wickedness, of our contemplated mutiny. I told them we had come on board the ship voluntarily, and we had no right to be judges in our own case; that we should have done a cruel thing in deserting a ship at sea, with women and children on board; that the Malays would probably have cut our throats, and the vessel herself would have been very apt to be wrecked. Of all this mischief, we should have been the fathers, and we had every reason to be grateful that our project was defeated. The men listened attentively, and promised to abandon every thought of executing the revolt. They were as good as their words, and I heard no more of the matter.

As for my hurt, it was not easy to say what it was. The doctor was kind to me, but he could do no more than give me food and little indulgencies. As for the captain, I think he was influenced by the mate, who appeared to believe I was feigning an injury much greater than I had actually received. On board the ship, there was a boy, of good parentage, who had been sent out to commence his career at sea. He lived aft, and was a sort of genteel cabin-boy. He could not have been more than ten or eleven years old but he proved to be a ministering angel to me. He brought me delicacies, sympathised with me, and many a time did we shed tears in company. The ladies and the admiral's children sometimes came to see me, too, manifesting much sorrow for my situation; and then it was that my conscience pricked the deepest, for the injury, or risks, I had contemplated exposing them to. Altogether, the scenes I saw daily, and my own situation, softened my heart, and I began to get views of my moral deformity that were of a healthful and safe character.

I lay on that grating two months, and bitter months they were to me. The ship had arrived at Batavia, and the captain and mate came to see what was to be done with me. I asked to be sent to the hospital, but the mate insisted nothing was the matter with me, and asked to have me kept in the ship. This was done, and I went round to Terragall in her, where we landed our passengers. These last all came and took leave of me, the admiral making me a present of a good jacket, that he had worn himself at sea, with a quantity of tobacco. I have got that jacket at this moment. The ladies spoke kindly to me, and all this gave my heart fresh pangs.

From Terragall we went to Sourabaya, where I prevailed on the captain to send me to the hospital, the mate still insisting I was merely shamming inability to work. The surgeons at Sourabaya, one of whom was a Scotchman, thought with the mate; and at the end of twenty days, I was again taken on board the ship, which sailed for Samarang. While at Sourabaya there were five English sailors in the hospital. These men were as forlorn and miserable as myself, death grinning in our faces at every turn. The men who were brought into the hospital one day, were often dead the next, and none of us knew whose turn would come next. We often talked together, on religious subjects, after our own uninstructed manner, and greatly did we long to find an English bible, a thing not to be had there. Then it was I thought, again, of the sermon I had heard at the Sailors'

Retreat, of the forfeited promises I had made to reform; and, more than once did it cross my mind, should God permit me to return home, that I would seek out that minister, and ask his prayers and spiritual advice.

On our arrival at Samarang, the mate got a doctor from a Dutch frigate, to look at me, who declared nothing ailed me. By these means nearly all hands in the ship were set against me, but my four companions, and the little boy fancying that I was a skulk, and throwing labour on them. I was ordered on deck, and set to work graffing ring-bolts for the guns. Walk I could not, being obliged, literally, to crawl along the deck on my hands and knees. I suffered great pain, but got no credit for it. The work was easy enough for me, when once seated at it, but it caused me infinite suffering to move. I was not alone in being thought a skulk, however. The doctor himself was taken ill, and the mate accused him, too, very much as he did me, of shirking duty. Unfortunately, the poor man gave him the lie, by dying.

I was kept at the sort of duty I have mentioned until the ship reached Batavia again. Here a doctor came on board from another ship, on a visit, and my case was mentioned. The mate ordered me aft, and I crawled upon the quarter-deck to be examined. They got me into the cabin, where the strange doctor looked at me. This man said I must be operated on by a burning process, all of which was said to frighten me to duty. After this I got down into the forecastle, and positively refused to do anything more. There I lay, abused and neglected by all but my four friends. I told the mate I suffered too much to work, and that I must be put ashore. Suffering had made me desperate, and I cared not for the consequences.

Fortunately for me, there were two cases of fever and ague in the ship. Our own doctor being dead, that of the admiral's ship was sent for to visit the sick. The mate seemed anxious to get evidence against me, and he asked the admiral's surgeon to come down and see me. The moment this gentleman laid eyes on me, he raised both arms, and exclaimed that they were killing me. He saw, at once, that I was no imposter, and stated as much in pretty plain language, so far as I could understand what he said. The mate appeared to be struck with shame and contrition; and I do believe that every one on board was sorry for the treatment I had received. I took occasion to remonstrate with the mate, and to tell him of the necessity of my being sent immediately to the hospital. The man promised to represent my case to the captain, and the next day I was landed.

My two great desires were to get to the hospital and to procure a bible. I did not expect to live; one of my legs being shrivelled to half its former size, and was apparently growing worse; and could I find repose for my body and relief for my soul, I felt that I could be happy. I had heard my American ship-mate, who was a New Yorker, a Hudson river man, say he had a bible; but I had never seen it. It lay untouched in the bottom of his chest, sailor-fashion. I offered this man a shirt for his bible; but he declined taking any pay, cheerfully giving me the book. I forced the shirt on him, however, as a sort of memorial of me. Now I was provided with the book, I could not read for want of spectacles. I had reached a time of life when the sight begins to fail, and I think my eyes were injured in Florida. In Sourayaba hospital I had raised a few rupees by the sale of a black silk handkerchief, and wanted now to procure a pair of spectacles. I sold a pair of boots, and adding the little sum thus raised to that which I had already, I felt myself rich and happy, in the prospect of being able to study the word of God. On quitting the ship, everybody, forward and aft, shook hands with me, the opinion of the man-of-war surgeon suddenly changing all their opinions of me and my conduct.

The captain appeared to regret the course things had taken, and was willing to do all he could to make me comfortable. My wages were left in a merchant's hands, and I was to receive them could I quit this island, or get out of the hospital. I was to be sent to Holland, in the latter case, and everything was to be done according to law and right. The reader is not to imagine I considered myself a suffering saint all this time. On the contrary, while I was thought an imposter, I remembered that I had shammed sickness in this very island, and, as I entered the hospital, I could not forget the circumstances under which I had been its tenant fifteen or twenty years before. Then I was in the pride of my youth and strength; and, now, as if in punishment for the deception, I was berthed, a miserable cripple, within half-a-dozen beds of that on which I was berthed when feigning an illness I did not really suffer. Under such circumstances, conscience is pretty certain to remind a sinner of his misdeeds.

The physician of the hospital put me on very low diet, and gave me an ointment to "smear" myself with, as he called it; and I was ordered to remain in my berth. By means of one of the coolies of the hospital, I got a pair of spectacles from the town, and such a pair, as to size and form, that people in America regard what is left of them as a curiosity. They served my purpose, however, and enabled me to read the precious book I had obtained from my north-river shipmate. This book was a copy from the American Bible Society's printing-office, and if no other of their works did good, thus must be taken for an exception. It has since been placed in the Society's Library, in memory of the good it has done.

My sole occupation was reading and reflecting. There I lay, in a distant island, surrounded by disease, death daily, nay hourly making his appearance, among men whose langauge was mostly unknown to me. It was several weeks before I was allowed even to quit my bunk. I had begun to pray before I left the ship, and this practice I continued, almost hourly, until I was permitted to rise. A converted Lascar was in the hospital, and seeing my occupation, he came and conversed with me, in his broken English. This man gave me a hymn-book, and one of the first hymns I read in it afforded me great consolation. It was written by a man who had been a sailor like myself, and one who had been almost as wicked as myself, but who has since done a vast deal of good, by means of precept and example. This hymn-book I now read in common with my bible. But I cannot express the delight I felt at a copy of *Pilgrim's Progress* which this same Lascar gave me. That book I consider as second only to the bible. It enabled me to understand and to apply a vast deal that I found in the word of God, and set before my eyes so many motives for hope, that I began to feel Christ had died for me, as well as for the rest of the species. I thought if the thief on the cross could be saved, even one as wicked as I had been had only to repent and believe, to share in the Redeemer's mercy. All this time I fairly pined for religious instruction, and my thoughts would constantly recur to the sermon I had heard at the Sailor's Retreat, and to the clergyman who had preached it.

There was an American carpenter in the Fever Hospital, who, hearing of my state, gave me some tracts that he had brought from home with him. This man was not pious, but circumstances had made him serious; and, being about to quit the place, he was willing to administer to my wants. He told me there were several Englishmen and one American in his hospital, who wanted religious consolation greatly, and he advised me to crawl over and see them; which I did, as soon as it was in my power.

At first, I thought myself too wicked to offer to pray and converse with these men, but my conscience would not let me rest until I did so. It appeared to me as if the bible had been placed in my way, as much for their use as my own, and I could not rest until I had offered them all the consolation it was in my power to bestow. I read with these men for two or three weeks; Chapman, the American, being the man who considered his own moral condition the most hopeless. When unable to go myself, I would send my books, and we had the bible and *Pilgrim's Progress,* watch and watch, between us.

All this time we were living, as it might be, on a bloody battle-field. Men died in scores around us, and at the shortest notice. Batavia, at that season, was the most sickly; and, although the town was by no means as dangerous then as it had been in my former visit, it was still a sort of Golgotha, or place of skulls. More than half who entered the Fever Hospital, left it only as corpses.

Among my English associates, as I call them, was a young Scotchman, of about five-and-twenty. This man had been present at most of our readings and conversations, though he did not appear to me as much impressed with the importance of caring for his soul, as some of the others. One day he came to take leave of me. He was to quit the hospital the following morning. I spoke to him concerning his future life, and endeavoured to awaken in him some feelings that might be permanent. He listened with proper respect, but his answers were painfully inconsiderate, though I do believe he reasoned as nine in ten of mankind reason, when they think at all on such subjects. "What's the use of my giving up so soon," he said; "I am young, and strong, and in good health, and have plenty of sea-room to leeward of me, and can fetch up when there is occasion for it. If a fellow don't live while he can, he'll never live." I read to him the parable of the wise and foolish virgins, but he left me holding the same opinion, to the last.

Directly in front of my ward was the dead-house. Thither all the bodies of those who died in the hospital were regularly carried for dissection. Scarcely one escaped being subjected to the knife. This dead-house stood some eighty, or a hundred, yards from the hospital, and between them was an area, containing a few large trees. I was in the habit, after I got well enough to go out, to hobble to one of these trees, where I would sit for hours, reading and meditating. It was a good place to make a man reflect on the insignificance of worldly things, disease and death being all around him. I frequently saw six or eight bodies carried across this area, while sitting in it, and many were taken to the dead-house, at night. Hundreds, if not thousands, were in the hospital, and a large proportion died.

The morning of the day but one, after I had taken leave of the young Scotchman, I was sitting under a tree, as usual, when I saw some coolies carrying a dead body across the area. They passed quite near me, and one of the coolies gave me to understand it was that of this very youth! He had been seized with the fever, a short time after he left me, and here was a sudden termination to all his plans of enjoyment and his hopes of life; his schemes of future repentance.

Such things are of frequent occurrence in that island, but this event made a very deep impression on me. It helped to strengthen me in my own resolutions, and I used it, I hope, with effect, with my companions whose lives were still spared.

All the Englishmen got well, and were discharged. Chapman, the American, however, remained, being exceedingly feeble with the disease of the country. With this poor young man, I prayed, as well as I knew how, and read, daily, to his great comfort and consolation, I believe. The reader may imagine how one dying in a strange land, surrounded by idolaters, would lean on a single countryman who was disposed to aid him. In this manner did Chapman lean on me, and all my efforts were to induce him to lean on the Saviour. He thought he had been too great a sinner to be entitled to any hope, and my great task was to overcome in him some of those stings of conscience which it had taken the grace of God to allay in myself. One day, the last time I was with him, I read the narrative of the thief on the cross. He listened to it eagerly, and when I had ended, for the first time, he displayed some signs of hope and joy. As I left him, he took leave of me, saying we should never meet again. He asked my prayers, and I promised them. I went to my own ward, and, while actually engaged in redeeming my promise, one came to tell me he had gone. He sent me a message, to say he died a happy man. The poor fellow—happy fellow, would be a better term—sent back all the books he had borrowed; and it will serve to give some idea of the condition we were in, in a temporal sense, if I add, that he also sent me a few coppers, in order that they might contribute to the comfort of his countrymen.

CHAPTER XIX

ABOUT THREE MONTHS AFTER THE DEATH OF CHAPMAN, I was well enough to quit the hospital. I could walk, with the aid of crutches, but had no hope of ever being a sound man again. Of course, I had an anxious desire to get home; for all my resolutions, misanthropical feelings, and resentments, had vanished in the moral change I had undergone. My health, as a whole, was now good. Temperance, abstinence, and a happy frame of mind, had proved excellent doctors; and, although I had not, and never shall, altogether, recover from the effects of my fall, I had quite done with the "horrors." The last fit of them I suffered was in the deep conviction I felt concerning my sinful state. I knew nothing of Temperance Societies—had never heard that such things existed, or, if I had, forgot it as soon as heard; and yet, unknown to myself, had joined the most effective and most permanent of all these bodies. Since my fall, I have not tasted spirituous liquors, except as medicine, and in very small quantities, nor do I now feel the least desire to drink. By the grace of God, the great curse of my life has been removed, and I have lived a perfectly sober man for the last five years. I look upon liquor as one of the great agents of the devil in destroying souls, and turn from it, almost as sensitively as I could wish to turn from sin.

I wrote to the merchant who held my wages, on the subject of quitting the hospital, but got no answer. I then resolved to go to Batavia myself, and took my discharge from the hospital, accordingly. I can truly say, I left that place, into which I had entered a miserable, heart-broken cripple, a happy man. Still, I had nothing; not even the means of seeking a livelihood. But I was lightened of the heaviest of all my burthens, and felt I could go through the world rejoicing, though, literally, moving on crutches.

The hospital is seven miles from the town, and I went this distance in a canal-boat, Dutch fashion. Many of these canals exist in Java, and they have had the effect to make the island much more healthy, by draining the marshes. They told me, the canal I was on ran fifty miles into the interior. The work was done by the natives, but under the direction of their masters, the Dutch.

On reaching the town, I hobbled up to the merchant, who gave me a very indifferent reception. He said I had cost too much already, but that I must return to the hospital, until an opportunity offered for sending me to Holland. This I declined doing. Return to the hospital I would not, as I knew it could do no good, and my wish was to get back to America. I then went to the American consul, who treated me kindly. I was told, however, he could do nothing for me, as I had come out in a Dutch ship, unless I relinquished all claims to my wages, and all claims on the Dutch laws. My wages were a trifle, and I had no difficulty in relinquishing them, and as for claims, I wished to present none on the laws of Holland.

The consul then saw the Dutch merchant, and the matter was arranged between them. The *Plato,* the very ship that left Helvoetsluys in company with us, was then at Batavia, taking in cargo for Bremenhaven. She had a new captain, and he consented to receive me as a consul's man. This matter was all settled the day I reached the town, and I was to go on board the ship in the morning.

I said nothing to the consul about money, but left his office with the expectation of getting some from the Dutch merchant. I had tasted no food that day, and, on reaching the merchant's, I found him on the point of going into the country; no one sleeping in the town at that season, who could help it. He took no notice of me, and I got no assistance; perhaps I was legally entitled to none. I now sat down on some boxes, and thought I would remain at that spot until morning. Sleeping in the open air, on an empty stomach, in that town, and at that season, would probably have proved my death, had I been so fortunate as to escape being murdered by the Malays for the clothes I had on. Providence took care of me. One of the clerks, a Portuguese, took pity on me, and led me to a house occupied by a negro, who had been converted to Christianity. We met with a good deal of difficulty in finding admission. The black said the English and Americans were so wicked he was afraid of them; but, finding by my discourse that I was not one of the Christian heathen, he altered his tone, and nothing was then too good for me. I was fed, and he sent for my chest, receiving with it a bed and three blankets, as a present from the charitable clerk. Thus were my prospects for that night suddenly changed for the better! I could only thank God, in my inmost heart, for all his mercies.

The old black, who was a man of some means, was also able to quit the town; but, before he went, he inquired if I had a bible. I told him yes; still, he would not rest until he had pressed upon me a large bible, in English, which language he spoke very well. This book had prayers for seamen bound up with it. It was, in fact, a sort of English prayer-book, as well as bible. This I accepted, and have now with me. As soon as the old man went away, leaving his son behind him for the moment, I began to read in my *Pilgrim's Progress*. The young man expressed a desire to examine the book, understanding English perfectly. After reading in it for a short time, he earnestly begged the book, telling me he had two sisters, who would be infinitely pleased to possess it. I could not refuse him, and he promised to send another book in its place, which I should find equally good. He thus left me, taking the *Pilgrim's Progress* with him. Half an hour later a servant brought me the promised book, which proved to be Doddridge's *Rise and Progress.* On looking through the pages, I found a Mexican dollar wafered between two of the leaves. All this I regarded as providential, and as a proof that the Lord would not desert me. My gratitude, I hope, was in proportion. This whole household appeared to be religious, for I passed half the night in conversing with the Malay servants, on the subject of Christianity; concerning which they had already received many just ideas. I knew that my teaching was like the blind instructing the blind; but it had the merit of coming from God, though in a degree suited to my humble claims on his grace.

In the morning, these Malays gave me breakfast, and then carried my chest and other articles to the *Plato*'s boat. I was happy enough to find myself, once more, under the stars and stripes, where I was well received, and humanely treated. The ship sailed for Bremen about twenty days after I got on board her.

Of course, I could do but little on the passage. Whenever I moved along the deck, it was by crawling, though I could work with the needle and palm. A fortnight out, the carpenter, a New York man, died. I tried to read and pray with him, but cannot say that he showed any consciousness of his true situation. We touched at St. Helena for water, and, Napoleon being then dead, had no difficulty in getting ashore. After watering we sailed again, and reached our port in due time.

I was now in Europe, a part of the world that I had little hopes of seeing ten months before. Still it was my desire to get to America, and I was permitted to remain in the ship. I was treated in the kindest manner by Captain Bunting, and Mr. Bowden, the mate, who gave me everything I needed. At the end of a few weeks we sailed again, for New York, where we arrived in the month of August, 1840.

I left the *Plato* at the quarantine ground, going to the Sailor's Retreat. Here the physician told me I never could recover the use of my limb as I had possessed it before, but that the leg would gradually grow stronger, and that I might get along without crutches in the end. All this has turned out to be true. The pain had long before left me, weakness being now the great difficulty. The hip-joint is injured, and this in a way that still compels me to rely greatly on a stick in walking.

At the Sailor's Retreat, I again met Mr. Miller. I now, for the first time, received regular spiritual advice, and it proved to be of great benefit to me. After remaining a month at the Retreat, I determined to make an application for admission to the Sailor's Snug Harbour, a richly endowed asylum for seamen, on the same island. In order to be admitted, it was necessary to have sailed under the flag five years, and to get a character. I had sailed, with two short exceptions, thirty-four years under the flag, and I do believe in all that time, the nineteen months of imprisonment excluded, I had not been two years unattached to a ship. I think I must have passed at least a quarter of a century out of sight of land.[1]

I now went up to New York, and hunted up Captain Pell,

1. I find, in looking over his papers and accounts, that Ned, exclusively of all the prison-ships, transports, and vessels in which he made passages, has belonged regularly to seventy-two different crafts! In some of these vessels he made many voyages. In the *Sterling,* he made several passages with the writer; besides four European voyages, at a later day. He made four voyages to Havre in the *Erie,* which counts as only one vessel, in the above list. He was three voyages to London, in the *Washington,* &c. &c. &c.; and often made two voyages in the same ship. I am of opinion that Ned's calculation of his having been twenty-five years out of sight of land is very probably true. He must have *sailed, in all ways,* in near a hundred different craft.—EDITOR.

with whom I had sailed in the *Sully* and in the *Normandy.* This gentleman gave me a certificate, and, as I left him, handed me a dollar. This was every cent I had on earth. Next, I found Captain Witheroudt, of the *Silvie de Grasse,* who treated me in precisely the same way. I told him I had *one* dollar already, but he insisted it should be *two.* With these two dollars in my pocket, I was passing up Wall street, when, in looking about me, I saw the pension office. The reader will remember that I left Washington with the intention of finding Lemuel Bryant, in order to obtain his certificate, that I might get a pension for the injury received on board the *Scourge.* With this project, I had connected a plan of returning to Boston, and of getting some employment in the Navy Yard. My pension-ticket had, in consequence, been made payable at Boston. My arrival at New York, and the shadding expedition, had upset all this plan; and before I went to Savannah, I had carried my pension-ticket to the agent in this Wall street office, and requested him to get another, made payable in New York. This was the last I had seen of my ticket, and almost the last I had thought of my pension. But, I now crossed the street, went into the office, and was recognised immediately. Everything was in rule, and I came out of the office with fifty-six dollars in my pockets! I had no thought of this pension, at all, in coming up to town. It was so much money showered down upon me, unexpectedly.

For a man of my habits, who kept clear of drink, I was now rich. Instead of remaining in town, however, I went immediately down to the Harbour, and presented myself to its respectable superintendent, the venerable Captain Whetten.[2] I was received into the institution without any difficulty, and have belonged to it ever since. My entrance at Sailor's Snug Harbour took place Sept. 17, 1840; just one month after I landed at Sailor's Retreat. The last of these places is a seamen's hospital, where men are taken in only

2. Pronounced, Wheaton.—EDITOR.

to be cured; while the first is an asylum for worn-out mariners, for life. The last is supported by a bequest made, many years ago, by an old ship-master, whose remains lie in front of the building.

Knowing myself now to be berthed for the rest of my days, should I be so inclined, and should I remain worthy to receive the benefits of so excellent an institution, I began to look about me, like a man who had settled down in the world. One of my first cares, was to acquit myself of the duty of publicly joining some church of Christ, and thus acknowledge my dependence on his redemption and mercy. Mr. Miller, he whose sermons had made so deep an impression on my mind, was living within a mile and a half of the Harbour, and to him I turned in my need. I was an Episcopalian by infant baptism, and I am still as much attached to that form of worship, as to any other; but sects have little weight with me, the heart being the main-stay, under God's grace. Two of us, then, joined Mr. Miller's church; and I have ever since continued one of his communicants. I have not altogether deserted the communion in which I was baptized; occasionally communing in the church of Mr. Moore. To me, there is no difference; though I suppose more learned Christians may find materials for a quarrel, in the distinctions which exist between these two churches. I hope never to quarrel with either.

To my surprise, sometime after I was received into the Harbour, I ascertained that my sister had removed to New York, and was then living in the place. I felt it, now, to be a duty to hunt her up, and see her. This I did; and we met, again, after a separation of five-and-twenty years. She could tell me very little of my family; but I now learned, for the first time, that my father had been killed in battle. Who, or what he was, I have not been able to ascertain, beyond the facts already stated in the opening of the memoir.

I had ever retained a kind recollection of the treatment of Captain Johnston, and accident threw into my way some information concerning him. The superintendent had put me in charge of the library of the institution; and, one day, I overheard some visiters talking of Wiscasset. Upon this, I ventured to inquire after my old master, and was glad to learn that he was not only living, but in good health and circumstances. To my surprise I was told that a nephew of his was actually living within a mile of me. In September, 1842, I went to Wiscasset, to visit Captain Johnston, and found myself received like the repentant prodigal. The old gentleman, and his sisters, seemed glad to see me; and, I found that the former had left the seas, though he still remained a ship-owner; having a stout vessel of five hundred tons, which is, at this moment, named after our old craft, the *Sterling*.

I remained at Wiscasset several weeks. During this time, Captain Johnston and myself talked over old times, as a matter of course, and I told him I thought one of our old shipmates was still living. On his asking whom, I inquired if he remembered the youngster, of the name of Cooper, who had been in the *Sterling*. He answered, perfectly well, and that he supposed him to be the Captain Cooper who was then in the navy. I had thought so, too, for a long time; but happened to be on board the Hudson, at New York, when a Captain Cooper visited her. Hearing his name, I went on deck expressly to see him, and was soon satisfied it was not my old ship-mate. There are two Captains Cooper in the navy,—father and son,—but neither had been in the *Sterling*. Now, the author of many naval tales, and of the Naval History, was from Cooperstown, New York; and I had taken it into my head this was the very person who had been with us in the *Sterling*. Captain Johnston thought not; but I determined to ascertain the fact, immediately on my return to New York.

Quitting Wiscasset, I came back to the Harbour, in the month of November, 1842. I ought to say, that the men at this institution, who maintain good characters, can always get leave to go where they please, returning whenever they please. There is no more restraint than is necessary to comfort and good order; the object being to make old tars comfortable. Soon after my return to the Harbour, I wrote a letter to Mr. Fenimore Cooper, and sent it to his residence, at Cooperstown, making the inquiries necessary to know if he were the person of the same family who had been in the *Sterling*. I got an answer, beginning in these words—"I am your old ship-mate, Ned." Mr. Cooper informed me when he would be in town, and where he lodged.

In the spring, I got a message from Mr. Blancard, the keeper of the Globe Hotel, and the keeper, also, of Brighton, near the Harbour, to say that Mr. Cooper was in town, and wished to see me. Next day, I went up, accordingly; but did not find him in. After paying one or two visits, I was hobbling up Broadway, to go to the Globe again, when my old commander at Pensacola, Commodore Bolton, passed down-street, arm-in-arm with a stranger. I saluted the commodore, who nodded his head to me, and this induced the stranger to look around. Presently I heard "Ned!" in a voice that I knew immediately, though I had not heard it in thirty-seven years. It was my old ship-mate—the gentleman who has written out this account of my career from my verbal narrative of the facts.[3]

Mr. Cooper asked me to go up to his place, in the country, and pass a few weeks there. I cheerfully consented, and we reached Cooperstown early in June. Here I found a neat village, a beautiful lake, nine miles long, and, altogether, a beautiful country. I had never been as far from the sea before, the time when I served on Lake Ontario excepted. Cooperstown lies in a valley, but Mr. Cooper tells me it is at an elevation of twelve hundred feet above tide-water. To

3. Ned Myers's discovery of his old shipmate provides an unorthodox but happy ending: character finds author, in New York. Cooper invited him to Lake Otsego where Ned told him his life story. For an interesting discussion of Cooper's writing of Myers's tale, see Egan, "Gentlemen-Sailors."

me, the clouds appeared so low, I thought I could almost shake hands with them; and, altogether, the air and country were different from any I had ever seen, or breathed, before.

My old shipmate took me often on the Lake, which I will say is a slippery place to navigate. I thought I had seen all sorts of winds before I saw the Otsego, but, on this lake it sometimes blew two or three different ways at the same time. While knocking about this piece of water, in a good stout boat, I related to my old shipmate many of the incidents of my wandering life, until, one day, he suggested it might prove interesting to publish them. I was willing, could the work be made useful to my brother sailors, and those who might be thrown into the way of temptations like those which came so near wrecking all my hopes, both for this world, and that which is to come. We accordingly went to work between us, and the result is now laid before the world. I wish it understood, that this is literally my own story, logged by my old shipmate.

It is now time to clew up. When a man has told all he has to say, the sooner he is silent the better. Every word that has been related, I believe to be true; when I am wrong, it proceeds from ignorance, or want of memory. I may possibly have made some trifling mistakes about dates, and periods, but I think they would turn out to be few, on inquiry. In many instances I have given my impressions, which, like those of other men, may be right, or may be wrong. As for the main facts, however, I know them to be true, nor do I think myself much out of the way, in any of the details.

This is the happiest period of my life, and has been so since I left the hospital at Batavia. I do not know that I have ever passed a happier summer than the present has been. I should be perfectly satisfied with everything, did not my time hang so idle on my hands at the Harbour. I want something to occupy my leisure moments, and do not despair of yet being able to find a mode of life more suitable to the activity of my early days. I have friends enough—more than

I deserve—and, yet, a man needs occupation, who has the strength and disposition to be employed. That which is to happen is in the hands of Providence, and I humbly trust I shall be cared for, to the end, as I have been cared for, through so many scenes of danger and trial.

My great wish is that this picture of a sailor's risks and hardships, may have some effect in causing this large and useful class of men to think on the subject of their habits. I entertain no doubt that the money I have disposed of far worse than if I had thrown it into the sea, which went to reduce me to that mental hell, the "horrors," and which, on one occasion, at least, drove me to the verge of suicide, would have formed a sum, had it been properly laid by, on which I might now have been enjoying an old age of comfort and respectability. It is seldom that a seaman cannot lay by a hundred dollars in a twelvemonth—oftentimes I have earned double that amount, beyond my useful outlays—and a hundred dollars a year, at the end of thirty years, would give such a man an independence for the rest of his days. This is far from all, however; the possession of means would awaken the desire of advancement in the calling, and thousands, who now remain before the mast, would long since have been officers, could they have commanded the self-respect that property is apt to create.

On the subject of liquor, I can say nothing that has not often been said by others, in language far better than I can use. I do not think I was as bad, in this respect, as perhaps a majority of my associates; yet, this narrative will show how often the habit of drinking to excess impeded my advance. It was fast converting me into a being inferior to a man, and, but for God's mercy, might have rendered me the perpetrator of crimes that it would shock me to think of, in my sober and sane moments.

The past, I have related as faithfully as I have been able so to do. The future is with God; to whom belongeth power, and glory, for ever and ever!

Index

ABOUT THE EDITOR

WILLIAM S. DUDLEY, a native of Brooklyn, New York, graduated from Williams College in 1958. Joining the navy, he served for three years in a destroyer-escort based in Newport, R.I. In 1963 he returned to civilian life, taught in secondary school, and entered Columbia University where he earned the M.A. and Ph.D. degrees in history. For seven years he was an assistant professor in the history department of Southern Methodist University. Since 1977, he has been a supervisory historian at the Naval Historical Center in Washington, D.C. In 1982 he became head of the Early History Branch and currently is the principal editor of two multivolume series, *Naval Documents of the American Revolution* and *The Naval War of 1812: A Documentary History.* His articles and book reviews have appeared in journals such as *The American Neptune, Naval War College Review, Maryland Historical Magazine, Hispanic American Historical Review,* and the *Journal of Latin American Studies.* He is an active member of the Society for History in the Federal Government, North American Society for Oceanic History, the American Military Institute, and other professional organizations. Dr. Dudley and his family live in Annapolis, Maryland, where he enjoys sailing and life in a historic maritime community.

CLASSICS OF NAVAL LITERATURE

JACK SWEETMAN, SERIES EDITOR

Richard McKenna, *The Sand Pebbles.* Introduction by Robert Shenk

Rear Admiral Charles E. Clark, *My Fifty Years in the Navy.* Introduction and notes by Jack Sweetman.

Rear Admiral William S. Sims and Burton J. Hendrick, *The Victory at Sea.* Introduction and notes by David F. Trask

Leonard F. Guttridge and Jay D. Smith, *The Commodores.* Introduction by James C. Bradford

Captain William Harwar Parker, *Recollections of a Naval Officer, 1841–1865.* Introduction and notes by Craig L. Symonds

Charles Nordhoff, *Man-of-War Life.* Introduction and notes by John B. Hattendorf

Joshua Slocum, *Sailing Alone Around the World.* Introduction by Robert W. McNitt

Marcus Goodrich, *Delilah.* Introduction by C. Herbert Gilliland, Jr.

Edward L. Beach, *Run Silent, Run Deep.* Introduction by Edward P. Stafford

Captain David Porter, *Journal of a Cruise Made to the Pacific Ocean by Captain David Porter in the United States Frigate* Essex *in the Years 1812, 1813, and 1814.* Introduction and notes by Robert D. Madison and Karen Hamon

Fred J. Buenzle with A. Grove Day, *Bluejacket: An Autobiography.* Introduction and notes by Neville T. Kirk

Filson Young, *With the Battle Cruisers.* Introduction and notes by James Goldrick

Herman Wouk, *The Caine Mutiny.* Introduction by Noel A. Daigle

Admiral of the Navy George Dewey, *Autobiography of George Dewey.* Introduction and notes by Eric McAllister Smith

Theodore Roosevelt, *The Naval War of 1812.* Introduction by Edward K. Eckert

Thomas B. Buell, *The Quiet Warrior: A Biography of Admiral Raymond A. Spruance.* Introduction by John B. Lundstrom

Richmond Pearson Hobson, *The Sinking of the* Merrimac. Introduction and notes by Richard W. Turk

Herman Melville, *White-Jacket.* Introduction by Stanton B. Garner

Edward P. Stafford, *The Big E.* Introduction by Paul Stillwell

Nicholas Monsarrat, *The Cruel Sea.* Introduction by Edward L. Beach

Arthur W. Sinclair, *Two Years on the* Alabama. Introduction and notes by William N. Still, Jr.

C. S. Forester, *The Good Shepherd.* Introduction by J. D. P. Hodapp, Jr.

Frederick Marryat, *Mr. Midshipman Easy.* Introduction and notes by Evan R. L. Davies

Samuel Eliot Morison, *John Paul Jones: A Sailor's Biography.* Introduction by James C. Bradford

Harold and Margaret Sprout, *The Rise of American Sea Power, 1775–1918.* Introduction by Kenneth J. Hagan